ABOUT THE AUTHOR

Born in London, Wendy Alec has pursued successful careers in advertising and television production, as well as writing books and screenplays. The cinematic scope and epic sweep of the Chronicles of Brothers series have won her legions of devoted fans around the world.

Also by Wendy Alec

THE CHRONICLES OF BROTHERS,
TIME BEFORE TIME SERIES
The Fall of Lucifer
The First Judgement

THE CHRONICLES OF BROTHERS SERIES
A Pale Horse
End of Days (September 2018)

*For a complete character list, please refer to the back of
the book.*

WENDY ALEC

SON OF PERDITION

THE CHRONICLES OF BROTHERS

INSP:RE

Harper*Inspire*, an imprint of
HarperCollins Christian Publishing
1 London Bridge Street
London SE1 9GF

www.harpercollins.co.uk

First published by HarperCollins*Publishers* 2018

2

A catalogue record for this book is available from the British Library

ISBN: 9780310090991 (TPB)
ISBN: 9780310097471 (ebook)

Set in Sabon Lt Std by Palimpsest Book Production Limited,
Falkirk, Stirlingshire

Printed and bound in the UK by CPI Group (UK) Ltd, Croydon CR0 4YY

MIX
Paper from
responsible sources
FSC™ C007454

PROLOGUE

They Cast No Shadows

2001
World Trade Club
107th Floor, World Trade Center
Lower Manhattan, New York

It was 10 September 2001, a day almost like any other, Lorcan De Molay reflected. At precisely 8.46 a.m. tomorrow, the entire world would change.

He pondered this fact as he gazed out of the vast expanse of glass at the breathtaking panorama of Manhattan's skyline from the private club room that rose a full quarter of a mile above New York City.

He stared silently across the spectacular vista of the Manhattan Harbour, his eyes fixed on the relentless passage of sleek 757 and 747 airliners arriving and departing from La Guardia, JFK, and Newark Airports.

Finally the priest drew his gaze away from the skyline and turned.

His face, although strangely scarred, was imperial. His features striking. The wide brow and straight patrician nose framed imperious sapphire eyes that held a haunting mesmerizing beauty. His thick raven hair was silvering at the edges.

On an average day, he wore it fastidiously pulled back from his high cheekbones into its customary braid bound by a simple black band.

On an average day, he wore the flowing Black Robes of his Jesuit order.

But today was not an average day and this dusk De Molay's gleaming raven tresses fell loose to his shoulders, skimming the exquisitely tailored, bespoke Domenico Vacca suit that accentuated the deliberately honed body beneath it.

The priest caressed the carved silver serpent on the top of his cane, slowly surveying the men seated before him.

The Grande Druid Council of Thirteen, the highest orders of the Committee of Three Hundred, The Black Nobility of Venice, The Supreme Mother Council of the Thirty-Third Degree Masons of the Scottish Rite.

He scanned the faces of the elite who controlled the Federal Reserve, the Bank for International Settlements, the World Bank, the Council of Foreign Relations, the Bilderberg Group, and the Club of Rome, his gaze finally resting on the Frater Superior and Grand Tribunal of the Ordo Templi Orientis.

The Grand Masters of the Illuminati.

The secret cabal that controlled the United States Government.

That controlled every government of the Eastern and Western world.

A slight smile flickered across his lips.

Who were in turn controlled by himself – Lorcan De Molay.

He flipped open a silver cigar case. Kester von Slagel, his emissary, materialized from the shadowed corner of the club holding a cigar guillotine. De Molay inserted the head of a cigar as Von Slagel cut deftly into the cap before vanishing back into the shadows.

De Molay put the cigar to his lips, positioning the end just above the top of the flame. 'La Corona, 1937.'

He puffed in gratification, then slowly removing the cigar, he let his gaze linger on the impassive faces of the chairmen of the most powerful banks in the world seated before him.

They were simpletons. Power-hungry despots.

But according to the Tenets of Eternal Law, the fallen angelic Dread Councils had no direct jurisdiction over the race of men.

He pursed his lips at the memory of the Nazarene.

He had no alternative. After his humiliating defeat at Golgotha, the Fallen's presence on this mud-spattered orb was illegitimate.

He had only one alternative – he had to use the craven masses. Beguile them – engage them in his masterplan. Dark Slaves of the Fallen.

At least until the Great Battle.

Until the defeat of the Nazarene.

After that, they would all be expendable. The thought gave him a rush of undiluted pleasure.

And Jerusalem would finally be his.

But now – to the business at hand.

De Molay spoke softly, his voice low and cultured. His accent was distinctly British, London W1K to be precise, but it carried a subtle exotic inflection that was indefinable.

'At precisely 8.46 a.m. tomorrow, our operation to subvert and destabilize the United States of America will have begun.' He caressed his cigar slowly between slender, elegantly manicured fingers. Every eye was fixed on him.

'By noon, there will be closings at the United Nations, the Securities and Exchange Commission, the stock markets,' he murmured. 'We will have struck at the foundations of the entire Western world.'

He turned to Charles Xavier Chessler, the silver-haired Chairman of Chase Manhattan.

'Our insider-trading account stands as we speak at fifteen billion dollars,' Chessler said. 'Untraceable back to the Brotherhood.'

De Molay puffed on the cigar until the outer rim began to glow.

'The towers will collapse like a proverbial house of cards,' he murmured.

'Freefall,' added Jaylin Alexander, former Executive Director of the Central Intelligence Agency. 'The evidence of controlled implosion buried forever in the debris.' De Molay gestured to an imposing figure, in military dress and with a shock of coarse white hair, who sat at his right hand. Omar B. Maddox, Commander General of NORAD, the North American Aerospace Defence Committee.

'Vigilant Guardian is in effect, General?'

The general saluted. 'NORAD is on standby, Your Excellency. At dawn, we execute the largest imaginary air defence exercise in our history, simulating an attack on the United States.'

The general smiled but his small hawklike eyes glittered hard.

'Vigilant Guardian,' he drawled. 'The simulation will create the distraction and confusion necessary while the real attacks succeed. NORAD's FAA technicians will be half blind.'

De Molay turned to Gonzalez of the United States Secret Service Presidential Protective Detail.

'The terrorists are in possession of the codes?'

'Air Force One codes and signals and our top White House codes, Your Excellency.'

'Access to the NSA's surveillance systems?'

Gonzalez nodded.

'In place, Your Excellency.'

'We must cast no shadows.' De Molay turned to Alexander.

'The car registered to Nawaf al-Hazmi will be ditched in the parking area at Dulles Airport the morning of the twelfth,' Alexander stated. 'Inside is a copy of Atta's letter to the hijackers, a cashier's cheque made out to a flight school in Phoenix, four drawings of the cockpit of a 757 jet, a box-cutter-type knife and maps of Washington and New York.

'The terrorists have accepted the cover story, hook, line, and sinker. They take over the planes. Their "bogus" mission – to return to the airports, where fuelled planes will be on standby for them and their hostages. Once we activate the primary control channel, they will realize they have been deceived. Hijacked from the ground. Too late.' Alexander smiled thinly. 'They will die unwilling martyrs of the Brotherhood. Textbook black-ops scapegoats.'

'Bin Laden?' Julius De Vere, Chairman of De Vere Continuation Holdings, queried.

'Osama bin Laden flew from Pakistan to Dubai on 4 July,' Lewis, Deputy Secretary of Defence replied. 'He was accompanied by his personal physician, four bodyguards, and a male Algerian nurse, and admitted to the urology department of the American Hospital. His family's evacuation is taken care of.'

'Two Boeing 777s are on standby as agreed,' Alexander nodded. 'The Bin Ladens will be evacuated on 18 September in the no-fly period.'

'*Then* we invade Iraq,' interjected Drew Janowski, Special Assistant to the President for Defence Policy and Strategy. 'Saddam's resistance to our oil-for-dollars programme permanently eradicated. We create the crisis, then willingly manage it. We introduce Homeland Security, then the Patriot Act.'

'In the Fall of 2008, we will crash the market,' Werner

Drechsler, President of the World Bank, said very softly. 'Plunge the dollar. There will be a deliberate contraction of all credit. We will instigate the single greatest economic crisis since 1929. Between 40 and 45 per cent of the world's wealth destroyed in less than eighteen months.'

Julius De Vere surveyed the assembly in satisfaction. 'By 2025 we finish the job. During the run on the banks, we intentionally collapse the Federal Reserve and replace it with our One World Central Bank. They will cry out to us to do anything to stop their pain.'

A bony, creased-looking man in his early fifties wearing horn-rimmed spectacles looked up from his papers.

'The United States' sovereignty permanently eliminated.' Piers Aspinall, Chief of British Intelligence Services, removed his spectacles and breathed on the lenses. 'The first phase of the North American Union. We launch the Amero currency. Introduce mandatory gun control.'

De Vere leaned back leisurely in his chair.

Aspinall continued: 'Then we divide the world into ten superblocs. Stage a false flag incident – nuclear or bio-terror – weaponized Avian flu; smallpox . . . ushering in martial law and mandatory vaccination.' He removed a perfectly pressed, monogrammed linen handkerchief from his suit pocket and polished the lenses. 'We eradicate resisters. Patriots. Constitutionalists.'

De Vere and Lorcan De Molay exchanged a fleeting glance.

'Christians,' added Aspinall.

'Then, gentlemen,' he continued, 'our coup d'état. The towers fall. The Securities and Exchange Commission for the first time in US history invokes its emergency powers under Securities Exchange Act Section 12(k), allowing our illegal covert war chest, due for settlement on 12 September 2001, to be cleared without meeting the legal demands for identification of ownership.'

Lorcan De Molay smiled faintly in the direction of Drechsler and Julius De Vere as Aspinall drew towards his conclusion.

'Eradicating the trail to our illegal covert fund of trillions and trillions dating back to the Second World War and the Bretton Woods international financial conference after it. Eradicating the evidence of every election we have engineered for the past five decades; every government we have destabilized; every covert black-ops operation we have financed.

'We remain invisible. The greatest criminal act of the industrial military complex in the history of mankind, dismissed by the American people in decades to come as nothing more than an *urban legend.*'

Aspinall held up a glass of vintage port.

'A toast to invisibility, gentlemen.'

The Brotherhood raised their glasses.

De Molay walked over to the floor-length windows and gazed out towards the Atlantic.

'We cast no shadows,' he murmured.

He turned from the window, his expression strangely distant.

'*Then* Jerusalem . . .'

The men stood as one and lifted their glasses.

'Jerusalem.'

To our New World Order,' Lorcan De Molay declared. '*Novos ordo seclorum.*'

The voices of every man in the chamber echoed in unison: '*Novus ordo seclorum.*'

Lorcan De Molay raised his glass a second time at unsuspecting Manhattan glimmering in the weak autumnal sun. His voice was barely a whisper.

'And to the reign of my only begotten son.'

The eye-catching brunette wearing enormous Prada sunglasses smiled and turned to the nervous olive-skinned young man in a blue shirt seated next to her. He stared straight ahead. Stony-faced.

She shrugged, ran slender French manicured fingernails through her long low-lighted hair, then glanced back at the half-empty plane. She yawned.

Since Alex's birth twelve weeks ago, Rachel Lane-Fox had been *obsessed* with sleep.

She stretched out her long shapely legs, wiggled her toes and sank down into her business class seat in row 8 of the Boeing 767.

Scrabbling in her bag, she removed her mobile phone, then scrolled down until she found Julia De Vere's number and dialled. It rang twice.

'Hey, Jules,' she grinned. 'Yes – I'm on my way back. We're on the tarmac at Logan.' She peered out of the window.

'We've been slightly delayed. Listen – yes – Dad's out of intensive care. I can't thank you enough for looking after Alex.'

A flight attendant stood at her elbow. Rachel looked up.

'I'm sorry, ma'am – your mobile phone and . . .' She gestured at the seatbelt.

Rachel fastened her seatbelt awkwardly, tucking the phone under her chin.

The flight attendant frowned. She studied Rachel intently. 'Aren't you the supermodel Rachel . . . Rachel Lane-Fox?'

'Yes – you got me,' Rachel sighed. 'Guilty.'

8

She removed her dark glasses and put her free hand on the stewardess's arm.

'Look,' she pleaded, 'it's my baby. He's only twelve weeks old. My dad had a heart attack. My baby's with a friend. I've never left him before.'

She pointed to the phone. 'Please?' She grinned disarmingly, her perfectly veneered white teeth gleaming.

The flight attendant looked down at her watch. She sighed.

'Okay.' She gestured to the aircraft doors. 'As soon as the doors close.'

'Thanks,' Rachel mouthed and winked.

The man in the blue shirt glanced at her, disapprovingly.

'Jules?' She glanced at the man, then lowered her voice. 'Look, did Alex sleep through the night or did he drive Jason *crrrrazy*?'

She stifled a giggle. The man next to her glared at her openly.

'Okay. I'll get a cab straight to the *Cosmo* office when we land in LA. Pick you both up for lunch.'

The flight attendant was back at her elbow.

'Miss Lane-Fox . . .'

'Have to go, Jules. Kiss Alex for me.'

Rachel clicked the phone shut, put it in her bag, and stowed it hastily under her seat.

She glanced down. *Strange*, she thought. The olive-skinned man was grasping the armrest as though his life depended on it. He was sweating profusely.

He must hate flying.

'Hey,' she said, softly, tapping him on the arm. 'When you do this regularly it's not so bad. You get used to it.' She gave him a soft smile. 'I did.'

Mohammed Atta stared right through her.

She shrugged, picked up a fashion magazine and flicked

9

idly through it as the aircraft taxied away from Gate 32 onto runway 4R.

Eight minutes later, Rachel Lane-Fox stared out of the window at the spectacular view of Boston Harbour as the Boeing ascended into the clear fall skies.

It was precisely 7.59 a.m., on Tuesday morning – 11 September.

L orcan De Molay glanced idly down at the gold chronograph face of the 1925 Grogan Patek Philippe watch on his right wrist.

'The only watch of its kind ever made for a left-handed wearer,' he reflected idly.

It was 8.14 a.m. precisely on the East Coast of America.

The hijacking of American Airlines flight 11 was now in process.

In minutes Mohammed Atta and his CIA patsies would realize they had been betrayed.

There would be no planes waiting for them.

He smiled thinly, dabbed at his mouth with a monogrammed linen napkin, then set it down next to his unfinished lunch – *millefeuille* of Catalan lobster.

The remote control protocol would kick in at any moment.

The primary control channel would be activated.

He stared out past the bronze lions supporting the 132-foot red granite Egyptian obelisk, past the Via della Conciliazione, past the murky green waters of the Tiber to Rome's seven hills, then checked his wristwatch one more time.

Four minutes and the 767's functions would come under the direct ground control of the 'Command Post'.

He smoothed his Jesuit robes and closed his eyes, raising his face to Rome's soft autumn breeze.

The Boeing's flight control system was about be reconfigured to fly directly into the World Trade Center in New York City.

The first phase of the One-World Government was under way.

Jordan Maxwell III, investment banker, checked his computer screen for the third time in as many minutes.

'Hey, boss!' Damien Cox, wet-behind-the-ears Harvard grad, leaned against the glass door of Maxwell's office, holding a Starbucks coffee in one hand. 'Something's up. We're locked out of the system.'

He grinned. 'Weird.'

Maxwell nodded to Powell, Neal Black's fifty-year-old VP of Information Technology, now standing in the doorway behind Cox.

'We're locked out all right,' Powell muttered.

'Everyone?' Maxwell raised his eyebrows.

'Every computer. All three floors: 318 workstations to be precise. We've been completely taken over. And something ... someone is downloading all our files.' Powell paused. 'Out of the building.'

'Hackers?'

'Nah.' He shrugged. 'Too sophisticated. Locked out by a program I've never seen before.' Powell shook his head. 'And I've seen everything.'

Maxwell rose, walking briskly to the expansive open-plan office floor of Neal Black, followed by Powell and Cox.

He scanned the computer screens as he walked, then glanced up towards the glass doors of the boardroom where

11

the Managing Director and two general partners of the securities brokerage firm were engaged in intense hushed conversation.

'You've informed Morgan?'

'Conference call with Europe. The big cheeses. No disturbances,' Powell replied.

'Okay, I'll inform him via the in-house line.' Maxwell turned abruptly, walked back into his office, and slid into his expensive leather chair, his eyes still riveted to the computer screen. He moved to press the in-house line, then hesitated.

The files were still downloading.

He was supposed to be in the dark, but he'd been tracking the abnormal transaction traffic since 6 September.

Over $200 million in illegal transactions had been rushed through the Neal Black WTC computers in the past forty-eight hours alone.

Then there was the single five-billion-dollar Treasury note trade that Von Duysen had mentioned over drinks yesterday.

He looked through the glass doors of his office over to the boardroom, troubled.

It was connected with Europe. The powers that were never to be disobeyed. Of that he was certain.

Maxwell tapped the key of his keyboard impatiently, then stared back at his computer.

There was no doubt about it. An extensive financial 'sacking' operation was in process.

Someone was covering their tracks. Every file was being downloaded out of the building at lightning speed. In front of his eyes. Out of the system. 'But to where?'

He shook his head, picked up his lukewarm coffee and walked towards the window.

He gazed out at the clear Manhattan skies.

'And why?'

He frowned. There was a strange sound. If it wasn't so ludicrous, he'd swear it was the roar of jet engines.

He turned his head to the left.

The coffee cup slid out of his hand onto the elegant berber carpet.

The 767 was heading straight towards him.

TWENTY YEARS LATER

CHAPTER ONE

Allah's Chariot

December 2021
Cistern Number 30
Temple Mount, Jerusalem

Grandfather! Grandfather!' Jul Mansoor tugged on the old Bedouin's tunic as his grandfather walked doggedly through the maze of surface cistern entries down towards Warren's Gate.

'Grandfather!' he cried. 'We should not be here – it is forbidden territory – the radiation!'

Abdul-Qawi turned, frowning darkly at his thirteen-year-old grandson, then suddenly his dark leathered face broke into a broad toothless smile.

'Jul.' He raised his gnarled sunburnt hands in the air in exasperation, then unclipped a hand-held radiation meter from his belt and held it up.

'Hah! No radiation!' he exclaimed. 'It is the UN's – how do you say – spin? The radiation is in Tel Aviv – in Jaffa – *not* in Jerusalem.'

'The soldiers will stop us, Grandfather.'

'Do you *see* the Israelis? Do you even see the Wakf?'

17

Abdul-Qawi gestured dramatically at the cordoned-off deserted Mount.

He spat on the ground, then wiped his mouth with the back of his hand.

'They are all gone – *gone* – since the war ended.' The old man continued walking the 150 feet towards the Gate.

'The soldiers are gone – but YOU are still trespassing, Jadd.'

At the sound of his name in Arabic, Abdul-Qawi halted.

'Ah!' He flung his hands in the air, this time in despair. 'Private school, European tutors . . . all it teaches you is to disrespect your grandfather. Now let your Jadd be your teacher.' He turned to face Jul, his hands on his scrawny hips.

'This old Bedouin archaeologist knows that at this very moment the Israelis and the Wakf lie dead and wounded in hospitals all across Jerusalem, while the Europeans recline in their opulent palaces, dividing the Mount as we speak.'

He raised one hand dramatically.

'This for the Jews – this for the Arabs – this for the UN. Pah! We take our chance.'

He pointed to the rubble ahead of them.

'The Israelis and the Wakf sealed the Gate; the earthquake has unsealed it. For the sake of Allah, for the sake of my archaeological diggings these past sixty-five years, I *must* search.'

Carefully, the old man began to climb through the rubble and into a great hall about seventy-five feet long with many exit tunnels running in different directions. His hawk-like eyes glittered with excitement.

'Hurry, hurry,' he gestured impatiently to Jul, who was ten feet behind him, and started clambering down the stone stairs.

Then he stopped, lit his lamp, and hunched down over a crumpled map.

Jul sighed heatedly. Suddenly, the old man clasped his free hand so tightly he winced.

'The Holy of Holies!' Abdul-Qawi's eyes shone with a strange ecstasy. Trembling, he clambered to his feet and scuttled through fresh rubble towards an already-excavated tunnel.

He frowned. His gaze was fixed thirty feet away on a glistening golden object jutting out of a small ravine.

Abdul-Qawi stepped tentatively closer, waving his grandson back behind him.

Awestruck, he stared at the glistening metal.

'Allah's Chariot,' he murmured.

He continued walking, muttering to himself in Arabic as though in a hypnotic trance, his hand outstretched until he was only inches away from the ornate gold handle protruding from the sand. He reached out his hand, trembling.

Jul watched in awe as Abdul-Qawi touched the handle. Instantly a ferocious blue lightning struck savagely from the casket.

'*Allahu Akbar*!' Abdul screamed as he closed his hand over the golden handle. The savage electric current surged through his body. Jul watched in horror as his grandfather's body thrashed violently from side to side in paroxysm.

'Jadd!' Jul ran towards him.

The old man stared at Jul through terrified, exhilarated eyes, then summoning all his strength, he wrenched his hand free from the casket and was thrown violently to the ground.

Jul pulled him through the rubble away from the pulsating chest.

'Jadd . . . Jadd!' Jul cradled his grandfather's head in his hands, trembling, tears rolling down his mud-streaked face.

Abdul raised himself up, looked through Jul, then uttered a strangled cry. 'The seal of Daniel.'

He fell back.

Struck dead by the Ark of the Covenant.

CHAPTER TWO

Aftermath

Jason
December 2021
Vox Communications Yacht
Upper New York Bay

It was the fourth of Vox Entertainment Group's illustrious PR launch campaigns in that week alone.

And the most lavish.

Despite the below-freezing temperatures, New York was in the mood for celebration. As was Jason De Vere, Chairman and owner of multi-billion-dollar media corporation Vox Entertainment.

The Third World War had ended fourteen weeks earlier after the nuclear strike by the West on Moscow. And Manhattan's countless multinational conglomerates were tentatively resurfacing. The constant threat of a nuclear strike in downtown New York was now a swiftly fading memory and the lowest deck of the largest of Jason De Vere's five corporate yachts was literally heaving.

Middle-aged Wall Street financiers, hedge-fund owners and managers, ageing TV news anchors and entertainment agents crammed the dance floor, mingling with the *crème de la crème* of New York's twenty- and thirty-something elites in the television, fashion, and publishing industries – all gyrating to the pounding music.

Jason De Vere had arrived by helicopter ten minutes earlier. An unusual occurence, which those who worked with him intimately knew could only be accounted for by the attendance of five billionaire Beijing media-investors, who were involved in Jason's latest venture.

His most recent hot button. The launch of Vox's multiple media networks and film conglomerates into China.

At forty-four, Jason De Vere was still ruggedly handsome but already well worn. His tanned face was creased and his cropped silvering hair unbecomingly severe.

As was his current demeanour.

He was unenthusiastically entwined in the clutches of a svelte, over-tanned blonde, trapped in the centre of the dance floor, gyrating awkwardly to the music, whisky glass in hand.

He glanced around at the dance floor. They were all so *young*. Nearer his daughter Lily's age than his. Where *had* time gone? The blonde clone, Vox's latest music awards presenter, entwined her arms more intensely around his neck, now making it *completely* impossible for Jason to drain the last swig from his ever-present whisky glass.

'Damn the need for PR.' He rolled his eyes in frustration, trying to locate one of his three executive assistants.

The newest and youngest, a stylish Asian beauty recently transferred to New York from Vox's Singapore bureau, was engaged in deep conversation with his Beijing clients.

Desperately he scanned the room for his trusty personal executive assistant of nineteen years – fifty-seven-year-old Miss Jontil Purvis, originally of Charleston, South Carolina.

Jontil was the salt of the earth and completely indispensable to Jason. She had joined Vox at its inception and rough-ridden through the hectic and chaotic start-up years.

Over the past two decades she had been involved in the inexhaustible task of endeavouring to make every aspect of Jason De Vere's brutal and unrelenting existence manageable.

From the complexity of his multi-billion-dollar mergers to organizing Lily De Vere's hospitalization and therapy after her accident, and, more recently, finalizing the unpalatable details of Jason and Julia's acrimonious and highly publicized divorce.

Jontil Purvis had given Jason the cold shoulder for a full year during the separation. She adored Julia St Cartier and had since she had first met Jason's sparky young journalist wife nineteen years earlier. She and Julia had forged a deep friendship and Jontil Purvis was loyal to a fault. She was also a devout Baptist who fervently believed in the sanctity of marriage. And believed in Jason and Julia.

Then there was his youngest brother Nick. Jason scowled. Jontil Purvis had no intention of making it easy for Jason De Vere, that much he was sure of. But she fielded Nick's calls and kept her opinions to herself. Jason trusted Jontil Purvis implicitly. And Jason De Vere trusted very few.

He finally spotted her impeccably coiffed blonde beehive. She was standing in the corner with her ever-present Xphone, two notebooks in her left hand, her rather matronly figure attired in a silk lilac suit. Composed as always.

'Purvis!' Jason shouted over his shoulder. 'Purvis!'

Jontil Purvis looked up from her call, looked the blonde and Jason up and down, nodded, and disappeared.

A split second later, a tall gangly brunette rushed out and extricated Jason from the furious blonde's grasp. Guiding him over to the cocktail bar, she pressed a remote screen. A man's face appeared on the screen.

'Jason . . .'

She clasped his arm tightly, barely able to contain her excitement.

'Jason!' She pushed the screen towards him. 'Matt's on the line from Tehran – it's your brother. We've got the *exclusive* – breaking news. The final date's just been set for the peace accord. This is a goer, Jason.'

'You're kidding, right, Maxie?' Jason frowned. 'This is Purvis's rescue ploy.'

She stared at him blankly. Jason's eyes narrowed.

'The Ishtar Accord.' He grasped Maxie's arm so hard that she winced.

'Israel – Iraq – Iran – Russia.' Maxie nodded vigorously.

'The Third World War peace treaty – You're *sure*?'

Jason pulled his Xphone from his belt and scrolled down until he reached a message marked ADV.

He opened the text that had been sent over an hour earlier.

'*Iran conceded. Ishtar Accord. 7 Jan . Your scoop. EXCLUSIVE.*'

'Damn!' Jason pushed Maxie aside.

'Matt, what's going on?'

His eyes bored into the image of Matt Barton, Vox's Tehran Bureau Chief, on the screen.

'There's virtually nothing left here, Chief. Tehran's the only city left standing. Mashhad, Tabriz – incinerated. Direct nuclear strikes. But the Iranians have still been as stubborn as hell. Until your brother arrived. They conceded an hour ago. It's confirmed.' Matt nodded. 'The Accord's set to coincide with the opening of the United Nations in Babylon. Three weeks' time.'

'Babylon, not Damascus?' Jason raised his eyebrows. '*Interesting*.'

24

He frowned.

'And Israel?'

'Intractable as always. I'll let Melanie give you the lowdown.'

Melanie Kelly, Vox's senior Middle East Correspondent, came into view.

'Israel *is* prepared to denuclearize, sir. We're sure.'

'How sure is sure?'

'As sure as sure can ever be, o great tycoon, but the rumour is your genius of a little brother has somehow got pre-signatures from Israel, dependent on some major concessions known only to himself. Sorry to say it – you know how cagey he is. Bit like a pre-nup, it seems. Anyway, trust me – Iran's in. Israel will be in by next week. It's watertight. We go on air in ten.'

Jontil Purvis placed her hand calmly on Jason's arm.

'Vox Central's online, sir. They're waiting for you downstairs.'

Jason snapped off the small TV screen, then wound his way through the crowded cabaret and lounge bar and strode down the spiral stairs into the lower deck executive quarters, stopping outside a leather-covered door.

'Lily,' he spoke into the system.

'Palm verification.'

Jason held his palm up to the reader and, a second later, the door swung open. He walked over to the vast bank of television monitors that straddled one entire wall of the deck.

The transmission controller flicked a switch and the Vox Manhattan broadcast centre came online.

Jason watched as dozens of baby-faced producers fresh out of media college hustled in and out of transmission clutching VCDs, shouting instructions over mobile phones. A twenty five year old with a West Coast tan and long highlighted hair came into view.

'Hi, boss. We're uplinking your brother live on Vox any second . . .'

'Turn it UP.' Jason threw his jacket down on the plush black leather sofa and slowly rolled up his shirt sleeves, his gaze locked on the running chirons on the TV screen.

Jontil Purvis stood in the doorway watching her boss intently. Twenty years in the business and he still got a high when it was a live exclusive scoop – Jason De Vere was in his element when he was hands-on.

Jason watched as New York lined up.

'Ten . . . Line it up – Nine . . .'

'Jason, we've got China.'

'Where's Al Jazeera?' Jason shouted into the mike.

'Al Jazeera's just come online, Jason.'

A lanky Ivy-League-looking executive strode in, exhilarated.

'They're all desperate for the feed: Reuters, Associated Press, CNN, ABC . . .'

'We make money.' Jason muttered. 'Good. Desperate is good. The BBC?'

'We're linking to London now – over to Mel in Tehran.'

Melanie Kelly, Middle East Correspondent, visible on two of the preview screens, cupped her hand over her earpiece.

'Clay's just finished wiring the President up – we'll be ready in eight.'

Jason stared exhilarated at Melanie on the television screen.

Next to her stood Adrian De Vere, newly inaugurated President of the European Union.

'Tell my little brother, hi,' he murmured into the mike.

'Will do, boss.'

Jason watched – Adrian smiled on the preview screen and lifted his hand in recognition.

'Ask him if Israel's in the bag.'

Adrian nodded, then gave Jason a thumbs-up sign.

Jason shook his head, grinned, then held out his hand to Jontil Purvis. She mixed him a whisky and passed it to him. He clutched it and slugged it down, his attention now fixed on the New York news anchor broadcasting from Vox's midtown Manhattan Studios.

'We have breaking news that a final date for the most tenuous peace treaty in the history of the Western world – the peace accord in the aftermath of World War III – the Middle East Ishtar Accord has been set half an hour ago in Tehran, Iran.'

Jason sat down on the sofa, his eyes fixed on the screens.

'All major participants from the bloodiest nuclear war in history, the Russo–Pan-Arab–Israeli War, are signatories: Iraq, Iran, Syria, Turkey, Egypt, as well as Russia, Israel, America, and the European Union.'

'We cross over to Melanie Kelly, Vox senior Middle East correspondent, reporting for Vox News live from Tehran.'

The camera zoomed onto the slight blonde figure of Melanie Kelly.

'With me here in Tehran, I have the United Nations chief negotiater of the Accord and newly appointed President of the European Superstate. At just thirty-nine years of age – hailed as the new John F. Kennedy – Adrian De Vere.'

The camera panned onto Adrian De Vere. Jason stood watching, elated.

'This is a historic day in the history of the Middle East . . .' Adrian smiled brilliantly with his easy relaxed charm. '. . . and the world.'

Jason studied his younger brother. Adrian's face was perfectly proportioned for the camera. Strong. Chiselled.

High cheekbones. Almost beautiful. He was urbane. Refined. His hair was a blueish-black and skimmed his perfectly tailored suit. He wore his usual summer Caribbean tan.

Jason frowned.

His teeth looked slightly different, perfectly veneered and whiter. Julia's influence, no doubt. Her newly established PR company in Chelsea, London, had signed up two major celebrity clients in less than two months: the England football team and Adrian De Vere, newly inaugurated President of the European Union. Jason scowled. After twenty years of marriage he was proud of the fact that, until their divorce, he had stubbornly resisted her every attempt to restyle him. But even he had to admit that, thanks to the efforts of Julia De Vere, Adrian was now the epitome of a modern movie star.

'Both the East and the West have longed for the day when we can rest knowing that our families and future generations will no longer face the threat of nuclear warfare, of suicide bombs, of hostages being murdered . . .' Adrian hesitated. 'Of the sons of the East and the sons of the West being killed in action.'

Jason shook his head. It had to be said. Never in the history of television had any one politician, anchor, or movie star come remotely close to the intense personal connection that Adrian generated with the individual viewer.

It was instantaneous. It was mesmeric. It was undeniably compelling . . . and effortless.

Adrian De Vere was the darling of the international viewing public. It had been the same during his recent two terms as British Prime Minister. Whether they watched him in Iraq, Syria, Germany, England, America, China, or France, he was their son, father, brother, neighbour, friend. In fact, he was – Jason shook his head, incredulous – whoever they wanted him to be.

He took another long slug and finished his whisky. His eye caught the headline on the business section of the *New York Times*. It read: '*European Union's 2021 GDP set to double the USA's.*'

'My, my, little brother,' he murmured, his eyes riveted to the screen, 'you're the most powerful man in the Western world.'

Nick
December 2021
Soho, London

Nick De Vere leaned back in the red crocodile-skin chair. He was handsome, almost pretty, with intelligent deep-set grey eyes above an aquiline nose and high cheekbones. His fine sunbleached hair grazed the collar of his leather jacket.

He sipped his espresso, enjoying the clamour of the unending clientele of A & R executives, record producers, artists, and the normal run-of-the-mill rock star wannabes that milled around the bar.

Soho. London at night.

Back in full swing after the end of the Third World War.

London had been living under threat of nuclear annihilation from Iran and Russia for eight nail-biting months. The atomic weapons site in Aldermaston, twenty-four miles out of the capital, and the Faslane nuclear submarine base in Scotland had both been razed to the ground by the Russian equivalent of the mini nuke B61-11. As for Manchester and Glasgow . . . Nick sighed.

Everyone was on tenterhooks waiting for the Ishtar Accord to be ratified. But all things considered, the theatres had reopened to the public last week and scores of creative agencies, record labels, post-production houses, and recording studios were all back in full swing.

It was business as usual in Soho.

Nick pushed the ever-straying dark blond fringe out of his grey eyes and surveyed the ground-floor restaurant, his innate archaeologist's sensibilities in gear. The boutique hotel had been carved from a pair of Soho townhouses once occupied by MI5. Private cinema. Roof garden. Cool vintage-style metallic leather banquettes. Altfield gold rose wall coverings.

He scanned the faces at the entrance for Klaus von Hausen. Still no sign of the lean stylish antiquities expert. Von Hausen, true to his Germanic heritage, was a stickler for promptness. And for detail. He was the youngest senior curator of the Department of the Middle East in the British Museum's existence, overseeing the most comprehensive collection of Assyrian, Babylonian, and Sumerian antiquities in the world. Klaus had been uncharacteristically guarded on the phone earlier. Nick would find out why over drinks.

He closed his eyes, a rare tranquillity on his features.

No sign of the invasive British paparazzi who dogged his every move. Today he had given them the slip. Four years ago, at twenty-five, Nick De Vere, brilliant archaeologist, heir to the De Vere banking and oil dynasties, and London pop culture icon, had been sex symbol of the year, feted by every gossip magazine in the Western hemisphere. He stared up at the bank of televisions that hung above the crimson leather bar, each broadcasting the familiar Vox branding in the top right-hand corner.

Vox. His eldest brother's monolithic, billion-dollar communications company.

He sighed.

Jason.

Jason had never forgiven him for the accident.

Nick put down his coffee cup, exchanging it for the John Smith's bitter on his left.

For that matter, he had never forgiven himself.

Lily De Vere, Jason's seven-year-old daughter had been permanently disabled. Julia, like the older sister he never had, had forgiven him instantly. But Jason. Jason hadn't talked to him from that day to this. The rich, pretty young playboy had drowned his sorrows and a large portion of the first tranche of his inordinate trust fund in a score of exclusive private clubs strung from London to Monte Carlo to Rome.

His antics had been splashed across the front pages of the *News of the World* and *The Sun*, much to his father's chagrin and his mother's despair, and to his elder brother's outright horror.

His father, James De Vere, a strict traditionalist, had found out about his affair with Klaus von Hausen and had frozen Nick's trust fund the week before collapsing with a fatal heart attack.

And now Nick had Aids. One evening too many – the sex, the heroin, the adrenaline of the chase.

Nick De Vere was dying.

'Hey!' A soft German accent broke into his reverie.

Klaus sank his tall, lean frame into the crocodile-skin chair opposite Nick. Their relationship had been intense but shortlived, yet they were still close.

'Hey!' murmured Nick. 'Good to see you.'

Klaus looked at his watch. 'I can't stay long. Have to pack. I've been seconded.'

Nick raised his eyebrows.

'Classified dig in the Middle East.' Klaus pushed his chair in. 'They've uncovered a historic ancient artefact of international importance.'

He lowered his voice.

'Look, Nick. I don't know what they've discovered, but it's huge. MI6 and Interpol. They were . . .' He frowned. 'How do you say it in English? "Swarming" all over the museum today. The Vatican's involved.'

'And you don't know where?'

Klaus shook his head.

'Iraq . . . Syria . . . Israel. The beginning of civilization. I know the way they work. It'll remain undisclosed until my arrival.' His eyes shone with exhilaration.

'No mobile phones. No laptops. All communications confiscated till I return to British soil.'

'Which is . . . ?'

Klaus shook his head.

'As long as it takes.' He signalled to a waitress. 'Espresso. When do you leave for Egypt?'

'Tomorrow,' Nick answered. 'I overnight in Alexandria, then meet St Cartier at the monastery.'

'Ah, Lawrence St Cartier.' Klaus raised his eyebrows. 'The *enigma*.'

He gestured up to the bank of televisions above the bar. 'It looks like your brother's actually got the Iranians to the table. It's all over the news.'

Nick stared up at the six screens, all transmitting the handsome angular features of Adrian De Vere.

'Thank god for Adrian,' Nick muttered.

Klaus laid his hand gently on Nick's frail forearm.

'He's still paying for your medication?'

Nick nodded. 'The meds, clinics, my apartments in Monte Carlo, London. LA, my Jags, the Ferrari . . . He's saved my life. Literally. The Jordanian monies are released this week. I'll be of independent means again. God.' Nick shook his head. 'Dad hated you and me; our relationship.'

'It's in the past, Nicholas,' Klaus said gently. 'We have

32

to get you strong. You know I'm always here if you need anything.'

Nick smiled faintly. 'Thanks, Klaus. You've been the best.'

'How's the Princess, the Jordanian?'

'Things are good,' he said softly.

'Serious?'

Nick took a sip of his bitter. 'Very serious.'

'And Jason?'

'You know Jason.' Nick shrugged. 'I don't exist.'

'*You've been given six months to live*. Not even a phone call? Leave him to it.' Klaus frowned, visibly upset. 'He has the problem.'

Klaus gestured back to the television screens.

'Germany's calling Adrian *der Wunderkind*, even my grandmother in Hamburg.' He shook his head. Ashen. 'It was so awful what happened in Berlin.' He fell silent.

'Hey, turn it up!' An unshaven A & R executive in a tight-fitting shiny black suit called out.

Nick watched, intrigued as the restaurant quieted.

All eyes were riveted on the former British Prime Minister, Adrian De Vere.

'For the first time in the history of the world since Hiroshima, major cities have experienced the utter devastation of a nuclear strike.'

Adrian's voice was very quiet but like steel.

'Moscow, St Petersburg, Novosibirsk, Damascus, Tel Aviv, Mashhad, Tabriz, Aleppo, Ankara, Riyadh, Haifa, Los Angeles, Chicago, Colorado Springs, Glasgow, Manchester, Berlin. The list goes on.'

He hesitated.

'Entire cities erased from the face of the earth. Communities. Families. Fathers. Mothers. Sons. Daughters. Their bodies consumed to ash.'

33

Adrian looked directly into the camera. The entire restaurant fell silent.

'Next month, in Babylon, a pact between Russia, the Arab nations, the United Nations, the European Union, and Israel will be signed. A nuclear disarmament pact that will last for forty years. The first phase – the seven-year Ishtar Accord – to be signed in Babylon. It is my personal and fervent aspiration. By that I mean that I am determined.' He paused. 'Let me repeat . . . I mean *determined* . . .'

His eyes blazed with intensity. With passion.

'. . . that under the guidance and protection of our formidable newly formed European Union Military Defence Force, and under my leadership as President of the European Union, the threat of nuclear warfare between the East and the West will be erased not only for an entire generation, but for all time.'

He paused.

'I can think of no better way to end this address than to quote directly from the thirty-fifth President of the United States. From John F. Kennedy's speech on 10 June 1963 to the American University.

What kind of peace do I mean? What kind of peace do we seek? Not a Pax Americana enforced on the world by American weapons of war. Not the peace of the grave or the security of the slave. I am talking about genuine peace – the kind of peace that makes life on earth worth living – the kind that enables men and nations to grow and to hope and to build a better life for their children – not merely peace for Americans but peace for all men and women – not merely peace in our time . . .'

Adrian looked straight into the camera lens, his sapphire blue eyes like steel.

'. . . *but peace for* all *time.*'

Nick looked on in amazement at the faces gazing up in adulation at Adrian.

The discriminating and frequently sceptical British public were hanging on his every word.

He shook his head in wonder.

It was an indisputable fact. His elder brother was, at this moment, the most influential public figure in the civilized world.

Nick had promised Adrian he would drop in on his way back from Egypt.

He'd book his flight to Paris in the morning.

Lorcan De Molay stood staring at the television screen, a slow smile spread across his face.

'*When the Accord of Men is signed,*' he murmured, '*and when Zion's Gates stand fast, the First Seal shall be broken . . . The Tribulation shall come to pass.*'

He drew deeply on his cigar.

'Three weeks until the Accord is signed in Babylon.'

He clicked the remote. Adrian De Vere's face disappeared from view.

'Three weeks until the First Seal of Revelation is broken,' he mused, turning to the Presidents of Iran and Syria.

Kester von Slagel appeared at his side.

'Everything is going according to plan, Your Excellency. Soon this parched tract of dust shall be a thorn in your side no more.'

De Molay walked out onto the balcony of the presidential suite of the King David Hotel. His jet-black hair lashed his cheeks in the icy Jerusalem winds that blew up from the west.

He wrapped his smoking gown tightly around his form and stared out past the Western Wall and East Jerusalem, over the Old City, in the direction of a nondescript rocky hill towards the north. Golgotha.

He would defeat the Nazarene in his own backyard. The Last Great Battle.

A thin hard smile flickered on his lips.

'In Jerusalem.'

CHAPTER THREE

Brothers

2021
Lincoln Memorial
Washington DC

Michael pulled his jade cloak around his lean, imperial form, scanning the horizon for what must have been the eighth time that hour. His imperial features were set. Gabriel stood just paces behind, his clear grey eyes lit with a rare intensity. His platinum locks blew in the sudden winds.

The intense aroma of frankincense permeated the air.

Michael frowned. There, striding towards them up the palatial staircase, past the monolithic fluted columns that soared above the porticoes, was a priest. His hair was pulled back from his cheekbones into a single braid and he wore the flowing black robes of the Jesuit Order.

Lucifer raised his hand in recognition to his brothers.

'I have *converted*,' he declared. He grinned maniacally at Michael. 'A soldier of Christ.'

Michael stared at him grimly.

Lucifer stopped directly beneath the immense, seated

sculpture of Abraham Lincoln, his six-foot form dwarfed by the sculpture carved from white Georgia marble.

His entire body started to transform into what seemed to be billions of atoms radiating at the speed of light as six monstrous seraph wings rose from his shoulders. He stood. Nine feet tall. Imperious. Lucifer. Seraph. Fallen Archangel.

Michael studied his elder brother. Still magnificent.

Lucifer's sculpted alabaster features had been scarred almost beyond recognition in the torrid inferno at his banishment from the First Heaven. Yet tonight, as he stood bathed in the soft moonlight of Washington DC, the haunting beauty of aeons past was strangely evident: the wide, marbled forehead, the high imperial cheekbones, the straight patrician nose. His gleaming raven tresses were loosed, devoid of their intricate gold braiding and had grown longer, now falling past his waist.

Lucifer's imperious steel-blue eyes held Michael's gaze. Abruptly he pushed his long raven mane back from his face, turned, and stared up at the sixteenth President of the United States who stared pensively eastwards down the Reflecting Pool.

Bowing melodramatically to Abraham Lincoln, Lucifer flung his arms in the air towards Washington's dawn skies, the ice diamonds on his white velvet cloak radiating with fire. An iniquitous smile flickered at the corners of his full, passionate mouth.

'*I have a dream,*' he cried, his cultured tones resounding through the Greek Doric Temple. '*I have a dream that one day every valley shall be exalted, and every hill and mountain shall be made low.*'

He watched Michael out of the corner of his eye.

'*The rough places will be made plain, and the crooked places will be made straight.*'

He strode to the very front of the memorial, staring out

at the Reflecting Pool, the indigo silk robes beneath his cloak billowing in the sudden gales from the Atlantic.

'*Let freedom ring, from the Stone Mountain of Georgia.*

'*Let freedom ring, from the snow-capped Rockies of Colorado.*

'*Let freedom ring, from every hill and molehill of Mississippi, from every mountainside, let freedom ring!*'

Grinning maniacally, he turned with a flourish and walked towards Gabriel.

'*And when this happens, brother,*' Lucifer grasped Gabriel's shoulders with both hands, his voice soft yet intense with emotion, '*when we allow freedom to ring, when we let it ring from every village and every hamlet, from every state and every city . . .*'

He released Gabriel abruptly, then closed his eyes, his imperial face raised to the heavens, his voice imbued with passion. '*We will be able to speed up that day when all of God's children, black men and white men, Jews and Gentiles, Protestants and Catholics, will be able to join hands and sing in the words of the old spiritual, "Free at last, free at last".*'

He stood, silent for a full minute, then turned to Michael, an irreverent smirk on his face.

'*Thank God Almighty, we are free at last.*' Lucifer bowed with a flourish.

'To Martin Luther King in whose symbolic shadow I stand.'

'A thorn in your side, I think,' Gabriel said, staring at him grimly.

'A barb, it is true, Gabriel. But I dispensed with the rabble-rouser.'

He bowed to Abraham Lincoln.

'As for Lincoln,' he murmured, 'his printing greenbacks became a real impediment to creating a central bank. It became essential to remove him.'

'As you did with John F. Kennedy and too many others to mention.' Gabriel's eyes narrowed.

'I reward the elite with power. They serve me unwaveringly. The race of men sell their souls *so* indiscriminately.' Lucifer shrugged. 'Power. Riches. Assets. Reserves . . .' He hesitated, then gave Michael a slow depraved grin. '*Sex*.'

'You are contemptible.'

Lucifer walked towards Michael. 'My sanctimonious brother, Michael.'

'Not all succumb,' said Gabriel, gazing back up at Lincoln.

Lucifer smiled. A wicked fire flickered in his eyes.

'Ninety-nine succumb. Then we exterminate the one.'

'You delude yourself, brother.' Michael stared at him coldly. 'Your kingdom ended at Golgotha. The Nazarene dealt you a deathblow.'

'But no one appreciates the *fact*, Michael,' Lucifer answered in a patronizing tone. 'The past two thousand years, I have painstakingly ensured that the sacrifice on Golgotha has been a mere myth for the weak and stumbling. For kindergarten. Except that thanks to my fervent disciples even *kindergarteners* no longer pray to the Nazarene.' He gave a derisive laugh, staring out over the water past the Washington Monument to the Capitol building which lay straight ahead.

'His influence wanes,' he murmured. 'I shall erase his name and face forever from the records of the race of men. Like Europe before her, I shall bring America to her knees.'

Michael held out a missive with the Royal Seal of the House of Yehovah.

'Yehovah offers mercy.'

Lucifer glanced down at the missive in Michael's grasp, then directly up into his clear emerald gaze.

'*Mercy?*' He frowned, momentarily taken aback.

'*If* you and the Fallen abandon your plan to annihilate the race of men.' Michael averted his eyes from Lucifer's.

'His unfailing compassions are infinitely more than you deserve, Lucifer.' Gabriel's voice was hard.

'Tut ... tut ... tut ...' Lucifer instantly regained his composure. A disparaging smile flickered on his mouth. 'I see the altar boys are here today.'

He snatched the missive from Michael's grasp and tore it open. He scanned it, then turned, his eyes searching Gabriel's face.

Gabriel held his gaze. He nodded, then bowed his head.

Lucifer walked over to the edge of the stairs and gazed out into Washington's dawn skies, beyond the Reflecting Pool to the Washington Monument, whose red light flickered in the dawn.

He stood a long time, his back to his brothers, the missive held tightly in his grasp.

Finally he spoke.

'He offers mercy,' he whispered. 'But he of all knows that I am long beyond redemption. He taunts me.' His eyes scanned the heavens. 'Tell my Father this is a war to the death. I will fight. At every turn. At every opportunity. I will *never* surrender.'

Michael stood staring at him for a long while, his fierce green eyes boring into Lucifer's back.

'Then it is war, brother.'

Lucifer stood silent. Finally he turned.

'*And there was war in heaven*!' he cried. He raised his scarred imperial features in ecstasy to the skies. '*Michael and his angels fought against the dragon; and the dragon fought and his angels*. The King James version.' He opened one eye. 'It has a certain turn of phrase, don't you think?'

He stared at Michael, a half-smile on his lips. Michael stared back, fierce.

'And prevailed not,' Michael said though clenched teeth.

'War between two brothers.' Lucifer moved closer to Michael. '*Such* a thing,' he murmured, 'such a thing should *never* be.'

Clasping Michael's shoulder, he pressed his lips to his brother's ear.

'*We, of all*, Chief Princes – brothers – should *never* be asked to choose.'

Lucifer's features contorted into a mask of disdain.

'It is malevolent.' He crushed the missive in his palm. 'It shows his weakness. His Achilles heel,' he hissed. 'It is *precisely* why he should vacate the throne; the throne *I* intend to occupy, Michael.'

Michael removed Lucifer's hand from his shoulder.

'That would be a cold day in hell,' he snapped.

Lucifer bowed mockingly in deference to Michael. 'Tell Yehovah,' he murmured, his voice carried across to Michael on the winds, 'he can still surrender to me if he chooses.'

He rubbed his chin, in deliberation.

'I may even offer him mercy.'

He swung around to Gabriel.

'But not the Nazarene!' he hissed.

He cocked his head to one side for a moment, studying his brothers intently.

'No, there will be no surrender,' he answered, suddenly matter of fact.

'My plan to annihilate the race of men is far more in advance than Yehovah dare to admit. My son rises even now in the ranks of the dissolute and wanton corridors of political power.'

He pulled his velvet robes around him. 'You will inform me of the time of our war.'

'You will receive a missive from the Royal Courts,' Michael said coldly.

'In the middle of the Tribulation,' Gabriel's voice was soft, 'when the Son of Perdition breaks his covenant with Israel – the war between Michael and the dragon draws nigh.'

Gabriel's eyes bored into Lucifer.

'You will lose, Lucifer, as you lost at Golgotha.'

Lucifer stared through veiled eyes at Gabriel's flawless features.

'That, my naive younger brother, remains to be seen.'

He pulled his cloak to his form, then turned.

'Tell him that if I lose, I shall set myself up a kingdom on their territory. In their midst – a seat of power. Babylon.' He shrugged. 'Although Washington DC holds a certain *callow* appeal. Either way, Michael, I shall wreak havoc among the race of men.'

Michael watched as Lucifer strode to the very edge of the Memorial.

'Before the First Seal is opened,' he said softly, 'you shall be summoned by Royal Missive to witness the reading of the Tenets of Eternal Law regarding the Seven Seals of Revelation.'

'I await his summons.' Lucifer's eyes flashed with a dark, evil fire. Six monstrous black seraph wings rose behind him.

And before their eyes, he vanished at the speed of light into the clear skies above the District of Columbia.

CHAPTER FOUR

Raiders of the Ark

Temple Mount
Jerusalem

The outside of the Temple Mount was heaving with activity. Rows of gleaming blue-lettered UN four-wheel drives, trucks, and helicopters stood around the perimeter of the Mount. All land for a mile around the Mount had been evacuated and was sectioned off with high-rise barbed-wire fences as armed special forces, wearing the familiar blue UN helmets, guarded the perimeter with their German shepherds. Inside the secure zone, high-ranking Israeli, Palestinian, and UN officials talked tersely among themselves. Nearer the dig was a second smaller cordoned area.

The sacred relic lay uncovered under a canopy on a raised dais in the second fenced-off area. Now fully visible.

It was an ornate chest, approximately four feet long and two and a half feet high, made of wood overlaid with gold. A decorated gold rim ran around the top and at the four corners were rings through which poles could be passed to carry it. On the lid, facing each other, were two figurines of angels: cherubim, in beaten gold, their wings outstretched towards each other.

Eight archaeologists were meticulously checking measurements and comparing them to diagrams.

Father Alessandro, a white-haired scientist priest from the Vatican, gazed at the enormous golden seal locking the casket.

'The seal of Daniel,' he whispered.

He shook his head from side to side in wonder.

Klaus von Hausen studied the priest intently from the far side of the casket, then took a step nearer.

'It's *what*, Father?' He frowned.

'The seal of Daniel.' The priest looked up into Klaus's clear gaze. 'Look – look closely.'

Klaus examined the engraving of four horsemen in fascination, then looked back up at Father Alessandro.

'The Four Riders of the Apocalypse.' He shook his head. 'Impossible.'

Father Alessandro nodded fervently.

'It is the the earthly seal. It replicates the Seals of Revelation. You have heard of it?'

Klaus nodded.

'The Apocalypse of Saint John, Father. Before I studied antiquities, I studied in Germany. The Theological College of Bethel.'

'Ah.' Father Alessandro raised his eyebrows. 'Then you *understand* that, according to the writings of the Prophet Daniel, Solomon's Temple must be rebuilt at the time of the End. "*The Son of Perdition will confirm a covenant with many for one 'week'. In the middle of the 'week' he will put an end to sacrifice and offering . . .* "'

Klaus gazed over to the Ark, then finished the priest's sentence softly.

'*And on a wing of the Temple he will set up an abomina-*

45

tion that causes desolation, until the end that is decreed is poured out on him.'

Father Alessandro smiled in approval. 'Ancient legend has it that when the First Seal of Revelation is about to be broken – the First Seal of the Seven-Sealed Scroll – the Ark of the Covenant will be rediscovered. It heralds the End of Days.'

'Just a legend, Father.' Klaus smiled.

He stopped in mid-flow, interrupted by the roar of gunships on the shimmering Jerusalem horizon. Father Alessandro dropped his instruments and moved nearer, shielding his eyes from the sun as six massive gleaming black Sikorsky CH-53E gunships hovered over the cordoned-off area of the Temple Mount, blowing up a dust storm.

The UN security forces stared perplexed, then in confusion aimed their weapons towards the gunships. Six Hellfire rockets screamed towards them in succession. Directly on target. Destroying everything in their detonation zone.

Only the casket itself and the small group of archaeologists surrounding it stood untouched. The archaeologists stared petrified at the mangled metal remains on the Mount.

'They are here,' Father Alessandro whispered, staring at the soldiers' incinerated bodies lying on the outer perimeter.

'Who?' Klaus whispered. '*Who* is here?'

He looked up to the huge black gunship hovering directly over the Ark.

A section of special forces mercenary commandos rappelled to the ground.

Father Alessandro gestured to Klaus. 'Stay close.'

The remaining archaeologists cowered in terror.

All except the Vatican Priest, who watched intently as the mercenaries executed a well-rehearsed operation to crate up the Ark of the Covenant.

Kester von Slagel appeared through the smoke. He nodded

to the commando leader, Guber, who turned from the crate and nonchalantly lifted his sub-machine gun.

Guber gave a thin smile.

Klaus watched in horror as he gunned down the archaeologists. One by one. Execution style. Until he came to the priest, who stood deliberately shielding Klaus von Hausen.

'A man of the cloth,' Guber leered. Moving alongside the priest, he pointed the machine gun straight at his temple. Father Alessandro thrust Von Hausen away from him as Guber pressed the trigger from point-blank range. The bullets ploughed straight through the priest who stood facing him, unharmed. Klaus stared at the priest, petrified, his body trembling uncontrollably.

Guber turned to Von Slagel, confused. Von Slagel walked over to Guber and laid his hand on the gun barrel.

'It seems we have an uninvited visitor,' he said. He took a step towards the old priest, looking into his eyes with undisguised hatred.

The priest gazed back at him fearless. He gestured to Von Hausen.

'Let him live.' He spoke softly in an ancient form of Syriac. 'It is enough slaughter for one day.'

'Unfortunately,' Von Slagel replied in Syriac, 'That is just not *possible*.' He paused, studying the priest. 'Father Alessandro,' he added scathingly, 'you of all are aware that I *always* obey my Master's orders.'

Von Slagel removed a small handgun, pointed it straight at Klaus von Hausen's head and pulled the trigger at point-blank range. Von Hausen fell to the ground. Lifeless.

The priest's eyes blazed with fury, he looked at Von Slagel in contempt, then sank to his knees. Gently, he closed Von Hausen's eyelids, then removing the cross from around his neck, he laid it on Von Hausen's chest.

'Seven years until your demise in the Lake of Fire,' he

said softly, rising to his full height. 'Your reign will not be long,' Father Alessandro paused, '*Charsoc the Dark.*'

A fleeting smile played on Kester von Slagel's lips.

'But longer than yours, I think,' he replied in Syriac. '*Issachar the Fool.*'

They exchanged a long hard look.

'And where *is* your Grand Master, Jether?' Von Slagel spat. 'I have sensed him,' he hissed. 'I know he is here, hidden somewhere on this muddy little orb. When the First Seal is broken, I shall find him.'

The priest closed his eyes, ignoring Von Slagel's question. 'Seven years till Christos' reign,' he said softly.

'Jerusalem is *ours.*' Von Slagel's face contorted in rage. '*We the Fallen* are the Kings of Earth. The Nazarene will never reign.'

Kester von Slagel metamorphosed until he stood, floor-length black hair flying, eight feet tall, and lifted his gleaming curved necromancer's blade high over Issachar's head.

'You revealed yourself before the First Seal is broken, Issachar. How *careless* of you. You now forfeit your right to walk as the angelic amongst the race of men.'

Charsoc's eyes fleetingly glowed an evil yellow. 'In the name of his son.'

He severed Issachar's head from his shoulders with one clean thrust.

Issachar's head rolled to the dirt. His body followed, plummeting to the ground, where it disappeared.

'Raven is here.' Von Slagel stared at a soft bluish glow on the horizon as four dome-shaped flying machines hovered over Jerusalem, and then just as suddenly vanished. A machine seared a strange black seal in the shape of a phoenix onto the side of the crate.

Underneath, it read: *Property of the New World Order.*

CHAPTER FIVE

Monastery of Archangels

19 December 2021
Monastery of Archangels
Egypt

Nick De Vere's open-roofed Jeep sped across the sands of the sprawling Western Desert, leaving huge dust trails in its wake.

Nick caught sight of the ancient granite monastery-fortress walls carved from the mountain three miles in the distance. He pushed the Jeep into a lower gear, as he sped up the dirt road for the final stretch of his journey.

Five minutes later, the Jeep came to a grinding halt outside the towering western gate of the Monastery of Archangels. Nick leaned on the hooter, then pried his tall, frail frame out of the Jeep and walked over to the gate.

The two Bedouin gatekeepers scrambled to their feet, their long robes billowing behind them, and began hauling the lift down by its system of pulleys.

There was a loud scraping and groaning of wood as the

huge lift contraption descended over the side of the monastery wall.

Nick stepped into the swaying lift.

Professor Lawrence St Cartier lay snoring loudly on an imported teak recliner in the lush monastery gardens, his knee-length fawn safari pants exposing his thin lily-white legs and their quintessentially British sandals and knee-length socks. At the sound of hooting, he lifted his white Panama hat from over his eyes and grudgingly raised himself on one arm, then frowned, swatting irascibly at the flies buzzing overhead with a large mesh flyswatter.

Rising reluctantly from the recliner, he walked over to the edge of the gardens, shielding his eyes from the winter sun as he peered through the gate.

He smiled broadly in recognition as Nick climbed out of the lift and walked into the garden.

St Cartier grabbed Nick in a crushing bearhug, his Panama hat awry on his head, then held him at arm's length.

Nick De Vere was a shadow of his former self. The 'pretty' young London playboy whose face had been plastered across the celebrity columns of the British tabloids for years had definitely changed.

Nick's cheeks were hollow, the intelligent clear grey eyes sunken, the thick blond streaked hair thinner. Lawrence gasped inwardly as his gaze fell to the outline of Nick's ribs visible beneath the T-shirt.

'Lawrence.' The irrepressible boyish grin was still there.

Lawrence noted the white area on Nick's tongue that was slightly raised, then stared in dismay at the reddish purple patches across Nick's body. Kaposi's sarcoma had already set in. Lawrence bowed his head. Nicholas De Vere had only weeks to live.

'Nicholas, dear boy! You look sicker than even "they" described.'

'They being Mother and Julia?' Nick sighed.

The professor nodded. He had known Nicholas De Vere since birth. The easy-going youngest son of the De Vere dynasty. Lilian had described to him in detail her beloved youngest son's deterioration, but even the pragmatic Lawrence had not been prepared for this.

'I'm so sorry, my boy,' St Cartier said awkwardly. 'Your mother is beside herself with worry and Julia phoned me from Rome.' Nick waved Lawrence aside.

'*Don't*, Uncle Lawrence. Compassion was never your strong suit. The antiretroviral drugs have stopped working,' he said matter of factly. 'I'm dying.'

The old man nodded, then pursed his lips.

'Death is an old friend to the likes of me.' He looked deeply into the deep grey eyes, then knitted his eyebrows. 'But a foe to you, Nicholas De Vere,' he muttered.

Nick rolled his eyes. 'Lay off, Lawrence. We've been through this since I was twelve.'

The professor swatted absently at four flies circling his nose.

'Your stubborn insistence on refuting the existence of a higher power in no way negates his existence, Nicholas.' Lawrence's beady blue eagle-like eyes glittered in dudgeon. 'Your ignorant repudiations are like the infinitesimal rantings of . . .'

'A bug on a windshield.' Nick grinned.

Lawrence glowered at him, then his expression softened. Nick smiled. *Lawrence St Cartier, CIA agent, antiquities expert, but at heart – still the Jesuit priest.*

'You said it was imperative I meet you here, Lawrence. What rare antiquity did you unveil in Bali?'

'Ah!' Lawrence signalled to a monk who walked out from under the cypress trees.

'I knew I could count on your incurable obsession with the rare antiquities market. I'll enlighten you at dinner. A nap and some sunlight will do you the world of good. Brother Francis, show Mr De Vere to his room. Number nine, if I recollect.'

The old monk bowed and gestured to Nick to follow him through the cypress grove.

Lawrence St Cartier watched, disquieted, as the frail young De Vere limped across the meticulously kept lawns of the monastery gardens, leaning heavily on an antique silver cane. A parting gift from Klaus von Hausen.

Lawrence sighed deeply, then walked over to a small open-air Coptic garden chapel ten yards to his left.

Kneeling before the exquisitely carved stone crucifix, Professor Lawrence St Cartier bowed his head in supplication for the soul of Nicholas De Vere.

CHAPTER SIX

Lily and Alex

Manhattan
New York

The landlines in Jason De Vere's private executive headquarters in midtown Manhattan rang incessantly, fielded by his three remarkably efficient executive assistants.

Jontil Purvis answered Jason's private line for the seventh time in succession, in her normal calm demeanour. She put the call on hold.

'Mr De Vere, sir.'

She watched Jason on the monitor in front of her striding across the tarmac of the penthouse roof towards his personal private helicopter. He fixed his earpiece into his ear.

'I said hold all calls,' he shouted above the roaring of the helicopter turbine and rotor.

'You'll want this one, sir,' Jontil Purvis purred in her unflappable southern accent. 'It's Lily.'

Jason climbed into the helicopter and settled down into the plush leather seat.

'Put her through,' he barked.

Jason glared at the striking dark-haired sixteen year old on the monitor of the helicopter communication system.

'Lily!' he growled.

Julia St Cartier stood in her faded Levi jeans and white cotton T-shirt watching Lily in amusement as she negotiated with her father, who was raging on the phone six thousand miles away across the Atlantic.

She stood at the enormous floor-to-ceiling windows of the Georgian townhouse looking out at the bustling Brighton promenade in southern England. It was still winter and the temperatures were just above freezing, but as usual the British public were out in droves in every public place, shopping, working, dining.

She smiled.

Strange how the Americans had been labelled 'loud'. She was in no doubt, after living on the East Coast for over half her life, that it was quite the reverse. The grocery stores and shopping malls in America were refined in their level of noise output. On her return she had walked into her local Sainsbury's grocery store and been amazed and amused by the loudness of British life.

The Americans dressed more conservatively too, except in hubs like New York or LA, but in Britain you found New York on every street of every British town. British idiosyncrasy.

She broke off from her meanderings and turned from the window. Lily was still on the phone arguing with her father.

'No, Dad, you knew months ago!' Lily scowled. 'Alex, Polly, and I are spending the summer at the townhouse in Georgetown. It's been planned since September.'

Lily rolled her eyes impatiently.

'No, we're not on our *own*, Dad. Mum's joining us the second week. Stop treating me like I'm nine!'

Julia studied her sixteen-year-old daughter with amusement and not some little admiration. Lily's long gleaming dark hair framed strong features and the high De Vere cheekbones. Her deep green eyes were flashing. They were her only leaning to the St Cartier side, from Julia's beloved late mother, Lola.

Everything else was pure Jason De Vere, right down to the cleft in Lily's chin. There was no fighting it. At sixteen, Lily was already almost a replica of Jason De Vere in both her looks and temperament. And Julia adored her.

It had been almost nine years since the accident that disabled Lily.

Julia sighed. She knew it to the day. It was one of the big De Vere family parties. Lily, only seven, was exhausted, and Nick had offered to drive her home early. A huge articulated lorry had jack-knifed in front of them from out of nowhere. They hadn't a chance. Nick, though concussed, had only bruises and scratches, but Lily had been paralyzed from the waist down. Wheelchair-bound, disabled for life. Nick had had two beers – below the legal limit. Julia never needed any convincing that it had all been beyond his control. But Jason – well, that was another matter. Jason hadn't talked to his youngest brother from that day on. And the vivacious seven year old, whose world had revolved around ballet, had spent six months in hospital and another six in physical therapy. The specialists had been unanimous; she would be bedridden for life. But typically De Vere, Lily had proved them all wrong.

In under two years, in a wheelchair, she had been inaugurated into life as a boarder at Roedean school for girls in Brighton, England.

Within three months, Lily De Vere had become the life and soul of the establishment, and Jason and Julia had purchased the house in Brighton so that Julia could come and go at leisure to be near Lily.

Lily was a true survivor. In the mould of her father Jason De Vere. Courageous. Tenacious. Sometimes tactless. She had inherited her father's bluntness, his lack of sugar-coating.

Julia knew her softer, more artistic nature tempered Lily. They were best friends, as close as a mother and daughter could be.

The only thing that had nearly destroyed Lily was her parents' divorce.

Julia bit her lip at the memory. She had heard Lily sobbing every night for a month after she and Jason separated.

'*Ask him how Lulu's doing,*' Julia mouthed.

Lily rolled her eyes.

'Mum wants to know how Lulu's doing, Dad.'

She put her hand over the mouthpiece.

'He says it's *his* dog. He's keeping the Ridgeback. No negotiation.'

Now it was Julia's turn to roll her eyes.

Lily winked. 'He says she's fine. She's sleeping on his bed every night.'

Julia raised her eyebrows. 'That's a first.'

She watched as Lily clicked off her phone, seething.

Lily manoeuvred her wheelchair over to the windows, scowling darkly at the stormy English Channel in the falling dusk.

Julia hid a smile and walked towards her.

'He'll calm down, sweetheart.' She placed her hand on Lily's shoulder. 'He always does.'

Lily glared up at her mother, her cat-like eyes flashing with indignation.

'He expects me to drop all my plans at the drop of a hat and to spend my summer in New York when he knows Polly and I are going to Georgetown with Alex.' She looked at her mother imploringly.

'We've planned it for forever, Mum; it's Polly's seventeenth.

Her parents are in Tanzania. Alex is *depending* on her being with him. She won't go without me.'

The doorbell rang.

'Speak of the . . .' Lily winked at Julia.

The tall lean young man walked into the expansive white living room, ducking under one of the several gold and crystal chandeliers that Julia had bought on one of her many antiquing trips to Sweden.

Alex Lane-Fox was six foot three. Tall, dark, and as handsome as his mother, supermodel Rachel Lane-Fox, had been gorgeous. His dark hair was sliced with blond, he wore torn Levis and a baggy jacket, and he was clutching his Apple laptop.

'Hey, Aunt Jules.' He kissed Julia affectionately on the cheek, then spun Lily's wheelchair around.

'Hey, Lils, looks like I got accepted by the *New York Times **and*** the *Washington Post.*'

Lily clasped his hand. 'Hey, Alex, that's fantastic. You've always wanted to go back to the US! Mum, Alex is following in your footsteps.'

Alex grinned.

'*No,*' he said emphatically, 'I'm going to be a *serious* journalist.'

Julia clipped him with her hand.

'Hey! Subservience, please. I've known you since you were in nappies!'

Alex walked past the immaculate silver and white French sofas through the living room to the kitchen.

'Is Polly ready?' he shouted.

'She's just showering,' Lily called back. 'She'll be out any minute.'

Polly Mitchell was Lily's bosom friend from Roedean School. Lily and Polly had been friends since the age of nine. Whereas as Lily was the vivacious leader, Polly had been

57

the perfect foil for her. Polly Mitchell was one of eight children, the daughter of a minister with a passion for social action, who supported Aids orphanages in Tanzania and Malawi, and fought vehemently against human trafficking in China and Eastern Europe.

Polly had been accepted at Roedean on a scholarship and instantly the quiet, soft-spoken, hardworking minister's child and the outspoken freewheeling tycoon's daughter had fast become inseparable. Julia had watched Polly in amazement as the thin slip of a girl had blossomed overnight at fifteen from a shy, retiring, pale waif into a literal supermodel lookalike.

And Alex Lane-Fox, son of Rachel Lane-Fox, Julia's best pal, had been completely smitten.

He and Polly had been an item ever since.

After Rachel Lane-Fox had died on American Airlines flight 11 on 9/11, Alex had stayed with Jason and Julia and then lived in Manhattan with his stockbroker father. Until his first new stepmother came on the scene, that is. Alex had fought violently with his father, packed his bags and shocked everyone by moving in with Rachel's parents, Rebekah and David Weiss, in the north-west of Ireland. He was just fourteen.

His grandparents had strongly encouraged him to pursue a career in journalism, and at seventeen he had a placement with the *Irish Independent* newspaper in Dublin, then spent two years with the *Guardian* in London. He had long since buried the hatchet with his father and had spent the past three summers with him and wife number three, but his grandparents were kindred spirits and he was fiercely loyal to them. As he was to Jason. And to Julia.

Alex grabbed himself a Coke from the refrigerator.

'I hate to disillusion you both,' his voice echoed through to the lounge, 'but *Cosmo* isn't serious journalism!'

He walked back inside.

'Well, which is it to be?' Julia frowned. 'The *New York Times* or the *Washington Post*?'

'*New York*, of course. I start on 8 January. My defining moment. Who knows, maybe Uncle Adrian'll give me an exclusive on the Ishtar Accord!'

'In your dreams!' Julia threw a set of keys at him. Alex caught them deftly in one hand. 'Present from Nick. To you. Keys to his London apartment.'

'South Bank?' Alex grinned.

Julia's eyes narrowed.

'No wild parties, Alex. You and the girls stay there while I'm in Italy. Nick'll pick you up on his way back from France. I'll meet you all at the manor for Christmas Eve.'

'I'm not in a partying frame of mind, Aunt Jules. Seriously, guys, there are things going down. Stuff . . .' Alex hesitated. 'Bad stuff going down. Stuff the man in the street has no idea about,' he added ominously.

'Oh, Alex, don't start,' Lily pleaded.

Julia raised her eyebrows.

'No – no – you *don't* understand!' He opened the Coke and slugged it down noisily.

'The public's being lied to, manipulated by a global elite that has as its ultimate objective world domination.' He looked up at Lily and Julia ominously. 'World depopulation.'

'Oh, come on, Alex,' Julia said, waving him quiet. 'We've been through all this a million times.'

'Respectfully, Aunt Jules, it's not about 9/11. I'm in the middle of uncovering explosive stuff.' He put the Coke down on the marble countertop and opened his laptop.

'Weaponized Avian flu produced in bio-terror laboratories in Maryland; covert deep underground military bases across America; $500 billion of drug cartel money run by the CIA, siphoned off into the black budget annually . . .'

Alex's eyes blazed with conviction.

'And *all* roads lead to a shadow government.'

Julia and Lily mouthed to each other. 'Shadow government.'

'You have to admit it, Alex,' Lily said, 'it's wild, even for you!'

Julia winked just as Alex looked up at her. He shook his head.

'Your head's respectfully in the proverbial sand, Mrs D. A shadow government. The global elite. The Federal Reserve, International Bank of Settlements . . .'

His fingers flew over the laptop keys:

'*I will splinter the CIA into a thousand pieces and scatter it to the wind.*'

Alex looked up from the keys. 'Who said that? he demanded.

Lily shrugged her shoulders. Julia shook her head.

Alex held up his hands. 'The thirty-fifth President of the United States.'

'JFK?' Lily frowned.

'Oh, come on, Alex.' Julia waved him quiet.

'Did you *know* he said that?' He glared at Julia fiercely.

'Well, no, but there's no proof, Alex. The fact that Kennedy disliked the CIA doesn't make a government conspiracy, we all know that. The Warren Commission put an end to it.'

'Closed minds. You serve to prove the point. Closed to anything beyond your comfort zone. Over 40 per cent of the Warren Commission were members of the Elite Council of Foreign Relations. JFK fired Allen Dulles, Director of the CIA, after the Bay of Pigs. But Dulles was appointed to the Warren Commission after Kennedy's death. *Look* at the motives to assassinate JFK. Kennedy had tried to control the agency by reducing its ability to act through National Security Memorandums 55, 56, and 57.'

Alex pointed to the screen.

'These documents literally eliminated the ability of the CIA to wage war. It threw James J. Angleton, who ran CIA counter-intelligence, and Allen Dulles into a panic. Their power would have been limited to handguns. And *who* stood to gain from a long drawn-out war in Vietnam? The Vietnamese had refused to allow the elite to establish a central bank in Vietnam. The elite wanted a central bank *and* access to the vast oil reserves off the Vietnamese coast.'

He stared at Julia and Lily in frustration. 'Don't you get it? Vietnam. The Cold War. The international bankers, the elite, the military industrial complex, the oil barons – all members of a shadow government totally dependent on a *Pax Americana* forced on the world by American weapons of war. They *all* stood to gain from his death.'

Alex pulled out a kitchen stool and sat.

'Within days of JFK's death, Lyndon Johnson signed a National Security Action memorandum instructing the Pentagon to keep the troops in Vietnam. By 1963, Kennedy had already called for general and complete disarmament in the Cold War. And, of course, there's the contested issue where on 4 June 1963 JFK issued Executive Order 11110, instructing the Treasury to issue Treasury silver certificates.

'Okay,' he shrugged, 'the disinformation surrounding this is common knowledge, but it seems evidence exists that a high-level meeting of the elite was called immediately. Kennedy had thrown the secret masters in Washington and London into a tailspin. Look at *this*.' His fingers flew over his laptop keys.

'A 1960 USA five-dollar note. Green Seal. Look what it says at the top.'

Lily steered her wheelchair closer.

'It reads *Federal Reserve Note*.'

'Okay. Now study the 1963 five-dollar USA note. The year Kennedy was assassinated. Look at the Red Seal. '

'It says *United States of America Note*.'

Julia peered at the screen, perplexed.

'You sure? It can't be: it's always *Federal Reserve*.' She studied the laptop screen.

'There it is, Aunt Jules. Documented in black and white. A real note. The year of Kennedy's death. *United States of America Note. Now* look at a 1964 note. The year after JFK was assassinated.'

Julia frowned.

'*Federal Reserve Note*,' she murmured.

'Exactly. Back to the Fed. The facts are – Issuance of *all* United States Notes ended in January 1971. *Everything* in circulation today is issued by the Fed: *nothing* by the US government. The powers that be got back control.'

Alex slammed the laptop shut.

'Federal Reserve aside, JFK signed the Test Ban Treaty with Moscow. He was going to stop the Vietnam War, drastically reduce the CIA's influence.'

He stood as Polly Mitchell walked into the sitting room, her pale blonde hair straightened and her exquisite face perfectly made up. Alex walked over and kissed her full on the lips.

'He was blowing their powerbase apart piece by piece.' He swung around to Julia.

'Kennedy defied the secret rulers. They made a deliberate example of him. Brutally executed in broad daylight in front of millions. He didn't have a chance,' Alex concluded matter of factly. 'The shadow government achieved its objectives. Look at the 2008 bailout. Prime example. The shadow masters pull the strings. The Congress, the Senate, all too terrified to get out of line. They learned their lessons well. They *know* the cost of disobedience.'

'C'mon, Alex. Enough,' Polly said.

'I just don't get it,' Julia said. 'What has JFK's assassination got to do with *anything*?'

'If the government has lied and covered up the assassination of JFK, Aunt Jules – ' Alex stared at her darkly, 'and they *have* – what else have they lied about?'

He looked at Julia straight in the eye.

'And *who really runs the government?*'

'Dad would go ballistic if he heard you,' said Lily.

'Uncle Jas,' Alex rolled his eyes at Lily. 'The great American patriot!

'Alex!' Polly glared at him warningly.

'If I'm not mistaken,' Julia said drily, 'it was the great American patriot who got you your place at the *New York Times*. And changed your nappies when you were four months old. You're going to be the scourge of Manhattan at this rate.' She looked at him and sighed.

'You are *so* like your mother, Alex Lane-Fox.'

Alex grinned.

'Gorgeous? Yeah, I get that a lot.'

'I was rather thinking, stubborn.' Julia clipped him on the shoulder, then stopped in mid-sentence. Frozen.

Lily was staring up at Alex in complete adulation. Lily and Alex had virtually grown up together. Holidays. Family festivities. They were like brother and sister.

Julia took a deep breath. All these years, she had never noticed. Her strong-willed, independent, wheelchair-bound daughter was totally besotted with Alex Lane-Fox.

Julia knew with a mother's instinct that it had nowhere to go.

Alex was deeply in love with Polly. Lily was disabled for life.

How had she not seen this?

Alex, through no intention of his own, was breaking her daughter's heart.

Julia caught her breath.

She was going to have to put some space between them.

The doorbell rang again. This time, eight teenagers stood in the hallway. Exact replicas of Alex, Polly, and Lily, they were distinguishable only by the colour of their hair.

Alex pushed Lily's wheelchair out through the doorway.

'Bye, Mum,' Lily said, waving. Julia smiled weakly.

'Bye, Mrs D.' Polly stopped. 'Habit. I suppose I shouldn't call you Mrs D. now.'

She shuffled embarrassed.

'Now that the divorce is through.'

'Aunt Jules?' Julia snapped back into realty.

Alex pushed Lily through the door, then poked his head back around.

'You should really start dating again, Aunt Jules. My dad's surgeon friend – the good-looking one in London, Callum Vickers – says you never return his calls.'

He winked. 'He thinks you should.'

The door slammed.

Julia walked over to the windows to draw the heavy cream curtains.

The skies were already darkening. She hesitated and frowned, staring at the strange white apparition in the skies above the English Channel.

She wondered if Jason was dating. Odd, the thought of Jason dating. She couldn't quite imagine it.

She had to admit he was still attractive in a worn kind of way. Strange how she missed him tonight.

She walked over to the mantelpiece and picked up the solitary picture of Jason and Lily in the apartment then walked back to the window, staring out at the waves breaking on the Brighton shoreline. She looked down at the photograph, studying his features. He was as he always was. Serious.

She ran her fingertips gently over his face.

Then turned the photo face down and scrolled down her Xphone to Callum Vickers' phone number.

She took a deep breath.

And dialled.

CHAPTER SEVEN

Mourir de Façon Horrible

Nick dried his freshly washed hair and upper torso with a bath towel.

There was a loud knocking on the door of the monastic chamber. Nick frowned, then walked towards the door and opened it. Lawrence St Cartier, now freshly changed into a crisply pressed shirt and cravat, stood clutching a dog-eared British newspaper in hand. He stared at the red weals and sores all over Nick's chest, then lowered his eyes.

'Lawrence, this place is in the Dark Ages.' Nick said in frustration. 'There's no mobile signal. I've tried to put a call via landline through to the UK six times and each time I'm told the lines are down.'

'Oldest monastery in Egypt; still operates on a local exchange. The lines stay down for days at a time,' Lawrence replied distractedly.

'Aren't you going to come in?' Nick frowned. He studied Lawrence's face. The professor looked strangely shaken. Ashen, in fact. St Cartier fidgeted uneasily in the doorway.

'I'm the bearer of unpleasant news, I'm afraid, Nicholas.'

He laid the newspaper on the table awkwardly.

'I came as soon as it was slipped under my door. I haven't had time to review the entire article.'

Nick stared down at the newspaper headline: *Massacre at the Temple Mount*. His eyes locked on to a black-and-white headshot of one of eight archaeologists murdered.

'Klaus,' Nick murmured, stunned. He grabbed the paper and scanned through the leading paragraph. 'Klaus . . .'

'Von Hausen,' St Cartier finished crisply. 'Rising star of the British Museum and intimate friend of Nicholas De Vere. Your association was splashed across the *Sun* and *News of the World*, if I recollect.'

'Look, Lawrence,' Nick muttered, 'I don't expect sympathy.' He sat down heavily on the bed, his hands trembling.

'If it makes it easier, Klaus and I were long over.'

'Don't waste your sentiment, Nicholas, dear boy.' St Cartier's voice was unusually soft.

'You can't bring Von Hausen back.' He grasped Nick's shoulder gently.

'I . . . I saw him two days ago,' Nick said. 'In London. We met for drinks. Hadn't seen him for months. He'd been seconded to a classified dig in the Middle East.' He looked up at St Cartier, suddenly vulnerable.

'He was exhilarated,' he murmured. 'It was classified "Eyes Only". He said MI6 and Interpol were swarming over the British Museum. His department – the Middle East. Something connected with the Vatican. Klaus knew the way they work – it would remain undisclosed to him until his arrival.'

St Cartier took the paper from Nick, put on his glasses and studied the article thoroughly.

'Hmmm. The papers only report it was an ancient Temple relic,' St Cartier said.

'All the marks of a massive mop-up job. Seven archaeologists mown down with sub-machine guns . . . execution-style. Special Forces. Trained killers.'

He scanned a smaller paragraph halfway down the page.

'And one Vatican priest beheaded . . .' His voice trailed off.

Nick studied the professor through narrowed eyes. St Cartier was pale. His right hand was trembling uncontrollably.

'Beheaded, Nicholas,' St Cartier said, crisply, swiftly regaining his composure. He folded the paper up neatly with three deft moves.

'*Most* barbaric.' St Cartier's eyes glittered with an uncharacteristic hardness.

'Islamic terrorists?' Nick asked.

'No.' St Cartier walked to the far window and gazed out beyond the rows of cypress trees to the vast expanse of sands.

'No, not terrorists, Nicholas,' he murmured. 'This has the mark of something far more sinister than terrorists. Someone would like the entire Western world to *think* it was terrorists.'

St Cartier fell silent, engrossed in his own reflections.

Nick eased a fresh white shirt over his head. He stared blankly at his hollow cheeks in the mirror. 'If not terrorists, then who, and what do they want?'

The bell in the tower chimed six o'clock just as the dinner gong sounded.

'Time runs down, Nicholas. Daniel's week is almost upon us.'

He looked grimly into Nick's face.

'I fear the End of Days has begun.'

68

The nib of Gabriel's quill scratched the heavy linen paper embossed with his crest Prince Regent. Gabriel's exquisite italic lettering filled the page.

My tormented brother, Lucifer,
I saw you in my dreamings this very dawn, a lone figure overlooking Golgotha.
So assured of your victory at Armageddon.
The White Rider, your Son of Perdition, coming forth to rule the race of men.
Heralding the Tribulation of the Apocalypse of the Revelation of Saint John.

Gabriel sighed. He pushed his long platinum locks back from his flawless features, then continued his intensive lettering.

And I remembered another dawn when you came to me in my dreamings.
The dawn when your iniquitous plan was conceived.
The dawn when you stood sleepless on the Portico of the North Winds.

The dawn of the Wizard Riders.

FORTY YEARS EARLIER

1981
One Thousand and Forty-Eight Years
after Golgotha

CHAPTER EIGHT

Diabolical Schemings

L ucifer stood, a lone figure, on the Portico of the North Winds under the great silver battlements of the Citadel of Gehenna.

He stared out grimly at the seven comets of Thuban, their flaming hoar-frost tails blazing indigo as they rose over the barren ice plains of Gehenna. Then he raised his head to the freezing arctic blizzards approaching from the White Dwarf Pinnacles of the north, venting their fury against the monstrous forbidding fortress.

His Winter Palace.

It had been almost two thousand years since Golgotha.

Since his humiliation at the hands of the Nazarene.

He scowled. He could still taste his acrimonious defeat, on the scorching black pitch plains inside the monstrous iron gates of hell, as though it were yesterday.

He had vowed by the dark Codices of Diabolos to embrace eternal winter until his allotted time was up according to the Tenets of Eternal Law.

Until the Final Judgement – *the Lake of Fire*. He shuddered.

His slumber had been fitful these past thirteen moons.

Marred by strange and sinister nightmares.

Charsoc the Dark had plied him wth myriad sleeping potions of belladonna, mandragora elixir, and hellbroths, furnished by the Warlock Kings of the West.

But nothing had eased the menacing spectres that tormented his dreamings.

He pulled his velvet gown tightly around his form and stared bleakly past the ice-capped crags of Vesper.

Since Golgotha, his power in the land of the race of men had been greatly curtailed by the Tenets of Eternal Law. His presence on their futile mass of mud and vapour was illegitimate. The race of men was plagued with infirmities . . . beleaguered by vanities . . . contemptible. But he had no alternative. He had to use the craven masses.

His time ran down. He sensed it.

Armageddon drew nearer.

And with it a thousand years incarcerated in the bottomless pit before his demise in the Lake of Fire.

His nails dug harshly into his palm.

At Golgotha, his fallen armies against Michael's warriors and the Nazarene's sorceries had been vanquished with ease. It would never happen again.

This time there would be no error. Deep beyond the Vaults of Vagen, his scientists had been building superweapons and manufacturing vast armies of monstrous hybrids these past thousand years – preparing for Armageddon.

He raised his face to the skies.

He would conquer the Nazarene. But there was still one more addition to his ambitious scheme.

The ice blizzards tore the hood from his head, exposing the once-exquisite imperial countenance, now scarred almost beyond recognition in the torrid inferno at his banishment from the First Heaven.

He *would produce a super legion of the Fallen.*

74

A two hundred million army.

He smiled malevolently.

To defeat the Nazarene in the Great Battle.

Armageddon.

His iniquitous contemplations were interrupted by the thunderous pealing of the monstrous bells of Limbo, echoing from the spire across the bleak ice plains of Gehenna.

A thousand jaundice-eyed demonic gargoyles soared from the spires into Gehenna's skies, screaming maniacally, their scaled wings beating like giant bellows, their great horn claws slashing the skies.

Lucifer swung around to the shadowed figure standing at one of the hundreds of hideous stained-glass windows lining the Eastern Wall.

'Who summons me at this infernal hour?' he hissed.

Balberith. Lucifer's Chief of Angelic Courtiers bowed deeply.

'Your Excellency,' he said, trembling, 'Charsoc the Dark requests an audience with you.'

'Charsoc the Dark,' he scowled. 'Bearing yet another ineffectual *potion*!'

A tall bony form moved from the shadows and stood in the portico entrance.

Charsoc the Dark, Chief High Priest of the Fallen, bowed deeply, his black hair swept the floor. Charsoc's fall from the First Heaven had been second only to his nefarious Master's. Formerly one of Yehovah's eight High Elders of the First Heaven and second only in rank to Jether the Just, Charsoc had sunk effortlessly to become the most depraved of Lucifer's Necromancer kings. He was Governor of the dreaded Warlock Kings of the West and the Governor of the Grand Wizards of the Black Court.

Iniquitous, cold-blooded, and scheming, he ruled from the Catacombs of Gehenna, second in command only to Lucifer.

'My Lord, esteemed excellency, it is no potion that I bring.'

Charsoc smoothed his vermillion taffeta gown. 'It is tidings: pleasant tidings.' Charsoc grasped Lucifer's sleeve with bony, pale, jewelled fingers.'

'What, Master, if your reliance on the Monarchs of the race of men were at an end?

'What, *Master*,' – Charsoc moved closer, so close that Lucifer could feel his hot tepid breath on his cheeks – 'if you could mobilize your armies . . . under a messiah . . . your *own* messiah?'

Lucifer grasped Charsoc's arm so fiercely that Charsoc winced in agony.

'Explain yourself,' he hissed.

'The Dark Cabal Wizards.' Charsoc exhaled. 'They ride from the Crypts of Nagor as we speak.' He hesitated. 'The Twins seek an audience.'

Lucifer's eyes searched Charsoc's face, instantly alert. 'The Twins?'

He released Charsoc from his fierce grip. Charsoc caressed his arm and bit his lip in pain as Lucifer strode past him under the colossal Ionic columns of the Eastern Portico.

Charsoc withdrew a black missive seemingly from mid-air, sealed with a silver pentagram.

'From the Twins' emissaries, Your Excellency.'

Lucifer snatched the missive and scanned it. It blazed fiercely in his palm, then evaporated.

'Release my vulture shamans from their hell cages as their welcoming parties. Send word to the Grand Wizard of Phaegos and the Grand Wizard of Maelageor that I prepare to grant them audience. Summon the Darkened Councils from under the earth.'

Charsoc bowed deeply.

'Your word is my command, sire,' he said, and vanished into thin air.

Lucifer moved to the very edge of the Portico, deep in contemplation.

Slowly, he raised his palm to the skies.

The form of Gabriel became visible, slumbering deeply in his chamber in the First Heaven.

Lucifer stared at his youngest brother. Captivated.

'Gabriel,' he murmured.

Gabriel's exquisite features were bathed in the glimmering radiance from the Western Wall. Serene. Undisturbed.

'Dream deeply, Revelator,' Lucifer uttered.

Gabriel's breathing became shallow. He tossed restlessly from side to side.

Lucifer smiled a slow evil smile.

'May the Wizard Riders infect your dreams, brother,' he whispered. 'My redemption draweth nigh.'

Gabriel stared up at the soaring gold-columned palace that towered high above the Western Wall of the First Heaven. His normally serene features were troubled. His grey eyes clouded.

The eastern and northern wings of the Palace of Archangels were still inhabited by him and Michael – but the great west wing, once occupied by the former Prince Regent, Lucifer, lay desolate. The magnificent mother-of-pearl chambers lay deserted. Their towering golden doors engraved with the emblem of the Son of the Morning had been shackled since the dusk of his banishment, in worlds long since departed.

The west wing had been unchained only once in all the millennia past. The day that Lucifer was summoned to appear at the First Judgement, nearly two thousand years before. He had dressed in these very quarters before he was delivered to the Great White Plains.

Gabriel ran his fingers through his pale gold tresses, uneasiness etched on his flawless features. He gave a backward glance at Zadkiel who rode a clear ten feet behind him, with Sandaldor by his side. Gabriel nodded.

As one, the small party rode through the Western Gates a full mile above the glistening diamonds that paved the winding roadway. Gabriel hesitated outside Lucifer's vast orangeries. Once vibrant with the heliotropes and lupins that his eldest brother had so loved, it was as it had been since his banishment.

Desolate. Bleak. Almost austere.

Nothing flowered and yet at the same time there was no decay. It was a vacuum. As though even the animated blooming flora of the First Heaven had sensed Lucifer's treacherous betrayal and declined to grow these hundred million aeons since his exile.

He pulled gently on the reins of his mare Ariel. They continued, past the drained Pools of the Seven Wisdoms, drawing to a halt directly in front of the two towering golden doors of Lucifer's west wing chambers.

Gabriel dismounted, followed by Zadkiel and Sandaldor. Zadkiel walked over and laid a hand gently on his arm.

'You are sure this is your wish, my prince?' he asked.

Gabriel bowed his head, then raised his gaze to meet Zadkiel's.

'It is my wish,' he whispered, his normally serene eyes awash with intense emotion.

Zadkiel studied the Prince intently, then bowed. He gestured to Sandaldor who moved forward. Zadkiel nodded. Together they raised their huge iron axe-hammers high, then swung them forcefully against the monstrous iron manacles, shattering them cleanly in two.

Slowly Zadkiel pushed open the heavy golden doors of Lucifer's quarters. Gabriel drew a sharp breath. The west wing lay untouched.

Zadkiel walked after Gabriel into the atrium, staring into Lucifer's chambers. They stood together a long while in silence.

'I cannot contend with this, Gabriel.' Zadkiel bowed his head, his hands trembling. Remembering.

'It brings back memories of all that damned my soul.'

He raised his tortured gaze to Gabriel.

'I plead with you, Gabriel.' Zadkiel's voice shook with intensity. 'Release me from this undertaking.'

Gabriel studied Zadkiel intently with compassion. Finally he spoke.

'I release you, old friend,' he sighed. 'Return with Sandaldor to my chambers and await me there.'

Zadkiel bowed deeply.

'May you find, my revered prince, that which you so earnestly seek,' he murmured.

He started to walk away.

'Zadkiel,' Gabriel called after him. 'Michael . . .' He hesitated. 'He has no knowledge I am here?'

Zadkiel held his gaze.

'He has no knowledge.'

Gabriel nodded.

'I will reveal it when I am ready. And Jether?'

'I have not revealed it to Jether.' Zadkiel smiled faintly. 'But his knowledge will be from a higher source.'

Zadkiel bowed once more, then remounted his steed. He tore at high speed back down the roadway followed by Sandaldor. Without a glance back.

Gabriel stood in the gateway staring after Zadkiel until he had completely disappeared from view, then retraced his steps, pushed open the chamber doors, and moved into the atrium. He secured the doors from inside, surveying the vast chamber.

He shook his head in wonder.

It was almost as it had been in aeons past before their world fell.

Lucifer's collection of pipes and tabarets.

His Sword of State still in its magnificent jewelled sheath.

Gabriel walked under the great frescoed Arch of Archangels and into Lucifer's inner sanctum, staring up at the magnificent trompe l'oeils – Lucifer's own handiwork, painted on the vaulted ceilings that soared a hundred feet. Heliotrope, damsons, and amethysts merging into magenta and vermilions covering the ornate carved ceilings.

His gaze fell onto the beautifully carved marble writing desk.

The very same desk where his elder brother had penned thousands of his beautifully italicized missives in worlds long gone.

He paled.

Leaning next to the desk was an enormous *objet d'art*, covered with gold cloth. It had not been there two millennia ago, the day of the First Judgement.

The answers to his disturbed dreaming of the night before lay there.

He was sure of it.

Lucifer and his infuriating sorcerers' games!

He strode over to the desk, then leaned over and untied the golden cords of the cloth. The gold muslin dropped from the frame onto the floor below revealing a life-size painting. Nine feet tall. Twelve feet wide.

Gabriel studied it intently.

Directly in the centre of the canvas was a perfect depiction of Christos. Exquisite, each feature captured in light. It was breathtaking, but for one thick, jagged, crimson line that severed the face from one side of the canvas to the other.

He lowered his gaze to the left of the image.

There they were. Just as he had known. The Dark Cabal Wizard Riders, astride their monstrous creations. Their destination, the ice world of Gehenna.

Lucifer had painted the scene unerringly down to the finest detail. It was exactly what Gabriel had witnessed in his disturbed dreamings of this dawn.

Directly below Christos was a precise depiction of Lucifer himself standing on the huge, ornately carved pearl balcony of these very chambers. Exactly as he had in aeons past when he watched his brothers race across the sands. His sculpted alabaster features were perfect in their beauty. Gabriel stared mesmerized into the cold sapphire eyes.

They were almost lifelike. His gaze dropped to the base of the picture where an enormous menacing serpent writhed across the entire canvas.

He shuddered.

'They ride the West Winds.' A soft voice shattered the silence.

Slowly, Gabriel turned.

Jether the Just, imperial angelic monarch and ruler of the twenty-four ancient kings of Yehovah, stood directly before him, resplendent in his striped scarlet robes.

He studied his old student intently, his ancient lined features filled with compassion.

Gabriel bowed his head.

'The Dark Cabal Wizards,' Jether said softly. 'They left the Crypts of Nagor before the dawn moons rose. They ride as we speak.'

Gabriel raised his face to Jether's, his features etched with anguish.

'Lucifer spoke to me in my dreamings, Jether,' he whispered.

'He said he has been sleepless many moons. He bade me come to him.'

Jether laid his veined hand on his arm.

'But you did not.' He smiled gently.

'No.' Gabriel bowed his head. 'But he came instead to me in my dreaming.

'"Gabriel," Lucifer murmured. "Gabriel, I would have you know I will be sleepless no more. The riders come." Then he smiled. A wicked evil smile. And said, "Tell Jether – my redemption draweth nigh." And he was gone.'

Gabriel looked at his mentor with imploring eyes. 'What dastardly scheme is afoot, Jether?'

'It is the fullness of time,' Jether murmured, his venerable features grave. He walked over to where Gabriel stood, his silvered hair and beard sweeping the sapphire floors. He studied the painting carefully.

'They prepare for Armageddon. The Grand Wizards ride through the underworld from the dead places. He grants them audience.' He walked to the balcony and parted the heavy velvet curtains.

'How did you know I would come?' Gabriel whispered.

Jether looked at him benevolently.

'The older seer discerns the younger.'

He felt for the huge set of keys at his waist and removed one engraved with the Son of the Morning's insignia. 'I could have saved Zadkiel and Sandaldor their exertions, magnificent though they were.' Jether smiled into his beard. With nimble fingers, he unlocked the immense glass doors, then walked out onto the balcony, staring out towards a towering, golden, ruby-encrusted door, ablaze with light, that was embedded into the jacinth walls of the tower – the entrance to the throne room.

Huge roarings of thunder and blue bolts of lightnings emanated from the Rubied Door.

'They meet,' said Jether softly. He bowed his head in reverence.

Gabriel walked out onto the balcony.

'Yehovah, Christos, and the Sacred Spirit.'

Jether turned, his watery blue eyes deep in thought.

'What Lucifer discerns and learns today, Yehovah in his omniscience knew aeons past. Yehovah summoned me this very moon. Lucifer gathers the Courts of Perdition in council even as we speak. This very hour the plan to conceive his own messiah, the Son of Perdition, will be set in motion.'

Jether's gaze became as steel.

'Make no mistake. Lucifer's grand schemings are transparent to Yehovah at every turn. There is nothing that is hidden from his gaze. He is omniscient. He is omnipotent. He knows the end from the beginning to the ages of ages. Lucifer well knows this. And trembles.'

His features softened.

'We rest in the brilliance of Yehovah's multitude of discernments and great and infinitely tender compassions. We rest in his infinite wisdom.'

Gabriel was quiet a long moment. Jether laid his hand on his arm.

'You have what you came for, Gabriel. He has delivered his message. The Seed of the Serpent. The seed that will become his son. His Son of Perdition. *That* is what disturbs your dreamings.'

Jether closed the balcony doors.

'Now, come. We have urgent matters to attend.'

Together they retraced their steps through the chamber ino the atrium. Gabriel glanced back at the painting.

'The Seed of the Serpent. His own? Nephilim?' Gabriel asked.

Jether shook his head.

'No, Gabriel. Not Nephilim.' Jether closed the doors of

Lucifer's chambers hard behind them and relocked them. Gabriel turned to him, confused.

'If not a hybrid mixture between the angelic and the race of man, then what?' His voice broke off as he caught sight of Jether's sombre expression.

'There will be no mixture of the seeds.' Jether's voice was soft, but it cut the air like a blade.

'That is what Yehovah well discerns. Lucifer's messiah will be fashioned neither of the seed of man nor the egg of woman. Lucifer mimics the Christ's seed – *ex nihilo*.'

Gabriel shook his head confused.

'He would create a clone, Gabriel. His clone. We have not much time. The Fallen ride even as we speak.'

Jether studied his face, then sighed, his expression softening.

'Tell Michael I will meet with him on the Pearl Sands. At dusk.'

Jether embraced Gabriel on both cheeks, then mounted his white-winged charger.

His eyes flashed with intensity.

'I go to summon the High Councils of Yehovah.'

Six hundred and sixty-six of Lucifer's Dark Cabal Wizards ascended from the blazing acid-green infernos of the labyrinths deep within the lowest Crypts of Nagor. Their sparse white hair was pulled back from their sunken foreheads and their monstrous feathered seraph wings thrashed the air as they rode the arc of the North Wind, astride their monstrous hybrid genetic creations.

A depraved ghoulish horde led by the two-headed Twin Wizards of Malfecium.

The super-scientists of the damned would reach the Ice Citadel of Gehenna by dawn.

CHAPTER NINE

The Vial of Sacred Progeny

L ucifer sat majestically on his enormous carved horn throne, his headrest one enormous ruby. He smoothed his glistening white robes of state, embroidered with diamonds and molten gold.

Four of his bearers appeared and deftly plaited his raven hair with ice-diamonds and amethyst lightnings, then slunk away. Balberith placed the diamond Satanic Crown of State on Lucifer's head and bowed.

Charsoc moved towards the throne. He bowed deeply, his jet-black hair sweeping the crystal floors.

'Your Majesty, the Darkened Councils have been summoned from under the earth. The Warlocks of the West gather as we speak.'

Lucifer caressed the coarse white fur of the six-headed ice-wulf at his feet. A gift from the Twins of Malfecium. He bit into the flesh of a large golden fruit, then held it out idly in his palm to the ice-wulf who wagged his serpent tail, then devoured it ferociously, his dark blue fangs visible.

He smiled in approval, then studied Charsoc through narrowed eyes.

'Long have I awaited this day,' he murmured.

'From the time I ruled through Nebuchadnezzar, I waited.'

He sipped delicately from his goblet.

'During my reign through Antiochus IV of Syria and Mesopotamia, I waited.'

He raised his head and stared up at sixty-six golden seraphim and carved gorgons above him. His gaze dropped to the magnificent frescos beneath the arches of the inner dome depicting Nimrod, Alexander, and Antiochus's kingdoms.

'Antiochus failed me,' he hissed. 'Alexander the Great, Charlemagne, Stalin, Adolf Hitler . . .' He scowled. 'All incompetent mewling parasites!'

He swung around to Charsoc, his eyes dark. 'I will tolerate no more error.'

Lucifer raised his sceptre in the direction of the mammoth black ice doors to the throne room.

At once they turned to vapour, revealing 333 cowl-hooded Magi led by Marduk, head of the Darkened Councils.

Marduk led the way down the western stairs to the West Portal of the Last Judgement. A magnificent ivory carving of Lucifer triumphant and the race of men burning in the Lake of Fire towered overhead. The Darkened Councils each took their carved horn thrones, two levels below Lucifer's own ornate throne.

A discordant droning filled the atmosphere of the throne room as a thousand hunched Black Murmurers entered through the gates, their black seraph wings concealed underneath their semi-transparent grey muslin cloaks.

They formed a sinister dark line, skulking up the 666 steps to the circular Whispering Gallery, directly beneath the open dome. Their cowled hoods blew under the swirling ice tempests.

The bells of Limbo pealed. The throne room instantly filled with a strange noxious green sulphur. The Dark Cabal

Wizards swooped down through the vast open dome on their biogenetically-engineered monsters until all 666 were gathered in the aisle of the North Wind. As one, they bowed low before Lucifer.

Lucifer raised his sceptre.

'I summon the Twins of Malfecium: the Grand Wizard of Phaegos, the Grand Wizard of Maelageor.'

The Twins stepped forward. They stooped exceedingly, their long, pointed chins resting only six inches from the ground. Each had two shrunken rotating heads.

Their physical features were almost identical. They stared up at Lucifer out of pale, bulbous, straw-coloured eyes that glittered malevolently from beneath their sunken foreheads.

Their flesh held a strange cadaverous green pallor and their sparse white hair fell to their waists. Under their muslin cloaks, their backs were knotted and each had three hunchbacks. Under their robes on either side of their hunchbacks grew six immense feathered seraph wings.

The Twins were Lucifer's super-scientists. His evil intelligentsia.

The Grand Architects of his depraved eugenics and biogenetic engineering schemes, their days and nights were spent huddled in their gruesome laboratories a thousand miles below the scalding ice rings of Mellenzia, in the barren wastelands of the Underworld in the Crypts of Nagor.

It was here they performed the most depraved of their iniquitous procedures: biogenetic engineering; poisonings; amputations; limb and head grafts; lobotomies. Agonized screams of torment resounded day and night from the Labyrinths of Angor as the harpies of Gilmagoth, under their tutelage, violated each rule of decency, and contravened every tenet of Eternal Law with their cloning of the bestial and the angelic.

The Twins were purists. They maimed, tortured, and

disembowelled banshees, trolls, and demon-vampires, and they experimented on all that roamed the underworld unaware. They spawned an army of misshapen inbreds. Millions of depraved new species – grotesque deformed monsters.

Winged Vampire-Behemoths, sixty-six-eyed Cyclops, Scaled Brobdingnagians – the foot soldiers of Gehenna. The monsters of the Army of the Fallen, prepared to be unleashed at the last great battle fought against the Nazarene – Armageddon.

But the Twins' greatest conception, their consummate work of genius, lay beyond the eight Great Vaults of Vagen. In the Sarcophagus of the Furies.

Behind the translucent shimmering veils that fell from columns of golden asps lay one single vial of gold emitting strange black lightnings.

The vial that contained a single genome.

The Seed of the Serpent.

Lucifer's genome.

Lucifer's angelic DNA, biogenetically re-engineered by the Twins of Malfecium to correspond precisely with the growth cycle of human DNA.

The Vial of Sacred Progeny.

It had lain for millennia beneath Mellenzia. Awaiting the day when technology in the race of men was advanced enough to complete the sacred task.

The Twins' journey this day was connected to the genome. This Lucifer sensed.

He gestured them nearer.

'Maelageor,' he said softly to the Twin at his left. 'You requested audience.'

The Grand Wizard of Maelageor stared out at Lucifer with veined hooded eyes.

'Your Excellency,' he slithered, his tongue distended and mottled.

'It concerns the Vial of Sacred Progeny.'

Maelageor bowed low. Lucifer stared intently at Maelageor. Waiting.

'Sire, we have found one in the race of men of skill beyond any other. His proficiency in the field of biogenetic engineering leads us to believe he could be suited to the sacred task.'

Phaegos stepped forward.

'Your Excellency, he is the race of men's leading expert in genetic engineering, genetic manipulation, and gene-splicing.'

He bowed deeply.

Lucifer rose. He paced restlessly before the throne, deep in contemplation.

Abruptly he turned to Maelageor.

'You are sure?' His gaze locked on Maelageor's. 'I will tolerate no more error. Hitler failed me,' he hissed.

'The Nazi eugenics programme, their manipulation of human DNA . . .' He spun around to stare at the fresco of the Nuremberg Rally above him.

'Mengele, Clauberg, Brandt . . . We gave them every blueprint crucial to the task of cloning. *All* led to failure!'

Maelageor raised his head.

'Your Excellency, the race of men's technological progress in the area of genetics has greatly accelerated. The year 1981 finds it still primitive, but this one is a fervent scholar.'

'He is a genius?'

Charsoc leaned over to Lucifer.

'He is a genius among the race of men, sire.'

Charsoc held a sheaf of documents in his hand.

'Your Excellency,' he bowed, 'I have studied the texts. It is as the Twins relay.'

Lucifer seized the documents from Charsoc's grasp and strode down the nave, scanning the papers, Charsoc at his side.

'He is sympathetic to our cause?'

Charsoc nodded.

'He was the scientist in charge of the Los Alamos cloning programme, sire. Black operations. He serves our dark slaves of the race of men with devotion.'

'His silence will be ensured?'

Charsoc stroked his beard pensively as he walked.

'He is an ambitious man, Your Majesty.' He hesitated. 'But not a curious man. He cares not who his masters are. He has no god. His only god is that of science.'

Lucifer swung around.

'Marduk! I seek a family of the race of men. Search the Lower Libraries of Iniquities. Seek out a hundred dynasties of the race of men. Dark Slaves of the Fallen. Those I have endowed with riches. Those I reward with power. Devoted servants of the Fallen.'

Lucifer paced back up the nave, deep in contemplation.

'I think I shall give him brothers. A stubborn Michael. A tender Gabriel. They shall be three, even as we three angelic brothers. Three brothers of the race of men.'

An insane fire lit his gaze. 'And *like* his father before him.'

He raised his arms towards the vast dome.

'My son shall be an insurrectionist. A renegade!' he cried.

Maelageor moved nearer.

'There *is* a family, Sire.' He held out a large black codex emitting silver lightnings. Lucifer recognized it instantly as one of the thirteen Codices of Diabolos.

'A most *suitable* family.' He stared up at Lucifer, his cruel bulbous eyes glittering. Lucifer studied him intently, then took hold of the Codex.

'One of the thirteen families of the Grande Druid Council,' Maelageor wheedled. 'Those who reign in the world of the race of men as Warlock High Priests.'

'The grandfather is familiar to me,' Lucifer murmured,

studying the Codex. 'He bears the "Warlock's Mark". He is a devoted servant of the Fallen.' He smiled slowly in approval. 'Pray, continue, Maelageor.'

'The host is with child, sire. Her second child. Eight weeks in the womb; a son. The infant will be exchanged at birth with your own clone.'

Six Dark Cabal Wizards entered through the ice doors, bearing a black sarcophagus on their shoulders. They set it down on the altar before the throne.

Lucifer nodded. Slowly, Maelageor opened the casket. In the very centre lay a single vial of gold emitting strange black lightnings. Lucifer circled the casket, staring at the vial enthralled.

'There is no time to lose, Your Excellency,' Maelageor continued. 'In anticipation of your sanction of the chosen family, we have re-engineered the DNA of your genome – the genome of the Vial of Sacred Progeny – to correspond precisely with the projected birth date of the human infant. The DNA reconstructor has already been activated. The genome must be transported to the world of the race of men by one you trust. Without delay.'

'You have excelled yourself as always, Maelageor.'

Lucifer raised his sceptre to Charsoc.

'Charsoc, you will deliver the genome to earth. Instruct the occultic time sorcerers to prepare for the unleashing of the time whirlwinds of the Eastern Vortex!' he commanded.

The Grand Wizard of Phaegos stepped forward, trembling.

'Your Majesty.' He bowed, his two chins scraping the floor. 'One hundred moons waxing and waning must pass before the whirlwinds of the Eastern Vortex are unleashed. And another three full moons before the Time Gates of the Eastern Vortex pass by the Second Heaven and open into the world of the race of men. Time is against us. The genome must be delivered in the dimension of matter *now*.'

He took two steps backwards.

'And by one of our own in *human form*.'

'Human form? Impossible, Phaegeor!' Charsoc exclaimed. 'Golgotha changed the conditions of our sojourning in the race of men. His Majesty alone, as archangel, retains the ability to sojourn in human form and only through the Time Gates. We – the Fallen – are forbidden!'

'The genome is set to the human growth cycle, Phaegeor. It *must* be delivered in the dimension of matter by one of our own in matter. In human form. There is no other way.'

Lucifer stepped towards Phaegeor. Incensed.

'*Find* a way, Phaegeor.'

'But . . . the Time Gates . . . It is impossible, sire.'

Maelageor grasped Phaegeor's trembling arm with the six long green rubbery fingers of his right hand. Phaegeor winced in agony.

'What my twin brother means' – he raised his sunken features to Phaegeor and gave him a dark glare – 'is that there *is* another means, Your Excellency,' he lisped, 'for us, the Fallen, to enter the race of men. In human form. One moon from now.'

'What means, Maelageor?' Lucifer hissed.

A cruel smile flickered on Maelageor's thin black lips.

'We enter by the Ascending Stairs.'

A horrified silence fell throughout the throne room.

Lucifer stared at Maelageor, a strange wonder on his features.

'The Portals of the Fallen,' he uttered, 'they are force fields. Each has its own interdimensional threshold.'

Maelageor nodded. 'The force fields are DNA reconstructors. They are our only way of entering the race of men in human form.'

Marduk walked towards them, his yellow eyes glinting from under his fawn cassock hood. He bowed to Lucifer.

'My liege lord.' He kissed Lucifer's black onyx ring.

'The traversing of the Portals by the Fallen into the land of the race of men is not only forbidden, it is impossible, Your Majesty. All eight Portals of the Fallen were permanently *sealed* after the defeat at Golgotha. There is no way in from the Second Heaven to the Earth's atmosphere.'

'There is one.' Charsoc exchanged a glance with Maelageor.

'One Portal that is more vulnerable, its force field between the land of men and the Second Heaven ruptured. Torn.'

Lucifer sat on his throne, stroking the ice-wulf's coarse white fur.

'The Angelic Portal that was torn in the Tower of Babel–Nephilim fiasco,' he murmured. A faint smile flickered on his lips.

'The Portal of Shinar.'

'Your Excellency, with all due veneration and respect,' Marduk whined, wringing his lizard-like fingers. 'It is forbidden.'

'It is forbidden, Marduk.' Lucifer looked out of the corner of his eye at Marduk. 'But it *is* possible.'

The ice-wulf licked Lucifer's palm.

'Nimrod and the Nephilim, incited by our demonic hordes, were well advanced in their plans to traverse the Shinar force field from the Land of Men into the Second Heaven.' Lucifer's expression darkened. 'Gabriel and his Revelators sent word to the High Council. Yehovah confused their languages by day.' He held out his hand to his cupbearer.

'By night Michael and his armies overthrew our battalions, took control of Shinar and sealed the Portal.' He flinched at the memory of his defeat, then snatched the golden goblet from his trembling cup bearer.

'The interdimensional force field was permanently ruptured in the battle.' He caressed the rim of the goblet with his fingers.

'If we could control the Portal we could *reverse* the restructuring process and enter through the fissure in the force field.'

'It has been sealed fast by Michael's warriors in the Second Heaven these twenty millennia since Babel,' said Charsoc, pacing the nave. An evil fire flickered in his irisless eyes.

'But to what extent is it protected all these millennia later, Mulabalah?'

Mulabalah, ruler of the Black Murmurers, Charsoc's spies, stood, a sinister dark figure in the centre of the Whispering Gallery.

'Report on the defences of the Portal of Shinar.'

The incessant mumbling of the Murmurers fell to a hushed drone.

'Sire, in our traversing of the time corridors, the vulture shaman scouts have frequented the time lock between the Portal of Shinar and Gehenna. From the time of the uprising of the Nephilim and the race of men at Babel, it was defended unremittingly with a thousand of the First Heaven's strongest battalions.' Mulabalah hesitated. 'And the White Winged Lions,' he said, ominously.

A ripple of horror ran through the Whispering Gallery.

'These past millennia, however, Prince Michael reassigned the armies from Babylonia to Jerusalem, sire.' He hesitated, trembling. 'In 1947 . . .'

'Nineteen forty-seven!' Lucifer hissed. 'Jerusalem. Ashdod was defeated by Michael.'

'But today only Zalialiel and a battalion of two hundred guard the gates,' Mulabalah reported.

'You are certain of this, Mulabalah?'

'It is corroborated by Darsoc and by the vulture shaman scouts, sire. I am certain.'

Marduk rubbed his pockmarked chin in agitation.

'Your Majesty. It is my solemn duty as Chief of Staff and

94

Legal Counsel to bring to your attention that the Tenets of Eternal Law as pertaining to the Portal of Shinar carry dire consequences to us, the Fallen, if they are broken.'

Marduk lifted his hood, his ravaged, pockmarked, sallow features clearly visible.

'*Dire* consequences . . .'

'I am well versed in Eternal Law, Marduk. The penalty is not expressly spelt out in the tenets,' Charsoc hissed.

'It is nebulous at best.'

Marduk stared coldly at Charsoc through jaundiced, straw-coloured eyes.

'I warn you, Charsoc, do not be deluded. My sources reveal that an addendum has been added, by decree of Yehovah to Jether of the High Council, in order to protect the race of men from the Fallen. The rumours are the *severest* of penalties will befall those of the Fallen who violate the tenets.'

'Jether and his rumours!' Charsoc hissed.

Maelageor shook his two shrunken heads.

'The genome,' he slithered. 'We run out of time, Your Excellency.'

Lucifer rose.

'Rumours . . . rumours!' He strode up the steps towards the Whispering Gallery. The Black Murmurers fell prostrate.

'The Portal of Shinar is our *only means* of getting the genome into the race of men in time. The plan *must* be activated without delay! We must get the Portal back under our control long enough to get Charsoc and the Vial of Sacred Progeny through.'

Lucifer stared down a hundred feet towards Marduk and Charsoc.

'Charsoc, you will leave at once for the Portal of Shinar. I have entered their world in past aeons as a priest of high standing. You, Charsoc, shall arrive in the world of the race of men as my emissary. In human form. You will convey to the Council of Thirteen my choice of the family. Ensure that every part of our strategy is executed with ultimate precision. We can afford no human error. When the plan is set, at the appointed time of my son's exchange, I myself shall enter the world of men through the Time Gates.'

'Astaroth! Escort Charsoc without delay.'

He raised his sceptre.

'Instruct Sargon the Terrible, the great Prince of Babylonia, and his hordes to meet you at the Portal and to hold it until Charsoc is through. By the time my brother Michael realizes our diabolical strategy, it will be too late. Zalialiel and his guard will be overrun.'

'It will be done, my Lord.' Charsoc bowed deeply.

Lucifer watched as Astaroth strode through the gates followed by Charsoc and the Dark Cabal Wizards bearing the casket that held the Vial of Sacred Progeny.

'Sire,' Marduk murmured, an evil glint in his jaundiced eyes, 'once Charsoc enters the world of the race of men through the Portal of Shinar, he cannot get back.'

Lucifer held Marduk's gaze.

'He will find out soon enough.'

Michael stood on the glistening Pearl Sands of the First Heaven's celestial white beaches. He stared out towards two immense pearl gates that towered far in the distance – the entrance to Eden. Yehovah's lush Hanging Gardens and waterfalls that dropped a full mile down were faintly visible through Eden's swiftly descending indigo mists.

Michael had ridden straight to the Pearl Sands after inspecting his battalions on the vast Onyx Plains. He was still dressed in his ceremonial warring armour.

His thick flaxen mane was unbraided and fell down his

broad shoulders onto his silver armour. The Sword of State hung at his side.

Michael removed his gauntlets, then closed his eyes and inhaled the soft fragrance of myrrh and spikenard that wafted from the the Plains of the White Poplars in Eden, an unusual tranquillity on his features.

Jether stood at the top of the gilded stairs studying the imperial warrior.

Michael. Chief Prince of the Royal House of Yehovah and commander of the First Heaven's armies. Jether smiled faintly. Lucifer had well met his match in his valiant, noble younger brother.

Michael's strong chiselled features were relaxed. Jether had caught Michael in one of his rarer unguarded moments.

Jether sighed. He hated to break the moment, but break it he must.

'Michael,' Jether called.

Michael turned, then raised his hand to Jether in greeting.

'Revered Jether,' he said, striding towards the white-haired figure descending the gilded steps.

'Why, it has seemed countless moons since our last fellow-ship,' he exclaimed, his incongruous dimples softening his chiselled features.

They embraced affectionately.

Jether nodded.

'I have been many moons in Sacred Council with Yehovah, Michael.'

He breathed in the scent of myrrh from the mists of Eden.

'Come, let us walk.'

Jether clasped Michael's arm, his coral slippers sinking into the pearl sands.

Michael glanced at Jether.

'You come on grave matters,' he said.

Jether looked into Michael's fierce emerald gaze. He nodded.

'Lucifer has chosen the family?'

'A dynasty. One of the thirteen ruling families of the Grande Druid Council. There is already one son. Another is two months in the womb.'

Jether stopped in mid-stride and looked earnestly into Michael's fierce intelligent gaze.

'That one will be slain, murdered in cold blood. Lucifer will place his own infant in his place.'

He closed his eyes.

'Then another son will be born. It is certain. It is written in the Blueprints of Yehovah.'

Michael's eyes narrowed.

'Three brothers.'

Jether nodded.

'Even as yourselves . . . by his deliberate design.'

'He is *diabolical*!'

'There is, however, another matter,' Jether continued, 'a matter of extreme concern.'

They strode across the pearl sands past the twelve immense white columns of the grand gazebo.

'Our scouts inform us that the Fallen devise a plan to enter the world of the race of men.'

'That is nothing new. They violate their right of entry constantly.'

Jether stopped in mid-stride. He turned his face to Michael.

'In human form.'

Michael froze.

'But it contravenes the Tenets of Eternal Law set in motion by Golgotha.'

Jether nodded.

'There is only one means by which the Fallen's DNA can

98

be altered to that of matter,' he said. 'Our immediate concern lies with the Portals of the Fallen.'

Michael stared at Jether. Appalled.

'But they have been sealed since our victory at Golgotha.'

Jether gazed out at the silver waves of the Sea of Zamar. Grim.

'We of the High Council have reason to believe that Lucifer may attempt to breach one of the dormant Portals. There is one that is more vulnerable than the others. One that could be more easily breached.' He hesitated.

'The Portal of Shinar,' Gabriel said softly.

Michael turned as Gabriel drew up on the sands beside them, astride his winged stallion.

He held out a missive to Michael.

'Intercepted only minutes ago by Joktan, ruler of my Revelator Eagles.'

Michael took the missive from Gabriel and scanned it, ashen, then handed it to Jether.

'Astaroth and his High Command surround the gates of the Portal of Shinar as we speak. I mobilize my Royal Guard.' Michael signed with his fingers and at once a magnificent winged black stallion flew across the sands, stopping a yard from where he stood.

Jether looked up from the missive, his wizened face pale.

Michael placed his foot in the golden stirrup and mounted the black stallion.

'A thousand of my finest battalions and the Winged Lions guarded Babylonia these nineteen millennia. This past seventy years, it has been two hundred warriors at best.'

Gabriel laid his hand on Michael's arm. 'Brother, that is not the worst. Sargon the Terrible, the great prince who is monster of Babylonia, travels with his hordes through the heavens as we speak. To meet Astaroth at Shinar.'

'Sargon? Zalialiel and his guards will be overrun,' Michael whispered. 'Sargon will massacre them in cold blood.'

Jether paced the sands.

'No.' He shook his head. 'Astaroth leads the Black Horde. He is commander-in-chief. He will keep Angelic Protocol.'

'Time is against us, Gabriel,' said Michael. 'Follow swiftly with my armies. I must leave with my Royal Guard.' He lowered his visor. 'I must leave *now*.'

'Yehovah be with you, Michael,' Jether whispered as Michael ascended into the sky on his winged black charger.

Jether sighed deeply and closed his eyes.

'He is too late,' he whispered, pale. 'I see the battle even as we speak. Zalialiel is surrounded. They surrender. Charsoc will enter the world of the race of men. Go, Gabriel. Marshall the armies of the First Heaven.'

Jether stared after Gabriel. 'Lucifer's new strategy. He plans to send Charsoc in human form to the race of men. But why?'

An icy chill of foreboding flooded his soul.

'I go to consult with Yehovah,' he whispered.

CHAPTER TEN

The Portal of Shinar

The mammoth door to the entrance of the Ascending Stairs had been razed from its hinges. Zalialiel and two hundred warriors were lined up against the platinum walls outside the stair entrance, their ankles and wrists chained in heavy iron shackles.

The great silver stairs were hung from one gilded thread, swaying back and forth in the blue-black heavens. At the very top of the thousandth silver stair, lying on the curving arms of a spiral galaxy, rose the immense Gates of the Portal of Shinar, sealed at the base by the great golden seal of the Royal House of Yehovah.

Astaroth, commander of the armies of Gehenna, turned to Charsoc.

'Michael will have received word of our assault. We have not much time before his armies descend.'

He stepped forward, his black-gloved hands grasping his broadsword.

'Sargon of Babylonia, Champion of Gehenna!'

The great prince of Babylonia stepped forward. His coarse unbraided red hair fell below his thighs. Thick yellow saliva dripped from his thin blue lips, his red eyes glinted. Astaroth nodded to him.

'Warriors of hell!' Sargon cried.

The Black Horde stepped forward, their black braids hung well down their backs.

They held their super-weapons, developed by the Twins of Malfecium, at the ready.

'Open the Seal!'

The warriors stepped forward, and with their combined strength, raised their huge tactical laser canons. As one they channelled the searing beams of the lasers towards the Seal. The air exploded beneath the huge Seal holding the gates of the Portal. The Portal remained firmly shut.

Charsoc frowned.

'Again!' Sagon screamed in frustration and a second battalion of Sargon's warriors stepped forward. They aimed their advanced electromagnetic pulse weapons at the golden Seal. Violent blazing rubied lightnings erupted from the Seal, hurling the entire battalion to the ground.

'Aaaaahh,' Sargon cried as he fell to his knees, clutching his head in agony. 'Yehovah's sorceries!'

Charsoc walked towards the Portal, his eyes narrowed.

'Let me try the good old-fashioned way,' he said, removing a ruby-hued stone from his breastplate. He held it over the very centre of the Seal. It fitted exactly, then he turned it two-thirds of a revolution and waited. There was silence.

Then came a deafening blast as the monstrous pulsating copper force field of the Portal of Shinar erupted a thousand feet upward into the Second Heaven.

Charsoc smiled. It was exactly as he had foreseen. A flickering electric blue laceration ran down the entire mid-section of the force field.

The interdimensional force field was torn.

He looked on in ecstasy as thousands of blazing crimson

102

electromagnetic waves ignited from the surface. The force field's DNA converter was reactivating.

Charsoc turned. Sargon and his battalions raced towards Michael and his Royal Guard, who were locked in ferocious combat with Astaroth's rearguard a thousand steps below at the entrance to the Ascending Stairs.

Charsoc watched intently as Sargon's battalions reached the Gates. Savagely they waded into the fray with Astaroth and his warriors brutally assaulting Michael's troops.

Sargon and eighteen of his horde surrounded Michael. Michael and his Royal Guard warred ferociously, but Charsoc knew that they were clearly outnumbered. He also knew that Gabriel would be following hot on Michael's heels with the armies of the First Heaven. He was only minutes away. Charsoc was certain. He must enter the world of the race of men with the genome at once. Time was short.

Charsoc nodded to Dracul, ruler of the Warlocks of the West and ancient leader of the Time Lords. The thirteen Time Lords stood in a full circle, then lifted their black cloaks. Scorching green lightnings erupted from the fingertips of the Warlocks striking the laceration of the force field. The Portal's interdimensional threshold was opening.

'Charsoc the Dark – you, the Fallen, enter the race of men – in their image!' Dracul hissed.

Charsoc glanced back just as Michael, still violently struggling, was heaved savagely up the Ascending Stairs by Sargon and his thugs, who flung him viciously to the ground at the base of the force field.

Charsoc rose two hundred feet into the air above Michael and hovered, completely immersed in the blazing crimson waves of the force field, his entire body vibrating at ultra-high frequency.

Michael, bruised and beaten, watched through clouded

eyes from the ground as Charsoc's DNA restructured before his eyes.

The blazing crimson waves passed through Charsoc's nine-foot form. He shrank to a mere six feet three inches. His floor-length beard disappeared and his long black hair turned silver and cropped to within half an inch of his scalp. His blind eyes developed irises and he now saw as men saw.

Dracul opened the casket and carefully removed the Vial of Sacred Progeny.

Michael looked on, appalled. He had no doubts as to what it contained. Charsoc opened his palm. The Vial flew up into his hand just as the interdimensional threshold opened fully and Babylonia became visible to the Second Heaven.

Charsoc disappeared.

Sargon grasped Michael from behind with his massive filthy hands, his broadsword resting at the Archangel's throat. The remainder of Sargon's hordes surrounded the shackled warriors.

He leered at Astaroth, thick yellow globules of saliva dripping from between his black stumps of teeth.

'We finish the job,' he snarled. 'We massacre their Prince and Commander. Send him to the Abyss.'

Michael stared at Astaroth from the floor, incensed.

'You break the Tenets of Eternal Law,' Michael shouted, struggling violently in the clutches of Sargon's savage grip.

'Astaroth! Gabriel rides as we speak with the armies of the First Heaven. Surrender while you can.'

Astaroth stood silent, his back to Michael and Sargon.

Sargon pressed his swordpoint into Michael's throat until a blue blood-like fluid dripped from Michael's neck.

'Astaroth.' Michael gasped for breath. 'The Protocol. You of all . . .'

'Lay down your arms, Sargon.' Astaroth's voice was soft. 'We have completed our task. Charsoc and the Sacred Vial have passed through the interdimensional threshold.'

He shook his head at Sargon.

'The Chief Prince has no weapon. He has surrendered. It violates Angelic Protocol.'

Sargon stared at Astaroth with hatred.

'We, the Fallen, do not abide by Angelic Protocol,' he roared.

Astaroth walked toward him and grasped his matted red hair in one hand. Prying Sargon's sword from his fist he reeled Sargon upwards until the two giant warriors stood face to face. Sargon's scarred craggy face was only an inch away from Astaroth's striking imperial features.

'We, the Fallen,' Astaroth spoke through gritted teeth, 'are not barbaric vandals. We are *warriors*. We adhere to disciplines.'

'Your sentimentality clouds your judgement,' Sargon snarled, looking from Michael back to Astaroth. 'You will pay with your *head*, Astaroth!'

He kicked Michael savagely.

'You were too long his compatriot!'

He turned to his battalions, an evil leer on his face.

With one violent thrust, he threw Astaroth to the ground, then licked his lips lecherously.

'We follow Charsoc into the world of men! We would have some sport.'

'No!' Astaroth cried.

Michael watched in horror as two great black wings rose from Sargon's colossal shoulders. Sargon rose into the blazing crimson waves followed by five hundred of the Fallen.

Astaroth stood, trembling, helpless as line by line his troops followed straight behind Sargon's, until only Astaroth himself remained.

Astaroth raised his gaze to the horizon. Gabriel and the armies of the First Heaven were descending towards them.

'It is too late,' Astaroth whispered. 'I cannot surrender.'

He walked slowly towards the Portal.

'You break Eternal Law!' Michael shouted. 'It will not go well with you. There is an addendum!'

Astaroth stood on the edge of the Portal, then turned one more time to look at Michael.

'My path is set.'

'Astaroth!' Michael reached for his arm just as Astaroth rose beyond his grasp and stepped through the threshold of the Portal of Shinar.

And vanished.

Into the world of the race of men.

CHAPTER ELEVEN

Council of Thirteen

1981
One Week Later,
The Square Mile,
London, England

Charsoc detested the colour black. He detested the sombreness of Earth. He detested the race of men. But for now, he was on his Master's business and all his options were severely limited.

He wondered how Jether was reacting to the news that he had now entered the world of the race of men. As one of them. He dug his nails deeply into his palm. The thought of Jether, however fleeting, incensed him. How much longer must he remain in this infernal inferior human body? Its blood pressure must be rocketing. He sighed.

The end justified the means. And his Master's ends were no doubt different from the ends of the thirteen men waiting silently in the chamber.

He leaned back in his ornately carved throne and surveyed the thirteen, dressed in charcoal robes, who were seated around the massive polished table.

The Grande Druid Council of the Illuminati.

Thirteen Warlock High priests.

The most powerful male witches and warlocks who existed in the world of the race of men, their ancestral lines steeped in the most heinous forms of satanic and occult practices dating back to Nimrod himself.

By night they engaged in covert and iniquitous occult practices, the conspirators behind thousands of satanic rituals and abuses, child abductions, blood sacrifices, drug and human trafficking, ritual murders.

They were the cold-blooded architects of the countless terrorist atrocities, assassinations, and bloody coups that filled the front pages of the newspapers of the Eastern and Western worlds.

By day they resumed their long-established respectable existences in London, Berlin, New York, Washington, Los Angeles, Rome, Tokyo, and Zurich.

They were global financiers, intelligence experts, oil barons, newspaper magnates, CEOs in the military and industrial sectors, Vatican bankers.

The controllers of the Illuminati.

Thirteen ruling families of the New World Order who answered to only one.

Their grand master – Lucifer.

Their heads were bowed, their eyes closed.

The only movement was the flicker of sixty-six black candles that surrounded the golden Sigil of the Baphomet lying in the centre of the table.

The race of men and their infantile sorceries, Charsoc thought.

Piers Aspinall stood.

'It is our privilege to have Baron Kester von Slagel, Lorcan De Molay's emissary, with us on this momentous occasion.'

He bowed to Charsoc.

'Baron von Slagel. If you would grant us the privilege of administering the Cup.'

'The family has been chosen by our Master, His Excellency,' Charsoc declared.

'Before His Excellency's choice is revealed, let us partake of the Cup of Diabolas.'

He slowly removed his pale grey gloves, one finger at a time, then raised his goblet.

'As we drink the blood of those innocents that were sacrificed for the partaking at this table, we reaffirm our commitment to the Left-Hand Path. We vow to avenge Golgotha. We vow to erase the blood sacrifice of the Nazarene.'

He sipped the fresh blood of the newly sacrificed infant.

'Golgotha.'

The thirteen warlocks held up their goblets.

'Golgotha!'

They drank as one.

Charsoc nodded and two men in livery moved to the windows and pulled back the heavy crimson velvet curtains, revealing the characteristic grey gloom of London's overcast skies, then exited leaving only a strapping six-foot-six body-guard with striking features by the door.

Sir Piers Aspinall, Chief of MI6, stood. He glanced over at the guard and raised his eyebrows to Charsoc.

'Travis is one of us.' Charsoc glanced back at Astaroth. 'Special forces.'

Aspinall nodded, then removed from his briefcase a black file marked *Eyes Only*, with an Illuminati crest on the cover, and handed it to Charsoc.

'We have waited century after century. Finally the family has been chosen.'

Charsoc gazed at the thirteen men around the table. Every eye was riveted to the file in his hand.

'The "Prince" will be placed into the family chosen by His Reverence.' Kester von Slagel smiled.

'Into the family of one at this very table.' He hesitated. 'Into the family of a *most* devoted servant of the Fallen.'

He raised his gaze to a tall distinguished-looking man in his late fifties with imperious features and a silver moustache who sat directly across the table from him.

Julius De Vere. Chairman of the De Vere banking dynasty and the European and New York communications industry.

'Into the De Vere Family.'

Xavier Chessler nodded. 'An advantageous start for our master's seed. Our Master's decisions are flawless.'

Raffaele Lombardi, patriarch of the Black Nobility Family of Venice and Director of the Vatican Bank, frowned.

'Julius,' Lombardi interjected. Julius De Vere sat across the table from Lombardi. Inscrutable. 'You are, as we are all aware, a most esteemed paragon of the Left-Hand Path,' Lombardi continued in his thick Italian accent.

'I remain eternally,' the older man murmured, 'our Master's devoted disciple.'

He ran his fingers lightly over his wrist. Instantly a strange blue brand illuminated.

The Warlock's Mark. Julius De Vere was one of only three that wore the brand, signifying a pact between Lucifer and certain of the race of men. He gazed at Lombardi through hooded eyes.

'Unfortunately,' Lombardi said, returning his cold gaze, '. . . unfortunately, your own son, conceived of your blood, does not seem to have upheld the Brotherhood's ambitions with the same . . . um' – he caressed the jewelled Masonic pin on his lapel – '*fervour*.'

'James De Vere is essential to our plan.' He paused. 'For the moment . . .'

Julius De Vere looked out at Lombardi from under bushy

silvering eyebrows. His black eyes glinted with intelligence. He smiled thinly.

'Your fervently harboured ambitions for your own four sons do not escape this table, Raffaelle.' Lombardi squirmed in his chair.

'I am well aware that my only son, regrettably, takes after my first wife. Although one of us, she became, let us say, *unresponsive* to our way of life. She met with an unfortunate accident. My son is weak like his mother before him. He holds a *righteous* streak.'

Julius De Vere's eyes hardened. 'He has no prospensity for getting his hands dirty. I am fully aware of his deficiencies. I shall make sure they are used to our advantage. Then he becomes expendable.

'I, as my father and his father before me,' he continued, 'have long awaited this day, in the expectation that our family would be chosen for the sacred task. To that end we have built through five generations our oil, banking, and communication arms in preparation for our "adopted" son's rapid ascension through the ranks of the race of men. All our resources remain entirely at the Brotherhood's disposal.'

Kester von Slagel gave a thin smile.

'You are *most* generous, Julius. Our Master is most gratified. Then we are assured of your family's complete collaboration?'

'My son will go to any length to protect his family. I shall ensure his full cooperation.'

'The plan must not be disclosed to James De Vere,' Vincent Carnegie added. 'We dare take no risks. He must not know of the infant's exchange.'

Julius De Vere nodded.

'My son cannot be depended on. He will bring up this infant as though it were his own, with no knowledge of the clone. We will make our demands. Though ignorant of our covert strategy, he will obey each instruction. His passivity will weigh in our favour.'

'He will be eliminated at the appointed time?' Lombardi inquired.

'In the event of my own demise, Chessler will ensure his silence.'

Xavier Chessler, blond, blue-eyed, all-American newly appointed Vice-Chairman of the Chase Manhattan Bank nodded.

'James De Vere roomed with me at Yale. A previous bonemaster. His ancestors were loyal adherents of our policies. James trusts me. I'll keep a close eye on him. Look after our interests. He won't be the least bit suspicious.'

'When the Lorcan clone turns forty years of age, the First Seal will be broken. He will rise to world power.' Dieter von Hallstein, ex-German Chancellor, turned to De Vere.

'After that point, they are *all* expendable.'

He turned to Julius De Vere.

'Your son, daughter-in-law,' His voice was soft but intense.

He paused. 'Your grandchildren, Julius. All to be exterminated. The first to be executed at the exchange of the clone, the remainder slain after the clone turns forty. This is acceptable to you?'

'My grandsons . . .'

Julius De Vere drew deeply on his cigar.

'They are to be sacrificed for a higher good,' Von Hallstein added. 'A New World Order. Our Master's Rule.'

Julius De Vere nodded.

'The terms are acceptable to me.'

Kester von Slagel nodded to Piers Aspinall who removed a document, then passed it over to Von Slagel. Von Slagel reviewed it then passed it to De Vere.

'Your signature. Their death warrants.'

De Vere scanned it, then took a fountain pen from his pocket and scrawled his name with four deep strokes in green ink on four pages. Von Slagel nodded to Aspinall.

'Thank you.' Aspinall replaced the document in his briefcase.

Ethan St Clair looked up.

'The boy will come of age in Europe, educated in the school of our fathers,' he said. 'Our Scottish brothers will let Gordonstoun know that they will be receiving a "special" pupil.'

Aspinall lowered his pipe.

'Our close friends in Washington will present James De Vere with an offer that he will not refuse: the ambassadorship to the United Kingdom. We will ensure that the boy grows to maturity in Europe. It is essential to our plan for one-world government.'

'My esteemed colleague, Julius, is, as we know, in charge of the International Security Fund.' Naotake Yoshido, Chairman of Japan's Yoshido banking dynasty spoke in soft cultured tones.

Julius De Vere nodded.

'During the next two decades,' Yoshido continued, addressing the table, 'under Julius De Vere's oversight, we will orchestrate the biggest, most secretive private placement financing operation in world history. My esteemed colleague, Julius De Vere and I, propose to start the fund as a token of our good faith.'

De Vere nodded to Yoshido.

'A small token of twenty trillion dollars,' Yoshido added.

A murmur of approval rippled round the table.

'Your generosity will be greatly rewarded by our Master,' Von Slagel said warmly.

'You are both devoted servants of the Fallen.'

'The fund will be based in Zurich,' De Vere continued.

'Its connections will be to a myriad of European Union institutions, untraceable back to the Brotherhood.

'By the year 2021, the trust will contain over two hundred trillion dollars. The year our clone will be in position. Equipped with such limitless resources, as well as the private fund of wealth I have amassed for him in the De Vere vaults, the Brotherhood will amass sufficient finance to bribe every president, prime minister, policymaker, intelligence operative, and political figure worldwide, for the rest of this century, in pursuit of our aims.'

Aspinall picked up a second file and passed it to Von Slagel who studied the papers.

'Lilian De Vere, your daughter-in-law, has suffered three miscarriages. She has been receiving fertility treatment from a top specialist in the Brotherhood's employ, Dr Morice. He has confirmed that she is eleven weeks pregnant. As per the agreed strategy, the family will travel as usual from New York to London in the fall.'

Von Slagel looked up from the papers.

'It is essential to our Master that to execute the Brotherhood's strategy for his political future, the Lorcan clone be born in Great Britain. Lilian De Vere will be advised in the strongest possible manner to see her term out in the UK and to stop all travel for the duration of her pregnancy.'

De Vere nodded. 'She has been managed since a child.'

Von Slagel continued. 'The birth is planned to coincide with the winter solstice and will be managed at the private and ultra-exclusive nursing home she frequents in London. We are aware that she will insist on Rupert Percival, her British obstetrician. Percival will be discreetly "replaced" by the Brotherhood's counterpart at the time of the exchange.

'The genetic scientist to incubate the Lorcan clone has been chosen after extensive investigation to fit our profile. The subject is a Scotsman. Fifty-six years old. Single. No children. A loner, dedicated to his field. He received the Nobel Prize in 1978 for his profound contribution to genetic research. He was the scientist in charge of the Los Alamos cloning programmes from '77 to '79.'

Ethan St Clair frowned.

'He is not one of the Brotherhood.'

Von Slagel's eyes narrowed.

'He is the world's foremost expert on animal and hybrid cloning. He is essential to our task. We can afford no mistakes. Last night,' Von Slagel continued, 'his Reverence's genome was delivered into the hands of the scientist at the laboratory at our safe house in Marazion, Cornwall. He has been provided with the cloning blueprints and all the technology he requires to complete the task. The DNA of the genome has been deliberately reconstructed to coincide precisely with the projected birth date of the human infant.'

Aspinall broke in.

'It is a classified black-ops operation. The identity of the genome will not be revealed to him.'

'The scientist is aware he is dealing with non-human matter?' Ethan St Clair asked.

'He is aware only that it is "alien" matter,' Aspinall replied. 'He spent years dealing with alien–human hybrid experimentation in the black-ops underground bases. He is a man who asks no questions. He expects no answers. He is a most brilliant man. Regrettably, as soon as the procedure is complete, he will suffer an untimely and catastrophic accident.'

Kester von Slagel rose.

'His Reverence has indicated his satisfaction with the proceedings. The Lorcan . . . clone' – he hesitated – 'will be conceived: a precise replica of his father.'

He paced the room.

'And now to our timeline, gentlemen. The "Prince" will

115

be dedicated in the crypts of the Vatican by His Reverence and the black elements of the Jesuits. He will then be transferred to London from Rome. The De Vere infant and the "Prince" will be exchanged the night of the infant's birth: 21 December 1981. The De Vere infant will be murdered. James and Lilian De Vere will never know of the exchange. They will bring the "Prince" up as their own.'

Von Slagel turned to the thirteen men in the room.

'A one-world government. Headed by our messiah.'

He nodded to Piers Aspinall.

'Pray, enlighten us as to the Brotherhood's aspirations for the City in the next four decades, Aspinall.'

Piers Aspinall removed a pair of wire-rimmed spectacles from a leather case. He placed the wire rims over his ears and read from a sheaf of papers marked *Eyes Only*.

'By the year 2008, we project daily turnover of foreign exchange in London's Square Mile will exceed 1.6 billion dollars; the City will house 22 per cent of the global foreign equity market; 70 per cent of all eurobond turnover; at least £263 billion of worldwide premium insurance income in the UK; 1.7 trillion pounds of pension fund assets under management. We predict a 43 per cent global share in "over the counter" derivatives market, and an 18 per cent share of all global hedge fund assets in the UK. By 2012, the Square Mile will be the leading Western centre for Islamic finance. All in the hands of the Brotherhood.'

Von Slagel walked over to the window, looking out at the 677 acres sprawled in front of him.

'The wealthiest square mile on earth,' he murmured. 'We have achieved our Master's goals this past century, gentlemen. The City. A privately owned corporation that is not subject to the Queen or Parliament, gentlemen,' Von Slagel said. 'Behold our secret. Remember that the end justifies the means.'

The men followed Von Slagel's gaze as he surveyed the Bank of England, the Stock Exchange, Lloyd's of London, Fleet Street, and the London Commodity Exchange. 'And the wise take all means . . .'

CHAPTER TWELVE

Disclosure

Jether walked the nameless secret passageway from the throne room of the First Heaven through the twisting labyrinths of the seventh spire, beneath the sacred vaults, to the Tower of Winds. Stopping in front of the small silver filigree door of the Walled Garden of Tempests, he placed his onyx ring over the keyhole. The door slid open onto the vast lush gardens of the Tower of Winds.

Obadiah, Jether's attendant, a youngling of an ancient angelic race possessing the characteristics of eternal youth, a remarkable inquisitiveness and bright orange curls, remained blissfully oblivious to Jether's arrival. He hung from a tree, his stocky little legs entwined around a bough, avidly plucking sweetmeats from a low-hanging branch hung with white blossoms and stuffing them, six at a time, into his already chock-full mouth.

'Humpf,' Jether cleared his throat. Obadiah stared at Jether with wide eyes, then fell with a loud thump onto a bed of cowslips beneath him, crushing the flowers. The cowslips let out a loud sigh. Obadiah jumped up and scurried over to Jether, grasped his satin train and wiped his sticky hands painstakingly on the satin.

Jether glowered at him, then strode at full speed past the water fountains and the manicured hedges.

Obadiah's tight orange curls flew in disarray as he desperately attempted to keep up with his sprightly master. He stared greedily at a second tree of strawberry sweetmeats, as they hurried past, then plucked at a large blue strawberry and opened his mouth. The strawberry flew forcefully out from his hand directly into Jether's palm.

'I told you, Obadiah,' Jether said, in a deliberately stern tone, 'I have *eyes* in the back of my head!'

Jether turned and shook his head at the languishing Obadiah, then popped the sweetmeat unhurriedly into his own mouth, his eyes twinkling with mirth.

Obadiah followed behind him meekly in a mixture of high speed and distinct awe, his squat little legs flying. He gaped at Jether's back in rapture.

Jether continued into the very centre of the tower gardens, to a large golden table where the Council of Yehovah sat on twenty-three golden thrones, their long white hair and beards blowing in the blue zephyrs.

Each elder wore a golden crown except one, Xacheriel, who wore a bright orange sou'wester.

Jether pried his train forcibly loose from Obadiah's sticky little fingers and stood at the head of the table.

He stared over at Xacheriel and frowned pointedly. Xacheriel scowled, then nodded to a second youngling, his own attendant, Dimnah, who ran forward holding the elder's golden crown. A strange piece of shredded jam-like mixture, that Jether thought looked suspiciously like remnants of Xacheriel's favourite breakfast – a remarkable mixture of tiffin and a blue marmalade-like substance he had concocted

– was smeared across the central ruby. Grudgingly, Xacheriel removed his orange rain hat that he donned for the messier of his scientific experiments. With a loud huff he grabbed his golden crown from Dimnah and put it on his head.

Jether surveyed the elders, bowing to each in turn before sitting heavily on his jacinth throne.

He raised his hand. Instantly the zephyrs subsided to a gentle breeze.

'Let us bow our heads in supplication, my fellow compatriots.' And as one, the High Council bowed their white crowned heads.

Dimnah was still bowing to Xacheriel profusely.

Xacheriel shook his head vehemently at Dimnah to no avail. Dimnah's eyes remained closed tightly in ecstasy while he continued his fervent bowing, his forehead slamming the grass with intense force at every bow, making a strange thudding noise.

Jether opened one eye to investigate the cause of the incessant thumping.

'Dimnah – STOP!' Xacheriel bellowed at last, with such force that Lamaliel the gentle, sitting on Xacheriel's right, fell off his throne onto the grass.

As Xacheriel reached over to help Lamaliel up, his over-sized galoshes got caught in Lamaliel's robe, whereupon Obadiah and Dimnah rushed to Xacheriel's aid. Xacheriel came crashing down with full force on top of the long-suffering Lamaliel, while Obadiah and Dimnah fell headlong on top of Xacheriel.

Jether hid his laughter in a napkin as Issachar and Methuselah gently helped up the sputtering Xacheriel and the blushing Lamaliel.

'A thousand pardons, a thousand pardons, revered Lamaliel,' Xacheriel gasped to Lamaliel.

'A great adventure. A great adventure to be sure, my dearest compatriot.' Lamaliel's eyes shone with sheer exhilaration as he dusted off his crown.

'You are recovered, venerable Lamaliel?' Jether tried to compose his features.

'An invigorating interlude from my holy supplications,' Lamaliel replied.

'Light entertainment has its place as always in Heaven,' Jether sighed. 'But today we have weighty matters to discuss. Obadiah. Dimnah. You are dismissed.'

He watched as the two younglings' stocky little legs carried them down the gilded stairs descending from the Tower of Winds. Jether sighed. 'Oh to be a youngling ... so uncomplicated an existence. But come, let us open the Council, revered compatriots. We are gathered here today on grave matters.'

He buried his face in the immense filigree golden codex that lay open before him. After a few moments, he raised his face to the elders.

'It has been nearly two thousand years since Lucifer's defeat at Golgotha.'

He paused to let his words sink in.

Maheel lifted his silver head.

'The Great Battle Armageddon draws nigh.'

Issachar nodded. 'Lucifer well knows this. At Golgotha, his third of the Fallen were resoundingly defeated by our armies.'

'Lucifer vowed this would never happen again,' Jether replied. 'And as we are all aware, he conceived a scheme. A diabolical scheme.'

He gazed out at the assembled elders.

'A scheme to conceive his messiah. His own Son of Perdition.'

All eyes were intent on him.

'My revered compatriot, Issachar. Pray relay the Council's findings.'

Issachar the Wise folded his hands, his normally gentle features grave.

'My honoured compatriots, our findings bode ill for the race of men. Through this messiah, Lucifer's intention is to control the world of the race of men by his institution of a New World Order. A one-world government. His goal is to control the banking systems, the military industrial complex, the secret government cabals and intelligence communities, pharmaceutical and drug cartels, mass communication.' Issachar sighed.

'His ambitions are endless.' He paused. 'Through this messiah, Lucifer himself plans to govern the world of the race of men.'

'Thank you, Issachar.' Jether surveyed the faces around the table.

'Up until now, the race of men did not possess the capabilities to produce a clone.' He paused. 'However, the world of men's technological advances has greatly accelerated this past decade. We have received word that Lucifer creates a clone in the world of the race of men,' Jether continued. 'A clone who will carry his own DNA.'

The High Council stared at Jether in shock.

Lamaliel spoke. 'He will no longer be reliant on the Stalins and Hitlers of this world who failed him.'

'You have spoken truly, honoured Lamaliel.' Jether turned to Xacheriel.

'Xacheriel, as Yehovah's revered curator of the sciences and universes, pray deliver the scientific facts as they stand.'

Xacheriel extricated his great yellow-galoshed feet from under the table and stood.

'Humph.' He cleared his throat loudly. Then putting his monocle to his eye, he thumbed through his scientific papers.

'Honoured compatriots. My revered Jether . . .' Xacheriel's

voice trembled with emotion. 'Unlike Christos' birth, the birth of Lucifer's messiah will not be supernatural. It will be a feat of biogenetic engineering . . . executed by Lucifer's iniquitous super-scientists of the Fallen. The Twins of Malfecium, my *own* protégés for years here in the scientific portals of the First Heaven.' Xacheriel turned beetroot red with indignation.

'Pray *calm* yourself, old friend,' Jether admonished him gently. 'The times of such treachery in our world are long past.'

Xacheriel glowered at the elders around the table from under huge bushy white eyebrows, then thumped his scientific papers down on the table.

'Lucifer's pets,' he scowled. 'At very *best* you could call them depraved biogenetic engineers.'

Jether gave him warning glance.

Xacheriel took a deep breath.

'Anyway, the point is,' Xacheriel muttered, rummaging through his papers again, 'for over two thousand years, beyond the Vaults of vagen, a thousand miles beneath the Labyrinths of Angor, has lain a sarcophagus safeguarded by the Twins of Malfecium. The Sarcophagus of the Furies. There lies the Vial of Sacred Progeny.

'It contains a single genome.' He stared ominously at the elders around the table.

'*Lucifer's* genome.'

Xacheriel sat heavily back on his throne.

'From which he would create a clone . . .'

'A replica of himself,' Jether continued. 'It is his most dastardly of all strategies.'

He gestured to the goblet at Xacheriel's right hand.

'Pray sip some elixir to calm yourself, then continue, old friend.'

Xacheriel took a loud slurp of harebell nectar. Issachar

123

held his hand to his ear as Xacheriel smacked his generously large red lips with relish and replaced his monocle. 'His super-scentists have been prepared since Alexander ruled the world. They were prepared during Stalin's purges, and they got very close during Hitler's reign of terror.'

Again, he rifled through his tiffin-stained papers.

'The Kaiser Wilhelm Institute of Human Heredity and Eugenics was a base for Hitler's more depraved genetic and eugenic experiments. Otmar von Verschuer, Grebe, Mengele . . . depraved monsters all!'

Jether frowned.

'They all had one aim instigated by their Dark Master. *Cloning*. But even the Nazi scientists, so technologically advanced, had not the technology to create the clone from the Lucifer seed.'

Xacheriel rose and strode through the flowering lupins, deep in thought, his huge galoshes crushing them. Instantly they grew back the moment he raised his foot. In perfection.

'In 1943, my compatriots, it was failure at every turn. Technologically impossible to create a clone in the world of men. These past few years, however, the Twins of Malfecium provided technological blueprints to the darker elements of the race of men, in order that their Black Intelligence units might start to conduct cloning experiments in secret facilities in North America. Los Alamos. Dulce. One scientist in particular . . .' Xacheriel threw up his hands in a mixture of repulsion and admiration.

'A genius!' Xacheriel declared. Jether sighed.

'But Lucifer's DNA is as ours,' Issachar interjected. 'It is angelic. It is not matter, esteemed Xacheriel.'

'That, honoured Issachar, is where the Twins' evil genius excelled itself. Maelageor, who was my *finest* protégé,' Xacheriel caught Jether's eye and hurried on, 'readjusted the DNA sequence of the genome of the Sacred Vial of

Progeny to correspond precisely with the growth pattern and cycles of human DNA. The clone will retain the angelic capability of spirit but will be confined in a body of matter. He will look like Lucifer. His human attributes, hair colour, eye colour, facial features will be a precise replica of his father, but his physical development will be as a man. In matter.'

Maheel spoke. 'Revered Xacheriel, he will retain the super-natural capability of the Fallen Angelic?'

Xacheriel nodded.

'His powers will be more confined, honoured Maheel. He utilizes them in matter. But yes, his clone will have access to the supernatural powers of the angelic.'

Jether surveyed the elders. 'However, Lucifer is well aware of the curtailing power of the presence of those who bear the Seal of the Nazarene. Until *every* follower of the Nazarene is removed from Earth, his clone's supernatural powers will be greatly restricted. Impeded.'

'*Every* follower?'

'Even the weakest follower of the Nazarene poses a threat, when they exercise their supernatural authority in the world of Men,' Issachar added.

'The transportation of the Nazarene's followers to the First Heaven is to occur in the middle of the Tribulation,' Methuselah said in his slow measured tones. 'Three and a half years after the First Seal is broken.'

'Yes,' said Jether. 'Until then Lucifer's clone will exercise limited supernatural power. Time is short. Word has reached us that Lucifer has already set his plan in motion. We have evidence that his genome was provided to the elite one moon ago. By one who sat at this very table in aeons past. Charsoc the Dark.'

He looked around the table. The elders stared back at him in stunned silence.

125

'Charsoc entered the world of the race of men to deliver the genome. In human form. As one of them. Through the Portal of Shinar. Charsoc is presently unaware of the addendum that was added after the Nephilim incident at Babel. Neither Lucifer nor Charsoc were privy to it.'

Jether turned to Gabriel who read from a codex.

'The addendum states that if the Portal of Shinar is ever again breached by the Fallen, any human form they take will be irreversible,' Gabriel stated, looking up at the elders. 'At first Charsoc will still maintain the ability to transform back into angelic form but with each passing decade in the race of men, this capacity will diminish. Until by the end of the Tribulation, he will lose his First Estate forever. By the end of the seven-year Tribulation, Charsoc will wander the desert places as neither fallen angel nor human . . . until his banishment to the Lake of Fire.'

'Unfortunately,' Jether said, 'Charsoc was not the only one who entered through the Portal. Michael, you saw it all firsthand.'

Michael stared grimly across to the Rubied Door.

'Sargon, Prince of Babylonia, and five hundred of his guard entered through to the world of men in human form, as did hundreds of Lucifer's Royal Guard. And Astaroth.'

There came a collective gasp from the table.

'We have regained control of the Portal,' Michael continued, 'but the Fallen now walk in human form, before their time.'

'This Lucifer well knows.' Methuselah spoke, his voice very soft.

Jether added. 'He has also already chosen a family to incubate his "son".

'One of thirteen ruling families of the occult society identified as the Illuminati.

'The family Lucifer has chosen to incubate the Son of Perdition is one of these.'

Jether looked down at the parchment of the Codex, and instantly reams of silver writings formed on the pages.

'Their designation in the race of men is De Vere.

'Three of us seated at this very table have been elected for a new task.' Jether rose. 'A dangerous task at hand. Three of us have been chosen as stewards – protectors of the family De Vere. Stewards who will now manifest in human form. *As angels unaware.*' He smiled faintly.

'We will now retreat to our chambers in supplications,' he said. 'Yehovah's Sacred Spirit himself will convene this very moon with each of the three chosen. The chosen ones will traverse between the world of the race of men and the First Heaven freely. They will leave the First Heaven at first moon.'

He gazed at the elders.

'I am one of those chosen for this sacred task,' he said, softly.

'Eternal Law decrees that none of us, the three chosen, is permitted to reveal himself to be angelic except in extenuating conditions – and then only on supreme authorization of Yehovah himself. Until the breaking of the First Seal of the Revelation of St John of the Apocalypse we must remain invisible to the Fallen.

'We will traverse the world of the race of men as is our common practice, through the Holy Angelic Portals. We will act as Watchmen. The Monastery of Alexandria in Egypt where the Christ child was given shelter will be a place of protection for each of us who journey between the First Heaven and the world of men.'

He closed the codex.

'If our existence is discovered before the First Seal is

opened, we will lose our entitlement to protect the chosen family and will be banished from the world of men until Armageddon. We must be circumspect. We must be measured.'

'We must be vigilant.' His features softened.

'Godspeed, my noble compatriots. He smiled gently at the grave faces in front of him. 'The Council is adjourned.'

SIX MONTHS LATER

CHAPTER THIRTEEN

The Seed of the Serpent

Vatican Heliport, Rome
21 December 1981, 5 a.m.

Kester von Slagel paced the icy tarmac impatiently, his black Jesuit robes blowing violently in Rome's freezing winter blizzards that had swept in from the north unexpectedly late this year. He hesitated briefly in front of a statue of the Madonna and Jesus, then continued his incessant pacing on the tarmac.

'December,' he muttered bitterly. '*Corto e maledetto*!' (Cold and cursed!)

He surveyed the Sikorsky UH-60 Black Hawk assault helicopter, barely visible through the driving sleet. It stood in the circle of floodlights on the tarmac of the Vatican heliport, guarded by six soldiers in SAS military uniform, all holding machine guns. The Brotherhood had financed the Black Hawk's prototype and maiden flight six years earlier and had been well rewarded. Over 900 gunships were now operational in Brotherhood hands. On every continent on Earth.

He smiled faintly in approval, then frowned, staring up at the medieval quarters of Torre San Giovanni.

Kester von Slagel rubbed his bony pale fingers together intensely, studied them, then pursed his lips in irritation. He felt a deep affection for his vast collection of vibrant-coloured opals and rubies. The fact that today his hands were completely bare of his usual flamboyant jewellery only served to deepen his present cantankerous mood.

And his irritation at having to presently reside in this infernal body as one of the race of men.

The single redeeming factor was that this undertaking was, without doubt, the single most momentous operation in the history of the Fallen.

Four cardinals bearing a sealed silver casket strode towards Von Slagel, their scarlet robes lashed by the violent winds. On reaching him, they bowed.

Von Slagel studied the casket's lid, exquisitely engraved with a golden inverted pentacle, and then surveyed the cardinals in front of him. Unlike these simpletons, *he* was well aware that inside the chest, sleeping soundly on indigo velvet, lay his Master's seed. The 'Prince'. The Lorcan clone.

There lay the Fallen's sole opportunity to destroy the Nazarene's illegitimate claim as King of the Race of Men. Von Slagel's pale eyes narrowed in satisfaction.

Unless Yehovah had some new-fangled line of attack up his sleeve. He nodded to the cardinals. They bowed again, then carried the small casket carefully up the helicopter steps and into the gunship.

The Black Hawk's sole occupant was a thick-set Teutonic-looking nun. Her pasty features were hidden under her wimple, leaving only her eyes, nose, and mouth visible.

Her habit fell to just below the knee and thick dark stockings were pulled over her hefty lower calves. She stared mesmerized at the golden image of a goat that filled the pentacle on the casket.

'The Sigil of the Baphomet,' she uttered, her pale eyes

wide with a combination of elation and terror. 'God of the Witches.' She clutched her own inverted crucifix with quivering fleshy fingers.

The pilot, a Jesuit priest, walked over to Von Slagel and knelt before him in the snow.

'My son,' Von Slagel said, 'you have been chosen for the highest order.'

'You have your instructions?'

'Si, Santo Padre,' the pilot answered, in reverence.

'The navigational system is set. You will transport the casket to the prearranged destination. Abbess Helewis Vghtred will conduct the exchange.'

Von Slagel laid his ringless hands on the priest's head.

'*Nel nome del Padre*,' Von Slagel said tersely. The priest wiped a tear from his cheek, saluted, then marched towards the cockpit.

Von Slagel walked over to the most decorated of the six SAS soldiers.

'Captain Granville, your final instruction,' he said softly. 'On receipt of the exchanged infant at St Gabriel's Nursing Home, exterminate it, then the pilots and the crew.'

Captain Nicholas Granville saluted.

'Yes, sir.'

Granville signalled to the soldiers and, as one, the mercenaries raised their MP5A3 sub-machine guns and fired a burst of 9mm rounds into the chest of each of the four unsuspecting cardinals. Then they loaded the bodies into the hold before climbing into the gunship.

Von Slagel smiled in approval, saluted, then turned sharply on his heel, and fought his way through the rapidly intensifying ice storm towards the shelter of the old Vatican fortifications.

All at once, Rome's skies filled with the rasping screams of a hundred thousand starlings. The glowing dawn skies

133

above Von Slagel turned black as the violent rotating dark column of starlings swooped across his path in a sinister swirling mass, twisting and turning like a great feathered cyclone. His master's iniquitous advance party.

The familiar aroma of frankincense permeated the heliport.

Von Slagel flung himself prostrate onto the tarmac as a tall form materialized from the centre of the savage churning flock directly in his path.

He raised his head, trembling, at the two feet that stood before him, shod in a pair of black Tanino Crisci patent leather shoes. He raised his head further to see a silver cane with a black gloved hand resting on the carved serpent handle.

'He is en route to London, Your Excellency.' His voice quivered. 'The infants will be exchanged. Executed, sire, according to your plan.'

He grasped his Master's ringed hand with his own bare trembling ones and kissed the golden seal of an immense onyx ring.

Lorcan De Molay smiled slowly in approval and adjusted the large crucifix that hung from a cord around his neck. He stared down at Von Slagel, his features hidden by the circular brim of his black *cappello romano*.

'You have excelled yourself, Charsoc the Dark,' he murmured.

He looked out from under the wide rim of the fur hat, his eyes riveted on the sleek black gunship gliding upwards into Rome's dawn skies. It circled the Vatican twice before flying out towards the Tyrrhenian Sea in the direction of London, its lights already just a speck in the shimmering blue-black horizon.

Lorcan De Molay walked over to the statue of the Madonna and Jesus, then stood perfectly still, his black Jesuit robes blowing violently in the raging blizzards.

'The Nazarene.' He ran slim manicured fingers over the infant Jesus' exquisitely carved iron features.

'An exquisite rendition; almost flawless,' he whispered, strangely captivated by the infant king's iron features. His intense sapphire gaze moved slowly upwards until it rested on the intricately carved golden crown on the infant's head.

Abruptly, he pulled his robes tightly around him, his steel blue eyes flashed with sudden venom. He raised his face to the heavens.

'*Your* son's kingdom comes to an end!' he hissed.

The King of the Damned stood in the blizzard, his face raised in wild abandon to the glowing dawn skies, his raven hair lashing wildly in the storm as he transformed to seraph. Archangel. Six monstrous black seraph wings billowed behind him.

'*My* kingdom come!' he cried.

OVER ONE DECADE LATER

CHAPTER FOURTEEN

Ancestral Ties

De Vere Ancestral Home,
Narragansett Bay,
Newport, Rhode Island
1994

The sleek black limousine was flanked by four black Lincoln SUVs. It purred past the three gatehouses, through tall cast-iron gates emblazoned with the De Vere family crest and on to the vast acreage of immaculately manicured grounds of the De Vere ancestral mansion. The limousine sped past the Pavilion and up the winding driveway, past grand overlooks and ornamental features, finally drawing to a halt outside a colossal Indiana limestone, gabled, fifty-room mansion overlooking the Atlantic Ocean at Narragansett Bay.

A tall, elegant, dark-haired man in his late forties exited from the back of the limousine holding a slim black briefcase. Four security men exited behind him. James De Vere stood completely still for a long moment, drinking in the sight of his East Coast childhood ancestral home. His handsome face was haggard, weary to the point of exhaustion.

James walked up the limestone steps just as one of the enormous yew front doors opened. An elderly, long-limbed British butler with a mop of unruly coarse silver hair bowed.

'Welcome home, Master James,' he said, in a cultured English accent. 'Excellent to have you back, sir.'

'It's been a long trip, Maxim,' James said, with a tired smile, handing Maxim his briefcase. 'Good to see you, too. The boys been behaving while I was gone?'

'Everything is quite in order, sir.' Maxim stared down at his white-gloved hands sheepishly.

James's eyes narrowed, catching sight of the charred patch on Maxim's pressed black trousers.

'No more scientific experiments while I've been away?' James studied Maxim intently.

A sudden pink flush started at Maxim's collar and spread up his neck.

'Maxim, when I agreed you were to take over the boys' scientific tutoring, I was meaning theoretical explanations and hypotheses, not advanced biochemistry experiments.' James sighed.

'We were merely studying biochemical reactions in the woodshed,' Maxim said, awkwardly.

'Let's see – in summer Nick blew up the aviary with nitroglycerine, in the fall Adrian exploded a mixture of acetone peroxide and sawdust in Frau Meeling's study, and at Thanksgiving Mrs De Vere discovered Jason assembling a homemade pipe bomb. Mrs De Vere's nerves will be intolerable.'

James turned to the security men, hiding a smile.

'Make yourself at home on the porch, gentlemen.'

He gave Maxim a pointed stare.

'Maxim will bring refreshments.'

Maxim scowled and looked the dark-suited entourage up and down sniffily.

'As you wish, sir.'

James walked inside into the spacious gilded hallway with its eighteen-foot vaulted ceilings. He stopped in the vestibule, his features visibly relaxing as he breathed in the aroma of bergamot and mimosa that wafted through the halls. Maxim eased him out of his overcoat.

'You are weary, Master James, sir?' He looked at James in concern. 'I took the liberty of placing your smoking jacket and slippers next to the fireplace as always.'

James laid a hand on Maxim's shoulder.

'Maxim, old friend, it's been a hard week.' He raised his eyebrows. 'Madam Lilian?'

'Madam Lilian is in the drawing room, sir.'

'Get the boys, please, Maxim. I have news that concerns them.'

James walked to the huge mahogany drawing room doors and slowly pushed them open.

Standing by the tall marbled log-burning fireplace was a slender, elegant, fine-featured woman. Her skin was alabaster-smooth, her make-up perfectly applied. Her shoulder-length glossy chestnut hair was swept up in a chignon. She wore a pale apricot silk dress that fell just above her well-turned ankle and a pair of apricot satin mules. Nothing was out of place. Lilian De Vere turned, instantaneously coming alive at the sight of James. She rushed over to him. They clung to each other. He closed his eyes, burying his face in her neck, visibly at peace.

Slowly he raised his head, unclasped his arms from her waist and walked over to the window, gazing out at the darkening thunder clouds building up over the Atlantic.

Lilian studied him intently.

'You were summoned?'

She walked over to him and placed her hand on his back. 'The Council of Three Hundred?'

James shook his head. 'No.' He turned to face her, his face ashen.

'Summoned by my father,' he said, his voice barely audible. 'To San Francisco. To the Grande Druid Council.'

'Julius.' Lilian pulled her hand away from James as though she'd been scalded.

'The Witch High Priests,' she whispered, looking up at James in dread. 'The Council came once to our house. On All Hallows. A Black Mass in my father's chapel.' She walked over to the wet bar and poured herself a Martini, her hands trembling violently. 'They conducted a child sacrifice on my behalf. What did they want this time?'

James took a deep breath. 'We leave for London in five weeks.'

'London?'

James reached out to clasp her arm, but Lilian backed away against the drinks cabinet.

'You said . . . you said you would do what we discussed. That this time you would tell them no,' she said, her voice dangerously soft. She walked over to the French windows, glass in hand, staring out over the beautifully manicured lawns, then turned to him emotional but controlled. 'You couldn't do it, could you?'

James nodded, suddenly world-weary. 'You knew when we married there would be' – he hesitated – 'demands: things that we would have to do.'

'We said we would tell them *no*.' Lilian stared at him, an unsettling wildness in her eyes.

'They made it very clear. If we refuse,' his voice was hard, 'they will kill us, Lilian.' He hesitated. 'If we refuse, they will kill the boys.'

'*The boys!*' Lilian whispered in horror. She turned from the window, a solitary tear escaped down her cheek.

'They will kill them like they killed my father.' Her slender shoulders shook with fury.

She raised her head, her soft grey eyes suddenly like ice. 'My entire childhood was *managed*: child sacrifices, mind control, my father's suicide ... And *they* managed it just like they manage *you*. We have to get out.'

She let out a strangled sob. 'For the sake of our sons we *have* to get out.' Her perfectly coiffed hair fell awry across her face.

James turned to her, ashen, his hands trembling.

'There *is* no out, Lilian.' James's voice was uncharacteristically harsh. 'You knew when we married, I was born into one of the thirteen Illuminati bloodlines. You knew the high price we would pay.'

She recoiled.

'I don't want this for my *sons*,' she sobbed,

James took her face in his hands. 'Listen to me,' he said, his voice like steel. 'I have their word. If we meet their demands, *every* demand they make, they will *not* touch our sons. If we do their bidding, all their bidding, the boys will exist outside of their clutches. Free to live a normal life. Free from covens and their depraved rituals. Free from things too unspeakable to utter.'

Lilian stared at James, her breathing shallow.

He continued, relentless. 'We sacrifice *our* freedom, that our sons live free from subterfuge. That our sons live free from their clutches.'

The Martini glass slipped from Lilian's hands, shattering on the floor. There was a soft knock on the drawing room door. A petite girl dressed in black maid's livery with crisp white apron entered with a gorgeous elfin-faced blond five year old in tow.

Nicholas De Vere peeked out from behind his long fringe.

He saw his mother, and broke out into a cheeky grin. Lilian turned and wiped the tears from her cheeks, regaining her composure instantly. She held out her arms.

'Nicholas, darling,' she said. 'Thank you, Laura. I had a slight "accident". Be a dear and clean it up, will you?'

Nick ran over to Lilian, then stopped in mid-stride as he caught sight of his father. Excitement swept across his features.

'Dad!' he cried, running full steam into James's open arms. James picked Nick up and lifted him high above his head. Nick screamed in exhilaration. James set him down on his lap.

A big-boned, Germanic-looking woman stood at the door, her blonde hair pulled severely back off her face. She wore an unflattering houndstooth suit and thick dark stockings pulled over hefty calves. Following immediately behind her was a handsome, almost beautiful boy of about thirteen.

His dark hair was cut short, framing high cheekbones. He was sweet faced. Serious.

'Adrian has done his homework, Frau Meeling?' Lilian asked, her eyes suddenly cold. Frau Meeling nodded briefly.

'Master Adrian has completed his social science, Madam. He has algebra homework.' Lilian nodded. Adrian walked over to his father who put his arm around him, slapping him on the back.

'Good to see you, Dad.' Adrian embraced his father warmly.

'Great to see you, Adrian pal.' James ruffled his hair.

Maxim entered with a tray of canapés.

James looked down and gingerly picked up a sticky green marmalade-looking hors d'oeuvre.

'A new recipe, Master James,' Maxim said, beaming proudly.

James exchanged a look with Lilian.

'It's Beatrice and Pierre's day off.' Lilian hid a smile, in spite of herself.

James grunted, took a bite and spat it immediately into his handkerchief.

Adrian winked at Nick who collapsed into loud giggles. 'Chilli, Maxim?'

'*Chilli*, sir.' Maxim glowed with pride.

James looked around and frowned. 'Where *is* Jason?'

Maxim raised his eyebrows.

'I have just been informed that Master Jason unfortunately had a technical hitch with his Mustang and had to *hitch*,' Maxim grimaced slightly, 'a ride home, if I may add, Master James.'

James sighed in irritation.

Suddenly there was a loud screech of brakes outside, accompanied by raucous laughter. Lilian walked to the window and watched the lanky, dark-haired seventeen year old ease his six-foot frame with difficulty out of a rusted lime-green Mustang crammed with high-school students.

A petite blonde entwined her arms around him flirtatiously and Jason smiled back with his usual rakish charm. He looked up to where Lilian was watching him through the drawing room window.

Blushing furiously, he glared at the window, slamming the car door. The girls in the back blew kisses at him while the guys shouted unintelligible insults.

Jason slung his satchel over his shoulder and strode up the front steps. A moment later he pushed open the drawing room door.

'Mom . . .' He scowled at her, then kissed her perfunctorily on the cheek. His eyes lit up when he saw his father.

'Hey, Dad! You're back!'

A genuine smile spread across Jason's face.

'Hey, Adrian, Nick!' He grabbed Nick's shoulder and

145

drew him to him. 'There're four security dudes on the porch.'

The boys made a scramble for the door.

'*Pow! Pow!*' cried Nick, shooting at Adrian with an imaginary pistol.

James held up his hand.

'Sit down, boys,' he said, suddenly serious. 'Your mother and I need to talk to you.'

With a groan, Jason slung his satchel onto the floor as the younger boys reluctantly retraced their steps.

Jason punched Adrian in the side. Glaring at him, Adrian punched him back.

'Boys!' Lilian glared warningly at Jason.

'Your father has news.' She looked over to him.

'Not another promotion.' Jason scowled. 'And another *move*.'

James spoke quietly.

'I have been offered and have accepted the post of Ambassador for the United States,' he poured himself a whisky from a tray next to the canapés, 'to the United Kingdom.'

The boys stared at him in complete astonishment.

'It necessitates our moving to London. We take up residence in Winfield House in Regent's Park in just over a month.'

'Aw, Dad, my baseball game . . .', Adrian moaned.

Nick ran around the room. 'The Queen. *Pow! Pow*! The Queen, *pow*!'

Jason sat, staring down at the floor. His shoulders shook with a cold fury. Lilian looked at him anxiously.

'Jason,' she said, softly.

He ignored her deliberately, looking straight into his father's eyeline.

'I'm not leaving.'

He stood up, his hands shaking.

'You'll have to kill me and drag me out of here.'

James took a sip of his scotch.

'Then I'll kill you and drag you out of here,' he said, matter of factly.

Jason turned to Lilian, trembling with uncontrolled rage.

'I *won't* go, Mother.'

Lilian looked at James imploringly.

'You'll do what we say,' James said, quietly.

'Do what *you* say?' Jason snarled. '*You're* no example. *You're* never here.'

His voice rose in decibels. 'My *life's here*; not in some backwater limeyland!'

'Your life's with this *family*!' James's voice rose.

'*What* family, Dad? You're never *here*! We've moved five times in five years.' He picked up his satchel. 'Thank god I'm in boarding school!'

He clenched his fists.

'*And* I'm not going to Yale. I'm going to film school in New York and *you* won't stop me.'

James moved towards Jason and grasped him firmly by the shoulder.

'And who *pays* for boarding school and film school? You'll do as I say, young man.'

'Go on, buy my subservience with *money* . . . just like you buy *everyone*.'

James turned to Lilian. Incensed.

'It's enough, Lilian! He sits in his room for days at a time watching god knows what. That Stanley . . . Stanley . . .'

'Cupcake,' shouted Nick. Then he buried his head in the down sofa cushions.

Jason threw his hands up. '*Kubrick*,' he shouted, red in the face. 'Kubrick to my unenlightened, media-illiterate family.'

'You're grounded and no allowance!' Adrian muttered under his breath. Lilian gave him a warning look.

'You're *grounded*,' James roared, thrusting Jason away from him in fury.

Nick and Adrian collapsed in uproarious laughter. Lilian gestured vainly to him to be quiet.

'And you watch that *temper*, Jason De Vere!'

Jason stormed out of the drawing room, slamming the door behind him.

'*Not one* of the De Vere's has a temper like his,' James exclaimed, heatedly.

The door reopened.

'*You do!*' Jason screamed. He raced up the stairs like lightning.

Lilian walked over to the windows, hiding her amusement.

'AND *NO* ALLOWANCE!' James roared up the stairs.

He strode back into the drawing room, slamming his glass of scotch on the table, and turned to Lilian, his face like thunder.

'He's coming to England, Lilian. My word is final.'

Five Weeks Later
New York Harbour, New York

The entire De Vere family gathered inside the huge embarkation hall in New York Harbour. They stood in front of a vast pile of trunks labelled *De Vere* directly in front of a large glass divider beyond which lay the massive berth of the *RMS Queen Elizabeth 2*.

Lilian took out a handkerchief, tears welling in her eyes. She clutched Jason to her.

'Goodbye, Jason, darling.'

Jason hugged her tightly.

'Bye, Mom. Take care.'

James slapped Jason on his back, 'I'll miss you, Jason.'

James stepped back, but his eyes moistened.

'Do us proud at Yale, son.' He clasped him in tight embrace.

'You pass Yale – you can go to film school, I've given you my word.'

Jason nodded, suddenly emotional.

'Thanks, Dad,' he said. He tousled Nick's hair, then slapped Adrian on the shoulder. James and Lilian turned and moved through passport control, up the embarkation gangway, followed by Adrian and Nick who clutched James De Vere's hand tightly.

'Hey, Nick!' Jason called.

Nick turned around.

'I'm not there to protect you now – and Adrian's off to Gordonstoun. You have to hold your own with the limeys!'

Nick let go of his father's hand and bolted back down the gangway, through the grasp of the unprepared passport controller and ran full tilt into Jason's legs, burying his face in Jason's ripped Levis.

Jason knelt down and gently raised Nick's tear-stained, heart-shaped face to his own.

'Hey, pal,' he whispered. 'I'm always here for you. No matter what.'

'No matter what . . .,' Nick stammered.

'No matter what,' Jason said. He held out his left hand to Nick.

'Remember. Brothers' pact.'

Nick placed his chubby nail-bitten hand on top of Jason's just as Adrian ran back down the gangway towards them. James was in intense conversation with the passport controller who nodded and waved Adrian through embarkation, back towards Jason. Adrian placed his left hand on top of Nick's.

'Brothers,' said Jason.

'BROTHERS!' Adrian and Nick echoed in unison.

'For eternity!' Nick added, emphatically.

Jason looked down at the sweet-faced five year old in affection and gave Nick his lopsided grin.

'For ever, pal,' Jason murmured. 'My word.'

Nick nodded earnestly.

A flashbulb went off as Maxim pressed the trigger of his latest invention. A large black digital camera with a myriad of impressive-looking silver gadgets on its top.

The ship's horn sounded.

'Boys! Come on!' James called. Nick and Adrian ran back up the gangway, then turned to Jason waving furiously.

'I'll miss you guys!' Jason shouted above the noise of the ship's engines.

The flash went off again.

James and Lilian stood at the entrance and waved, Lilian crying and blowing Jason one last kiss.

He took a deep breath, watching the back of his father, James De Vere, as he finally disappeared into the ship.

Maxim walked towards Jason, camera in hand.

'Master Jason, you're my responsibility now.'

'Let's pack for Yale.'

TWENTY-SEVEN YEARS LATER

CHAPTER FIFTEEN

Brothers

King David Hotel
Jerusalem
Saturday, 18 December 2021

Jason De Vere paced the marbled floors of the lobby of the King David Hotel, barking instructions into the headset of his mobile phone. He checked his watch for the third time in short succession, then reluctantly sank into a large leather chair and idly picked up the business section of the *Washington Post*. He glared in distaste at the cup of weak Israeli coffee on the table. Thank god the Third World War was finally over. The Ishtar Accord couldn't come soon enough for his liking, and he knew he echoed the sentiments of hundreds of conglomerate owners throughout the Middle East and the West. At least the media industry was fast returning to normal. He took a sip of the lukewarm black coffee, and grimaced. Vox's Jerusalem offices had escaped the worst of the war but his entire Tel Aviv staff had been killed in the nuclear blast from Iran. He sighed. And the King David Hotel stood unscathed. He snapped out of his reverie at the wailing of sirens drawing up outside the hotel.

Adrian had finally arrived.

Three open-backed black vans carrying six armed EU secret service men led the cavalcade, followed by the European President's sleek black armoured Mercedes. Four additional Mercedes and three more enormous open-backed convoy protection vans screeched to an abrupt halt outside the discreet hotel entrance, their ear-splitting sirens still wailing.

Six bodyguards armed with MP5 machine pistols jumped out of the first van and tore into the lobby while four Israeli police helicopters chatter-chattered overhead.

Immediately, six armed secret service men surrounded the armoured Mercedes as Adrian De Vere exited. He walked through the entrance of the hotel shielded by his ear-miked bodyguards through the lobby, straight to where Jason sat.

Jason put down the paper and grinned, studying Adrian as the head waiter nervously gestured to the plush velvet sofa newly refurbished in his honour.

Adrian took off his jacket, handed it to his personal bodyguard and leant back in the sofa, observing Jason affectionately.

He seemed relaxed. He wore an easy air of sophistication, a man at home with his presidency. Trim, tanned, and immaculately groomed, his playboyish good looks took eight years off him. Jason grimaced. Where his brother passed for thirty-two at forty, Jason was well aware he looked fifty for his forty-three.

'God, you're good, kid!' Jason leant over, clasping Adrian's shoulder. 'The last time you got this much attention was when you burned down Dad's greenhouse and the Newport firefighters came down! The historical centre of the city of Jerusalem's totally blocked off. Airspace over Ben Gurion Airport is closed. The whole city's crawling with police units and snipers.'

Adrian grinned and loosened his tie.

'Cappuccino.' Adrian smiled at a waiter hovering anxiously next to him. The waiter shook his head nervously.

'No cappuccino, Mr President, sir. It's Shabbat,' the waiter replied in a thick Israeli accent.

Jason held up his cup and sighed. 'Even a European President has to bow to Shabbat.' He sighed again. 'No milk.'

Adrian looked up at the waiter. He nodded. 'Black coffee.'

Jason raised his eyebrows. 'It'll be lukewarm.' He picked up the *Washington Post*. A photograph of Adrian covered the front page.

'You're the big news in this town, pal.'

'In fact, you're the big news *everywhere*. The most historic peace accord in seven decades of the Middle East; the charisma of JFK; the statesmanship of Kissinger.' He put the paper down on the table. 'You got the European Presidency, pal, and you deserve it.'

Adrian grinned. 'Not bad for someone who nearly failed his O levels. You should see the security brief.'

He called over his shoulder. 'Travis.' A tall, muscular, clean-shaven man with close-cropped blond hair and clear blue eyes stepped forward.

Jason nodded in recognition. Neil Travis, former SAS, Adrian's soft-spoken head of security had been in the security detail for Adrian's entire eight-year term as British Prime Minister. Travis pulled out a three-hundred page dossier, then nodded respectfully to Jason.

'The greatest security operation ever in operation in Israel, Mr President, sir.'

'Bigger than Bush in 2008, Travis?' Jason teased.

'Respectfully, much bigger than President Bush, Mr De Vere, sir.'

'Thank you, Travis,' Adrian said.

Travis stepped back out of sight.

'It's exhausting to be President,' Adrian laughed.

'Sounds more exhausting to be your security detail,' Jason said dryly.

Adrian grinned. 'He's a good man.' He looked around the lobby.

'I haven't been here for years . . . to the King David, I mean.'

'I heard they've given you the Royal Suite,' Jason said. 'Mother would bite your hand off.' He grinned. 'You know they turned me and a thousand other lesser mortals away on account of the President?'

'Sorry, pal, you should have let me know you were out here.' Adrian shook his head. 'Independent as always – you should have used my name, Jason. Chastenay booked every room four weeks in advance – more easily secured. You know the drill.'

'It's okay,' said Jason. 'I've booked out the fourth floor of the Colony. I prefer it.'

'Melissa and I used to stay there a lot when I was . . .' Adrian broke in mid-flow. 'I didn't want to go back.' His voice trailed off.

Jason studied his younger brother as the waiter returned with the coffee. When was the last time he'd seen Adrian? Four months ago at Melissa and the baby's funerals in London. Briefly at the Aqaba press conference. Business. But as brothers, they hadn't had a personal one-on-one since the last De Vere summer vacation house party in Martha's Vineyard when James De Vere had still been alive.

Jason studied his younger brother.

Adrian had changed. It was subtle, but unmistakable.

Two years ago, after two terms as British Prime Minister, he had been worn down, beaten down by the relentless British cynicism and the mandatory attacks on his character

156

and policy. He had taken a year off after resigning from the Labour Party and had holidayed for three months with Melissa in the Carribean. She was already five months pregnant.

Then four months ago, the unbelievable had happened.

Melissa Vane Templar De Vere, Adrian's wife, died in childbirth and the son who Adrian had so eagerly awaited had been stillborn.

Adrian had thrown himself furiously back into politics and was appointed Europe's envoy to the Middle East during the Russo–Pan-Arab–Israeli war. It had finally ended two months ago. A month later he had been inaugurated as European President with a ten-year term. The most powerful man in the West.

The Third World War – the bloodiest war in history – had ended. And Adrian De Vere had been almost single-handedly responsible for strategizing the most complex and ambitious peace process in the history of the Western and Middle Eastern world.

After five separate last-minute cessations, three by the Iranians and the most recent two by Israel, the final accord was due to be signed on 7 January, in Babylon.

'How much time have you got, pal?'

'I meet the King of Jordan here in twenty minutes. Then the Russians, dinner with President Levin, coffee with the Turkish Prime Minister, then fly out at midnight to Tehran. It's good to see you here, Jas. What is it, – a Vox merger?'

Jason shook his head.

'A buyout. The Israeli cable platforms Yes and Hot are up for grabs. Vox closes on it tomorrow. And I'm considering purchasing Israel's largest satellite provider. Once the Accord is signed, media shareholding here will go through the roof.'

'Impressive.'

Adrian frowned.

'Let's hope the Accord goes without another hitch.'

'The Israelis still not buying in to the peace process?' Jason asked.

'The truth *is*, Jas, if I don't get the Israelis to the table this time, the entire process is finished.'

Adrian set down his cup. 'Destroyed.' He looked straight ahead, grim.

'I thought you had it in the bag,' Jason said, puzzled.

'I have. But it's complicated.' Adrian stirred his coffee slowly.

'The major challenge to the whole peace process' – he leant back in his chair and sighed – 'is that the Israelis won. Single-handedly defeated the combined Russian and Arab military in twenty-two months.'

He lowered his voice.

'The earthquake was the event that threw it their way. We all *know* that. But, of course,' he nodded in the direction of the resident Rabbi overseeing the Shabbat observance regulations, '*they're* attributing that to the hand of the Almighty. And who can blame them? I mean it was a show-down: Iran, Russia, Turkey, and Syria decimated on the mountains of Israel. An unmitigated victory. It makes the war of '67 pale in comparison.'

Adrian drew his head closer to his brother.

'They've got enough nuclear fuel to power Israel for seven years. Truth is the Israelis want *total* capitulation from both the Arabs and the Russians. Nothing less. To them the peace accord is an admission of defeat. Capitulation. We had them at the point of signing three times.'

He drank his coffee down.

'When it comes to the issue of Jerusalem, they won't concede an inch. In their terms, they defeated the Arabs and they're demanding some major concessions. They want the entire Temple Mount back, East Jerusalem returned, and a watertight military commitment from the EU, UN, and NATO to protect Israel and her borders for the next seven years.' He sighed. 'The old 1967 borders.'

'Whew! Tough, little brother! And the Arabs – they're going to accept that?'

'They have already. It's the Israelis. They've agreed to all our demands but they refuse to denuclearize.'

Adrian suddenly looked worn beyond his years.

'I've worked day and night for this, Jason.' He nodded to the waiter and pointed to his cup. 'But I think I have it covered.'

The waiter reappeared and filled up Adrian's cup with lukewarm black coffee from a flask.

Adrian smiled at the waiter. He watched as the waiter disappeared back towards the bar.

'I have . . .' He lowered his voice. 'I have attained access – how do I put it? – to something of extreme value to the Israelis.' He paused.

'I intend to lock it down by the end of the week. I'm sure they'll be persuaded. I'm not prepared to let anything stand in my way.'

Jason idly noted the speed with which his younger brother had moved from relaxed charm to man of steel in less than five seconds.

'I heard about the Temple Mount fiasco.' Jason gestured to the papers. 'Some ancient relic stolen. It was all over this morning's local papers.'

Adrian lowered his voice below the hearing of the EU support staff, civil servants, and secret service agents now positioned all over the lobby.

'It should have been kept under wraps. The Israelis are blaming the Arabs. The Russians are blaming the Israelis. The Arabs say it's a set-up by the Mossad. The issue is – they aren't taking it with a pinch of salt.'

'You think it was terrorists?'

'We don't think. We're sure.' He sipped at his coffee again. 'It had all the hallmarks of a terrorist group.'

'And no sign of the artefact?'

Adrian shook his head.

'It's evaporated, into thin air. Interpol, every agency in the world is on to it. Nothing. Just nothing. To all intents and purposes it may as well never have existed. And every scientist sent to verify it was murdered by the terrorists.'

'Know what it was?'

'If I tell you, Travis has to kill you.' Adrian grinned. 'Classified.'

'But you think Israel would do almost anything,' Jason's eyes narrowed, 'to get it back into their hands?'

'Oh, yes, I think,' Adrian smiled, 'one could safely say they would sell their very soul.'

Jason studied his younger brother intently, but as usual Adrian was inscrutable.

The sound of loud wailing sirens drawing up outside the hotel echoed.

Jason watched as the elderly King of Jordan exited from the Jordanian Royal limousine. Adrian rose. Immediately ten Secret Service men materialized across the room.

'Julia's on the *New York Times* bestseller list this week.'

Jason shrugged. Travis appeared from the shadows and placed Adrian's jacket over his shoulders. Adrian grinned.

'I could have sworn the ruthless New York media tycoon with the zero people skills was based on you.'

Jason scowled, then they both laughed.

'Drop in to Normandy on one of your London trips.'

'I'll try, Adrian, really.'

Adrian smiled in affection at his elder brother.

'You've helped me get up the ladder of politics, Jason, and I'll never forget it. Whatever I can do for Vox – it's yours. The deal with China State TV's still on. I meet in Beijing in two weeks.'

Jason rose and slapped Adrian on the back.

'Hey, what are big brothers for?'

They walked together through the lobby. Adrian turned to Jason, suddenly grave.

'Look,' Adrian hesitated. 'There is something, Jas . . .' He looked his brother straight in the eye. 'It's Nick. His body's stopped responding to the antiretroviral treatments.'

Not a muscle of Jason's face moved.

'He's dying, Jason. He's been given six months. He needs you.'

Adrian walked a few steps, then turned back in exasperation.

'Hell, you're a stubborn son of a—'

He shook his head at Jason, then turned on his heel and disappeared down the hall in a flurry of black suits. Jason watched as Adrian and the King of Jordan embraced.

His jaw clenched at the thought of his youngest brother. Nicholas De Vere.

CHAPTER SIXTEEN

The Revelation

Monastery of Archangels
Alexandria, Egypt
19 December 2021

Nick and St Cartier sat at a corner table on the rooftop of the monastery. Sixteen round tables were covered in pristine white tablecloths. They were the only guests.

Around the perimeter of the cupola four hooded Egyptian monks stood quietly at attention. Nick laid down his knife and fork. Instantly, two monks hurried forward, unobtrusively clearing away his plate and glasses. Nick pulled his leather jacket over his shoulders.

'Eleven degrees. Bracing, dear boy. Good for the system,' the professor declared.

A third monk stepped forward holding out a huge platter of fresh watermelon and baklava.

'Dessert, sir?' he asked, in broken English.

Nick shook his head. He sipped on his mineral water.

'The usual, Professor?'

St Cartier licked his lips and gazed with relish at the baklava.

162

The monk placed a large piece onto his plate.

'I saw Jason,' St Cartier said matter of factly.

Nick shrugged.

'Fleetingly, when I dropped your mother off in New York. She said you're spending a week with her.' He pointed again to the tray. 'At the manor.'

The monk nodded respectfully and placed a second piece of baklava next to the first.

'Yes, I drop in to Adrian's place in Normandy tomorrow, back to London, then down to the manor for Christmas.'

Nick leant back in his chair, watching his old friend tuck in zealously to the first piece of baklava. 'You should watch your cholesterol, Lawrence.'

St Cartier waved him away, chewing intensely.

Nick looked up at the Milky Way glistening in the inky sky.

'*You* dabble in astronomy, Lawrence.' He frowned. 'What *is* that?'

He pointed below the full moon glowing high in the Egyptian night sky at a strange white apparition that hung in the heavens.

'It was in the skies over Alexandria last night. I watched it from the Cecil Hotel balcony.'

St Cartier dabbed gingerly at his carefully waxed moustache.

'Yes, yes. I know, my boy.'

He took out a spectacle case from his inside pocket, removed his glasses and rubbed them with a soft cloth, then placed them over his ears and studied the apparition. He became suddenly grave.

'Spectacular. Its appearance is unprecedented.'

Nick followed his line of sight up to the rotating telescope dome on the observatory of the Monastery of Archangels. Three monks gazed through a telescope, transfixed by the apparition in the night skies above the monastery.

'Astronomers have received reports of its sightings from London, Washington, Berlin – sightings as far away as Beijing. Through our Coronado Solar Telescope, it has been possible to actually distinguish a waxen spectre astride a white stallion.' Nick frowned.

'In apocalyptic discourse, Nicholas, it is a marker. A precursor if you will. Its appearance in the heavens heralds the advent of the White Rider,' he said softly.

'The white *what*?' Nick looked at him strangely.

'The First Seal is about to be broken. The White Rider will come forth. The Four Horsemen of the Apocalypse.'

The professor sighed. 'Your disdain for the supernatural aspects of life only serves to reinforce my belief that your ignorance of theological and paranormal affairs is more wanting even than it appears, Nicholas.'

Nick glared at him darkly. 'Give it a break, Lawrence.'

The professor's pale blue eyes glittered with exhilaration. He removed his glasses.

'White, Red, Black, and Pale . . .'

He placed the second baklava in his mouth and closed his eyes, savouring it.

'Sublime,' he murmured. 'Almost as good as junket.'

'As I was saying . . . Horses – white, red, black, pale horses – representing War, Famine, Conquest, and Death,' he said, crisply. 'The forces of men's destruction described in chapter six of the Book of Revelation.'

Nick stared at him blankly. St Cartier lowered his voice condescendingly, but his eyes twinkled with mischief.

'The Bible.'

'I *know* what the Book of Revelation is,' Nick retorted. 'Some raving fundamentalists waving sandwich boards quoting the end of the world, hustling their end-time wares on TV. Fundamentalist delusions. A scam for the weak and vulnerable.'

A monk hovered over them with a large silver pot of Turkish coffee.

'Your gross delusions, Nicholas De Vere' – St Cartier nodded to the monk, completely unperturbed – 'only serve to reinforce my belief' – the monk poured the thick steaming liquid into two small cups and passed them to Nick and St Cartier, who picked up his and breathed in the aroma – 'in your complete *ignorance* of philosophical, ethnographic, and historical analysis.' He took a long slurp before setting the cup back down, then put his glasses back on and studied the white apparition.

'I have been a student of Greek and Latin for over forty-five years, since my early tenure as a Doctor of Sacred Theology. I spent thirty-eight years using every form of analysis and argument to test and critique the vivid and disturbing imagery of disaster and suffering' – he hesitated – 'that is the Apocalypse of Saint John.

'The Apocalypse predicts the Battle of Armageddon, the Four Horsemen of the Apocalypse, the infamous beast whose number is 666. Some believe it predicts nuclear warfare, solar superstorms, even Aids. The Book of Revelation is a *map*, Nicholas.' His eyes flashed with fervour. 'A map to the end of the world,' he proclaimed ominously.

St Cartier gestured up to the white apparition far above them in the Egyptian skies.

'When the First Seal of Revelation is broken,' he murmured, 'the White Rider of the Apocalypse – the Son of Perdition – will come forth to rule.'

Nick looked at St Cartier, flummoxed. He shook his head.

'You've lost me completely.'

St Cartier sighed impatiently. 'The signs of the end of the world – the Apocalypse. In the time of the end, a ruler of immense stature, of immense power, will arise. A ruler who will gather ten rulers around him to create a one-government system. A world government. The Son of Perdition.'

'Oh god, Lawrence.' Nick raised his hands, incredulous. 'This is the kind of teenage brainwashing *The Omen* propagated in the seventies. What's he going to rule? North Korea, with "666" tattooed on his scalp?'

'He will for a short time rule the world,' St Cartier declared, ignoring Nick's sarcasm and pushing the dessert plate to the side. He opened his briefcase and removed a tiny palm-sized computer which he placed in front of him. He switched it on.

'Does the term "New World Order" mean anything to you?' Nick played idly with his spoon.

'Ah, *now* the light's come on,' St Cartier exclaimed.

'The *New World Order* refers to a belief or conspiracy theory that some powerful secret group has created a secret plan to rule the world via a single world government,' Nick rattled off.

St Cartier nodded, raising his eyebrows. With a sigh, Nick continued.

'Some groups are religiously motivated,' Nick raised his eyebrows deliberately at St Cartier, 'and believe that the agents of *Satan* are involved. There are others without a religious perspective on the matter.'

St Cartier nodded slowly. 'Impressive,' he murmured. 'Gordonstoun taught you well, Nicholas. You've no doubt heard of the Illuminati?'

Nick shrugged. 'According to last decade's pop culture, they were a Renaissance-era society of great thinkers who were "expelled from Rome and hunted down mercilessly" by the Vatican.'

'Poppycock! Fiction writers.' The professor pursed his lips in annoyance. 'A flagrant flight of the imagination.'

His fingers flew across the small keyboard.

'The Order of the Illuminati came into existence centuries after Michelangelo's death on 1 May 1776. Its nominal founder was Adam Weishaupt. Their plan was to use the Grand Orient Lodges of Europe as a filtering mechanism to set up a secret brotherhood; an elite that would infiltrate every corridor of power with the goal of one-world government. Weishaupt and his Illuminati were eventually banned and forced to work underground. They resolved that the name Illuminati should never again be used in public. Instead they would use front groups to fulfil their goal – world domination.'

He turned the computer towards Nick. 'Study it.'

Brother Francis stood at the table holding out a large silver platter of fruit. St Cartier's eyes narrowed in anticipation as he examined the platter intently. His hand hovered over the fresh figs and red dates. Finally, he picked up an orange fruit the size of an apple.

'Dom nut,' he exclaimed, holding it out to Nick. 'Your mother's favourite.'

Nick shook his head.

'Orange juice.'

Brother Francis signalled to a second monk who hurried over to the table and poured Nick a glass of freshly squeezed oranges, sweetened with cut sugar cane, from a large jug while St Cartier took a crisp white napkin and tied it around his neck.

Nick glared at St Cartier, then grudgingly scanned the computer screen.

'Financiers, dating back to the bankers during the times of the Knights Templar, financed the early kings in Europe, and funded the Illuminati,' the professor explained. 'They still operate today outside of social, legal, and political restraint. They control the international banking systems, the military industrial complex, worldwide intelligence agencies, the media, pharmaceutical cartels, drug cartels . . . the list goes on. Their infiltrators are positioned behind the scenes at every level of government and industry. Both American and British intelligence have *documented* evidence that they have financed both sides of every war since the American revolution,' Lawrence continued.

St Cartier took a large bite of the dom fruit. The juice slid down his chin and onto the napkin as Nick watched in amusement.

'Ah, gingerbread. No, caramel!' St Cartier smacked his lips. He chewed vigorously.

'Abraham Lincoln,' he said between mouthfuls, 'put a damper on their activities.'

He dabbed his mouth and moustache gingerly with the napkin.

'He refused to pay their exorbitant rates of interest and issued constitutionally authorized, interest-free United States notes. He was gunned down in cold blood.

'Their plan is to unseat the present powers of hereditary aristocracy and replace them with an intellectual aristocracy, using a staged revolt of the masses.

'The French Revolution, the Russian Revolution, the assassination of John F. Kennedy – he didn't tow the line. After the Bay of Pigs, Kennedy threatened to close down the CIA and transfer power back to the Joint Chiefs of Staff, and remove power from the Federal Reserve. The powers that be sent out a note.'

St Cartier undid his napkin and wiped his hands fastidiously. He glowered out at Nick from under his eyebrows.

'Some say 9/11 . . .'

Nick gave him a dark look.

'You were doing pretty well, Lawrence. Don't push it,' he warned. St Cartier ignored him.

'Today the same organization exists unidentified, covert,

and unseen. Hardly recognizable in 2021. But more powerful than ever. The Iluminati are the controllers. In tandem with organizations such as the Committee of 300.'

'Committee of *what*?' Nick stared at him in disbelief.

'An upper-level parallel government ruled by the Council of Thirteen. They dictate policy, determine the issues; their orders are executed by the lower levels of the food chain – the Council of Foreign Relations, the Bilderberg Group, Club of Rome, Trilateral Commission, and their offshoots. The Controllers don't get their hands dirty. The more sinister operations – executions, assassinations, coups, money laundering, drug running – are covertly enforced by renegade factions of the intelligence agencies under their control and the Illuminati's network of private armies. The ruling powers supply inordinate amounts of arms and money to both sides to achieve their objectives. Their primary goal: to form a one-world government. To obliterate all religions and governments in the process.'

'What's this got to do with anything, Lawrence?'

'While the Illuminati work behind the scenes to create conditions favourable to a New World Order,' St Cartier gulped down the remains of his coffee, 'the Illuminus gather evidence and take direct action, influencing groups to prevent the New World Order from attaining a foothold. These Illuminus believe that the totalitarian society has already arrived in a subtle form.'

Nick stared at St Cartier in disbelief. 'You're . . . you're a believer?' St Cartier nodded.

'I have followed their trail for over three decades, both as a Jesuit priest before I left the order and as a CIA officer. Yes, Nicholas,' St Cartier declared, 'I am an Illuminus.'

St Cartier continued. Unrelenting.

'Today there are thirteen families of great influence who rule the order. They are the Controllers. They meet on a regular basis to discuss finances, direction, and policy. Influential dynasties with *old* money.'

St Cartier removed a tin of tobacco from his jacket. He lit a match, then lit his pipe. 'Switzerland was in fact created as a neutral banking centre so that Illuminati families would have a safe place to keep their funds without fear of destruction from wars or prying eyes.'

St Cartier looked directly at Nick.

'Your *family*, Nicholas,' St Cartier paused, 'is one of these financiers. One of thirteen ruling families of the Illuminati. A Controller.'

Nick looked around at the monks standing respectfully silent on the rooftop.

'Lawrence.' He lowered his voice. 'Are you stark, raving mad? Dad was a complete sceptic. He never believed in conspiracy theories, let alone . . .'

St Cartier ignored Nick's comment.

'The De Vere family is one of thirteen that maintain a stranglehold on the political, financial, and social administration of the United States. They exert major influence in the global business of nations through a consortium of power brokers – private investors, defence contractors, renegade factions of the CIA, the Council of Foreign Relations, International Monetary Fund, the World Bank. The list is too long to mention.'

'That's pushing it, Lawrence,' Nick warned, '*even* for you.'

'Your family has financed these operations for centuries through their treasury and bullion trading, resource and mining banking, and investment banking.'

He looked at Nick pointedly. 'De Vere Asset Management. Leopold De Vere and Sons Limited.'

'Look, Lawrence, I grew up with all of this at the breakfast table.' Nick was becoming aggravated. 'Conspiracy theories involving my family are a thriving industry. De Vere

Asset Management New York, De Vere Ventures Middle East, De Vere Ventures East Asia, De Vere & Cie France, De Vere Reserve . . .' He raised his hands. 'It's all transparent. Been in the public arena for decades.'

'All of them subsidiaries of the De Vere family controlled De Vere Continuation Holdings AG,' Lawrence continued quietly, 'established in Switzerland in the early part of the twentieth century to protect your family's ownership of its banking empire. De Vere Continuation Holdings AG, however, is *not* in the public arena. And has never been transparent.'

Lawrence studied Nick intently. Nick frowned.

'Who runs De Vere Continuation Holdings, Nick?'

Nick glared at him.

'What *is* this, Lawrence? Some form of obsessive inquisition left over from your Jesuit training?'

Lawrence held his gaze.

'Humour me. Pacify an old man's curiosity.'

'Look, Lawrence, I was never interested in the details,' Nick snapped, losing his patience. 'None of us were. We weren't interested in the family banking dynasty. I studied archaeology. Jason went into media. Adrian into politics. Dad ran the banking dynasties until his death. At his death, all power of attorney was transferred to Mother. Simple. Satisfied?'

'Unfortunately, Nicholas. No.' His tone was unusually gentle.

'The De Vere Continuation Holdings was established by your ancestor, Leopold De Vere in the 1790s. He held a vast secret subterranean vault full of gold beneath his house in Hamburg. In 1885, Ephraim De Vere handed it to his son Rupert, your great-great grandfather. In 1954 your paternal grandfather, Julius De Vere, took the reins and ran it with an iron fist. He, as his ancestors before him, cornered the world's gold supply. By the time of Julius De Vere's death in 2014, De Vere Holdings held over five per cent of the world's gold hidden in its private vaults.

'Your father was allowed by the powers that be to dabble in it but Julius deemed him unfit to take the reins. Before Julius's death, he handed total control to his trustees. Nameless, faceless members of the Brotherhood.'

'That's patently untrue. Mother–'

'Your mother, shrewd businesswomen as she is, is their token. Nothing more, and she knows it. She has full autonomy on the charitable side and runs the De Vere Charitable Foundation with her unparalleled brilliance and expertise. Everything else is *clandestine*, Nick.'

Nick stared at the professor in disbelief.

'How much is your family worth, Nick?'

'Around five hundred billion dollars,' he replied. 'I know we lost 40 per cent of our net worth in the 2008 crash and over half our wealth in the run on the banks in 2018. Satisfied?'

St Cartier looked at him straight in the eye.

'The De Vere Family's assets amount to two hundred *trillion* dollars, Nick. Completely intact. There were no real losses. A PR ploy to keep prying eyes of undercover financial investigators at bay. The De Vere's secret financial records are never audited and never accounted for. And they are most assuredly *not* controlled by your mother.'

Nick's eyes flashed with fury.

'What *is* this, Lawrence? Some *sick* joke?'

'Would that it were, dear boy,' said the old man with a sigh. 'Your family owns more than 40 per cent of the worldwide bullion market, operates an aggressive monopoly on the diamond industry, has undisclosed stakes in Russian oil – estimated at over 50 per cent. It operates at the centre of the illegal global drug and arms trade.'

Nick shifted uneasily in his chair.

'Do you want me to continue?'

Lawrence removed a sheaf of papers bearing the seal of the CIA from his briefcase.

Nick glanced down at the top page.

'The International Security Fund? Never heard of it,' Nick said.

'Then you haven't been paying attention.'

St Cartier pushed the papers over the table to Nick.

'It was set up in the 1980s under the auspices of your grandfather Julius De Vere. Read.'

Nick scanned the pages.

'A *journalist*, Lawrence,' he said scathingly.

'No,' replied St Cartier. 'A top European Bank fraud investigator, Nicholas.'

Nick sighed. He picked up the papers again and read word for word from the article.

'By 2001, the Illuminati had orchestrated the raising of a targeted hundred and fifty trillion from at least three hundred international institutions, in the biggest, most secretive private-placement financing operation in world.' Nick paused.

'Read on, Nicholas.'

'The mainstream media unfortunately failed to report this operation, so the general public is ignorant of it. The aim was to provide finance for the New World Order's use throughout the twenty-first century,' Nick continued. 'Equipped with such limitless resources, the Council has now amassed sufficient financing to pay off or blackmail every leader, policymaker, and intelligence operative worldwide, for the rest of this century, in pursuit of their goals.'

Lawrence took back the documents and continued reading aloud from the article.

'It is a Zurich-based fund. It does not trade. It is not

listed. It has been used, since its inception, for geopolitical engineering purposes. There is strong evidence about the alleged involvement by the European Union's own institutions and intelligence resources in its management.'

Lawrence took off his glasses.

'In simple terms, Nick, it is the Illuminati's illegal slush fund, estimated today at over two hundred trillion dollars, directed on behalf of the Brotherhood.

'They bankroll most of the world's pre-emptive wars. Iraq. Afghanistan . . . That way they control the oil and the drugs. After its liberation from Taliban rule, Afghanistan's opium production soared from 640 tons in 2001 to 8,200 tons back in 2007. Afghanistan now supplies over 93 per cent of the global opiate market.'

His voice dropped to scarely more than a whisper.

'Who stood to gain from the invasion of Afghanistan?'

'The drug cartels,' Nick replied. 'Organized crime. It's obvious.'

Lawrence shook his head.

'No. The intelligence agencies in amalgamation with the powerful business syndicates of the elite, including your family.'

Lawrence looked at him pointedly.

'The Brotherhood deposits multi-billion-dollar revenues from narcotics in the international banking system, using its affiliates in the offshore banking havens to launder large amounts of narco-dollars. In tandem with covert factions of the intelligence agencies, they also bankroll Nicaragua's cocaine trafficking. In Columbia, they finance international paedophile rings, the hiring and selling of assassinations, billion-dollar nuclear component shipments. Ali Bhutto's assassination. Maybe Benazir's. Who knows the depths they stoop to? A hundred other false-flag terrorist attacks. They fund secret intelligence armies. Black-ops. NATO's Operation

Gladio. Italy's Department of Anti-terrorism Strategic Studies. The list is endless. All this to divert attention from their banking mafia. To divert attention from the Council.'

He dropped the papers down on the table.

'From the plans orchestrated before his death by the Brotherhood's grand architect – your paternal grandfather, Julius De Vere.'

Nick shook his head in disbelief. Silent.

St Cartier stared at Nick grimly.

'What is *not* common knowledge is that your grandfather was one of the most powerful warlocks of the twenty-first century.'

Nick looked back at St Cartier, incredulously.

'Warlocks? You have finally snapped, Lawrence. You're out of your mind.'

St Cartier removed a photograph from his briefcase and pushed it over the table.

'Study it. It's quite genuine.'

Nick studied the photograph of a black-robed Julius De Vere, the brand on his wrist fully visible. Next to him stood a fresh-faced nineteen-year-old James De Vere.

'Your grandfather was one of only three Witch High Priests on the Earth that wore the Warlock's Mark, an indelible mark which, when visible, is a seared branding. It was imprinted on your grandfather's left wrist. A seal signifying his obedience and devotion to his only master – Lucifer.'

St Cartier paused. 'A seal denoting that he had sold his soul, by a blood transaction that could never be revoked.

'The De Vere assets belong to the Brotherhood. To the Illuminati. Your father, James, made a pact with the Brotherhood, that he would execute every nefarious demand made of him, do their bidding to every last detail. His sons were to be left untouched.'

175

'I only met Julius twice,' Nick said quietly. 'He died when I was ...'

'Twelve.' Lawrence smiled.

Nick nodded.

'Dad never talked about him. Said he was very secretive. *Hard*, he called him. That's why Dad's relationship with us was always open. He vowed he'd never make the mistakes his father had before him.'

'Your father was a good man, Nick. Your grandfather, Julius, viewed him as weak, but it wasn't weakness, Nicholas, it was morality. Strength of character. He was an impediment to their plans for world dominion.'

St Cartier put away the photo and took a large brown envelope from his briefcase.

'The day before your father died, he sent me this.'

He opened the envelope and held out a folded linen bond letter to Nick.

Nick stared at the silver monogram of the De Vere family and the Air Force blue seal underneath the precise italicized handwriting of his father. Slowly he took it from St Cartier's outstretched hand. Ashen.

The last time Nick had ever seen James De Vere alive was four summers ago: 4 August to be exact. The day Nick had called off his engagement to top British model Devon, for his fling with the tall, lean stylish Klaus von Hausen, rising star of the British Museum.

He had brought Klaus to his mother's annual garden party, and while Klaus was playing tennis, lower down the estate, Nick and James De Vere had argued violently on the manicured lawns of the De Vere's country mansion in Oxfordshire.

James was old school, homophobic, no mincer of words, and they had both said passionate brutal things which could never be taken back.

That afternoon, James had frozen Nick's trust fund. A week later, he was dead. Collapsed in his study from a heart attack. Nick had been devastated.

From the time of his birth, he had been James's unspoken favourite, his adored and gifted youngest son.

And Nick in turn had adored his outspoken, entrepreneurial, generous-hearted father. But the brutality of that last encounter would never be undone.

Nick looked at St Cartier fiercely, then slowly unfolded the letter.

He looked back up at St Cartier and frowned.

'The date – it's the thirteenth; the day before he died.'

St Cartier nodded.

'Go on.'

Nick pushed his ever-straying fringe off his forehead. He could imagine James now, seated at his mahogany writing desk, his thick silver hair awry, writing intensely.

My dear Lawrence . . .

Nick looked up at Lawrence. St Cartier smiled gently.

'Keep reading, Nicholas.'

. . . Even though we have not always seen eye to eye, I appeal to you, my long-time friend – in the event of my ensuing death in unnatural circumstances, reveal these contents that justice may be served. Look after my beloved Lilian for me, Lawrence. They will get to her eventually. Look after my sons.

Bring evil to justice.

Protect the innocent, I implore you.

You are well aware, I know, that for the past four decades I and my father, and my ancestors before him, have been deeply involved in the shadow government and its plan to rule the world with a New World Order.

I was a man of little conscience.

I am now a man of many regrets.

Nick looked up at St Cartier, stunned. Cartier motioned to him to continue.

I have an arrangement tomorrow to disclose these contents to X.

If what I dread is confirmed, I shall do whatever lies in my power to protect the innocent.

It has been my lot to uncover one of the most base and nefarious plans ever conceived in the history of the human race.

I can no longer toe their line.

I have prepared a file of gathered evidence which is in a safe and undisclosed place. A file that discloses the horrors orchestrated in the dark halls of defence research. Weaponized Avian flu. Depopulation plans. I have detailed evidence of financial audit trails concerning the International Security Fund. Offshore bank accounts . . .

It is just the tip of the iceberg

You and I both know that I am laying my life on the line.

I intend to divulge this to the press, Lawrence, and save both the United Kingdom and the United States of America from certain annihilation.

Two days ago evidence came into my hands. Damning evidence, of what they have cold-bloodedly done to my adored son.

I enclose the documents.

They have broken their pact.

Now I break mine. At the risk of my own demise.
I shall be in contact when my investigations are
complete.

Your friend always,
James De Vere

The letter fell from Nick's hand onto the table.

'Your father was dead by the next evening,' St Cartier said, softly.

'It was decided Jason was to be kept in the dark. As were you. He was never interested in the banking aspect of your family holdings. He presented no immediate threat. The Brotherhood was satisfied he would content himself running the communications conglomerate. His Vox board is made up almost entirely of your father's closest colleagues. The Brotherhood, Nick. They have access to Vox communications at a moment's notice whenever necessary.

'But *you* were an irritant, Nicholas. The British papparazzi's fixation with the inner workings of your private life drew attention to the De Vere family. Far more attention than was acceptable to the Brotherhood.'

With shaking hands, St Cartier held out a paper.

'They had to dispose of you. Your father found out.'

Slowly, Nick took the document and read it.

His hands shook uncontrollably. He looked up at Lawrence, shaken to the core.

The professor nodded, then leant across and took Nick's arm, gently.

'The needle in Amsterdam that night was a plant, Nicholas. They deliberately gave you and your acquaintances full-blown Aids. Created in one of their covert bio-terror laboratories.'

Nick stared at Lawrence. Uncomprehendingly. Suddenly nauseated.

'When your father discovered their unspeakable act, he broke his pact. They killed him for it.'

Trembling, Nick stared back down at the incriminating document and reread it.

'It was deliberate,' he whispered. He ran his fingers through his hair, then looked up at Lawrence through reddened eyes.

'I'm so *so* sorry, my boy.' Lawrence stared at him, his eyes welling with tears.

'But who . . . *who* would want to kill me?' he said, his breathing suddenly shallow. 'Why? Who *are* these people Lawrence?'

He slammed the papers onto the table. 'It's my *life* they're playing with. Dammit!'

Nick broke off in mid-flow. The roaring of a helicopter's turbine drowned the conversation. They stared up at the landing lights of the rapidly descending helicopter. As it flew past the tower floodlights, Nick recognized the Royal Hashemite insignia of Jordan's ruling family.

Lawrence frowned. 'The royal helicopter is not in today's log.'

Nick stared as eight monks materialized, as if out of nowhere, then scattered in three different directions. Immediately lights switched on all across the monastery.

There was the sound of heavy footsteps. He turned.

Four muscular soldiers holding sub-machine guns materialized, as if from nowhere. Their heads were clean-shaven and Nick immediately recognized the digital pattern on their uniforms. Jordan's elite special operations command. Jotapa's Royal Guard.

The professor placed his napkin on the table. He stood up, pushed his chair back and bowed.

'Your Highness.' He bowed again. Nick turned.

Jotapa, Princess of Jordan, stood in front of him.

'I'm so glad I caught you, Nicholas. Professor,' Jotapa addressed Lawrence St Cartier.

'Professor, would you be so kind as to give Nicholas and me a moment? I have some pressing business.'

Lawrence St Cartier picked up his computer and papers, then put on his panama hat.

'The privilege is all mine, Your Majesty.'

'Nicholas, I'll retire early.' He looked down at him in concern. 'I suggest you do the same, dear boy. You've had quite a blow. See you for breakfast. Six a.m. sharpish.'

And bowing once more to Jotapa, he walked spryly across the roof and down the stairs.

Nick pushed back his chair. Ashen, his mind churning with the evening's disclosures.

'Nick?' Jotapa frowned. 'A blow?'

Nick stared at her blankly, still toying with the document in his hands.

'You okay? You don't look too good.'

'I'm okay,' Nick said quietly. 'Just some bad news, that's all.'

He looked up at Jotapa, distracted.

'I'll be fine by morning.' He folded the document into two, precisely, then placed it in the inner pocket of his leather jacket. He studied her heart-shaped face.

'You don't look so hot yourself.' He frowned. The fiercely independent strong-willed princess seemed somehow different tonight. On edge . . . vulnerable. The unspoilt twenty-four-year-old Princess of Jordan in jeans and T-shirt had disappeared. Tonight Jotapa wore a pale pink knee-length dress of shot silk that clung to her slim hips. Her long svelte legs were stockinged and she wore a pair of pale pink stilettos. The epitome of a young Jordanian monarch.

'Nick . . .' She placed her small slim hand on his tanned

one, her wrists laden with gold. 'You know I wouldn't have come unless it was really important.'

Nick nodded. Jotapa motioned the soldiers away and, as one, they retreated to the perimeter of the terrace.

'It's my father – the King. He arrived back late last night from Jerusalem. He met with your brother.' Tears welled up in Jotapa's eyes. 'He passed away at four this morning. A heart attack.'

Nick grasped her hand. He could feel it trembling.

'Your father. I'm so sorry, Jotapa.'

'I needed to see you.'

'Of course.'

'Look, Nick, I can't stay long but I had to tell you in person. Nicholas, I won't see you again.'

He stared at her in disbelief.

'I know we spoke on the phone.' Jotapa lowered her eyes. 'I feel as strongly as you. Nicholas, you just have to trust me.'

'We've only just . . .'

'I'm sorry, Nick.'

'It was my relationship with Klaus von Hausen, isn't it? You found out.'

'Nick, I have "eyes only" files,' she said softly. 'I knew who you were before I ever laid eyes on you. I knew what I was getting into.'

'Is there someone else?'

'No, there's no one,' she said softly. 'No one at all, Nick. I'm quite alone.'

Nick drew her nearer. He looked at her intently.

'Are you in some kind of trouble?'

'The entire course of my life is about to change.'

Jotapa glanced around, clearly on edge.

'My father was my protection – while he was alive. My elder brother Crown Prince Faisal will be crowned King in a matter of hours. It was not my father's wish.'

182

She paced up and down in front of Nick.

'Faisal was from my father's first marriage over thirty years ago. Two years ago, behind closed palace doors and in front of witnesses, my father the King designated my sixteen-year-old brother Jibril as his heir. He knew that Faisal was both ruthless and cunning and would be a bad king to the Jordanian people.'

She stopped, choked up, fighting to maintain her composure.

'All those who witnessed this or who are loyal to my father have already been silenced by bribes or other means. The ones who could not be bought or blackmailed were executed this morning before dawn.' Tears welled in her eyes.

'The Prime Minister, my father's royal aides, his trusted ministers. All dead.'

Jotapa walked over to the edge of the roof and looked up into the night skies over Egypt.

Her voice dropped to a whisper.

'I told them I had unfinished archaeological business here at the monastery. I was allowed one final trip. Safwat . . .' Her voice choked up.

Nick frowned. He knew Safwat, Jotapa's trusted head of security who had safeguarded her since birth.

'Safwat protected me since I was a toddler.' She raised both hands in despair. 'Executed at dawn.' She turned to Nick, tears streaming down her cheeks.

'Nicholas, my father was a great and noble king. Just. Courageous. Filled with wisdom. Without his protection – both I and my brother Jibril are in grave danger.'

She stopped, struggling to regain her composure.

'Faisal has given my hand in marriage to Crown Prince Mansoor of Arabia. My younger brother, Jibril, is being exiled and sent there also. We fly to Arabia at dawn.'

Nick stared at Jotapa in horror, slowly comprehending.

'Mansoor is a criminal,' he exclaimed. 'His own father, the King of Saud, has renounced him publically. The stories of his atrocities circulate throughout the Arab media. You *can't* go!'

He caught hold of her arm. 'I won't let you.'

'Nicholas, you are not one of us! You cannot understand our world.' She stared at him fiercely. 'Our world is not like your Western world. Faisal hates Jibril. Jibril is good and kind. Just and true just like my father. Faisal will not dare kill me, Nick, but he *will* kill my younger brother – that is certain. As soon as Jibril disappears behind the curtain of black gold, his life is in danger. Jibril is the only challenge to Faisal's throne.'

Jotapa stood silent, her breathing heavy. 'I *have* to protect him.'

'You're the only one I have left, Jotapa!' Nick cried. 'You'll never come out of that hellhole.'

'He's my *brother*.'

A bodyguard came up quietly behind them.

'Your Majesty.'

Jotapa nodded and held up her hand.

'One minute,' she said.

He bowed and disappeared.

Taking out the small silver cross that lay hidden under her dress, Jotapa hurriedly undid the clasp.

'In Mansoor's Palace, there is no place for this.'

She took Nick's hand, gently opening his fist and laid the cross inside.

'Keep it always.' Jotapa put her hand up to Nick's face. 'And remember me, Nicholas De Vere.'

She walked away from him.

'Jotapa!' Nick shouted. He ran after her and clasped her to him.

She raised her tear-stained face to his.

'You don't understand.' His voice broke with emotion. 'You're all I have left.'

She closed her eyes in anguish, then broke from his embrace and walked away.

'Jotapa . . .' he cried in desperation.

She stopped after eight steps and turned, tears streaming down her face.

'Nicholas,' she pleaded, 'you *must* let me go.'

And then she was gone.

Nick clenched his hand over the cross so hard it hurt. He opened his hand, hot tears stinging his eyes, and watched it slip from his grasp down onto the stone floor.

Jotapa was gone. He would never see her again.

They had murdered him. In cold blood. In the cold light of day.

Everything he had known as truth had been exposed as a lie.

Nick De Vere's entire life was on shifting sand.

CHAPTER SEVENTEEN

Dark Night of the Soul

Nick tossed and turned in the small iron bed, mumbling incoherently. Sweat poured from his chest and limbs, drenching the pressed white sheets. Slowly, he raised himself on one arm, groggy. In pain. He felt the soaking sheets and sighed in exasperation.

A brilliant white light illuminated the room, then faded.

Weakly, he manoeuvred both feet onto the floor, then fumbled for his watch. The luminous numbers in the semi-darkness read 3 a.m. He'd been asleep for just over two hours.

He felt for the bottle of pills on the wooden table beside him, unscrewed the cap and popped two in his mouth. Then froze.

He heard hushed voices whispering in a strange language he couldn't place. He listened intently. It wasn't Arabic or the local dialect. Of that he was certain.

Intrigued, he moved over to the smaller open window on the right-hand side of the chamber. As Lawrence had pointed out, room 9 had a magnificent view of the desert from the front but a bird's-eye view of the rooftop terrace from the back window. The hushed voices were coming from that direction.

He watched intently as three figures walked in the direction of the watchtower on the cupola. The same blinding light illuminated the room again.

There was no doubt about it. The activity was coming from the rotating telescope dome on the observatory of the Monastery of Archangels. Through the open window, he could hear their conversation more clearly. He stepped back. Astounded. It was precisely the same dialect as the mysterious angelic language in the Secret Angelic Annals he had discovered at Petra four years ago. He was certain of it.

Illuminated against the light, two tall figures became visible in the watchtower.

Nick pressed his face up to the old panes of the cloister window and rubbed his eyes.

They must be eight – no – more like *nine* feet tall.

'Get a grip,' he told himself.

He could have sworn on his father's grave that he saw wing-like projections extending from two of the forms.

It had to be the new medication. He must be hallucinating. He looked back through the window. The figures had disappeared.

Hastily, he flung on his jeans and pulled a T-shirt over his head, then opened the door, scanning the cloister corridors. They were empty.

He hurried down the winding passageway, following it through the terrace, past the monks' refectory, until he reached the cupola. The dinner tables and benches were now stacked neatly against the wall and the cupola was bare. Nick stared up at the watchtower, now strangely deserted.

Then he caught sight of a tall, robed figure standing on the far side of the cupola, staring out into the Egyptian night skies.

187

The figure spoke without turning.

'You seek for ancient truths, Nicholas De Vere.'

Nick stared, taken aback at the robed monk in front of him. He must be over eight feet tall. They stood in silence on the rooftop together for a long moment. The monk was still staring at the spectre of the White Rider now risen high in the inky Egyptian skies.

Finally he spoke again.

'Yet these truths may lead you on a path you may not wish to follow.'

A cold breeze blew. Nick shivered. It must be well below 10 degrees. He should have worn his jacket. He watched as the monk walked towards the very edge of the cupola.

'This monastery is a portal, Nick De Vere.' He knelt and picked up a handful of sand in his palm.

'A portal that bridges two worlds.'

The stranger turned. 'The world of the angelic and the world of the race of men.'

'Lawrence.' Nick gasped. It was unquestionably Lawrence St Cartier, but on second reflection, Nick realized that this could never be the Lawrence St Cartier that Nick had grown up knowing. Nick stared, his mouth hanging open. Lawrence was a spry five feet nine.

The figure that now stood before him towered above him – and Nick was a lanky six feet two. *He must be* – Nick hesitated – *at least eight feet tall*. He rubbed his eyes with his palms. *Definitely the meds.*

'I'm delusional,' he muttered.' They had warned him this might happen in the final stages.

The monk reached for Nick's hand.

'Feel me, Nicholas.' He walked towards Nick and placed Nick's hand on his chest. 'I am flesh and bone.'

Nick stared, bewildered, into the ancient imperial face. The wizened features were reminiscent of Lawrence St Cartier, the intense watery blue eyes glittered like an eagle's from underneath his bushy white eyebrows. But the countenance before him was gentler, much gentler and the eyes exuded a deep compassion that was rare in the eyes of the old professor.

'I am no hallucination.' Nick stared at the silken white spun hair that hung almost to to his feet. The stranger's skin glowed with a mysterious luminosity.

'*Who* are you?' Nick's eyes flashed in fear and infuriation. Again, the stranger smiled.

'My name is Jether,' Jether said, gently. 'Ruler of twenty-four ancient angelic kings. In worlds you do not yet comprehend, Nicholas De Vere.'

Jether looked upon Nick with deep compassion and understanding.

He gestured upwards to the waxen image in the sky high above them.

'The White Rider. It designates the opening of the First Great Seal of Revelation. The time of the Great Tribulation that comes swiftly upon your world.

'It is also the ignition key to activate the Angelic Portals connecting the world of the race of men and the other worlds. Portals that have lain dormant since the inception of time are to be activated.' He paused. 'Both for good and for evil.'

Nick stared at him in disbelief.

'Doorways between worlds, if you will,' Jether continued. 'C. S. Lewis – his wardrobe. He was close enough.'

'And Lawrence?' Nick blurted in frustration.

'We, the angelic, appear in human form as needed. You know me in my human form as Lawrence St Cartier.'

Jether smiled down at Nick, a great benevolence in his gaze.

Turning, he walked across the cupola, then motioned to Nick to follow him. He walked down the iron stairs through

189

a walled garden of sycamore trees onto a small stone path that twisted past a vast pond filled with exquisite pink lotus blossoms that rose above the murky waters. Nick stared after him in frustration, then followed, his mind racing with unanswered questions.

Jether stopped at a rusted metal gateway, the entrance to the sprawling ancient wing of the monastery.

'Your journey of enlightenment will begin this very night, Nicholas De Vere.'

He walked straight through the iron gate, rematerializing on the other side, then raised his hand to the sophisticated security system.

'It will be perilous.'

The metal gates swung open directly in front of Nick.

'But more glorious than you could ever conceive.'

Jether bowed his head, then disappeared down the smallest of the numerous winding ancient corridors of the ancient monastery.

Nick stared about him in exasperation. Hallucinations, riddles. Lawrence was at the bottom of this. Someone was playing games with his mind. He was going to get to the source of this madness. Lawrence. Where *was* Lawrence for that matter? Dammit!

He walked through the open gate. It immediately clicked shut behind him.

The lower crypt. He somehow knew beyond any shadow of a doubt that was where Lawrence, Jether, or whoever this monk was, was headed.

He had been there with Jotapa the last time he had visited the monastery and he vaguely remembered the way. He followed Jether's path, walking through the narrowest of the winding ancient corridors. He recalled the distinct aroma of inks and leathers mingled with myrrh.

He turned right and entered the enormous monastery

library, typically occupied by hundreds of monks archiving data into computer systems. Tonight it was deserted.

Portals . . . Wardrobes . . . Angelic Kings. What kind of a fool did Lawrence take him for? Nick leant against the wall, suddenly exhausted, sweat pouring down his chest.

He waited several moments until he felt recovered enough to continue, then ducked through a low dank tunnel, steadily descending a stone staircase.

He continued down the winding steps until he reached the lower crypts of the ancient wing of the monastery, then stopped outside a solid steel door, barely four feet high.

The Jordanian vault that housed the Royal Family's priceless antiquities.

Normally, the crypt was heavily guarded by the Jordanian Royal Guard. He looked up and down the corridor. It was eerily deserted. No sign of any Jordanian soldiers or Jether . . . Lawrence . . . or whoever he was.

He examined the one-foot-thick steel door. The only access was a secret electronic code altered every twenty-four hours and accessible only to the two special forces duty guards and one Benedictine monk. And Jotapa herself.

Nick suddenly doubled up in pain, as his body shook with violently wracking coughs. He reached his hand out to the door to steady himself. It slid straight open before his eyes to reveal an ancient wooden crypt door, the sole entrance to the high-tech archaeological vault.

Nick steadied himself, then gave the door a tentative push.

He saw it immediately.

In the far left corner of the chamber, resting against deep-blue velvet under a glass dome. The small cross carved from acacia wood was no larger than a DVD. The cross that legend said Jesus had carved as a child for Aretas, King of Petra, more than two thousand years ago, when Aretas aided the holy family in their flight from Egypt.

The cross that legend said possessed strange magical powers.

The cross of the Hebrew.

The door swung closed with a loud thud. Nick flinched.

The arsenal of sophisticated security devices employed by the Jordanian Royal family to protect their illuminated manuscripts and antiquities was state of the art. Unbreachable.

But there was complete silence. No alarms.

He stood frozen for a full minute, then slowly inched his way over to the glass dome.

He surveyed the room once more. He was completely alone.

It was now or never.

Throwing caution to the wind, he grasped the lid of the glass dome with both hands and raised it.

He held his breath. Incredulous. Nothing triggered.

The infrared and ultrasonic sensors must be immobilized.

He lifted the wooden cross carefully out of the case.

Jotapa had said that for centuries it had held a strange power. A curative power. Like Lourdes.

He clasped the wooden cross tightly with both hands and waited.

Nothing. He turned the cross over in his palm.

A powerless piece of very old wood. Exactly as he'd known it would be.

It was all a legend. A farce. Nick stared down at the simple wooden artefact in disgust, seething with a sudden inexplicable rage.

He swayed, doubling over with intense wracking coughs, desperately weakened.

'You stand in a sacred place, Nicholas De Vere.'

Nick froze. The voice was coming from behind him. But how? The steel security door had clicked shut and not reopened.

Whoever it was knew his name.

'Legend has it that our Lord carved this cross when he was but an infant.'

Nick swung around.

The stranger raised his head. His features were covered by the cowled hood of a monastic order.

'Right here in this spot,' the stranger said softly. 'He used to sing to his Father . . . an infant's lullabies.'

Very gently, the tall stranger reached out his hand. 'The power is not in the cross you hold, Nicholas De Vere.'

He gently took the cross from Nick's fierce grasp.

'It lies with the One *who carved* the cross.'

A strange inexplicable agitation coursed through Nick's being.

'*You* don't think they are legends, do you?' he said, fiercely, moving towards the stranger, seized by a sudden strange rising fury. His voice was strangely hard.

'No,' the stranger murmured, gently. 'There are no legends in this place, Nicholas De Vere.'

The stranger's hessian robe fell open.

Nick gazed, suddenly confused by the indigo silk robe now plainly visible under the simple handspun garment. He stared in disbelief at the stranger's feet, which were emitting a strange unearthly glow. Nick's gaze travelled upwards – from the hem of the stranger's indigo silk robe, past the girdle of gold around his chest and, finally, to his head.

'There is only grace, Nicholas.'

The stranger raised his head to Nick, his features still concealed by the cowled hood.

'And truth.'

The stranger's hood fell back from his face. Nick gasped. He shielded his eyes, suddenly blinded by the blazing, shimmering waves of light that emanated from the stranger's countenance.

193

Trembling with terror and ecstasy, Nick raised his head, transfixed by the settling light. He could faintly distinguish the stranger's hair and beard, which seemed a deep brown, almost black.

On his head was a golden crown embedded with three great rubies.

But it was the stranger's face that held him completely mesmerized. It was as though Nick was staring into the face of a long-distant sweetheart, or an old childhood best friend, who he hadn't seen for more years than he could remember, but who had known and loved him forever.

He stared transfixed at the strong, imperial countenance, the high, bronzed cheekbones, the blazing dark eyes that flashed like flames of living fire.

He had seen the stranger's face a thousand times before.

In the Sacred Heart picture of Christ, at mass when he was a ten-year-old altar boy.

In Michelangelo, Raphael, Fra Angelico, Leonardo da Vinci, Rembrandt, Botticelli.

At Christmas and Easter. In Lilian's private chapel.

In Lawrence's monastic chamber.

It was the most familiar face in the world. And yet, there was nothing familiar at all.

He was looking into the face of a king. Imperial. Courageous.

The stranger reached out his hand to Nick and touched his chest.

Nick's entire body shuddered violently as he struggled desperately for breath.

It felt as if arcs of flaming fire were surging through his veins like a violent electrical surge. He fell against the glass dome, clutching the stranger's indigo robe.

And still Nick De Vere stared into the stranger's face.

The all-consuming waves of light engulfing him. Bathing him. Washing over him.

He felt as if he were submerged in some inconceivable deluge of light coursing through every cell of his body. As if he were alive. Alive for the first time in his whole existence.

Images of his life flashed before him. The night of Lily's accident. Nick and Jason fighting. Nick injecting heroin in Amsterdam. In Rome. In Monte Carlo. Snorting cocaine in Miami. In Soho.

A thousand nights. With a hundred nameless, faceless bed partners. Men. And women.

And still he stared transfixed, into the stranger's face.

The afternoon Nick and his father had argued violently. The morning James De Vere died. The day Nick received his death sentence. Aids.

And still he stared into the stranger's face. Fully accepted. Fully embraced.

Sin not condoned. Yet wholly identified with. Every weakness fully exposed. Every vulnerability apparent.

And yet still the stranger gazed back at him in sheer adoration.

And Nick remembered the far-flung days of innocence.

'Forgive me,' Nick gasped. Tears streamed down his face. He collapsed to the ground, prostrate, trembling violently.

Desperately, he strained to open his heavy eyelids for just one more glimpse of the face that he instinctively knew he would never see again this side of eternity. Just one more glimpse . . .

He held out his trembling hand to the stranger.

His eyelids were growing heavy . . . *so* heavy.

Just one more glimpse . . .

The stranger reached for his hand.

And as he fell . . . fell, into the darkness of oblivion, suddenly it became crystal clear to Nick De Vere.

He had not been looking into the face of a stranger at all. He had looked straight into the face of Jesus Christ.

Gabriel stood quietly watching Jether, who was bent over Nick De Vere.

The ugly weeping sores on Nick's body were disappearing. The thin torso was filling out before their eyes.

Gabriel stared at the luminous white mark on Nick's forehead.

'He wears the Seal,' Gabriel whispered.

'Oh, what is man that he is mindful of them?' Jether said softly. He reached out his hand and gently pushed Nick's matted hair away from his forehead. Every sign of his earlier stress and pain had disappeared. And now on Nick's face was a deep tranquillity. Even in his deep slumber, he smiled.

'He must rest.' Jether stood up. 'Then he will enter the dark night of his soul.'

Leaning down, he picked Nicholas De Vere up in his arms as easily as if he were lifting up a child, and carried him like a babe down the ancient winding corridors to Nick's chamber on the far side of the monastery.

Just as dawn was breaking in the Egyptian skies.

'Nicholas! *Nicholas!*' Lawrence St Cartier gently shook Nick awake.

Nick was still collapsed in a deep stupor. Groggily he opened his eyes.

'Nick, wake up.'

Nick raised himself to a sitting position.

Lawrence opened the curtains behind Nick's bed. Daylight flooded in. Nick turned his face from the light.

'How long have I been asleep?'

'Two days.'

'Two *days*?' Nick frowned. 'Was I sick? I dreamed so strangely, Lawre–'

His voice broke off in mid-word. He stared down at his arms. The pus-red weals all over his forearms had vanished. In their place was brand-new, baby-soft skin. He stared up at Lawrence, a strange unsettling apprehension coursing through his entire body.

Trembling, he lifted his T-shirt. The ribs that had already been partially visible through his chest were undetectable. His chest had filled out overnight.

He swung his legs around onto the floor, then stared up at Lawrence, completely unnerved.

'My hips,' he stammered.

Nick walked over to the mirror. He looked up at Lawrence in disbelief. 'My hip joints . . . they're free from pain.'

He stared into the mirror, then opened his mouth. The invasive thrush and ulcers had vanished. The raised white patch on his tongue was gone.

He tore off his T-shirt, his breathing shallow. The reddish-purple blotches that had ravaged his limbs and chest had disappeared. He stared at Lawrence, disorientated, an incredible ecstasy on his face.

Every ravaging hallmark of Aids was gone. Tears pricked his eyes.

'Lawrence . . .', he uttered.'

Lawrence St Cartier grasped Nick's shoulder. Nick buried his face in the old man's chest.

'Was he . . . ?'

Nick's tears soaked Lawrence's immaculately pressed linen shirt.

'He was here, Nicholas,' Lawrence whispered. 'He was here.'

Fifteen full minutes later, the professor extricated himself from Nick's grasp, trying to compose himself.

'Come, Nicholas, dear boy.' He held Nick at arm's length, a solitary tear falling down his old, weathered cheek.

'It is time to discuss many things.'

Nick and Lawrence St Cartier walked side by side down the avenues of date palms. Lawrence stopped, gazing out at the vast expanse of desert that stretched before them.

'There is so much more that I want to divulge to you, Nicholas.' He stopped. 'But I cannot. The Tenets of Eternal Law forbid us, the angelic, to interfere first-hand in the affairs of the race of men. Even the Fallen have to adhere to the Tenets of Eternal Law. They are legally binding. I can only point you in the right direction – steer you – but I cannot operate in full disclosure.'

'And Jotapa?' Nick said softly, his face ashen.

Lawrence looked at him gently.

'Jotapa has faith. Faith burns brightest in the face of adversity. Her faith is more powerful than the strongest evil. The Royal Household of Jordan has been chosen. Jibril has been chosen for the end times to be a great king, like his ancestor Aretas before him. Jotapa's mission is to prepare him. This she knows. Her faith will prevail.'

Lawrence closed his eyes. 'And she will not be alone. Your family has been chosen, Nicholas. Chosen for repercussions of great good or terrible evil. Great good must triumph. If it fails, the consequences are inconceivable.'

Lawrence's expression softened.

'Your mother lives daily in the knowledge that her own life is in danger,' he said softly.

'She has comprehension of many of these things, Nicholas. My task was to protect her until her allotted time in the race of men is at an end. Her time draws to a close. She will of her own accord unveil some appalling truths.' He hesitated. 'At a terrible cost.'

Lawrence felt inside his jacket and brought out an old photograph.

He handed it to Nick.

'Your grandfather.'

Nick studied the photograph of Julius De Vere standing with four other men.

Xavier Chessler, Piers Aspinall, Kester von Slagel, and Lorcan De Molay.

He turned the photograph over.

On the back was written in James De Vere's precise lettering: 'The Robes are behind the Suits.' And then a single word – 'Aveline'.

Nick handed the photo back.

'It's Dad's writing.'

St Cartier took the photograph and slowly circled De Molay with a pen.

'Lorcan De Molay – Jesuit priest – a member of the Black Robes. Your father knew I had been on his trail for decades.'

Nick gave him a puzzled glance. 'His trail?'

'Your father knew they were going to kill him, Nicholas. He enclosed it with his letter. He was giving me a clue.'

St Cartier brought out a yellowed photograph from his wallet and circled the same face. He handed it to Nick.

Nick studied it. It was a photograph of De Molay and seven men all in Jesuit robes. Nick studied it more closely. The caption at the bottom read 'Class of 1874'.

'1874!' He glared at St Cartier. 'A common fake.'

St Cartier looked calmly back at Nick.

'*You're* the archaeological photography expert. You can tell these things apart. Go ahead – put it to the test.'

Nick took a small loupe from his leather jacket and studied the photograph.

The magnified lettering read: 'The London Stereoscopic & Photographic Company, 108 & 110 Regent Street and

54 Cheapside. Photographers to HRH, The Prince of Wales . . . 1874.'

Two rows of Jesuit priests stood in black robes. In the centre was De Molay.

Nick stared stunned. He turned it over.

'It can't be. It would make him over a hundred and thirty years old.'

'Over two hundred years,' St Cartier said quietly. 'De Molay was excommunicated from the Jesuits in 1776. Legend has it that he was the hooded figure who delivered the great seals of America to Thomas Jefferson one misty Virginia night in 1782. In 1825 he disappeared without a trace – all records erased. Rumours among the Jesuits held that in 1776 he sold his soul to the devil and was granted immortality and became custodian of the New World Order.'

He looked again at the image of Lorcan De Molay standing next to James De Vere.

'Some legends have it that he *is* the devil incarnate.'

Lawrence watched Nick's face closely. Nick shivered.

'And?'

'I left the order in 1986. The Jesuits have become "untouchable" over the years. The ruling members are very, very wealthy and powerful.'

Lawrence held out the photograph to Nick.

'Take it. It's yours.'

Nick looked at him questiongly.

'The men in the photograph hold the answers to your father's death.' Lawrence paused. 'And your attempted murder. I can tell you no more.'

Nick placed the photograph carefully in the inside pocket of his leather jacket.

'Come with me, Lawrence,' he pleaded.

'I have a prior engagement, Nicholas,' Lawrence said, softly. 'I cannot.'

They took the wooden lift, which landed on the ground with a jolt.

Nick and St Cartier got out and walked towards Nick's Jeep, still parked under the monastery walls.

'Bring evil to account. Protect the innocent, Nick. Find the truth.'

Lawrence looked into his face intently.

'You enter a time of great danger, Nicholas. Nothing is as it seems. The most evil now adopts the facade of the most noble. He who you trust implicitly will cold-bloodedly beguile and deceive you. He who you presently regard with misgiving will become your greatest benefactor. Trust no man's appearance readily.' St Cartier's eyes flashed with fervour.

'Not friend. Not brother.' Lawrence hesitated. He studied Nick intently. 'Not even Adrian, Nick,' he murmured.

'Don't even go there, Lawrence.' Nick warned. 'Adrian's kept me alive.'

He opened the Jeep door and flung his rucksack onto the back seat, then eased his lanky frame into the Jeep and slammed the door.

'Remember – the robes are behind the suits,' St Cartier said, intensely.

Nick put the Jeep in reverse, then leant out of the open window.

'You're way off the mark about Adrian, Lawrence,' he shouted, grinning, and waved.

St Cartier watched with misgiving as the silver Jeep roared off down the road into the desert haze, heading towards Cairo.

Nick De Vere might just make the last flight to Paris.

CHAPTER EIGHTEEN

Dark Clouds on the Horizon

21 December 2021
Western Coast Of Normandy
France

Adrian De Vere's Sikorsky S-76 Shadow flew towards the Abbey Fortress of Mont St Michel built near the mouth of the Couesnon River. Adrian stared transfixed at the fairytale Gothic castle that rose dramatically 260 feet above the ocean. No matter how many times he made his trip home, it never failed to strike a chord in him.

'You are prepared . . . ?'

Adrian looked up at the man he had trusted since he was a teenager at Gordonstoun. The man who over his formative years had become his closest spiritual adviser.

'I have lived prepared.'

'Once the Seventh Seal is broken, they are all expendable.'

Adrian nodded.

'My brothers suspect nothing. The Jewish whore chosen as my mother will be eliminated,' he said without a single trace of emotion.

Kester von Slagel smiled.

'Your father awaits you.'

Adrian looked down at the vast medieval fortress. There, on the very edge of the jagged cliffs, playing the violin, his black Jesuit robes billowing violently in the gales blowing off the winter North Atlantic, his face raised in ecstasy to the darkening Normandy skies . . . stood Lorcan De Molay.

22 December 2021
Normandy Autoroute
France

Nick put his foot down. The rented, metallic red Aston Martin surged ahead down the A84 autoroute, past the rolling Normandy wheat fields. He dictated a number into the car's voice recognition system. Like every vehicle in the European Union satellite footprint, it was linked up to supercomputer databases in Brussels which had universal access to all internet servers, private records, and global satellite networks in the EU.

Five hundred million citizens' personal data, accessible at the touch of a button. The 'superbeast' also recorded every citizen's personal ATM and debit card transactions within 57 seconds.

The refined robotic voice replied first in French, then in English.

'Julia St Cartier. Current GPS location: New Chelsea, London. King's Road. Last purchase: Starbucks. Item: vanilla latte, skimmed; lemon pound cake, slice, one. Purchase completed two minutes ago. Subject mobile. On foot. Dialling.'

Nick grinned. Typical Julia. He pressed her purchase history. Then smiled, amused. Only 10 a.m. in London and from her records she'd already visited Starbucks twice today.

Julia's phone rang once.

King's Road
New Chelsea, London

'Hi, Nick,' Julia spoke into her mouthpiece, handbag and lemon pound cake in her leather-gloved right hand, latte in the left. She glanced at her mobile screen, which showed Nick's GPS location in Normandy.

'Hi, Nick – you've left Alexandria already. On your way to Adrian's?'

Nick's face appeared on the screen. 'Yeah, sis, only forty miles away. Enjoying the latte?'

Julia frowned. Her expensive black patent leather boots pounded the pavement. She wore a snugly fitting charcoal wool coat that accentuated her slim form, a fake fox hat and big Chanel sunglasses that drowned her face. She walked with long strides down King's Road, her bleached blonde hair flying.

'Not good for the diet, lemon pound cake.'

Julia grimaced in frustration, then took a sip of latte.

'You tell Adrian from me, that the newfangled Big Brother he introduced before he left Downing Street is an infringement on our personal rights in the UK.'

Julia took a ravenous bite of the pound cake.

Nick watched her savouring every mouthful.

He grinned, amused. Through all the years he had known her, Julia had dieted constantly. Her resolve was legendary and she reaped the rewards with her svelte figure, but Nick remembered Julia avidly tucking into fry-ups with him and Jason in his summer holidays often spent with them at Cape

Cod. In reality he knew that Julia St Cartier adored her food. Abstinence was the high price she paid for a flourishing career in a communications industry where cake and carbs were illicit. Lettuce and Perrier water were the staple diet of the thousands of constantly starving industry icons, of whom Julia St Cartier was one.

He had caught her out this morning.

'When you can't have a piece of lemon pound cake in privacy, that's an infringement, sis. But very informative, all the same.' His tone changed. 'Look, Jules, jokes aside, I need some information.' He hesitated.

'On Lawrence St Cartier.'

'On Uncle Lawrence?'

Julia walked at a steady pace past the upmarket Jaeger and Habitat stores.

'What kind of information?'

'Did he grow up with your mother?'

Julia frowned.

'Strange question.' She took a second long sip of the latte.

'No, they were twins. My grandmother died at their birth; grandfather had died in the war. The twins were placed with social services in London, then separated during the Blitz, in the evacuation. My mother went to Kent, Lawrence to Ayr in Scotland. Mother only met Lawrence again when I was seventeen. He was already a Jesuit priest. Living in New York.'

'How old were you when you first met him, Julia?'

'I've known him all my life, but I only saw Lawrence on birthdays, Christmas . . . you know – occasions. He was in Rome as a priest when I was born, then when he joined the CIA, he was always travelling. Why?'

'Listen, Jules, I need you to find Lawrence's birth certificate.'

'Nick, his records were lost in the war.'

205

'Julia, listen. This is really important. You simply *have* to get your hands on Lawrence's birth certificate or some certified proof of his birth.'

'Nick, I tried years ago, before the wedding. He gave me away. There are *no* records for Lawrence St Cartier.'

Normandy Autoroute
France

'That's impossible!' Nick sighed. 'Look, there must be something: orphanage records, school records,' he persisted. 'Local authority records.'

'The most plausible explanation is that his records were erased from public records when he joined the CIA. It's logical. Look, Nicky, what's the big deal with his birth certificate?'

Nick looked into the phone's camera.

'Julia, look, I need you to answer me something?'

There was a long silence.

'Something personal?'

Nick hesitated, then took a deep breath.

'Do you believe in Christ?'

Julia stared into the phone's camera. Speechless. There was a long silence.

'Do I believe in *what*?'

Nick watched as she ducked into the door of the Designers Guild store. She removed her earpiece and spoke into her mobile. Her face disappeared off Nick's screen momentarily.

'Nick,' she said anxiously, 'are you on new medication?'

'It's not the meds, sis,' Nick said, softly.

He smiled at her gently into the camera. Then shrugged.

'Look, Jules, get what you can for me. I'll see you at the manor on Saturday with Lily at Mother's Christmas shindig.'

'You're sure you're okay?' Julia asked, still uneasy.

She held the screen away from her, her eyes searching Nick's face.

'You're looking good, Nick. In fact you're looking great. The medications *are* working then.'

'I've never felt this good in my whole life, sis.' He smiled gently into the camera at Julia. 'And I'm clean. No drugs,' he said, softly.

'Look, Jules, find out what you can. Email me any info on Lawrence. Also an updated list of who's who on Jason's board – the Vox board. I'm going to need your help when I get to London.'

'Of course, Nicky. Anything. Anytime.'

'You're my leading light, Julia.' He grinned.

Julia grinned back. 'Okay, little brother. Ciao.'

'Give my love to Lily. Tell Jason . . .' His voice trailed off.

He blew her a kiss, then clicked the videoscreen off and put his foot down flat.

CHAPTER NINETEEN

The Rubied Seal

The Great White Plains of the White Poplars radiated with a soft light that hung in the blazing mists rising from Eden's immense lush lawns of white lilies and foxgloves that stretched as far as the eye could see. In the very centre of the plains, the high angelic elders of the First Heaven sat on twenty-four carved silver thrones beneath a great canopy of the finest spun gossamer. Gabriel paced the lush white plains alone. Restless.

The stately white poplars encircled the canopy, their branches hung heavy with glistening white blossoms, with diamond stamens filled with spikenard. The exquisite fragrance permeated the First Heaven. The elders sat in silence. At last Jether raised his head.

'He has been sighted,' he murmured.

Michael dismounted inside the gates and strode towards Jether. Each head turned in the direction of the magnificent translucent Pearl Gates. The entrance to Eden.

'He is riding the Arc of the West Winds with his Royal Guard.' Michael removed his silver gauntlets as he walked.

Jether frowned.

'How many?'

Michael sat on a carved pearl throne to Jether's right, removed his helmet and placed it on the enormous pearl table in front of him.

'A *large* contingent of his Royal Guards.'

Xacheriel scowled.

'His thugs.'

'They will remain outside the gates,' Gabriel said. 'He is permitted only one witness, as stated by Eternal Law.'

Jether's gaze hardened.

'It will be Charsoc,' he whispered.

Michael frowned. 'Charsoc the Dark violated the tenets on his entry into Babylonia through the Portal of Shinar. He is confined to Earth. Yet he rides with Lucifer.'

Jether sighed.

'Charsoc is a master of the interpretation of Eternal Law. Today they journey to us straight from Earth. He well knows that the penalty regarding his violation of Shinar applies only to his readmission into the Second Heaven. It is not applicable to his being summoned to the First Heaven. He will suffer no ill effects while he is here.'

The roaring of a hundred chariots broke the tranquillity.

Lucifer's monstrous black chariot descended through the indigo mists of Eden, towards the Pearl Gates, pulled by eight of his dark-winged stallions.

The chariot tore through the gates, its huge silver wheels ploughing through the white plains, their war blades slashing savagely through the lush lawns of white lilies and foxgloves that grew beneath the poplars.

It drew to a halt only yards from the table of the High Council. Lucifer stood on the chariot, hands on his hips, staring down at his brothers. And at Jether.

'Your entrance befits you, brother,' Michael said, striding toward the chariot, his expression grim. 'Here, in the First Heaven, you make *no* mark at all.'

Lucifer followed Michael's gaze over to the the lilies and foxgloves springing up from the jagged tracks of his chariot.

'Ah.' Lucifer smiled, brilliantly. 'The *wonders* of the First Heaven.' He sprang agilely from his chariot down onto the Great Plains.

'Here I make no mark, brother.' He walked up to stand directly in front of Michael.

'But, believe me, in the land of the race of men I shall raze, tear down, corrupt . . . until I have completely annihilated that muddy little orb.'

Gabriel looked at him in quiet disdain.

'Well spoken, Lucifer,' he said. 'How eloquent. An auspicious start to the proceedings. You are in a *subtle* mood, I can see.'

Lucifer raised his hand dismissively.

'My mood is good, Gabriel. The First Seal is soon to be broken. My son rises in the world of men.'

Michael gestured over to the gate.

'*They* stay outside.'

Moloch leered at him from his chariot.

'Michael, my pretty,' he yelled, 'we have unfinished business.'

Unsheathing his monstrous sword, he drew blood from his thigh, then licked it. He grinned monstrously.

'Master,' he growled. 'Please.'

Lucifer raised his hand.

Immediately Moloch fell silent.

'Their manners are *still* impeccable, I see,' Michael noted.

'They have other aptitudes.' Lucifer smiled thinly. 'They will wait for me here. But I require my witness. Even the Lord Chief Justice would surely agree.'

Gabriel nodded.

Lucifer walked past Michael over to the table where Jether waited. Silent.

Charsoc stood up from his litter.

'My witness.' Lucifer bowed dramatically to Jether.

'Show them to their respective seats,' Jether said icily.

'I would sit with my brothers,' Lucifer declared.

Jether nodded. 'As you would have it.'

Michael showed Lucifer to a seat next to himself as Gabriel strode over to the table and sat on Lucifer's right. Taciturn.

'Gabriel,' Lucifer murmured. He kissed him deliberately on both cheeks.

'My presence disturbs you,' he said, enjoying his brother's discomfort.

Charsoc sat down opposite Jether, and laid his carpetbag in front of him on the table.

'You are returned from Earth?' He studied Jether intently.

Jether ignored him.

Charsoc smiled thinly, inhaling the breeze. 'Spikenard.' His eyes closed, his face in rapture.

'I *know* you reside on that muddy little orb, Jether.' He opened his eyes, studying Jether closely. 'I shall yet find your abode and we shall have' – he hesitated and took off his gloves finger by finger – 'a little tête à tête.'

'We do not take tea with cold-blooded murderers, Charsoc,' Jether said, coldly.

Charsoc's eyes fell onto Issachar.

'Ah, Issachar. How pleasant it is to see you under more' – he paused – '*auspicious* circumstances.' Charsoc opened his carpetbag and removed a small silver object. 'A souvenir from our little . . . run in.'

He flung it on the table in front of Issachar.

Issachar stared enraged at the silver cross, remembering Klaus von Hausen and the executed archaeologists.

'Issachar ran into – shall I say, the *thin* end of the blade.' Charsoc smiled broadly at Jether. 'Your stewards really need to exercise more *vigilance*, Jether. No niceties. No hors d'oeuvres. Biscuits?' Charsoc scanned the faces around the table, a malevolent smile on his thin lips. 'Who *else* at this table sojourns on the Earth, I wonder?'

His gaze rested on Xacheriel.

Lucifer played idly with his quill.

His gaze fell onto Issachar's cross. He raised his gaze to Jether.

'You are *peeved* by my methods. You feel I am barbaric.' He grinned maniacally at Jether. 'But this is *war*, Jether. Issachar was on the wrong side.'

'Your dark slaves commit untold murders in the race of men, Lucifer. You contravene the Tenets of Eternal Law. You are not above the Law. You will answer for each violation at the Last Judgement.'

'Ah,' Lucifer replied. 'I have been too long in the race of men. Their short-lived pleasures are so much more agreeable, don't you think? No consequences, just do as you please.' He hesitated. 'Until they get to the Lake of Fire,' he snarled. 'Too late, they will realize their folly.'

'Your concern for the race of men's welfare is simply awe-inspiring, Lucifer.' Gabriel stared at him coldly. Lucifer glared back.

Jether opened the codex and surveyed the table. 'Let us address the business at hand. Daniel's week is finally upon us. In three moons, the Seven Seals of Revelation will be broken. In three moons, the Four Horsemen of the Apocalypse will come forth.'

'They will be removed?' Lucifer's eyes narrowed. 'All those that bear the Seal of the Nazarene?'

'I will spell out the conditions,' Jether stated coldly. 'At the traversing of the Kármán Line by the Pale Rider, all those who wear the Seal of Christos will be transported to the First Heaven.' He looked Lucifer straight in the eye. 'Relocated from the land of the race of men.'

'Each and every wearer of the Seal.' Lucifer persisted. 'His subjects. *Every* subject.' His eyes grew dark. 'They damage my kingdom in the race of men. I must be rid of them. It is the agreement.'

'The Nazarene's followers will be removed,' Jether said slowly. 'They are his subjects. He is their king. He loves them. He will not in any measure allow them to experience the torment, the distress of all that lies ahead when you wreak your destruction on the race of men and the righteous Judgements of Yehovah follow.'

'He is *too* soft,' Lucifer snarled. He rose, circling the table. 'He is *prejudiced* towards them: he looks out for his mewling *pets*, but discards me, his Seraph, second only to his throne.'

Michael pounded the table with his fist.

'Those days are long gone, Lucifer. Restrain yourself. You have lost your estate forever.'

Lucifer bent over Michael, his eyes gleaming vindictively. 'They destroy my kingdom.' He placed his face a hair's breadth from Michael's own. 'Their prayers impede my strategies in the world of the race of men,' he hissed, nodding to Charsoc, who withdrew a ream of sealed papers from his carpetbag.

'Missives from the Dark Underlords, the Darkened Councils of Hell, Powers, Principalities, Thrones, Satanic Princes, Shaman Kings, Warlocks, Witches. Attached legal evidence that their advancement in the race of men is greatly impeded by those who bear the Seal,' he hissed. 'The Dread Councils of Hell demand watertight guarantees.'

'You have the Rubied Seal,' Gabriel said, quietly.

Lucifer stared in astonishment at Gabriel. 'The Seal of the Rubied Door?'

Jether nodded to Lamaliel who removed a golden missive from the Codex of Eternal Law.

Lucifer's eyes lit up. 'Yehovah's Seal.'

'Then it is certain,' Charsoc said, passing the missive to Lucifer.

'So he *rescues* his wretched subjects,' Lucifer hissed. 'How considerate, but it bodes auspiciously for me. It is promising.'

'If they are so wretched, so ineffectual, why your haste to rid yourself of them, brother?' Gabriel said, softly.

Lucifer glowered at him.

Charsoc frowned. 'They are redeployed to the First Heaven, Your Excellency. But they return to fight at Armageddon.'

Lucifer clenched his fist. 'The Return. I want the explicit conditions as laid out by Eternal Law. *Explicit*. No hidden clauses.'

'On the breaking of the First Seal, the Tribulation of the race of men will begin,' said Jether. 'Eternal Law states that you, Lucifer, Tempter, Adversary of the race of men, have been allotted seven years.

'The race of men has existed under the Tenets of the First Heaven's protection these past two thousand years. Now there shall be seven years. Seven years with no intervention from Yehovah. No arbitration from the First Heaven.

'Seven years when you and your dark disciples have free rein to wreak your havoc on the race of men. Seven years during which, according to the Tenets of Eternal Law, Yehovah's presence will be removed from the race of men.' Jether paused.

'*Unless* he is called upon.'

'And the Nazarene?' Lucifer snarled. 'He will no longer visit the race of men?'

Jether looked at Lucifer.

'He visits only those who are his subjects. Those who seek his cause.'

'There will be none left.' Lucifer looked around in triumph. 'Not one! They will be too busy blaming him for the anguish and torment I am about to rain upon them. Even the seven bowls – Yehovah's execution of Judgement on my reign. They will *lay it all* at his door. An Act of God!' he cried, a maniacal gleam in his eye.

'And if any *try*,' he hissed. 'If any remnant seeks him as their king, I shall force them to take my mark under threat of death.'

He smiled.

'You know the race of men.' He shrugged. 'Expediency comes easily to them. My disciples already prepare the death camps. I shall incarcerate everyone who resists. They will not sacrifice their lives so readily for him. You have answered my question. I am satisfied.'

'And Armageddon?' asked Charsoc.

'At the end of seven years, the Great Battle will be fought,' said Jether.

'My status if I win?' Lucifer queried.

'If you win, you reign as Eternal King over the race of men. Your incarceration in the Bottomless Pit and your demise in the Lake of Fire, a distant, fast-receding memory.'

'Nightmare,' Charsoc muttered, coughing into his handkerchief.

'And if I lose?'

'You will be held in the Crypts of Conflagration until Michael delivers you to the Abyss, where you will be incarcerated for a thousand years. After one thousand years, according to the Tenets of Eternal Law, you will be released for a short season, then meet your fate at the White Gorge of Inferno, on the eastern shores of the Lake of Fire.'

Jether turned to Charsoc, his eyes like steel.

'As for you, upon your defeat at Armageddon, you will be delivered straight to the Lake of Fire.'

'If I pass Go' – Charsoc opened his carpetbag and toyed with a small golden notepad and a quill feather pen – 'do

I collect two hundred?' Charsoc spoke nonchalantly. He and Jether exchanged a long, icy look.

'Just as an afterthought.' Charsoc cleared his throat. 'In the event of our actual defeat, what *are* my visiting rights in the Lake of Fire?'

Charsoc smiled thinly at Jether who refused to meet his gaze.

'And,' Charsoc continued, enjoying Jether's discomfort, 'please note that there are several,' he paused, '*indulgences* in the race of men I've grown partial to. *Minor* comforts.' He dabbed his pale face with a harlequin patterned handkerchief. 'Earl Grey Tea . . . Sushi . . .'

'What do you *want*, Charsoc?' Xacheriel glared from under his crown. 'A Harvey Nichols hamper? Barefoot Dreams blankets?'

He stared darkly at Charsoc's ever-present carpetbag. 'Or is that what you carry to your sorcerers' tea parties?'

Charsoc regarded Xacheriel with thinly disguised loathing. 'You seem rather *au fait* with the commodities of Earth, Xacheriel. You wouldn't by any chance have taken up residency *there yourself*, would you?' he hissed.

'If the tables are turned, I'll be sure to send you a Mason Pearson hairbrush.' Charsoc looked in disdain at Xacheriel's unkempt thatch of coarse white hair that stood awry beneath his crown. 'First class post.'

Jether sighed in frustration.

'Please. *Please*, compatriots. We speak of weighty things. This is no time for frivolous entertainments.'

Jether followed Michael's gaze to Lucifer.

Lucifer was staring in dread at the blood trickling from his right palm onto the table in front of him. The blood seeped onto his white silk ceremonial robes. Lucifer stared in horror at the darkening red stain.

'Christos,' he muttered.

He rose from the table, sweat glistening on his forehead, then paced restlessly up and down.

He turned back towards Michael, then walked away over the plains past the groves of great white poplars. He stood, a lone figure, bathed in the soft white light that hung in the blazing white mists, his gaze fixed ahead on the the Eastern Gates of Eden.

Jether looked after Lucifer. Grave.

'His soul seeks still for that which it can never have,' he whispered to Michael.

'He goes to Christos' garden.'

'No!' Michael rose to his feet, his hand on his sword.

'It is enough!' he cried. 'I shall put an end to his folly!'

Jether laid his hand gently on Michael's.

'No,' he said, shaking his head. 'It is Christos himself who draws him.'

Michael walked to the edge of the great plains, staring after Lucifer.

Lucifer turned, stared at Michael distractedly, then walked through the Eastern Gates.

He followed the familiar path that wound towards the Gardens of Fragrance that grew far below the plains. He walked under the narrow pearl arbour covered with pomegranate vines laden with lush silver fruits, his breathing shallow, treading frantically over beds of gladioli and frangipani trees, across lawns of golden bulrushes and buttercups with fine crystal stamens, towards the intense shafts of blinding crimson light radiating from far beyond. Across the vale, he came to an inconspicuous grotto at the very edge of the cliffs of Eden, surrounded by eight ancient olive trees.

He was there. Just as Lucifer had known he would be.

With trembling fingers, Lucifer pushed open the simple wooden gate.

Standing in the centre of his garden, his back faintly visible through the rising mists, stood Christos.

Lucifer leant against the gate, suddenly weakened. He struggled for breath.

Slowly Christos turned. Lucifer fell to his knees, his arm shielding his face from the glorious white light emanating from Christos' countenance.

'It was here that you kissed me so many aeons past', Christos said softly, 'before your treason.'

Lucifer's hands trembled uncontrollably.

'It was here that your treachery began.'

Christos walked towards him through the hanging mists. Lucifer stared up at him, ashen.

'The hour you learned of the advent of the race of men.'

Christos gazed out as the shimmering rays settled to reveal, a hundred feet ahead, across a vast chasm, the magnificent Rubied Door, ablaze with light, embedded into the jacinth walls of the tower – the entrance to Yehovah's throne room.

Lucifer followed his gaze to the shimmering rainbow that rose over the crystal palace.

At length, Christos spoke.

'In the midst of the Tribulation, there will be war between Lucifer and Michael in heaven. For surely you will be cast out from heaven. Never to return.'

Christos stared out towards the great Rubied Door. Slowly it opened, and with it the lightning and thunder grew in intensity, and a tempestuous wind blew.

'Mark well the sights and sounds of the First Heaven, Son of the Morning. They are nigh your last.'

Lucifer stared after Christos frantically as he vanished into the white, rushing mists. Then he reappeared across the chasm and walked through the Rubied Door, leaving Lucifer sobbing wretchedly under the eight olive trees of Christos' garden.

CHAPTER TWENTY

Mont St Michel

22 December 2021

Nick rounded a bend in the road. The bell tower spire of Mont St Michel became visible, the golden statue of Archangel Michael on the spire towering 560 feet above the English Channel. Soaring above the Normandy wheat fields, the fortress abbey of Mont St Michel rose like a Gothic apparition through the fading morning mists.

Nick stared transfixed at the towering mass of granite 3,000 feet in circumference. The new European Superstate had appropriated the island from UNESCO for the sole use of the European President. And Adrian now divided his time equally among his palaces in Normandy, Rome, and, recently, Babylon.

It was low tide. The mile-long embankment of the early 2000s had been bulldozed and replaced with a shorter one and an 800-yard low bridge. And the dam at the mouth of the Couesnon had recently been replaced by a hydraulic dam double its size. A feat of hydrological engineering with a price tag of 164 million euros. Nick shook his head in wonder. But it had stopped the island quite literally from sinking into the sand.

The Aston Martin crossed the new dual-lane causeway and slowed down in front of a huge black iron gate with the Mont St Michel crest scrolled in gold at its top.

Nick looked up at the six remote cameras positioned above the gate. He turned to the black iris scanner that automatically lowered diametrically to his eye level on the left-hand side of the car. He looked directly into the camera lens.

Six seconds later, the gates opened electronically and he drove slowly past the newly erected gatehouse with its polycarbonate-layered bulletproof windows.

He was well aware that in the ten seconds he waited outside the gate, every intricate detail of both his private and public life had been transmitted to 'The Core' – the President of the European Union's secret operations base, a sprawling underground city directly below Mont St Michel, over a mile beneath the Atlantic, where the notorious Guber, Adrian's autocratic Director of Security Operations, reigned supreme.

Nick drove through the old medieval village on cobbled winding roads reconstructed in accordance with Guber's exacting presidential security procedures. The village housed over two hundred of Adrian's presidential executive staff, including the head of the European Security Agency and his top economic and legal advisers. The medieval facade was precisely that – a facade. Surveillance cameras and sensors spied from every rooftop, window, and doorway. Unending teams of military police and guard dogs patrolled the perimeters of the double chain-link fence.

Nick finally drew to a halt outside the stables.

He got out, slammed the car door, and threw the car keys to a slightly built man in chauffeur's livery, who caught them neatly.

When James De Vere had been alive, Pierre had been James's manservant, second only in his affections to Maxim.

'Be a pal, Pierre,' Nick said. 'Park her for me, will you?'

Pierre bowed slightly.

'Of course, sir,' he said, smiling with affection at Nick. 'So good to see you, Master Nicholas.'

He opened the Aston Martin door, sat down and adjusted the seat.

'How is Beatrice?' Nick asked.

'Stubborn as ever.' Pierre grimaced, though his eyes twinkled in affection. 'She was up at dawn cooking sweet bread.' He lowered his voice. 'Drop into the kitchen on your way out or my life won't be worth living.'

Nick smiled, remembering the Rhode Island family mansion and his childhood Christmases when he would sneak into the kitchen where Beatrice, the De Vere's formidable French housekeeper was baking sweet spice bread, and be summarily ejected and threatened with a rolling pin.

'Those were good days, Mr Nicholas, sir ... the days with your parents.'

He turned the keys in the ignition. 'Good days,' Pierre muttered.

Nick watched the red Aston Martin disappear in the direction of the fifth garage in the stables. He filled his lungs with the soft damp Atlantic air, then walked the short distance to one of the looming Gothic doorways of Mont St Michel.

He stood beneath the huge ivy-covered Gothic ramparts, in front of the facial recognition scanner, then waited for one of the four security service agents to clear his access.

Slowly, the huge iron Abbey doors opened. An elderly man in tails nodded curtly to Nick.

'Hi there, Anton,' Nick greeted him nonchalantly.

'Your brother is expecting you, Mr De Vere.' Anton's

English was stilted and guttural. He scanned Nick's torn jeans and faded leather jacket disapprovingly. 'Follow me.'

Nick followed Anton through the vestibule, down Mont St Michel's huge vaulted Gothic hallways, down a series of long stone corridors hung with priceless old masters until they arrived at two huge steel doors.

He stood in front of a second facial recognition computer scanner. Seconds later, the steel doors parted, revealing eighteen-foot mahoghany doors.

Two of Guber's special forces materialized.

'I know the drill,' Nick muttered, removing his satchel and camera. He waited while Guber's men ran them through a high-tech scanner and returned them to him.

Anton pushed open the doors to the European President's enormous, magnificently furnished foyer.

Adrian's chief of staff, Laurent Chastenay, walked over to Nick. He was tall and well spoken. He carried a slim laptop.

'Follow me, if you please, Mr De Vere,' he said crisply. 'Your brother is waiting for you in the drawing room.'

Chastenay looked down at his watch, then walked down yet another corridor and turned a sharp left. Holding a door open, he gestured Nick through to a magnificent chamber.

Nick scanned the salon's priceless tapestries embroidered with Picardy wool and Italian silk and gilded silver threads, pastel Aubusson and Savonnerie carpets. Chesterfield sofas. He stared up at the enormous canvas by the iconic artist Francis Bacon.

Nick smiled. Typical Adrian. A complete juxtaposition.

On his last visit, the drawing room was being refurbished in preparation for Adrian's inauguration. It was magnificent. A reflection of Adrian's impeccable style.

Adrian stood, his hands behind his back, gazing out of the enormous opened cherrywood doors at the monumental view across the bay to the open sea. Gunships circled overhead.

'May I present your brother, Mr Nicholas De Vere, Mr President, sir.'

'Why, thank you, Laurent.' Adrian turned and Chastenay bowed.

'Your video conference with the Russian Premier is in fifteen minutes, Mr President, sir.' He bowed again slightly, then disappeared from the room.

'Nicky,' Adrian said, smiling in delight. He gestured to the bay.

'The wonder of the West,' he murmured. '"*À la vitesse d'un cheval au galop*."' Victor Hugo: 'the tides move as swiftly as a galloping horse.'

He turned back to face Nick. 'Three feet a second, the most dangerous tides in the world,' he declared. 'In depth and speed.'

Nick studied Adrian. He was immaculate as always. In fact he looked the epitome of a modern-day royal. All the way from his Oliver Sweeney custom-made ostrich skin shoes to his obscenely expensive Alexander Amosu suit, crafted from gold thread and Himalayan pashmina with its nine 18-carat gold and pavé-set diamond buttons.

Adrian's weakness for designer suits and modern art were his only leanings to indulgence in his normally spartan regime. While Nick had been the proverbial spendthrift, Adrian had hoarded his cash since he was young, a tendency that had become more ingrained through the years.

Nick attributed it to Adrian's rigorous background in economic analysis, his BA (Hons) in politics, philosophy, and economics from Oxford, two years at Princeton, and a year specializing in Arab Studies in Georgetown, before four years as Director of De Vere Asset Management.

Nick frowned, Lawrence's disclosures about the family business still ringing in his ears. Politics was Adrian's passion, but economics was his aptitude. His genius.

Adrian had become Chancellor of the Exchequer two

223

years after the crash of 2008 and had single-handedly revo-
lutionized the British economy. Then came two terms as
British Prime Minister. Until his tenure as European President,
Adrian had no yacht, stately home, beachfront mansion, or
classic car collection. He had lived in Downing Street with
Melissa, with their second home a functional semi-detached
house in Oxford.

Instead of living in evident luxury, he donated millions
to the Marie Curie Hospice, to children's charities in South-
East Asia, to both Georgetown and Oxford Universities, to
the United States Holocaust Memorial Museum, and financed
the restoration of Michelangelo's frescoes in the Vatican's
Pauline Chapel.

Adrian walked over to Nick. He held him at arm's length
and surveyed his brother. Jeans and T-shirt as always. Leather
jacket, satchel, bleached hair. The ever-present camera. Still
the pretty celebrity boy, even though the Aids had had a
devastating effect on him. In fact he was looking better than
he had for months.

'It's good to see you, Nicky,' he said.

Nick grinned and looked down at his torn Levi's.

'I think your butler disapproves of my attire.'

Adrian smiled. 'They said the antiretroviral treatments
stopped taking effect – but you look good, Nicky. You've
filled out.'

Nick hesitated. He turned to look at the three paintings
above Adrian's desk, uncomfortable. It was the first time in
his life he had made a deliberate decision not to confide in
his brother.

'New?' he asked, changing the subject.

Adrian smiled sheepishly. 'I indulged on my fortieth.
Warhol self-portraits.'

Nick frowned. 'Not exactly what I'd call pretty.'

'That's rich, coming from someone who hangs Edvard

Munch's *Vampire* in pride of place in his penthouse,' Adrian retorted, with a grin.

'It's tongue in cheek, Adrian. A numbered print, by the way,' Nick grinned back. 'It hides a safe.'

Adrian looked back up at the Warhol. 'Jason says they're a monstrosity,' he chuckled. 'Of course, what he *doesn't* know about art would fill the Louvre.' He stared up at the three portraits. 'Incredible investment. Worth forty million dollars.'

Adrian walked over to the drinks cabinet and picked up a chilled bottle of cider.

'All goes to developing world children's charities on my demise. It soothes my conscience. Cider? It's local – very good.'

Nick shook his head. 'Nah, Perrier, thanks. I'm detoxing. By the way, happy birthday.'

'Thanks, Nicky. Sorry you can't stay longer – I should have let you know. We've got dignitaries and government officials arriving from six continents.'

He poured Nick a Perrier. 'All classified – preparations for the Ishtar Accord.' He handed Nick the glass.

'It all happens in less than three weeks. *If* there are no setbacks,' he murmured distractedly.

He walked to his desk and started sifting through a sheaf of papers.

'You said it was urgent.' He looked up. 'You need money?' Adrian opened a drawer and drew out a chequebook. Nick shook his head.

'Adrian, listen, I'm fine. I got paid excessively by the Jordanians. I'm of independent means again.'

Adrian frowned. 'Then what, Nicky? You said it was important.'

Nick walked towards the window.

'Look, Adrian, it concerns Dad . . . his death.'

Adrian looked at him, perplexed.

'Dad died over four years ago. Look, I don't want to seem crass, but couldn't this wait?'

'Look, Adrian, I'll get straight to the point. Lawrence St Cartier believes Dad was killed' – Nick hesitated – 'by a group of elitists. Globalists. An extremely powerful cabal. You could be in danger.'

Adrian looked up from his papers. 'Killed?' He frowned. 'As in murdered?'

He stared at Nick in disbelief. 'That's ludicrous. He had a heart attack. There was an autopsy.' He shook his head. 'The old professor's been feeding you his conspiracy theories,' he said, gently. 'Dad used to rag him mercilessly behind his back.'

'Yes, I know it looked like that, Adrian, but . . .'

'Look, thanks for your concern, Nicky . . .'

He drew Nick with him to the windows, pointing to a ship in the English Channel far in the distance.

'See that ship? It's one of eight NATO naval craft that patrol the bay day and night – backed by round-the-clock air surveillance, four helicopters, four fighter bomber aircraft, dozens of cutters and speedboats, 121 magnetic gates, 60 X-ray machines, 132 metal detectors, 18 explosives detectors, 196 CCTV cameras, and 62 vehicle-tracking systems. Guber monitors the C41 system – digital communications radio network and IT systems that give picture, sound, and data to 36 security commanders at any given time – all to protect the European Pres–' He stopped in mid-flow, recognizing James De Vere's signature on the paper in Nick's hand.

'What *is* this, Nicky?'

'A letter from Dad to St Cartier and a document he enclosed to St Cartier. Sent the day before he died,' Nick explained. 'The document enclosed is evidence that the Aids virus was deliberately placed in the needles used that night in Amsterdam. Look. Requisition from Fort Detrick. Monies paid to low-level thugs in Amsterdam.'

Adrian put down the letter and scanned the document. He turned it over and frowned.

Nick pointed to part of the document.

'Live virus delivered 4 April 2017. Injected 12.07 a.m. Signed warrant for my execution. They gave me Aids.'

'Who, Nicky?' Adrian's fingers tightened around the document. 'Think about it. *Who* would want to give you Aids?'

For a split second, Adrian almost lost his geniality. 'Forgive me, little brother. This is nothing more than a common fake. To be brutally frank, Nick, you're innocuous. No one would go to this much trouble to eliminate you.

'You know St Cartier. Ex-CIA, Jesuit priest. Hell, he's over eighty. When they leave the agency, it's hard for them to tell fantasy from reality. He must be in the first stage of dementia. Using Dad's name to give this credibility.' Adrian shook his head. 'The old man's losing his marbles.'

Adrian's intercom buzzed on his desk at the far end of the room. Adrian chose to ignore it.

Nick reached for the envelope in his pocket, and the photograph of Julius De Vere, Lorcan De Molay, and the three men fell from his grasp out onto the Aubusson rug.

Adrian bent down and carefully picked up the photograph.

'Do you recognize anyone?'

'No one. Except Grandfather and Chessler, Jason's godfather. No.' Adrian's voice was soft. 'I've never seen any of them before in my life.'

'There's a woman's name, on the back of the photograph . . .'

Slowly, Adrian turned the photo over.

Nick pointed. 'It's Dad's handwriting.'

Adrian studied the writing. Ashen.

'Aveline,' he murmured.

He shook his head slowly.

'A woman's name. It's Dad's writing all right. But what it means, I've no idea.' He looked at Nick strangely. 'Where did you get it, Nicholas?'

'In some old boxes at Mother's,' Nick lied. Immediately his conscience pricked him, but these were extenuating circumstances.

Nick studied Adrian. He never called him Nicholas unless he was irritated. It was now or never. He had to push it as far as he could.

'Tell me something, Adrian. Is it true that we're so wealthy?'

Nick placed his glass on a cabinet, walked over to Adrian and took the photo from his brother's hands.

'I mean – inordinately wealthy?'

'You know how much we're worth, Nicky.' Adrian's eyes narrowed.

Nick shook his head.

'No. No, I don't think I do, Adrian. How much *are* we worth?'

Adrian caressed the rim of his cider glass.

'Around five hundred billion dollars by today's standards. Half our wealth was decimated in the run on the banks in 2018.' He gave Nick a penetrating look. 'What are you doing? You *know* all this.'

Nick paused, then decided to fling caution to the wind.

'Does that take into account that we own more than 40 per cent of the worldwide bullion market, have an effective monopoly on the diamond industry, and undisclosed stakes in Russian oil?'

Adrian looked back at Nick. Inscrutable as ever.

The intercom continued its high-pitched buzz. Adrian held his hand up to Nick to wait and strode over to his desk.

He hit the button with uncharacteristic impatience.

'What *is* it?'

228

'Your two o'clock video conference call, Mr President: the Russian and the Iranian Premiers are both on hold, sir.'

Laurent Chastenay walked in through the door. Adrian looked down at his watch and sighed.

'Put them through.'

He pressed the mute and looked over to where Nick stood at the far end of the room, then studied the document in his hand a second time. He folded it up and placed it in his pocket.

'Have you shared this with Jason?'

Nick shrugged.

'You know Jason. He hasn't returned my calls for years.'

'Get some fresh air, Nicky.' Adrian gestured towards the terrace doors. 'Give me thirty minutes.'

The buzzer started again. Adrian hit the button. He pressed a remote and twelve enormous flat-panel display television monitors slid down the far wall. Two tiers of state-of-the-art computer terminals and leather seating ascended from the floor.

Immediately, the head of Adrian's International Security Agency entered, followed by the European Secretary of Defence.

Adrian settled back into one of the custom-made grey leather seats.

Nick walked out of the cherrywood doors just as the Iranian Premier's face materialized on the huge screens.

He walked onto the huge overhanging terrace that surrounded the Abbey and gazed out at the smooth grey expanse of ocean, then slowly walked towards the northern wing. Taking his sunglasses out of his jacket pocket, he put them on. He looked downwards some fifty feet towards the cloisters where military police sprawled across the lawns except for the manicured square of courtyard directly outside the cloister arches.

Standing in the centre of the courtyard was a tall lean

man with severe features and badly dyed jet-black cropped hair, wearing a poorly fitting black suit. He'd know that haircut anywhere.

It was Kurt Guber.

Guber disliked Nick intensely. Nick knew he had reason enough.

Six years ago, at twenty-four, rich, pretty young playboy Nick De Vere's prime occupation had been to dissipate the first tranche of his inordinate trust fund in every exclusive private club from London to Monte Carlo. Unluckily for Nick, he was not only a De Vere but Adrian's youngest brother, and his antics had been splashed across the gossip pages of UK newspapers by the tireless London celebrity spindoctors.

Nick's antics had fast become detrimental to Adrian's fast-tracking political career and it had fallen to Guber, as Adrian's head of security, to clean up Nick's dirt. For months, Guber had warded off the savage London paparazzi, buried Nick's cocaine habit in a slew of lies and false witnesses, and salvaged what little was left of Nick's reputation. All in the interest of Adrian's future glistening career as President of the European Union.

Guber despised Nick almost as much as Nick despised Guber and his thugs.

Guber had been with Adrian for years, first as head of security at Downing Street, and now as Director of EU Special Service operations. Exotic weapons specialist.

Guber's grandfather had been in charge of one of the Nazis' most advanced covert weapons programmes. Who knew *what* Guber was concocting in his sprawling underground city directly beneath Mont St Michel?

Nick stared at Guber lazily through the sunglasses. He must be up for air. Guber looked pallid. Too much time in the bunker. Nick grinned.

Guber walked across the cloister lawn.

He happened to look up towards the balconies. Nick waved deliberately in his direction.

Guber's expression hardened as he recognized Nick.

He continued walking, deep in conversation with a second man, whose face was masked by Guber's head.

Nick continued staring lazily out to the Atlantic, then looked back down at Guber again. The man had vanished. There was just his companion, gazing up at the palace.

Nick looked at the man, then looked again to be quite sure. Trembling, he reached inside his pocket. He took out the photograph of Julius and his four companions, then looked back through the doors at Adrian, seated at his desk in intense conversation. Nick moved swiftly towards the grand arched steps.

He hurried down one flight, then the next until he was on a balcony just ten feet above where the man stood.

Again he took out the photograph.

There was no mistaking it. The man had a high, domed forehead, his silver hair meticulously cropped to half an inch from his scalp . . . hawk-like nose. But it was the eyes . . . so pale they seemed to be almost colourless.

The man standing below him was the very man standing on Julius De Vere's left in the photograph in Nick's grasp. And he was connected with Guber.

He needed to tell Adrian immediately.

Nick stiffened as Guber walked back towards Kester von Slagel.

Von Slagel surveyed the helipad.

'The preparations are in order?'

Guber nodded.

'All everyday staff are declassified, Your Excellency. By 6 p.m., only our private army will be within the grounds.'

Von Slagel nodded. 'My Master's orders must be adhered to.'

Guber nodded again.

'No-fly zone from 4 p.m. Airspace surveillance. The Hawks land at 8 p.m. The Eagle will land at 8.20 precisely. Delivery of the Ark to De Vere will be complete by 9 p.m.'

Nick aimed his digital camera directly in line with Von Slagel's face.

'His Excellency's orders are my command. As always.'

'He is comfortable?'

'The West Wing is entirely at his disposal. He lacks for nothing.'

Von Slagel smiled. 'My discussion with De Vere last night clarified the remaining details.'

Nick gaped in disbelief. Adrian *did* know the hawk-faced stranger with cropped white hair. He had lied to him about the photograph. He had not only *seen* Von Slagel before. He *knew* him. Nick's heart sank. He raised the camera, looked through the lens and clicked the camera switch.

Von Slagel looked up, directly connecting with Nick's eyeline.

He frowned. Guber followed his gaze.

'Lost your way, Mr De Vere?' Guber stared in irritation at the camera clasped in Nick's hand. Unsmiling.

'Gorgeous view, Guber,' Nick grinned deliberately. 'Don't you think?' he shouted.

Guber scowled, then ignored him.

'You know, you really should get some more sun, Guber,' Nick shouted over the balcony, his heart racing. 'Looking a little pasty. You know what they say – all work makes Kurt a dull boy . . .'

Nick retraced his steps up the first flight of stairs, hands trembling.

Von Slagel turned to the scowling Guber.

'What is De Vere doing here? I want no interference before our plans are complete.'

'Last-minute decision. It wasn't in the schedule. He's a low-lying parasite. Perfectly harmless.'

'Get rid of him,' Von Slagel muttered. 'Off the property. Now.'

Kester von Slagel limped across the lawn towards the arches then disappeared.

Nick stood outside the cherrywood doors. His hands shaking, he replaced the brown envelope in the satchel then walked back into the drawing room.

Adrian was still immersed in conversation with the Iranian Premier. Nick looked around then headed to the men's room. On his way he picked up a blank compliments slip.

He locked himself in the bathroom, safely out of sight of the surveillance cameras.

He swung round, trembling. Someone was in the room with him. He was sure of it. Uneasy, he stared around. No one was there. Nick hesitated, as a strange wild euphoria infused his senses. He recognized it. It was the same presence that he had sensed in the lower crypt of the monastery. He smiled.

Someone was watching over him.

With trembling fingers, he took the photograph of De Molay, Von Slagel, and Julius out of the brown envelope and replaced it with a blank Mont St Michel compliments slip. Then with a glance at the photograph, he stashed it in his satchel.

He washed his hands, then hesitated, loath to walk out on the mysterious presence. He shook his head, then walked back into the drawing room just as the TV screens disappeared into the ceiling.

Adrian clicked off the remote, smiled at Nick and stood up. Weary.

'Sorry, bro, bad day for a social visit.' His voice rose above the ear-splitting whine of helicopter turbines. 'That's my lunch appointment arriving. British Foreign Secretary.'

He put his hand on Nick's shoulder. 'Look, leave me the photograph. I'll make some discreet enquiries.'

'You're *sure* you've never met any of those men?' Nick studied Adrian's face intently.

'The what . . . oh, the photograph . . . Nope. Never in my life.'

He held his hand out.

'I'll give it to Guber – he'll pass it to the Interpol operatives in the Core.'

Nick handed him the envelope with the blank compliments slip.

Adrian tucked it in his inside jacket pocket.

'You know what, Adrian?' Nick said, lowering his voice. 'I think you've hit the nail on the head. I think Lawrence is senile. I noticed a deterioration when I was with him.'

Nick put on a false smile. 'Maybe he concocted Dad's letter. The documents.'

Adrian relaxed. He put his arm around Nick.

'He needs psychiatric evaluation. We've got units here that can help him.'

Nick nodded. 'I'll talk to Mother this weekend about having him checked out.'

Nick stuck out his hand.

'I'd like the document back. Avoid any confusion.'

'Too late, Nicky. You were so concerned, it's already on its way to Interpol. Thought it would ease your mind.'

Nick tensed.

'Look. No harm done. I'll call them and tell them it's a hoax.'

Nick nodded. 'Do that, Adrian.'

Chastenay materialized at the door and Nick walked towards him. He turned.

'Oh, and one more thing. De Vere Continuation Holdings

234

AG – can you get a set of management accounts for me? And the latest audit?'

Adrian frowned.

'Why, Nick? You've never shown any interest in the financials before.'

'I am now. Dad always said I should take personal responsibility. It's never too late.'

Adrian gave him a strange look.

The comms buzzed again. Adrian pressed the buzzer.

'The British Foreign Secretary is now on the premises, Mr President, sir.'

Nick smiled and waved. 'It's okay, Adrian.'

Two security men dressed in the pale blue uniform of the European Superstate's elite forces entered and moved towards Nick.

'Keep your minders off,' Nick grinned. 'I'll see myself out.'

Adrian shook his head at the security men and Chastenay.

'Clear my brother through the gate,' he said, quietly. 'Red Aston Martin.'

'By the way,' Nick said over his shoulder recklessly, 'ever heard of the International Security Fund?'

Adrian stared grimly after Nick's swiftly disappearing back, then pressed the remote.

Nick walked as fast as he dared back down the corridors, making a sharp left before he reached the foyer, evading Anton, then exited through a small side door into the vegetable gardens.

'Idiot,' he muttered, knowing he had overstepped the mark. He walked evenly in the direction of the old kitchen wing alongside the stables.

As he passed the scullery, he peered through the window then walked around to the open back door.

'Beatrice,' he whispered.

A stout red-faced woman with grey braided hair looked at Nick out of beady twinkling eyes.

'Why, Master Nicholas!'

She wiped her hands on her apron, then flung her plump arms around his waist in delight and surveyed him, tidying her unruly grey braids with fleshy fingers.

Nick put his finger to her thin lips. 'I'm not meant to be here. Our little secret.'

Beatrice giggled and nodded vigorously.

'I bake Christmas sweet spice bread for you.' She shuffled over to the oven and took out the plaited breads.

'Beatrice?'

She nodded eagerly.

'Is Pierre still here?'

'He and I are the last to go. As usual.'

'The main gate?'

'Our men left at one. Special forces took over the shift.' Beatrice scowled.

'Good, the car's already cleared through the gate. Pierre has the keys. Tell him to close the roof and keep his head down. Once he's past the gate, tell him to park in the old dock shelter. Our little secret from Guber. Do you understand?'

Beatrice nodded.

'What's going on tonight, Beatrice?'

'Classifed function. The usual procedure. Private caterers – Guber's private army – his battalions in charge.' She scowled. 'So different from your father.' She pursed her lips.

Nick looked out of the window, searching uneasily for signs of the European Secret Service.

'I need an envelope,' he said.

Beatrice walked over to an old mahogany dresser and,

unlocking a drawer, removed one of a pile of linen envelopes with the Mont St Michel crest on the back.

Nick nervously took out the photograph of De Vere and De Molay from his satchel and pushed them hurriedly into the envelope. 'Paper.'

Beatrice passed him another compliments slip, again bearing the crest. Nick wrote in a hurried scrawl:

Dear Jules,

Dad was on to something. Something big. They killed him for. They gave me Aids, Jules. Deliberately. I think they know I'm on to them. A group of elite powerbrokers. I'm doing some investigating of my own. In the event that I don't make it out of here – you must get this to Jason. He's the only one I trust.

The sound of voices drew closer.
'Master Nick. Hurry.'
Nick continued in a hurried scrawl.

Tell Lily I'll always be sorry. Be my leading light, sis.

Always, Nicky

P.S. I'm not sure if Adrian's . . .'

The sound of voices was at the door.

Hurriedly, Nick sealed the envelope, turned it over and scrawled Julia's name and New Chelsea address just as a short, red-faced youth walked in.

Beatrice sighed with relief.
'It's all right. It's Jacques, the groom.'
'What time does the post van pick up?'

237

'Pick up from the main house was at 10 a.m. The staff mailbag is picked up at 2.35 p.m. from the stables, Master Nick, sir.'

Beatrice looked up at the kitchen grandfather clock. 'Ten minutes. It's not checked.'

Nick placed the letter in Beatrice's hand and closed her plump, work-worn, red fingers over it. He looked into her eyes, addressing her like she was a child.

'Beatrice, this is very important,' he said. 'Put this in the mailbag before you go through the main gate. You *must* get it into the mailbag before you leave. I need you to do this for me. For my father.' Beatrice nodded earnestly.

'I promise, Master Nick.' Nick planted a big kiss on Beatrice's jowled cheeks.

'Is the East Wing suite vacant?'

She nodded. 'No one's staying there tonight.'

Nick groped in his pocket and pulled out a small plastic container and shook out two white pills, slinging them back in his throat.

He leaned his head on the large oak kitchen table in paroxysms of deliberate and faked coughing. He had felt perfectly well since his encounter at the Monastery in Alexandria, fighting fit in fact, but he was sure he would be forgiven for his present deliberate melodrama. It was essential to his plan.

'Beatrice . . .' He grasped her hand. 'You know I've been sick.'

She nodded vigorously.

'I'm in no state to go through all Guber's laborious security measures.'

Beatrice looked at him earnestly.

'Master Nick, what can I do?'

Nick looked up, between his hacking coughs.

'Get me to the East Wing. Our little secret. Guber mustn't know I'm here.'

Beatrice scowled. 'Stuck-up Guber.' She glowered.

'You're absolutely sure it's vacant, Beatrice?' Nick persisted. 'I thought there were heads of state flying in?'

'Some high-flown royal prince arrived around midnight last night. A presidential order was issued. No one is to occupy the main house while he's in residence, apart from Master Adrian. All visitors leave immediately after dinner. The fancy prince is in the West Wing. Guber's thugs are crawling all over it.'

She bustled over to the corner of the kitchen and picked up a key card with a gold Mont St Michel seal embossed on it.

'But the East Wing's deserted till the weekend,' she declared.

She pushed a wisp of grey hair out of her eyes.

'At 3 p.m., all staff security clearances are declassified.'

Beatrice punched in the key card through the security code. It emitted a green light.

'I need the surveillance system dismantled in the East Wing,' Nick said. 'Guber mustn't know I'm there.'

'I can't do that.' Beatrice raised her face to Nick's. 'I don't know how.'

'But I do.' They both turned to find Pierre standing watching them from the scullery door.

Pierre had known Nicholas De Vere from the time Nick was a sweet-faced three year old, and had loved him always. Pierre took the key card from Beatrice, passed it back through the scanner and punched in the number 666. A purple light appeared directly above the green.

'Today's privacy code,' Pierre said softly. 'Surveillance cameras have been disabled throughout the East Wing.

239

You're invisible to the Core, unless there's a power shortage.'
He handed the key card to Nick.

'Then you're on your own.' He made the sign of the cross.
'May God protect you, Nicholas De Vere.'

Nick, all signs of pallor and sickness now vanished, opened the shutters and stared out of the East Wing attic windows. From his vantage point, he had a bird's-eye view from the stable to the main gate. He looked down to the kitchen block as Beatrice walked out of the scullery door, over to the stables' entrance and placed the letter in the Mont St Michel staff mailbag. She climbed on her bicycle and cycled towards the main gate. A few minutes later, the red Aston Martin, its roof closed, sped down the winding Abbey lane.

Nick watched as Pierre cleared the main gate and roared off in the direction of the dock.

He paced the room back and forth, then walked back over to the window as a nondescript French post van drew up to the stable gates.

A uniformed officer placed the mailbag in the back of the van, which then meandered back up the drive and out through the main gate of Mont St Michel and towards Pontorson.

He sighed in relief.

The photograph was safely on its way to Julia in England.

Nick walked down the spiral staircase, through the master bathrooms with their custom water-lounger baths, through the sumptuous master bedroom to the drawing room, and checked that the East Wing suite doors were fully secured.

And waited.

Somehow he knew he was in danger. Grave danger.

Tonight he knew he would find out why.

CHAPTER TWENTY-ONE

Loose Ends

Jotapa sat on the plush leather sofa of the Royal Household's Gulfstream jet's lounge area, staring straight ahead. The only sign of her unease was her constant checking of her watch. She looked over to Jibril, who was playing games on the jet's media centre.

He looked up at her. In the face of his banishment he was rational. Calm. Just as her father would have been. Jotapa's eyes flashed with anger. Jibril shook his head, then put his finger to his lips. She sighed.

'Faisal.'

She knew her father had done his utmost to be even-handed in his affection for his offspring, but Faisal's character deficiencies were not easily overlooked.

In his twenties, much to her father's dismay, Faisal had run wild for months at a time with the younger Saudi princes on their fleet of luxury Boeings. Her father had received constant reports of the clubbing, the orgies, the drugs. Just as Nick's father had. Jotapa's expression softened.

But unlike Nick, Faisal was both cunning and ruthless. And dim. And in time, the noble elderly king came to despise his oldest son. Jotapa was born when Faisal was eleven, then seven years later Jibril came along. The eighteen-year-old Faisal had loathed the calm and sunny infant, the jewel of the King of Jordan's latter years.

She studied Jibril as he concentrated on the game. He was so like their father. A clean, angular face, thick black straight hair and clear, piercing brown eyes. He was only sixteen, but he had wisdom beyond his years. And far beyond his older brother.

'Your Highness . . .' A steward leant over. 'We are preparing for descent.'

Jotapa looked out of the Gulfstream's window. Thousands of feet below, the sprawling runways of the King Fahd International Airport, eight miles north-west of Damman, became visible through the early morning haze.

Jotapa looked back once more at Jibril, still engrossed in his game, then down at her jeans. A banned item in the Royal Household of Saudi Arabian princes. She closed her eyes, trying to shut out the dreadful foreboding that the twenty-first century and all that was safe and familiar was about to be wrenched away from her forever.

And the dreadful foreboding that Jotapa, Princess of the Royal Household of Jordan, was about to cease to exist.

Adrian and the British Foreign Secretary relaxed in the orangery under the balmy winter sun. Two butlers cleared the lunch crockery, while a third poured Earl Grey tea into porcelain cups monogrammed with Adrian's initials. Guber and Chastenay were in deep conversation outside the orangery entrance.

'Still can't persuade you to reconsider becoming a member of the euro zone?' Adrian said in his usual easy, disarming tone.

'You know our stance on it, Adrian,' the British Foreign Secretary replied. 'Nothing's changed since you left office.

The people would lynch us if we surrendered the pound. The Lisbon Treaty pushed it as far as we dare.' He smiled. 'Sorry, Adrian. Your "London Pact" lies gathering dust in some Downing Street archive.'

'Some day, George,' Adrian said, grinning.

'I'm betting it's not in *my* lifetime.' The Foreign Secretary leant back in his chair, relaxed. He sipped his tea. His aide stepped forward and whispered surreptitiously in his ear.

Nodding to the aide, the minister said, 'An urgent phone call – the Prime Minister.' Adrian smiled graciously.

'Chastenay, show Mr Hayes to the secure area.' The Foreign Secretary hastily left the room, his aide in tow, following Chastenay to a series of glass-encased booths directly outside the orangery.

Adrian pressed a button on a writing desk.

'Guber.'

He took the envelope from his inside pocket and placed it on the orangery bureau.

Guber appeared at his side almost instantly.

Adrian spoke without turning.

'A minor hitch.'

He gestured to the envelope.

Guber opened it, staring mystified at the blank compliments slip. He frowned, turned it over, then held it out to Adrian.

Adrian snatched the envelope.

The photograph was gone.

'When did my brother leave?'

Guber pressed the intercom line to the main gate.

'When did the Dauphin leave the building?'

'Forty minutes ago, sir. The Dauphin's red Aston Martin left through the front gate.'

'A problem, Mr President, sir?' Guber waited.

243

'My brother had in his possession a photograph,' he said, quietly. 'Supposedly from our father, James De Vere.'

He looked up at Guber.

'A photograph of my grandfather with our current house guests.'

He let the words sink in.

'And this . . .'

Guber scanned the execution document and turned ashen.

'James De Vere sent it to St Cartier. Apparently, your hoodlums left their tracks uncovered.'

'I'll deal with it.'

'You'd better.' Adrian raised his hand and Guber clutched his throat, struggling for air.

Adrian watched him dispassionately for a moment, then walked over to the orchids in the orangery and nonchalantly picked up a handheld mister. He began spraying the orchids as Guber started to choke violently.

At last, Adrian laid the watering can back down, then walked over to Guber. He laid his hand on Guber's shoulder. Instantly Guber caught his breath.

Guber's voice quavered.

'It will never happen again, Your Excellency.'

'Good,' Adrian said, softly. 'Then we understand each other.'

The British Foreign Secretary returned onto the terrace followed by two waiters carrying fresh tea and locally produced Camembert.

'Let me know when my brother arrives in London.' Adrian smiled genially to Guber and gestured to the Foreign Secretary to sit. 'And tidy up any loose ends in Egypt. I have it on good account that our professor friend winters in Cairo.'

'Yes, Mr President, sir,' Guber replied, and walked briskly out of the orangery.

The two waiters neatly removed the used crockery, reset the table, and poured the freshly brewed tea into clean teacups.

'Earl Grey? Glad to see you're still supporting English exports, Mr President,' the British Foreign Secretary quipped.

Adrian smiled faintly and stirred his tea. Lost, deep in thought.

'Aveline', the name of Hamish MacKenzie's biogenetics foundation, had been scrawled by James De Vere on the back of the photograph.

Nick had requested the De Vere Asset Management's financials.

He knew about the International Security Fund.

Nicholas De Vere was becoming quite the private investigator. Just *what* did his little brother think he was up to?

Nick gazed out of the vast Gothic drawing room windows onto the floodlit helipad far below, directly outside the cloister arches.

The noise of the gunship's engines hovering above the mansion was almost as deafening as the violent Atlantic storm now raging overhead. He watched as the huge black gunship landed. The fourth so far that evening.

He had already recognized seven dignitaries: princes of three European states, the queen of a fourth. The Crown Prince of Saudi Arabia. He studied the fifth figure exiting from the gunship. Assad, Crown Prince of Syria, followed by the head of Russia's FSB.

Nick frowned. He recognized the chairman of the Federal Reserve Bank followed by the head of the International Monetary Fund. Strange.

He gazed up to where three more gunships were hovering over the stormy black Atlantic.

Nick poured himself a mineral water.

Adrian had been more than economical with the truth. He had lied to him. But why?

Jotapa stepped out of the first black limousine in a convoy of eighteen black limousines. She stared down at her feet. The streets of heaven were paved with gold, but the streets of the Royal Palace of Mansoor were paved with solid Italian marble. She watched as Jibril exited. They were instantly surrounded by a dozen swarthy armed men wearing ghutrahs and black uniforms – Mansoor's brutal private army.

Jotapa stared up at the high-walled, mile-long compound of monolithic Versailles-like buildings surrounded by hundreds of palm trees. She braced herself, then smoothed down the black georgette abaya that she had been required to change into upon her arrival at the royal terminal – the attire demanded by Crown Prince Mansoor for all his four hundred wives.

Jotapa and Jibril followed the uniformed soldiers up the marble walkway beneath swaying palms, past magnificent pools and through a massive forty-foot gilt door into the foyer of the palace.

A soldier gestured her forward into the foyer with his machine gun. Jotapa stared up at the forty-foot ceilings of painted glass in an art-deco frame. They walked past gilt marble pillars, beneath crystal chandeliers and swathes of gold leaf. Twenty-first-century Islamic, she noted, staring up at the framed Koranic verses about the glory of God.

They marched down unending corridors, past Mansoor's harem of hundreds of women, and continued until they reached a smaller section of palaces, then stopped outside a vast silver gilt door. The soldier gestured to Jotapa to remove her jewellery. Slowly, she took off her bracelets and plain gold ring, then emptied the contents of her bag into a glass chamber. A second soldier pushed Jibril roughly towards the door. Jibril's eyes flashed. Jotapa stared, a dark fury rising in her heart.

They passed through a scanner. Jotapa turned to retrieve her phone.

'No,' a swarthy-looking soldier said in a clipped Arabic accent. 'No phone.'

Jotapa glowered at him.

'My phone,' she said coldly.

He smiled a slow nasty smile and reached out his big hand, caressing Jotapa's neck. She stared up at him, her eyes filled with loathing.

'No phone, Princess.'

Jibril moved forward just as two more soldiers grasped him. One held him while the second slammed a fist into his solar plexus. He crumpled to the floor.

There was the sharp sound of clapping. The first soldier released Jotapa's neck instantly.

She turned to see a tall, thick-set figure looking down at them from the marble balustrades. He smiled a slow smile.

'Hadid,' the stranger spoke in soft seductive tones, 'give the Princess her phone.'

With trembling hands, Hadid took the silver mobile from the glass chamber. Jotapa snatched it from him, then tucked it out of sight, deep in one of the abaya's pockets.

She watched as the tall stranger came towards her. She recognized him from the previous year's *Al-Hayat* newspaper photographs of his public disgrace. It was Mansoor. His dark features were coarse and cat-like. He had a full beard and a thin hawk-like nose. His beady eyes were cruel. He walked like a panther towards her.

'My Princess.' He turned to Hadid and with one vicious blow knocked him unconscious. His head smashed violently onto the floor.

Mansoor spat on the marbled floor, then smiled at Jotapa.

He reached out his huge palm and caressed her long dark hair. She struggled away from him violently.

Mansoor's eyes hardened.

'Bring me the boy,' he ordered. The soldiers kneed Jibril up from the floor and shoved him toward Mansoor.

'A piece of important information, Your Highness.' Mansoor grabbed Jibril in a vice-like grip. 'In the event of your non-cooperation, I am not averse to games with boys.'

'No wonder your father loathed you,' Jotapa hissed.

Mansoor looked at her with contempt, then reached his hand out to Jibril, sucked his fingers, then caressed Jibril's face.

'You take me,' Jotapa snarled, 'but don't you ever' – her entire body trembled with seething rage – '*ever* touch Jibril.'

Casually, Mansoor dealt a savage blow to her face. Blood seeped from her mouth. Mansoor disappeared down the hall.

CHAPTER TWENTY-TWO

The Robes Are Behind the Suits

Nick watched through the camera lens, unseen from the window in the darkness, his eyes riveted to a pulsating blue glow moving rapidly in from the sea. It stopped a hundred feet above the cloisters, hovering directly above Mont St Michel.

The enormous, silent dome-shaped object stayed suspended in mid-air for a full minute. There was complete silence apart from the rapid-fire clicking of Nick's camera.

Adrian strode past the columns of the refectory, followed by Laurent Chastenay and Guber.

'Our guests are well tended?' Adrian continued at his steady pace.

'Yes, Mr President, sir,' Chastenay replied, 'They are gathered in the Room of the Knights. Dinner is being served as we speak.'

'We must have no interruptions until we have taken delivery.'

He stopped in mid-stride and turned to Guber.

'Everything is proceeding according to plan?'

Guber nodded.

'Like clockwork. The Phoenix has landed. The package will be unloaded in precisely three minutes and twenty seconds.'

Adrian nodded. 'Return to your posts.'

The three men disappeared in three directions.

Adrian walked alone through the deserted corridors to the huge doors of the drawing room terrace and flung them wide open.

A deafening howling erupted from the Rottweilers and Dobermans guarding the perimeter. The powerful beams of the Mont St Michel searchlights went black.

An instant later, every light in the mansion switched off.

Adrian walked out onto the moonlit balcony and stared out at the hanging garden between sea and sky – then looked up to the blue pulsating light hovering over the ocean, covered by low mist.

He stared across the Atlantic, mesmerized by the descending object.

Then smiled. Inscrutable.

Nick walked through the master bedroom to the library and games room with views over to the West Wing and the Atlantic Ocean.

He stopped in front of rows of massive yew bookshelves, and ran his hand over the palace's vast collection of first editions, just as the whole wing plunged into pitch darkness.

Walking over to the window, he gazed out to the magnificent Gothic West Wing, now shrouded in darkness.

Who was Adrian's special guest? Beatrice had said he was staying in the West Wing. A prince? Adrian hadn't said a word to him. Nick frowned.

To his right, on the West Wing terrace that jutted out directly over the raging ocean, Nick could make out the silhouette of a man.

He grabbed his camera and pressed his face to the window.

Standing at the very edge of the master balcony of the West Wing stood a tall, lean figure dressed in black robes.

'A prince? No. More like a priest.'

He zoomed the digital camera in on the form.

Yes. Definitely a religious order. Maybe Jesuit.

The man's face was raised in ecstasy to the skies, his black robes blowing violently in the Atlantic winds. His raven hair was loose and fell past his shoulders, lashing against his face in the fierce storm.

Nick stared in fascination through the camera lens.

The priest swept a carved horn bow with long, passionate strokes over the strings of a violin. Turning, Nick hurried to the far side of the library and cranked open the huge casement windows. The West Wing terrace was now directly opposite him. The rain lashed through the windows, drenching his hair and T-shirt.

Nick stared, oblivious to the rain, lost in wonder.

The sound of the single violin echoed on the ocean winds.

Haunting. Exquisite. Poignant. Almost lonely.

He watched mesmerized as the priest's long fingers moved deftly across the fingerboard. The priest's eyes were closed in utter rapture, his mouth moving softly to the exquisite refrain.

And still Nick stood in the lashing rain. It was as though the music drew his soul. It was mesmerizing. Hypnotic. Then abruptly, the priest stopped playing and turned slightly, the light from the gunships illuminating his features.

Nick stared transfixed. The man was somehow strangely but indefinably familiar. Though the face was strangely scarred, the features were almost beautiful. The rain lashed the strongly chiselled cheekbones, the full passionate lips.

De Molay lowered the violin and turned, as though sensing something. Someone.

Nick stood frozen. He knew he was now directly in the priest's line of sight.

Suddenly, De Molay dropped the violin, cradling his head as though in agony. Then he stared up at Nick, his features turning from utter torment to ferocious rage.

It was the priest from St Cartier's photograph.

Nick slammed the window shut and flung himself against the wall in the darkness, his breathing shallow, his mind racing. For the first time in his entire life, Nick sensed an overshadowing evil.

'*The Robes are behind the Suits.*'

The old man's words rang unmistakably in his ears.

'*Some legends have it – he IS the devil incarnate.*'

There was no doubting it. There, on the terrace of the West Wing, less than fifty feet away, stood Lorcan De Molay.

Adrian walked through the drawing room into his private elevator. A minute later, he walked out from the columns into the cloisters. He shielded his eyes from the lights and wind.

The huge, domed flying object, some two hundred feet in diameter, hovered a full ninety feet off the lawn. Adrian stared in awe as the massive metal ship's doorway opened. A brilliant arc of light radiated over the Abbey.

The entire East Wing balcony lit up as though it were broad daylight.

Nick shielded his eyes from the intense flashing strobe. His head throbbed intensely from the electromagnetic rays it was emitting. An eerie, low-frequency humming sound filled the air.

He scrabbled for a lens in his satchel, adjusted it, then lifted the camera back up in line with the unidentified hovering craft as it descended nearer the cloisters.

Nick stared through the lens, fascinated. He'd never seen anything like it in his life.

He could make out the outline of a figure dimly visible in the brilliance, standing in the centre of the open doors. Zooming in with the lens, he saw that it was the man with the high-domed forehead that Guber had addressed as Von Slagel. Nick clicked shot after shot as a metal crate came into view. Click.

It was lowered by steel cables down onto the cloister lawn. Click.

Nine men in uniform holding machine guns spilled out of the lower cloisters and manoeuvred the crate to the edge of the lawn. Click.

A seal on the outside of the crate was plainly visible under the floodlights. The crest of Mont St Michel. Click.

Nick stared, stupefied, as the craft's doors closed and the dome-like ship ascended back into the sky and vanished. He gazed after it, bewildered. It must have been travelling at more than three thousand miles an hour.

Immediately, the power returned to the entire East Wing.

Nick looked up at the surveillance camera positioned directly above him and moved out of its line of sight.

Time was running out.

Guber walked out from the cloisters towards the crate. 'Prepare to unload the merchandise,' he ordered the soldiers.

The special forces levered open the crate and one by one the metal sides fell to the ground.

Nick stared in disbelief as the ornate chest became fully visible. It couldn't be. He rubbed his eyes, bewildered. Instantly, every instinct sharpened by his years of training as an archaeologist kicked into gear.

Checklist.

Length, four feet long. Check. Height, two and a half feet. Check. Carved of wood overlaid with gold. Check. Decorated gold rim running around the top. Check. Rings at four corners through which poles could be passed. Check.

Nick trembled. He ran his fingers through his hair, almost afraid to check the final unmitigating factor. He took a deep breath, exhaled, then looked through the camera lens.

There they were. On the lid, facing each other, their wings outstretched, were the two figurines of angels: cherubim – in beaten gold. Double-check.

'The Ark of the Covenant,' he breathed. Stunned.

Then steadied the digital camera.

Adrian walked back into the lift just as one of Guber's Special Service soldiers reached out his hand to the Ark. Guber raised his hand to stop him, but it was too late. The man fell to the floor like stone. Electrocuted.

Adrian smiled faintly.

Guber nodded to a group of soldiers standing at attention. 'Use the winch,' he said.

A second crate was lowered from the open doors. The seal read *MOSSAD*.

Nick, his hands shaking, sat cross-legged on the carpet. He tried for the fifth time to email the camera memory file through to Dylan Weaver.

'Busy,' he muttered in frustration and tried again.

As the electrocuted Special Service officer's body was being stuffed into a hessian sack to Guber's right, his walk-talkie buzzed.

'What is it, Von Slagel?' Guber said curtly.

'It seems there is an unauthorized visitor in the East Wing.'

'Impossible.'

'He's sending unauthorized information out of the grounds. It appears the low-lying parasite is more astute than you gave him credit for.'

Guber scowled and turned to Travis.

'Cut the circuitry,' he said, unholstering his Sig Sauer P225 semi-automatic pistol. 'Ill take care of him myself.'

'You'd better. His Excellency is most displeased.'

There was a hesitation on the end of the line.

'De Vere wears the Nazarene's Seal.'

Nick froze. The sound of thudding footsteps was drawing nearer through the corridors of the East Wing.

Frantically, he uploaded the digital film into his laptop and punched in Weaver's encrypted email address for the ninth time. There was a loud knocking on the secured East Wing entrance.

He pressed the send button.

'De Vere, I know you're in there,' Guber shouted.

The banging became more violent.

'Use the charges,' Guber's voice filtered through to Nick.

The email started to upload as Nick heard Guber shouting instructions in German.

He watched, as this time, the file uploaded successfully into cyberspace.

Then pressed delete.

Delete. Delete. Delete.

He was painstakingly deleting single photographs from the hard drive just as the door blasted open.

Guber flung open the back entrance of the Abbey Church and shoved the now secured Nick up the nave straight towards Adrian, who was pacing the floor behind the altar.

Adrian stared at his violently struggling younger brother, then at Guber.

He looked back down at the restraints on Nick's wrists.

'Release my brother, Guber,' Adrian said, softly.

Guber scowled. Grudgingly he unlocked the double-locking steel handcuffs.

Nick dusted himself off, still glaring at Guber.

'Nicky,' Adrian said, quietly, 'I thought you'd already left Mont St Michel.'

He paused. 'This afternoon. Your car went through the gates. It was verified.'

'You mean you *checked*?' Nick glared at him.

'He was hidden in the East Wing,' Guber scowled, 'watching, or rather, *filming* the proceedings.' He held up Nick's camera.

Nick raised his face to Adrian's.

'You're a thief, Adrian!' he muttered through clenched teeth, all fear suddenly lost in his outrage. 'A common thief.' Nick's voice rose with his fury.

'The Ark of the Covenant, for god's sake!' Nick shouted, tears of rage pricking his eyes. He struck out blindly in rage, striking Adrian in the chest.

Adrian stared at Nick in disbelief, frozen, as a violent electrical shockwave surged through his body. Lorcan De Molay was right. His little brother wore the Seal.

He loosened his tie, sweat breaking out on his forehead. It was undeniable. He had felt the power of the Nazarene in Nick's hand.

Nick was unaware of the force he possessed – of that, Adrian was certain. It needed to stay that way.

Adrian stared straight back at Nick, not a muscle of his face moving.

'The Ark's a sacred relic, Adrian,' Nick cried. 'It belongs

256

to the world's heritage, for god's sake – you can't *own* it!'

Adrian grasped Nick's arm in a vice-like grip.

'Calm *down*, Nick,' he said, warningly. 'You're making a fool of yourself.'

'You want *me* to calm down?' Nick shouted. He jerked his arm free from Adrian's grasp. 'All this power has gone to your head.' He glared with loathing at Adrian, emotionally charged. 'You've just stolen the most coveted archaeological antiquity in the world, and you want *me* to calm down. It's not yours to take – or buy – or steal.'

'Keep your voice down, Nick.' Adrian gave him a warning look.

Nick swung around to Adrian.

'It belongs in an antiquities museum!' Nick yelled, totally out of control and not caring.

Adrian stood directly in front of Nick and stared into his eyeline. Fierce.

'It belongs . . .', Adrian took a deep breath, '. . . to the *Jews*.'

He gestured to his right and slowly Nick turned.

The lights triggered on. Nick could make out around fifty elegantly attired men and women sitting at sumptuously decorated tables across the length of the transept, all staring at him in silence.

He looked back at Adrian in confusion. Adrian put his right arm paternally around Nick's shoulders.

'My brother . . .', He paused, '. . . is an archaeologist.'

He placed his left thumb in the small of Nick's back and pushed him forward.

'A *brilliant* archaeologist. He pours out his entire life on the quest for antiquities such as the one in our midst.' Adrian raised the glass of port with his free hand.

'A little understanding tonight, please, ladies and gentlemen.'

Adrian released Nick's arm, sipped his port, then pulled Nick aside as the dignitaries murmured among themselves.

Nick looked at him in utter bewilderment.

Adrian sighed.

'Look, Nicky. Let's calm down, shall we?' He motioned to the guests.

'Levin.'

An elderly, statesman-like figure with a mane of coarse white hair rose to his feet, followed by a fashionably dressed, olive-skinned man in his early forties who stepped forward and put out his hand to Nick. Nick stared at him, mystified, instantly recognizing him.

Adrian nodded.

'Daniel Rabin, Israeli Ambassador to the United Nations.'

Rabin shook Nick's hand.

'Moishe Levin, President of Israel.'

The eagle-eyed old patriach bowed slightly.

Nick rubbed his forehead with his palm, suddenly exhausted. He recognized Levin, the dignified ex-Israeli general, from the *Jerusalem Post*. Slowly, he scanned the faces in the room. One by one.

He recognized three Pentagon senior generals, the British Prime Minister, the Secretary General of the United Nations, the Director of the CIA, and the President of the Council of Foreign Relations.

Adrian gestured to a second table. Seated there were the three eldest sons of the Lombardi banking dynasty and their father Raffaele Lombardi; Naotake Yoshido, Chairman of Japan's Yoshido banking dynasty; and Xavier Chessler, now Chairman of the World Bank – James De Vere's closest friend; Jason's godfather.

Nick sighed. He scanned the faces around the room, half

of them had been close friends and associates of his father, James De Vere, for years.

Adrian gently steered Nick to one of the largest tables near the window.

'Gentlemen, I would like to introduce my brother, Nicholas De Vere.'

'King Faisal of Jordan.' Nick looked through him. 'Jotapa's elder brother.' Adrian steered him around. 'The Russian President, the Crown Prince of Iran, the President of Syria. All the major participants in the Ishtar Accord are our guests tonight.'

Levin touched Nick's shoulder.

'The second phase of the Middle East accord demands that Israel denuclearizes over a seven-year period,' the old man said in a thick, guttural Israeli accent. 'We demanded an equally high price for our participation in the negotiations with the terrorists.'

Adrian nodded to Levin to continue.

'The return of our nation's most sacred possession,' Levin's eyes gleamed with fervour, 'once belonging to our monarch King David. The Ark of the Covenant.'

Rabin stepped forward.

'Our government has been searching for it for generations – spent hundreds of millions of dollars ... in Axum ... on the Temple Mount. It was discovered ten days ago, on the Temple Mount, then stolen by mercenaries in the pay of terrorists bent on destroying our nation.'

Levin grasped Nick's upper arm. 'Your Mother, Lilian, has been a good friend to Israel, Nicholas. She never forgot her roots.' He looked deeply into Nick's eyes. 'Neither has your brother.'

'We made your brother's life extremely difficult.' Rabin smiled gently at Nick. 'We demanded nothing less than the

259

return of the Temple Mount – the most controversial piece of real estate the world has ever known – and the return of the Ark.'

Rabin looked to Adrian, who nodded.

'The Ark will be transported back to Jerusalem under Mossad's protection tonight. Your elder brother is a *miracle worker!*'

Levin shook his right forefinger in Nick's face.

'In return for Israel's agreement to denuclearize, six weeks ago, at a top-secret summit, your brother drew up the Concordat of King Solomon,' Levin exclaimed, 'to be initiated on 7 January 2022.'

Rabin continued. 'The Concordat is modelled on the Lateran Treaty which ended an intense dispute that began in 1871, when the then newly constituted kingdom of Italy took over Rome after centuries of papal rule.'

The softly spoken Rabin hesitated.

'Your brother, with his customary brilliance, drew up a similar concordat. An agreement in which Israel will declare unilaterally, by virtue of its sovereignty, that it is granting a special status to the Al-Aqsa Mosque and the Dome of the Rock sanctuary on the Temple Mount.'

Adrian smiled self-effacingly. 'Each of the three great monotheistic religions will be self-governing and will rule autonomously over the edifices sacred to them,' he explained. 'Israel will grant "free right of passage to the holy places regardless of religion, gender, or race".'

'It is a move that we believe will be unanimously accepted by the international community,' Levin said, 'and Israel reverts back to her boundaries of 1967 – Jerusalem undivided.'

He motioned to the presidents of Syria and Iran. 'In return for Israel's solemn assurance to engage in the first stage of denuclearization over a period of seven years, our Arab brothers have agreed for a UN peacekeeping force to occupy Temple Mount and Israel's boundaries.'

'And agreed to our rebuilding of Solomon's Temple in the Northern Quadrant,' Rabin added.

Adrian turned to Nick. 'We announce the first stage of Israel's nuclear disarmament on 7 January at the signing of the treaty in Babylon.'

Nick looked at Adrian, and then, one by one, at the gathering of men and women in the drawing room.

'You see, Nicholas,' Adrian said, softly, 'I'm the *good* guy.'

Levin shrugged his shoulders and raised both his palms.

'To denuclearize, is it such a terrible price for the Ark of the Covenant?'

At Adrian's signal, Chastenay pressed a remote switch and an enormous plasma screen descended at the altar giving a 360-degree animation of the architectural drawings of the new Solomon's Temple.

'But the massacre on Temple Mount?' Nick stared at Adrian, perplexed.

Adrian took out a cigar from a silver case.

'Terrorists who would thwart our plan and destroy the peace process.'

He rolled the cigar between his manicured fingers.

'We had ways of retrieving it.'

'They could not stand to see Israel with its most sacred possession back in its hands,' Levin said, shaking his head.

'This is a day to be proud. Your brother is a *great* friend to our nation.'

Adrian put his arm around Nick and walked him to the door.

'But the . . . the UFO?' Nick said.

Adrian smiled as he guided Nick out into the hallway.

'The Nazis were working on this form of sophisticated technology as far back as 1941, Nick.' Adrian smiled. 'After

World War II, Operation Paperclip brought over hundreds of rocketeers, nuclear physicists, and naval weaponeers to America. It led to the founding of NASA. Gerlach, Debus, Werner Von Braun – they all continued their research. Antigravity propulsion ... quantum physics ... secret atomic research ... the point is, everything's *perfectly rational*, Nicholas.'

Adrian's expression changed.

'Now you know this is a classified summit. Who did you email, Nick?'

Nick rubbed his forehead. Tired. Perplexed.

'I'm very tired.'

Adrian shifted his tone smoothly, becoming empathetic.

'Look, Nick, we know you're sick. Stay in the East Wing through the weekend, then go on to join Mother. We can play indoor tennis. Swim. Like old times.'

Nick shook his head. 'Thanks. But I need to leave.'

'Your car?'

'It's parked in the Dock Bay.'

'Chastenay, have someone bring the car to the front entrance.'

'My brother's belongings.' Adrian nodded to Guber who dumped Nick's satchel and the contents of his pocket down on the hall table.

There was no sign of the photograph of Julius De Vere and Adrian's current house guests.

Guber picked up Nick's camera.

'You realize, Nicholas, that we have no alternative but to confiscate your camera,' Adrian said. 'This is a classified summit.'

He looked down at the silver cross lying on the mahogany tabletop and watched as Nick grasped it in trembling fingers. Adrian rubbed his hand over his chin, deep in thought.

'See Mr De Vere through security. Nick,' he added, 'phone me when you reach London.'

Nick walked away from Adrian, his satchel over his shoulder, escorted by Anton. Without a look back.

Guber stared out of the second-floor hall window as the red Aston Martin sped out of the gates for the second time that day. Adrian walked up behind him.

'He knows too much,' Guber frowned.

Adrian stubbed out his cigar slowly and deliberately in a silver ashtray.

'It would seem my little brother wears the Seal. Use the neuro-electromagnetic frequency weapons. They are untrace-able. You know the procedure. He flies from Dinard. Wait until the pass.' Adrian stretched, then yawned.

'Tell my Father our little problem is resolved.'

Nick screeched through the Mont St Michel causeway gate, the engine of the Aston Martin screaming, then scrolled down to the number for Lawrence St Cartier at the Monastery in Alexandria and dialled.

There was a loud, insistent engaged tone. He clicked the phone off, then punched redial. The same flat tone rever-berated through the car.

'Damn!' he cried. 'Primitive exchange,' he muttered, putting the car into high gear. Nick punched in a different number. The phone rang three times.

'This is Jotapa. I'm sorry I . . .'

Jotapa sat clutching her knees, rocking from side to side on the edge of the gilt four-poster bed. She stared at the flashing light on her phone, then reached for it.

She read the black letters for the fifth time that hour.

263

'Call barred'. She threw the phone onto the bed in frustration.

The vaulted ceilings of the Crypt of the North Wind under Mont St Michel soared a hundred feet upwards and were fashioned with spectacular trompe l'oeils reminiscent of the indigos and heliotropes and soothing lilacs Lucifer had loved so well in his Palace of Archangels in the First Heaven.

At the far end of the crypt's nave towered a colossal garnet altar, its onyx surface covered with blazing black tapers, sputtering their intense aroma of frankincense, permeating the chamber.

The Ark of the Covenant lay gleaming on the onyx altar. Adrian stood silently in the shadows watching Lorcan De Molay stare mesmerized at the cherubim and seraphim.

He reached out his hand, almost hypnotized, to the beaten gold cherubim, then slowly withdrew it.

Adrian walked towards De Molay.

'The Ark will be transported at midnight to Jerusalem by the Sayeret Matkal. It will be held in the archaeological vaults under Jerusalem.'

'Until the Temple is complete,' De Molay murmured. 'Then it shall be restored to the Holy of Holies.'

Slowly he circled the Ark.

'And he shall make a firm covenant with many for one week: and in the midst of the week he shall cause the sacrifice and the oblation to cease; and upon the wing of abominations shall come one that maketh desolate . . .'

He knelt before the Ark, his head resting against the black garnet, muttering in a strange, guttural tongue, neither of angels nor of men.

'Then I crown myself King. In the Holy of Holies.'

He raised his head to Adrian and smiled.

'In Jerusalem.'

Nick had been driving for nearly an hour. He was dying to take a break but couldn't afford to slow down. He knew his life was in danger.

Two sets of car headlights appeared in the Aston Martin's rear-view mirror. Frantically, he punched in Jason's mobile number again.' He waited.

'This is Jason De Vere.'

'C'mon – pick it up, Jason!'

'I can't take your call right . . .'

Jason sat at the marble table, his tuxedo jacket hung over the back of his chair, his shirt sleeves rolled up. He took a swig of his whisky, then reclined back in his chair listening to the vapid blonde clone delivering her monosyllabic thank-you speech at the biannual Vox music awards ceremony.

He yawned, clapping half-heartedly.

His phone vibrated, then lit up in cobalt blue. He picked it up.

Nick's mobile number was displayed on the screen.

Jason took a long draw of his cigar.

Then clicked it off.

Nick looked in the rear-view mirror. The two sets of headlights were closing in on him. A black helicopter flew overhead. The exchange at the monastery was ringing through.

A voice answered in garbled Arabic.

'I need to speak to Lawrence St Cartier,' Nick shouted in Arabic. 'St Cartier – *yallah*!'

Two more garbled Arabic voices came on the line followed by Lawrence's voice as clear as a bell.

'Nicholas. It's Lawrence. Hello, my boy.'

'Lawrence . . . Lawrence I'm in troub–'

Nick broke off in mid-sentence. His head felt as if it was exploding into a million shards.

His heart pounded violently like a jackhammer in his chest as he entered the bridge to the oncoming pass.

His thoughts were suddenly in total disarray. Nick felt like he was physically losing control of his limbs. This was crazy. What on earth was happening to him?

Images of Lawrence, Jotapa, Adrian, the Ark of the Covenant, James De Vere, Lorcan De Molay competed with each other.

He wanted to throw up from the sudden nausea. He could hear Lawrence calling his name, but for the life of him, he couldn't answer.

Jason . . . Jotapa . . .

He tried to put the car in a lower gear but the entire left side of his body felt strangely paralyzed. Sweat broke out on his forehead. Seeing Jotapa's cross dangling from the mirror, he grasped it with trembling fingers, then let go of the steering wheel, clutching his head as an agonizing pain struck his eyes. He was blinded by the intense searing light that all at once filled the Aston Martin.

He could still hear Lawrence's voice dimly in the background reciting the Lord's Prayer.

Nick closed his eyes. He knew he was dying. Yet he felt strangely calm.

'Thy kingdom come . . .'

Just one more glimpse of that glorious face . . .

He smiled faintly as the red Aston Martin crashed through the steel barrier.

'Thy will be done . . .'

Just one more glimpse . . .

He smiled as the sports car plunged down the sheer embankment. Down.

'Forgive us our trespasses . . .' He and Lawrence were speaking in unison.

Down . . . Down . . . towards the raging black torrent.

'Deliver us from evil . . .'

Down . . . towards the jagged rocks.

Just one more glimpse . . .

Down towards utter darkness.

Nick reached out his right hand towards Christos . . .

'For thine is the kingdom . . .'

And then there was no more light.

CHAPTER TWENTY-THREE

Shock Wave

23 December 2021
New York

Jason was splayed out across the bed, his face crushed against the pillow. The phone rang incessantly. He stirred, opening one eye, then scowled, feeling for the phone with his right hand. He slammed on the mute button and put the pillow over his head.

The phone rang again, this time from the hall. It rang and rang. Then a message.

He opened one eye. The phone rang again. His fat, spoilt Rhodesian Ridgeback dog bounded in next to him and licked his unshaven face insistently.

Jason scowled.

'Off, Lulu!' He raised himself up groggily, then looked at his watch. It was barely 6 a.m.

He stumbled out of the bedroom into the hallway followed by the doting Lulu, sighed and rewound his messages. Then he hit the 'play' button on the phone.

'Sunday 7.04 p.m,' the electronic voice informed him.

'I'm in trouble . . .' Nick's voice echoed through the hall.

'... *real* trouble Jas ...' There was a hesitation. '*We're* in trouble. Uncle Lawrence was right. They killed Dad, Jason.'

Jason sighed and opened the fridge, listening as Nick's voice rose in intensity.

'We're involved in it, Jason – *our* whole family – you and me – it'll blow your mind ...'

Jason reached for the orange juice. He shook his head and poured a glass.

'Listen, Jason, you've got to listen to me. I got it all on camera. I've emailed it to Weaver. They've got the Ark of the Covenant. He's masterminded some insane barter deal with the Israelis.'

Jason set down the glass.

'Jas, listen to me. The needle was a plant. They wanted me dead. They gave me Aids ... Adrian's involved in ...'

There was a strange static noise and the message cut off.

'For god's sake, Nick, get a life.' Jason took a big slug of orange juice, then put a frying pan on the stove. Lulu cocked her head at him.

Jason frowned at her, then cut half a slice of bread and buttered it.

'Sit,' he commanded. She stared up at him, her dewy brown eyes riveted to the bread, her tail wagging vigorously, then took it gently from his outstretched palm. Jason fondled her ears distractedly, then threw two eggs in the pan and hit the message play button again. He sat down heavily on a kitchen chair and picked up yesterday's *New York Times*.

'Monday 6 a.m.'

'Jason, it's Mother. Please phone me immediately.'

Jason frowned. It was Lilian. She sounded on edge.

'Monday 6.03 a.m.' It was Lilian again.

'Jason,' her voice was shaking, 'I need you to call me right away.'

'Monday 6.10 a.m.'

Jason went over to the stove and flipped the frying eggs. 'The whole world's going nuts,' he muttered.

'Jason, it's Mother.' There was a long silence. Lilian sounded strange, as though she'd been crying. Her voice was so soft, Jason had difficulty making out her words.

'There's been a terrible accident.'

There was another long silence.

'It's Nick ... Jason ... his car plunged over a bridge in Normandy. There was a fire.'

Jason stood frozen.

'Jason ... Nick's dead ...'

Jason's chest constricted so violently he struggled to breathe.

The spatula slipped from his hand and clattered onto the floor.

He closed his eyes but all he could see was Nick. Nick as a six year old gazing up at him with clear grey eyes from a gangway in New York Harbour. Nick in high school. Nick at sixteen with him and Julia at the house in Cape Cod. Nick's first day at Oxford. Nick and himself fighting violently after Lily's accident.

And then there was no more Nick. Jason had cut him out of his existence.

He slid in slow motion down the stove, tears streaming down his unshaven face onto the marble kitchen floor, oblivious to the new maid from the agency, who stood staring down at him in alarm. And to Lulu who was whining in concern.

Then – for the first time in his entire adult life – Jason De Vere lost all self-control. Closing his eyes, he clutched his head in his hands.

And sobbed like a baby.

Lawrence St Cartier sat at the immaculately laid breakfast table, his eggs untouched on the plate before him, staring out into Cairo's dawn haze. Waseem, his assistant, laid out the *Middle East Times* carefully beside his plate.

'Today's paper – Egypt,' Waseem said.

He spread out the *Daily Telegraph* on top of the first newspaper.

'Yesterday's paper – London.'

Finally he placed a copy of the *News of the World* on top of the *Telegraph*. 'Yesterday's sensationalist – London.'

St Cartier adjusted his monocle.

The headline read: 'Youngest De Vere magnate in fatal accident.'

He picked it up.

Waseem watched Lawrence St Cartier intently.

'You must eat, Malik. You insult Waseem.'

St Cartier smiled weakly.

'Your stomach is weak today, Malik. It is Nick, Malik?'

St Cartier folded up the newspaper and sighed. Waseem continued. Relentless.

'Malik, you insult him by your great tragic. Today he is with the angels.'

St Cartier looked out into the Cairo haze, a strange exhilaration in his gaze.

'Yes, Waseem. Today, he is with the angels.'

Julia walked out of the luxurious white marbled bathroom, freshly showered after her early morning flight from London to Milan. She was wrapped in a soft, pink lambswool robe. She surveyed the rich blue damask silks of the luxuriously appointed suite in approval. She loved Milan. And she loved the Hotel Principe di Savoia with its imposing neoclassical facade.

One of the many perks of her having landed the England football team's PR account was that, on days like this, she stayed in a suite in the Principe Tower at their expense, just a stone's throw from Milan's elegant shopping district.

Great for her last-minute Christmas shopping.

She sat at the ornately carved Italian dressing table and towel dried her wet, blonde hair, then plugged in her flatirons, Julia's most indispensable item, next to her state-of-the-art Xphone 2022. She walked into the sitting room to the writing desk and checked the Xphone. Still charging.

She picked at a croissant from her breakfast tray, then distractedly picked up the remote and switched the television on.

Julia watched as Nick's face appeared on the flat screen. She frowned. What had Nick done to make the news *this* time?

The announcer spoke in fast, fluid Italian. Julia couldn't make head or tail of it.

Then she put her hand to her mouth in horror. A red Aston Martin was being dredged up by police boats in Normandy. She grasped the remote and flipped channels until she reached Vox UK 24.

She stared, frozen, at the efficient brunette presenter. This time there was no mistaking it.

'The charred remains of a red Aston Martin were discovered in Normandy in the early hours of this morning after a search through the night by French police. The rented car was identified as belonging to the youngest of the De Vere magnates – Nicholas De Vere.' The remote fell from Julia's hand.

Tears rolled down her face as she sank slowly onto the sofa, and the presenter's well-modulated British tones became a haze.

Nick was dead.

She had to tell Lily.

Royal Palace
Damman, Saudi Arabia

Jotapa lay face-down on the pale gold silk covers, fresh purple welts covering her arms and upper legs. The Koran lay unopened next to her bed.

'Our Father,' she murmured. 'Who art in heaven . . .'

Jibril leaned over her, stroking her dishevelled hair.

'Hallowed be thy name,' he whispered.

Slowly, Jotapa opened her eyes and turned her head. She looked at Jibril in amazement.

He smiled gently down at her.

'Thy Kingdom come . . .'

'You know it?' Jotapa whispered.

Jibril nodded. He clasped her hand. Tears streamed down Jotapa's cheeks.

'Thy will be done,' she murmured.

The door flung open. Jotapa sat bolt upright, staring at Mansoor with fear and hatred. He stood over them, an evil smile on his face.

He looked at the phone on the floor.

'Waiting for your playboy Prince Charming to rescue you, Princess?'

'You're barring my calls,' Jotapa said.

'It will no longer be necessary.'

He held out an Arabic newspaper in his right hand, then smiled and threw it onto the bed. He walked out slamming the door behind him.

Jotapa reached out her hand, a strange fire coursing through her limbs. Trembling she picked up the paper, staring at the headline, then down at the picture of Nick.

The paper slipped out of her hands onto the floor.

She sat screaming noiselessly, rocking herself from side to side.

Nick De Vere was dead.

Now she knew it for certain. She had landed in hell.

CHAPTER TWENTY-FOUR

The Cold Light of Day

La Guardia Airport
New York City

J ason De Vere got out of the helicopter and strode across the tarmac towards his newly acquired Bombadier Global Express business jet, sunglasses on, his earpiece in, firing instructions into a silver headset. Jontil Purvis marched at his side, calmly fielding three simultaneous conversations.

A few paces behind strode Liam Keynes, Vox's Senior General Counsel, and Levine and Mitchell, his aides.

'I want our bid raised to 1.6 billion,' Jason shouted over the roaring engines of the jet concourse. 'You tell Simons from me, we can't afford to lose. I'll do the Beijing meeting, but I *won't* move it again.' He glared again, this time at Jontil Purvis who was still talking on the phone. He signed to her impatiently to hurry, then sighed loudly, still talking into his headset.

'No,' he declared. 'Not even for the Chinese Premier.' He was in full stride again, straining against the freezing New York winter wind, towards the steps of the lone, gleaming

Global Express on the sectioned-off runway at La Guardia.

'I don't give a *damn* about the protocol. I'm in the middle of a family crisis.'

Jason beckoned to Keynes.

'Tell Geffen to get his lawyers out to Beijing today. Get the Beijing platform deal account at any cost, Keynes. Do you understand me?'

'Yes, sir.' Keynes backed away. 'Understood, sir.'

Jontil Purvis held out her mobile. 'Call from London. I'm transferring to you.'

'Who *is* it?'

'Aunt Rosemary.'

Jason scowled. Rosemary was James De Vere's British second cousin, now Lilian's companion. She had lived with Lilian since James's death and known Jason since he was three – and still treated him as such. His headset lit up an electric blue.

'Aunt Rosemary . . . Yes . . . It's all a nightmare . . . *No* press activity on arrival in London. Is that crystal clear?' Jason continued his striding. 'Yes . . . Tell mother I'm on my way. I'm giving you to Purvis.'

The small party arrived at the steps of the jet.

Jontil Purvis clicked off her phones.

'Aunt Rosemary will meet us with a car at London City Airport.'

'Well that's something to look forward to,' Jason said drily as they walked up the jet's stairway.

Jontil Purvis's quiet efficient tones continued, 'You go directly to the house in Knightsbridge. The funeral's on Tuesday . . . 11 a.m. . . . All Souls, Langham Place. Christmas lunch is arranged for tomorrow, Saturday. With your mother and Lily.'

Jason's mobile rang again. He clicked it off.

A distinguished-looking man in pilot's uniform stood at

the entrance to the Global Express. He nodded in deference to Jason.

'The headwind's on our side, Mr De Vere, sir,' he said, his voice tinged with a soft Scottish burr. 'All things considered, we should be in London by 8 p.m.'

'Good man, Mac,' Jason said, softly. 'Let's make good time.'

The pilot nodded. 'Good flight, Mr De Vere, sir.'

Jason took off his dark glasses. His eyes were bloodshot and ringed by dark circles.

'I'm sorry about your brother.'

Jason walked past the conference area towards the centre of the Global Express. He glanced up wearily at the eight customized television monitors broadcasting VoxDigital, then passed his briefcase to a young man with a large gaudy tie. 'Levine, make sure Phillips follows up with Jenkins in Tokyo.'

Levine headed towards the conference area with the briefcase.

'Where'd you get the tie?' Jason grimaced.

Levine grinned. Jason swayed slightly. He waved him away, then rubbed his eyes. He'd been drinking since yesterday morning on an empty stomach.

An air attendant put out two bottles of mineral water and a glass then scuttled off.

'Oh, and Levine, pour me a whisky from Macdonald's stash at the back, get me Mitchell, then join me.'

Jason sank into the chair.

He picked up the *Wall Street Journal*, then flung it down again. Restless.

A second, slightly built young man wearing glasses appeared.

'Mitchell, I want a damn good explanation what the Legal Channel's still doing on our platform.' Jason gestured to one of the Vox channels broadcasting above him. 'Get hold of Keynes *now*.'

Mitchell scuttled back towards the customized conference centre. Jason sighed deeply, rolled up his shirtsleeves, then stared at the television.

'Adrian De Vere, President of the emerging European superpower . . .'

Jason turned up the volume.

'. . . cut talks with the Russian President Oleinik and Syrian President Assad in Babylon short this evening after his brother's tragic death in the North of France earlier today. Police are investigat–'

Jason snapped the remote off, his eyes moist. He heaved a heavy sigh and ran a hand through his greying, short dark hair, then put on his reading glasses and picked up a sheaf of papers.

Levine came back down the aisle carrying a thick file and Jason's whisky. He was followed by Jontil Purvis. Levine handed the whisky to Jason, who immediately slugged it down. Jontil Purvis settled herself opposite Jason. She looked at the empty whisky glass and frowned.

Jason held the empty glass out to Levine.

'The same.' He glared deliberately at Purvis. The engines began to warm up.

'Mr De Vere, sir,' said the flight attendant holding out a menu.

Jason waved it away.

'Give it to Purvis,' he slurred.

'Jason,' Jontil said, softly, 'you've refused everything but whisky for the past forty-eight hours. You *must* eat.'

'Not hungry, Purvis,' he slurred. 'Stop mothering me.'

She sighed, stowed her handbag, then took off her elegant peach lambswool cardigan from her rather full form and fastened her seatbelt. Jason pushed his glasses down onto his nose and studied her. It never ceased to intrigue him.

Jontil Purvis had been flying with him for fifteen years and each flight she did the same thing. He watched as she put on her reading glasses, patted her immaculate blonde beehive, opened the pages of a small, weathered brown leather pocket Bible and immersed herself in its pages.

'I should have taken his calls,' he grunted, shuffling through the sheaf of papers.

Jontil removed her reading glasses. She studied the haggard face intently. She knew him so well. Nick's death had hit him like a sledgehammer. In the entire twenty-two years she had known Jason De Vere, she had never seen him so unglued. So rattled. Or so drunk.

Clutching the leather pocket Bible, she closed her eyes and bowed her head as the jet took off into the brilliant blue New York skies.

'Purvis?' She followed Jason's gaze to the slim weathered book in her hand. '*You* believe in redemption.' His bloodshot eyes searched her face. Jason's voice was so soft, she almost missed it. 'Say one for me.'

Communications Network
London

Dylan Weaver's stubby fingers flew effortlessly across his laptop. He looked down at the photo of the mangled sports car and the story of Nick's death on page five of *The Sun*, then zoomed down his inbox for what must have been the tenth time that hour to Nick De Vere's email from 9.19 p.m. GMT yesterday evening. He hit 'Detach' and 'Launch'.

'C'mon, baby,' he murmured.

The encrypted icon flashed on his laptop screen. Weaver slammed the laptop shut in frustration, scrolled down his phone and dialled.

CHAPTER TWENTY-FIVE

Lilian

New London City Airport
London

Jason stood at the top of the Global Express's steps, staring bleakly out at the sleet lashing down from the grey, overcast London skies onto the tarmac. It was Christmas Eve and his head felt as though it was exploding from his hangover.

'Damn British weather,' he muttered, grudgingly descending the steps. He strode across the tarmac, followed by a grimacing Levine, shielding his head from the sleet with Jason's briefcase, and with Jontil Purvis following closely behind.

A tall, bony, dowdy woman in her late sixties, wearing a plastic rain hat and a houndstooth tweed coat, rushed up to them holding out two umbrellas.

'Jason, Jontil,' she called out impatiently in a refined, clipped British accent, 'Follow me, the Bentley's waiting.' She embraced Jontil, then held out an umbrella to Jason.

'Hurry!' she snapped.

'Nice to see you, too, Aunt Rosemary,' Jason muttered as a horde of press photographers stampeded towards them.

'Damn, Rosemary!' Jason scowled. 'I said no press.'

Rosemary turned to give him a dark stare.

'It's *Nicholas*, Jason,' she said, crisply. 'He was celebrity fodder in London when he was alive; he's celebrity fodder when he's dead. He's the ex-Prime Minister's brother, for pete's sake.' Jason was still looking at the umbrella. 'Well, don't just stand there,' she snapped.

'What do you need? Three assistants?' She looked around at Levine, Mitchell, and Purvis. 'I should have known.'

She pursed her lips.

'Americans – can't do anything without an entourage.' Turning, she narrowly missed poking Jason's eye out with the umbrella.

'Well, you're in Old Blighty now. Here it's hands-on. Take it.' She thrust the umbrella at him. 'You don't think I'm standing here for my health, do you?'

Meekly, Jason took the umbrella.

'And don't think it'll get any better at the funeral,' she warned, striding away from Jason. 'Adrian's presence is going to attract every journalist in Europe.'

Jason shot Jontil Purvis an annoyed glance. He was well aware how much it amused her to see him bossed around by his father's cousin. Lilian always said they were as stubborn as each other. Hewn from the same block.

'Cooper. Grayson.' Aunt Rosemary directed Lilian's bodyguards. She nodded at the rapidly approaching press corps. The two ex-SAS soldiers warded off the rapacious British press as a third ploughed a way through the pushing and jostling paparazzi towards the waiting Bentley, twenty feet away.

'De Vere. The *Mirror*.' A lanky, fresh-faced journalist flashed his credentials in Jason's face. 'How long did you know your brother was gay?'

A flash went off directly in Jason's face. 'Damn British paparazzi.'

'Do you believe your brother was murdered?' a thin balding photographer shouted. 'A crime of passion?'

A crimson flush of anger spread from Jason's face to his neck.

'He had a car accident, for god's sake.'

The *Mirror* reporter smiled.

'Is it true you were estranged from your brother?'

Jason shoved the *Mirror* reporter roughly out of his way just as more camera flashes erupted.

'Aggressive as always, Mr De Vere.' The young man in torn jeans and T-shirt spoke politely in a refined English accent. 'Great cover picture for the Sunday edition. *Thank* you.'

'Did you know your brother was dying of Aids?' Jason stopped in mid-stride, his temper raging. Jontil placed her hand on Jason's arm gently. He stared at the paparazzi scathingly. She tightened her pressure on his arm.

'Jason,' she said. He looked at her, reading the expression in her eyes. Another flash went off.

'Let's get out of here!' Jason put his head down as the third bodyguard pushed through the reporters. Jason followed him blindly to the open door of the Bentley and climbed in, sinking into the soft leather seat.

Aunt Rosemary was taking charge outside. 'Push off!' she commanded. 'I said *move* it.'

She pointed her umbrella at a young cameraman.

'You leave my nephew alone,' she said, menacingly.

Levine passed the briefcase through the door, then hurried through the sleet to join Jontil in a second waiting car as Aunt Rosemary climbed into the Bentley.

A reporter battered on the Bentley window.

'British guttersnipe press,' Jason snarled.

'You play *right* into their hands, Jason.' Aunt Rosemary frowned at Jason in disapproval. 'You always have.'

More reporters battered on the darkened Bentley windows.

'*Don't* lecture me, Rosemary.' Jason glared at her, then tapped impatiently on the smoked glass divider. The Bentley lurched ahead still in clutch. Jason stared blindly ahead at the compartment door as Rosemary poured him a mineral water. Grudgingly, he took it, as another lurch rocked the Bentley. Hearing a loud hooting from behind them, Jason turned to see a London cab driver, his head sticking out of the window glaring at them aggressively.

'Get a move on, mate,' the cabbie shouted.

Jason raised his eyebrows in disbelief.

Rosemary nodded.

'He *insisted* that he pick you up. No one could stop him.'

For the first time in two days, a glimmer of a smile spread across Jason's face.

'But he hasn't driven since the war.'

The dark glass of the compartment divider opened slowly and Maxim, now in his early eighties, patted his twirled waxed moustache. He nodded respectfully.

'The *Falklands* War, Master Jason. You were, if my memory serves me, studying at Yale.'

Jason grinned in affection.

'Good to see you, Maxim. You're sure you can drive this beast?'

They passed Westminster and the Houses of Parliament. Maxim looked back at Jason in the Bentley mirror.

'Piece of cake, Master Jason, sir,' he said, narrowly missing a red London bus.

'How good to see you. My deepest condolences for our Master Nick, sir.'

Jason became instantly grave again.

'Thank you, Maxim. How's Mother?'

'She's the picture of composure, Master Jason, sir, but I must confess to have instigated a little spying operation, of

283

which, of course she has no inkling. Each night, after her bedtime drink, I confess that I hear her sobbing. I have been most concerned, Master Jason.'

The Bentley lurched violently, followed by another huge lurch, then a screech. Cars hooted from all around them. Jason and Rosemary exchanged a look as a cab driver rolled down his window and shook his fist at the Bentley. He glared at Maxim.

'Go back to the bloody old-people's home.'

Maxim rolled down his window most indignantly just as the cab driver made a vulgar sign at him.

'The impertinence!' Maxim spluttered, made a fist with his own hand and shook it at the cabbie, who had long gone.

'Now, now, Maxim.' Jason grinned.

As they got under way again, Aunt Rosemary opened her briefcase.

'Funeral's at All Souls, Langham Place – the north end of Regent Street – next to the BBC. The only central place available at such short notice.'

She took out a stack of notes typed on an old ribbon typewriter.

'The usual. Your mother's dreading it. Security'll be a nightmare with Adrian there.' She took out a small black book. 'Your mother's list: seven Labour MPs and four Conservative. The Prime Minister. Speaker of the House. Seven minor royals. Nine Lords. You know. The norm.'

Jason looked ahead disbelievingly as they sailed through a set of red lights amid more hooting.

Unconcerned, Aunt Rosemary continued. 'Peers, one or two minor European royals, seven US senators and congressmen, chairmen of the Bank of England, North Sea Oil.'

She removed a second ream of paper.

'Your list, courtesy Jontil Purvis. Adrian's list – huge. And of course, Nick's *personal* friends' She grimaced. 'Needless to say, *they* won't be in black tie. Oh, and Julia.'

Jason steeled, perceptibly.

'I thought she was in Rome.'

'She is. She flies into Heathrow tonight. Alex, Lily, and her friend meet her there and go back to New Chelsea.' Aunt Rosemary checked her watch. 'We just missed her. Lily arrives tomorrow at 2 p.m. sharp at your mother's for Christmas lunch. She'll stay with you till 7 p.m. Adrian's been held up in Babylon. He'll arrive in London the morning of the funeral.'

Which is . . . ?'

'Tuesday. The twenty-eighth.'

The Bentley jolted, braked, then screeched to a halt outside a sprawling mansion in Belgrave Square. Jason caught his mineral water just as it flew off the Bentley table.

Jason climbed out onto the pavement as Maxim was still struggling to open his own Bentley door. Jason leaned down and opened it. Maxim extricated his size-sixteen shoes from under the brake.

'Most appreciated, Master Jason, sir.'

'Maxim,' Jason said, sternly, 'I think a refresher course is in order.'

Maxim eased his six-foot-four frame out of the car and surveyed Jason in approval.

'Master Jason, may I say how *very* smart you look.'

Jason smiled, gazed up at the old London six-floor, white stucco-fronted Georgian mansion, then walked the short distance to the commanding portico. Maxim followed with Jason's briefcase. Rosemary turned the key in the lock.

The door opened onto an enormous marble hallway, with twenty-foot-high ceilings adorned with imposing Georgian coving. An arrangement of forty-eight ivory roses sat on the antique hall table.

A young girl in livery appeared.

'Ceci,' Aunt Rosemary instructed, 'help Maxim with Mr De Vere's cases, will you.'

Jason removed his gloves, his face alight with memories.

'Maxim,' he said, 'I thought Mother said in her last letter that you were retiring.'

Maxim's brows furrowed in disapproval.

'*Retire* is a word that only Madam Lilian used, I believe.'

'No, Maxim,' Aunt Rosemary glared at him, 'she mentioned nothing at all about retiring. All she did was suggest you take a well-earned holiday!'

Maxim gave Jason a long-suffering look.

'I said to Madam Lilian,' he declared sniffily, 'if my services are no longer required, I shall assume that my skills are slipping. I have been with this family for over thirty-five years.'

'There, there Maxim.' Jason hid a smile. 'You're a part of the furniture. How would Mother cope without you?'

'Well, I'll be going,' Aunt Rosemary said, drying off Jason's umbrella. 'Staying with my niece,' she declared. 'Thought I'd give you and your mother a little privacy.'

Rosemary rubbed her hands, then leaning over, she pecked Jason on the cheek and disappeared out of the front door.

'Forgive me for my petulance, Master Jason,' Maxim said, taking a perfectly pressed white hanky from his pocket. He wiped his eyes and then blew his nose at a thousand decibels.

'It's Master Nick. His death.' He blew his nose again. 'It's quite thrown me off.'

Jason put a hand on Maxim's shoulder.

'It's thrown us all off, I know, Maxim.'

Maxim removed a well-worn photo from a battered black leather wallet. 'Master Nicholas when he was four. After he exploded the woodshed.'

Jason took the tattered photo of a very singed Nicholas from Maxim's trembling grasp.

'Dad was livid,' Jason recalled, smiling faintly.

'And my favourite of Master Nicholas,' Maxim murmured.

Jason stared, transfixed at the photograph of himself, Adrian, and Nick together at the gangway in New York.

'You still have it,' he said in wonder.

Maxim gave a watery smile.

'It's from my scrapbook.'

'Brothers,' Jason murmured.

He looked up to the first-floor landing towards two large, closed mahogany doors.

Maxim nodded.

'Madam Lilian hasn't left her quarters since she received the news of Master Nicholas's death.'

Jason sighed.

'The South Wing is prepared for you as usual, Master Jason. My room is still on the sixth floor. Upper right. If you need me, ring the bell in your drawing room. Breakfast will be served in Madam Lilian's dining room at 8 a.m. sharp.'

'No breakfast, Maxim.'

Maxim looked at him sternly.

'I shall be preparing a separate breakfast tray for you at 7 a.m. precisely, Master Jason. Three eggs. Over easy. Orange juice. The nutritionless white toast you insist on.' He scowled. 'And porridge, with cream and whisky. And may I be so bold, Master Jason, having looked after you since you were in second grade, to *strongly* recommend that you partake of no spirits until after the funeral.'

Jason looked at Maxim, strangely emotional.

'You may be so bold, Maxim, old friend,' he said, softly.

Maxim dabbed his eyes again.

'I shall return with Madam's sedatives,' he said. 'Good night, Master Jason.'

Jason walked slowly up the stairs to the first-floor landing.

'Mother,' he whispered.

He pushed open the set of mahogany doors and peered into the large sitting room, elegantly decorated with antiques, tapestries and throws.

Lilian De Vere sat alone in the dark, staring at video footage of Nick in his schooldays, Nick at Cape Cod with Adrian and Jason, Nick at the last De Vere family party when James De Vere had still been alive.

Very gently, Jason leaned over and took the remote out of her hands.

'Mother,' he said, softly.

Lilian started and turned to Jason. Her eyes misted over and she clasped his hands. 'Jason, darling.' Her thin hand trembled as she switched on a side lamp.

Jason looked down at her gently and drew in a deep breath. She had aged overnight. Always elegantly very thin, she now looked gaunt. Her silver hair was impeccably braided and pinned up in a chignon, and she wore a tailored black dress with a diamante brooch on her lapel. But tonight she looked so vulnerable. So frail.

Lilian clasped him tightly to her and for a fleeting moment Jason struggled to keep his composure. She released him.

'You were always like your father – so strong . . . stubborn – focused . . .' Her voice trailed off.

'But Nicholas . . .' She picked up a photograph of Jason, Adrian, and Nick on the antique table next to her. Her eyes grew distant.

'Nicholas . . . was a free spirit.' She took Jason's hand and clasped it tightly in her own.

'First your father.' She drew Jason down next to her. 'Then Nick.'

There was a soft knock on the door. Maxim bowed slightly, then wheeled in a silver tray of canapés.

'Refreshments, Madam Lilian.' He studied Jason in approval.

'And your sedatives.'

He frowned at her then looked at Jason.

'She refuses to take them, Master Jason.'

Jason held his hand out.

'Here. She'll take them.'

Jason placed the two tablets gently in Lilian's palm, then gave her the glass of water.

'Drink it, Mother,' he instructed. 'You've got a stressful few days ahead with the funeral.'

Lilian smiled faintly.

'Lily's coming for Christmas lunch with us.'

'I know. Now drink up.' He smiled gently at her. Lilian drank the sedative.

'Good girl.'

'Madam Lilian, I am on the other end of your bell if you require me in the night,' Maxim said, and bowing, he disappeared through the drawing room doors.

Jason stood.

'It's late, Mother. You've got a long day tomorrow. You need your rest.'

He helped Lilian to her feet and they stood together in the dark for a long moment.

Finally, Jason spoke. 'I miss Nick,' he whispered.

Lilian held his face in her hands. She looked deeply into his eyes.

'When he was very young, Jason,' her voice was very soft, 'you were his hero. All his life until the accident, he relied on your strength – the strength he knew he never had.'

She clasped Jason to her.

'He loved you, Jason.' She kissed him tenderly on his head as she had done when he was a boy.

'He was too soft,' Jason mumbled. 'He was a fool . . .'

Tears streamed down Jason's cheeks.

'A fool. But I loved him, Mother.'

Jason strode from the room, leaving Lilian staring alone into the darkness.

CHAPTER TWENTY-SIX

The Funeral

Three Days Later
All Souls Church
Langham Place, London

Jason stood inside the foyer of the church, safely out of sight of the media circus. Adrian's black cavalcade drew up outside the circular columned portico of All Souls, Langham Place. Jason squinted as the light from the paparazzi's ever-present cameras flashed, illuminating the bleak, grey London skies overhead.

Adrian De Vere had arrived.

Jason turned and walked down the aisle towards the front row of the church. It was crammed to overflowing with the *Who's Who* of both British and American political and corporate society. A combination of the dual influence of both the De Vere banking empire and the fact that Adrian was the fastest-rising political leader in the entire Western world.

Jason took mental notes as he walked. On the right-hand side of the aisle he recognized four British MPs, the Chancellor of the Exchequer, the newly elected Conservative

Prime Minister of the UK, the President of France, the Queen of the Netherlands, and four lesser-known UK royals. On the left-hand side sat the chairmen of the Bank of England and North Sea Oil, along with four US congressmen and three senators he recognized from the news, including the one from New York with whom he played golf every month.

His expression softened. He recognized the elegant features of Xavier Chessler, President of the World Bank, his godfather.

Jason paused and leaned over Xavier Chessler's shoulder.

'Uncle Xavier,' he said. Xavier Chessler looked up.

'Jason.' He stood and embraced him. 'I'm so sorry, my boy. It's devastating. Nick was so young.'

Jason nodded.

'I had breakfast with your mother this morning,' Chessler said. 'You know we'll look after her.'

Jason smiled.

'You've been a brick, Uncle Xavier. I don't know what she would have done without you.'

'Your father was my oldest friend, Jason.'

Jason turned to see Lily, who had turned around in her wheelchair and was beckoning to him. He turned back to Xavier Chessler.

The elegant old man looked worn.

'I'm here for you, Jason,' he said. 'You know . . . anything I can do. Why don't we catch up this week in New York?'

'I'll be back Thursday. The usual. Two-thirty, Fifth?'

'How about that eclectic bar? Nick's favourite?'

Jason nodded.

'The Gramercy,' he said, softly. 'The Rose Bar.'

Chessler smiled.

'I met him there with Marina. In the summer.'

He looked down at the date on his watch.

292

'Thursday night. Nine-thirty. The Rose Bar. A toast to Nick.'

'A toast to Nick,' Jason echoed.

He clasped Chessler's hand, then walked past the remaining two rows. At last, Nick's friends. Jason recognized two international models, a leading British recording artist, three famous Hollywood actors, celebrities from a top British reality TV show and . . . He stopped. He'd know that profile anywhere, even covered by a black veil.

Julia.

He turned abruptly away and made his way past the minders to the front pew, where Lilian sat staring straight ahead, her face covered by a black veil, dabbing her eyes with a lace handkerchief. Lily sat on her right. Alex and Polly on her left.

'Dad.' Lily pulled Jason down next to her, her eyes red-rimmed from sobbing. She clasped his hand.

'Dad, I'm worried about Alex. He's closed us all out.' Jason frowned. He leaned over to Alex.

'Sorry, bud.' He touched his arm. 'I know how close you were.'

Alex scowled at Jason, then returned to his morose staring into his hymn book.

Adrian sidled into the pew, while his Secret Service entourage took the pew behind. He looked worn to the point of exhaustion.

Reaching Lilian, he clasped her in his arms for a long moment. He kissed her softly on the forehead, then sat her down and bent down next to Lily. He kissed her on both cheeks, then sank into the pew next to Jason. Directly behind Adrian sat Guber and Travis.

'Dad, don't you even feel bad you never even returned Nick's calls?' Lily whispered.

Lilian shook her head warningly at her grandchild.

'Of course he feels bad,' she said, softly.

Adrian took Lily's hand. 'He just can't admit it. You know your dad. Stubborn as always.'

Lilian smiled faintly.

'Just like his father.'

Jason scowled, but then his expression softened.

'Poor Nick.' Adrian sighed deeply. 'Last time I saw him at Mother's birthday supper in Rome, he was skin and bone.'

Jason frowned. 'Wasn't he with you the night of his accident?'

Adrian shook his head. 'He was on his *way* to the Abbey when he crashed. But, no, he didn't arrive.'

Jason frowned. 'He was travelling late.'

Adrian opened the Anglican Book of Common Prayer.

'You know Nick,' he shrugged, 'no rhyme nor reason. He was meant to arrive at noon. Phoned, said he'd been held up, would arrive late, and stay the night.'

He looked at Jason.

'He never arrived.'

Jason nodded. 'Just strange, that's all.'

He picked up a hymn book.

'He left me a message. Sounded like he'd just been with you. Some incoherent rambling about you masterminding some insane barter deal with the Israelis. And the Ark of the Covenant. In fact those were his exact words.'

'He say anything else?' Adrian riffled through the Prayer Book.

'Nah.' Jason glanced back in the direction of Julia. She was gazing directly at him. He immediately immersed himself in the hymn book.

'Who's that with your mother?' he whispered to Lily.

Lily smiled weakly at Jason.

'It's Callum. Callum Vickers. Good looking, isn't he?' She waited for effect. 'And young.'

294

Jason turned round again, on the pretence of getting Xavier Chessler's attention.

Julia was now in deep conversation with the man who he presumed was Callum Vickers. He frowned. *The guy must be at least ten years younger than Julia. Longish blond hair, tan. Thirty; thirty-two max.* He scowled. *Probably an actor, a model. Typical. One of Julia's PR celebrity types.*

Lily looked at him intently. She read her father like a book.

'He's actually a top London surgeon, Dad,' she declared.

'Plastic surgeon, I'll bet.'

Lily heaved a sigh.

'Neuro, actually.'

Jason looked at Lily sheepishy. Lily shook her head at him and put her arm around Lilian.

Jason turned back for one more look at Callum Vickers, then stood up to pray for the soul of his youngest brother – Nicholas De Vere.

Maxim was bent over the Bentley bonnet, painstakingly polishing the winged badge.

'A butler.'

The familiar dulcet tones were coming from directly behind him. Maxim froze.

'How appropriate.' Charsoc clasped and unclasped his long fingers, cracking his knuckles loudly and deliberately.

'My, my, Xacheriel. From taking my throne at the right hand of Jether the Just to buffing automotive bonnet ornaments of men.'

Charsoc circled the Bentley.

'Oh, how thou hast fallen.'

Maxim continued his deliberate polishing.

Charsoc raised his eyebrows, then opened his carpetbag. He studied Maxim's untameable mop of wiry silver hair for a moment, then fished out a Mason Pearson hairbrush.

'My promise.'

He held it out to Maxim.

At that moment, Jason rounded the corner with Lily in her wheelchair, followed by Jontil Purvis.

He frowned.

'Von Slagel.' Charsoc bowed slightly.

'Mr Jason De Vere.'

Jason looked at the hairbrush. He raised an eyebrow.

'You *know* Von Slagel, Maxim?'

Maxim rose from the Bentley bonnet to his full height. He turned to face Charsoc.

'I have had the displeasure of his acquaintance in my former life.' He glared down at the hairbrush. '*Before* I went into service, Master Jason.'

Maxim opened the car door for Lily and eased her into the Bentley as Jason folded up the wheelchair. Jason shook his head, baffled.

'Maxim worked for you, Von Slagel?'

Charsoc smiled thinly. 'Many years ago. He served me well.'

Charsoc doffed his hat to Jason. 'Mr De Vere.'

Jason took another look at the hairbrush, then at Maxim's hair, grinned and climbed in next to Lily.

Maxim closed the door, then turned to face Charsoc.

'You have no place here.'

'Oh, but you see, Xacheriel, I do. Jason De Vere's demise after the Seventh Seal is opened is essential to our strategy.'

He looked at Maxim through narrowed eyes.

'I know Jether resides somewhere on this muddy little orb.'

Maxim stood expressionless.

'I shall find him.'

Maxim climbed into the front seat and drove off, leaving Charsoc standing in the falling rain.

Jason stood at the far side of the conservatory under the high glass roof, watching Adrian make small talk with Lord Kitchener, former chairman of BP, a towering man with a ruddy face and a waxed moustache. Behind him was the normal line-up of politicians, industrial magnates, and oil barons, all fawning over the newly inaugurated President of the new European superstate.

Jason read his brother at a glance. Anyone watching the animated young politician would conclude he was vitally engaged in conversation, but Jason knew that he was bored to death. His left hand was tapping rhythmically on an antique table next to him. Adrian tapped indiscriminately when his interest level was waning. Had done since he was twelve. Jason hid a smile, then walked towards him, side-stepping the discreetly placed Secret Service men under Guber's vigilant gaze.

'Hey, pal,' he whispered. 'Need a drink?'

He put his arm around Adrian's well-secured back. Guber frowned. Jason frowned back. Adrian and Jason exchanged a glance.

Jason surveyed the escape route to the bar. Adrian hid a smile, then shook hands with the effusive Lord Kitchener and nodded to Guber, who relaxed as Jason guided his younger brother beneath the elegant chandeliers, past numerous potted palms to the well-stocked bar.

'Sir James Fulmore,' Jason muttered, indicating a stout gentleman with a bow tie. 'He'll be wanting your support.'

'And Owen Seymour – ex-governor of the BBC – he'll be wanting my support.'

'Babylon?' Jason asked as they entered the bar.

Adrian nodded. 'After the Treaty's signed on 7 January, the oil will start flowing again like Niagara Falls. Everybody wants a share in Babylon.'

Jason turned to the bartender. 'Whisky.' He looked enquiringly at Adrian.

'Perrier.'

Jason shrugged. 'Perrier water for the European President.'

The bartender nodded, staring at Adrian, awestruck.

Jason leaned against the bar.

'Levine told me the New York and Moscow Stock Exchanges move permanently in July.'

Adrian nodded. 'And Bombay. The entire Asia Pacific exchange moved last month. Shanghai, Hong Kong, Tokyo, Milan, Frankfurt, and London. Been permanent fixtures in the new International Exchange Edifice since January.'

'You've got to admit, though,' Jason continued, 'the "Babylon" catalyst was the United Nations' move from New York to Babylon in July.'

Adrian nodded.

'That and the fact that the EU and the World Bank pumped in over two trillion dollars to reconstruct the city.' He sipped his Perrier water.

'And to bulldoze Saddam Hussein's prehistoric blot on the landscape,' Jason added, 'as Nick used to call it!'

They both fell silent at the mention of Nick's name.

'Seriously, you okay, pal?' Jason asked. 'The funeral I mean. It must bring back memories.'

Adrian looked out at the view of Hyde Park.

'You mean Melissa – the baby?' Jason nodded.

Adrian continued his staring, expressionless.

'It'll take years, Jason . . .' he hesitated, 'to get over it, I mean. Their deaths.'

Jason studied Adrian intently. Adrian wiped his eyes with the back of his hand. 'Sorry, pal. Didn't mean to upset you.'

Adrian clasped Jason's shoulder, instantly regaining his composure.

'It's okay, Jason. I have to live with my own ghosts.'

Jason took a slug of his whisky and slammed the glass down on the polished countertop. He surveyed the room.

'I hate these things. My social skills have completely slipped.'

A faint smile glimmered on Adrian's lips. He put his hand on Jason's arm.

'Aw, c'mon. You never had any social skills, Jas.'

Jason grinned just as Lilian caught sight of them. She walked across the conservatory, followed by a posse of well-heeled 'suits'.

'Jason, Adrian – Lord and Lady Kirkpatrick. John, Margaret – my sons: Jason.' Jason nodded politely. 'Adrian.' Adrian shook the outstretched hands.

Owen Seymour rushed over to them.

'Jason, please accept my sincerest regrets.'

He bowed slightly. 'Mrs De Vere.' He put his hand out to Adrian. 'Mr President, sir.'

Jason scowled.

'Well, Mother,' he said, drawing Lilian to his side and leaning closely to her. 'Between Adrian and me, it looks like we've got both the political arena and the media sown up.'

Lilian frowned at him.

Jason continued. Relentless.

'They all want something, Mother,' He downed the whisky. 'And it isn't Nick.'

Lilian removed the glass from Jason's hand and placed it fimly on the bar countertop. She signed to Jontil Purvis, standing discreetly behind Levine and making phone calls.

Adrian rested his hand affectionately on Jason's shoulder.

'It's politics, Jason. We all play it.' He grinned. 'You do, too. Ah, there's the Queen of Spin ... as you so aptly put it.'

He looked at Jason, mischief in his eyes.

'Julia.'

Jason paled, took a deep breath and steeled himself.

'Levine, another whisky.' He took another look at Julia coming towards him with Lily in tow. 'A big one.'

Lilian turned round from her guests.

'That's your third, Jason,' she whispered. '*And* you refused breakfast.'

'Trust me, Mother,' he muttered, watching Julia glide towards him in her five-inch Chloe heels and a close-fitting black Chanel suit. 'This is no time to be sober.'

Lilian reached out her hand to Julia.

'Julia. Margaret, this is the daughter I never had – Julia St Cartier.'

Jason seethed, watching as Julia charmed Lord and Lady Kirkpatrick. Her long ash-blonde hair was swept up beneath a classic black hat with a long black tulle veil.

He tapped Levine on the shoulder. 'Make that a double.'

Julia turned to Adrian. She lifted the veil away from her face, revealing red bloodshot eyes.

'Hey, sis.' Adrian clasped her hands, gently kissing her on both cheeks.

'I'm so sorry, Adrian.' She smiled up at him weakly.

She turned to Jason whose mouth was set in a firm line and her eyes immediately lost all warmth.

'Jason.' Jason stared bleakly at her.

'Julia.'

'I'm so sorry about Nicky, Jason.'

Jason gave her a blank look.

The tall blond surgeon from the funeral came up behind Julia and put his arm around her waist.

'Adrian, this is Callum,' she said. 'Callum Vickers. Callum, this is Adrian De Vere. No introductions needed.' Callum offered his hand to Adrian who shook it firmly.

300

'And this is Jason,' Julia said, curtly.

Callum held out his hand to Jason who stared at him, then unenthusiastically shook his hand.

'Very sorry about your brother,' Callum said, softly.

'Thanks,' Jason answered, monosyllabic.

'How's the media empire doing?'

'Well enough, thank you.' Jason turned and narrowed his eyes at Julia. 'I'm sure that Julia has told you I'm a slave to the industry.'

'No,' Callum said, in his calm manner, 'Julia hasn't really mentioned you.'

Jason grunted as Levine reappeared with the full whisky glass. 'Lily said you're a surgeon.' He took a swig.

Callum nodded and smiled at Jason in his easy relaxed fashion.

'A consultant surgeon, at St Thomas'.'

Jason looked over the glass at Julia, a sarcastic smile on his lips. 'That'll please Daddy, I'm sure.'

Julia glared at him.

'You're drinking,' she said frostily. 'Callum, we need to leave.'

The PD on Callum's waist emitted a loud consistent chirp.

'So sorry, I'm on call. If you'll excuse me.' He walked towards the window, talking into an earpiece. Jason took another slug of his whisky, deliberately staring at Julia. She glared at him, pulled the black veil back down over her face in annoyance and walked away from Jason over to Callum at the window.

'Dad,' Lily hissed, 'behave. Can't you be civil to Mum just this once?'

Jason stared ahead, grimly. 'The short answer is no.'

'De Vere.' A low voice broke through into his reverie.

He turned to find a fat pasty-faced man at the bar. He was in his late twenties, early thirties, wearing a badly fitting black suit that had seen better days, covered by a grubby yellow anorak.

Jason's eyes narrowed in slow recognition.

Weaver. Of course, Dylan Weaver, Nick's schoolboy friend from Gordonstoun. Now some top European IT specialist.

Jason held out his hand. Weaver ignored it. He looked around the room, clearly ill at ease, his eyes lingering on Guber.

'You don't like me much, do you?' Jason said.

He stared at Jason impassively.

'No, De Vere, I suppose I don't.'

Weaver glanced furtively around the room, as though looking for someone.

'Meet me at the Singing Waitress, Shaftesbury Avenue, Soho, in three hours.' He picked up a handful of appetizers. '10 p.m. Alone. I'm on the move.'

Jason stared at Weaver stuffing the cocktail sausages into the pockets of his anorak. Incredulous.

Weaver walked away from Jason. Then turned.

'It's about Nick.'

Julia unlocked the door to the quaint London cottage, situated in what was formerly known as the Artists' Colony of the New Chelsea Studios.

She deactivated the alarm, then removed her hat and hung up her fake fox fur coat. Bending down, she picked up the small pile of letters from the doormat and sifted through them casually, then froze. She stared at a cream linen envelope addressed to her. The writing on the envelope was familiar. Extremely familiar. It was Nick's writing. She'd know it anywhere.

Trembling, Julia dumped the rest of the post on the hall table, then walked through to the drawing room.

She turned the envelope around, studying the familiar

302

Mont St Michel crest and stared at the postmark on the envelope. She recognized *Pontorson*, the name of a small town near Mont St Michel.

She'd visited the Pontorson market on her last visit to the Abbey, before she had flown with Adrian to the Aqaba press conference. She frowned. The postmark was dated the twenty-second. The day of Nick's death.

Picking up a silver letter opener, she slit the letter open and slowly sat down on her ivory, slip-covered sofa. A photograph fell out onto the hardwood floor. She picked it up and placed it on the side table, then took out Nick's note. It was written hastily. In a scrawl. But it was definitely *Nick's* scrawl.

Dear Jules,

Dad was on to something. Something big. They killed him for. They gave me Aids, Jules. Deliberately. I think they know I'm on to them. A group of elite powerbrokers. I'm doing some investigating of my own. In the event that I don't make it out of here – you must get this to Jason. He's the only one I trust.

Tell Lily I'll always be sorry. Be my leading light, sis.

Always, Nicky

P.S. I'm not sure if Adrian's . . .'

The sentence was unfinished. Julia turned the slip over, there was nothing on the back. Tears streamed down her cheeks. She picked up the photograph.

There were four men. She recognized one of them as Jason's grandfather, Julius De Vere. Another as Xavier Chessler, his godfather. She turned the photograph around and read the writing.

'The Robes are behind the Suits.' Then a woman's name – Aveline.

Julia replaced the photo in the envelope, then walked over to the French doors, staring out at the Italianate walled gardens, her thoughts in disarray.

She took out the note once more and studied it.

Then reached for the phone.

Jason sat in the upmarket bar below the street patio that was the cigar room of the Lanesborough. A waiter hovered discreetly.

'Lagavulin 1991,' Jason muttered. The waiter smiled in approval. Jason leaned back in the leather chair, puffing on an expensive cigar and stared up at the tent-top roof. Lily wheeled herself next to Jason.

'Okay, all sorted. Gran's tired. She just left with Uncle Xavier. Alex'll drop Polly and me in New Chelsea, then spend the night at Nick's apartment.'

'Why don't you stay with me?' he asked.

Lily shook her head.

'Mum's expecting me, Dad. Next time.'

She looked around. 'Where did Uncle Adrian go?'

Jason looked up from his cigar.

'Conference call . . . Babylon,' he murmured.

Polly walked towards them, pulling her sleek, long blonde hair back into a ponytail.

'Hi, sweetheart.' Jason smiled. Polly stowed her mobile in her bag, then leaned over to Jason and gave him a hug. Jason trusted Polly. She was straightforward. Down to earth. No guile. Rare today. She'd been a good friend to Lily. The best.

'Keeping Lily in check, Polly?' Jason raised his eyebrows.

'I try.' Polly smiled back at Jason. 'She's a chip off the old block, Mr D.'

Alex caught sight of them and made his way through the cigar smoke.

Jason frowned. 'Still an item?' he asked.

'Alex wants to get engaged when I turn eighteen.'

'I hope you know what you're doing,' Jason muttered. 'God knows I didn't at that age.'

'You've known him since he was eight weeks old, Mr D.' Polly smiled brilliantly at him.

'Precisely.' Jason raised his eyebrows.

'I always know what I'm doing, Mr D.'

'He doing all right? He looked like hell at the funeral.' Polly took Jason's hand.

'Look, Mr D. I know he's really mad with you for cutting Nick off. But you're like the only real dad he's ever had. Don't be too hard on him.'

Jason turned to watch the tall, lean twenty-year-old striding towards them in his black funeral suit, laptop slung over his shoulder, carrying five cans of Coke in his two hands.

'I'll try not to beat myself up over it,' Jason said, wryly.

Alex finally arrived at their table.

Jason watched as Alex stowed the five cans of Coke deep in his satchel.

'Testing for fluoride?' Jason said, sceptically. He winked at Polly, then firmly removed the cans from Alex's grasp and placed them on the granite counter. '*I'm* paying for those. Investigative journalism not paying so well?'

Alex glowered at him, then sat down morosely in the chair next to Polly.

Jason puffed on his cigar, then looked up to see Alex still glaring at him.

'Look, Alex.' He stubbed out his cigar in the ashtray. 'Nick's dead. I should have been there for him. I wasn't. You going to hold it against me the rest of my life?'

'Maybe.' Alex scowled at him darkly.

'Have it your way.' Jason shrugged.

'Alex has been investigating something, Mr D,' Polly said, trying desperately to ease the tension. 'Something *big*.'

Jason yawned.

Lily glared at Jason. Polly nudged Alex. 'Alex . . .'

'The global elite – Bilderberg, the Feds, World Bank, UN – they're engineering world economic collapse. The fall of 2008 will look like a walk in the park compared to what's coming up,' Alex mumbled.

'Famine, rolling blackouts, looting, rioting – Katrina back in '05 is nothing compared to what's coming,' he added, ominously.

'Okay, Alex,' Jason steeled himself, 'tell me what's coming.'

Alex took back a can of Coke, flayed open the top, and took a long slug. 'Martial law, that's what. That's how it's all going to start. Military policing our streets, curfews, they'll just pick you up and put you in prison.'

Alex was picking up steam.

'If people only knew the truth.'

Jason rolled his eyes.

'It's not the *truth*, Alex. People already *know* the truth. I'm the media. That's my job: to *inform* people of the truth. Don't you think if there were any accuracy in anything you're saying that at least one out of ten thousand of our correspondents would have got hold of this?' He groaned in exasperation.

'When everything's already in chaos,' Alex continued, rashly, 'they'll stage a false-flag operation. A secret operation when government forces pretend to be an enemy while attacking their own forces or people.'

Jason caught sight of Adrian winding his way through the granite and glass-top tables towards them.

'I know what false flag means, Alex Lane-Fox,' he said, icily.

306

'You know your problem, Uncle Jason?'

Jason stared at him darkly, then moved his head an inch away from Alex's.

'No, Alex. Why don't *you* tell me my problem, Alex?'

Lily and Polly exchanged an uneasy look.

'*Your* problem, Uncle Jas,' Alex continued, recklessly, 'is that you're a puppet of the New World Order.'

Lily rolled her eyes in despair.

'And *your* problem, Alex Lane-Fox is . . .'

Lily glared pointedly at Jason. He bit his tongue just as the waiter returned with his dram of Lagavulin.

'Look, Alex . . .' Jason sighed, his expression softened. He put a hand on Alex's arm. 'No matter how much you investigate a shadow government, nothing's going to bring your mother back, son.'

He picked up the glass, savouring the intense, peaty smoky bouquet from the thirty-year-old single malt whisky.

'Produced on the island of Islay, Lily.' He sipped it slowly. 'Queen of the Hebrides.'

'Did I hear "false flag", Alex?' Adrian said, grinning.

Jason signalled to the waiter, who opened a mahogany box of the hotel's finest cigars and presented it to Adrian.

'In the 1960s, the Joint Chiefs of Staff signed off on a plan codenamed Operation Northwoods,' Adrian said, sitting down in between Alex and Jason. 'A plan to blow up American aeroplanes using an elaborate plan involving the switching of aeroplanes, and to commit a wave of violent terrorist acts on American soil – Washington DC and Miami – then to blame it on the Cubans to justify an invasion of Cuba.'

Adrian hesitated, his fingers skimming over the cigars, then selected a pre-Castro Havana. 'Northwoods never happened.' The waiter produced a guillotine and cut into the cap of the cigar. 'Kennedy refused to implement the Pentagon plans.'

Adrian paused for effect and placed the cigar in his mouth. The waiter lit it and Adrian puffed on the cigar.

'But he *could* have.'

Alex glared at Jason in triumph. Jason glared back.

'Uncle Ade – I mean, *Mr President*,' Alex pulled his chair nearer to Adrian's. 'To consolidate power into their hands, the global elite needs to stage a false-flag incident: either a nuclear incident in LA, Chicago, or the East Coast, or a weaponized bio-terror agent released from their own laboratories – say smallpox, Ebola, weaponized Avian flu – to gain control of the mass population.'

Alex pulled out his laptop and set it on the glass-top table in front of Adrian.

His fingers flew over the keys.

'Take the case of a false-flag bio-terror attack. Avian flu. Millions of deaths occur. People are so demoralized they cry out to the shadow government to save them.' Alex paused dramatically. 'Then it starts – the real introduction of martial law. A one-world currency. Bodies piling up, mandatory vaccinations.' Alex's voice rose in intensity. 'Look at the past. By 2009, thirty-two states had passed laws that made resisting inoculation once it's ordered by the governor a felony; unlimited quarantine mandated for any who resist.'

Adrian took a long draw of the cigar, then said: 'Vaccinations contain the RFID chip. People are frantic, they willingly accept it.' Adrian looked around at the table. 'They become legitimate trackable property of this "New World Order". All by their own volition.'

Lily stared at Adrian, appalled.

'You can't be saying the government *is* in the know. *You're* not in the know, Uncle Ade.'

Adrian smiled. 'Alex's premise is that the government is merely a pawn for the system. Its strings are being pulled covertly by a shadow government. Bankers. Oil barons. The military industrialist complex. According to this same premise, the dissenters – whoever refuses vaccination – are rounded up by military police into FEMA concentration camps as threats to the health of the community. Quarantined.'

Adrian looked around the table, his expression grave. 'It's completely plausible. With millions of people dead, martial law declared, complete control of news media, no one will care.'

'Exactly!' Alex said. 'By 2008, there were over six hundred FEMA concentration camps in the USA,' he declared, gaining steam. 'Multiple sources confirming rumours of prisoner boxcars from China: forty-foot cargo containers, with shackles and a modern guillotine at the head of each one. No windows. Guillotines in Georgia. In Texas. Unsubstantiated rumours that they were ordered under secret contract through a congressman in the pay of the elite who met with officials in China.'

Jason held up his hands. 'Unsubstantiated rumours! Boxcars! guillotines!'

He slammed the Lagavulin down on the countertop. 'Alex Lane-Fox. This takes the cake *even* for you. Concentration camps. Rubbish! *Absolute* drivel! Conspiracy theorists run amok!'

He looked at Alex in disbelief.

'And *who* do the global elite intend to put in these boxcars? Little Aunt Betty from Georgia and her peach pie?' Jason, in spite of himself, looked deeply into his whisky and hid a smile, though he could feel Lily glaring daggers at him.

'Constitutionalists,' Alex declared, recklessly. 'Patriots, gun owners, who refuse to relinquish their Second Amendment rights; anyone who rejects the concept of world government control.'

He looked at Polly.

'And Christians.' He winced, then glared deliberately at Jason. 'Of course, *you* don't have to worry about *that*.'

He scrabbled in his satchel, then put a thin stack of paper bearing the FBI seal down on the table.

'Sorry, Pol. There goes you and your dad. Read this. Project Megiddo: FBI strategic assessment of potential for domestic terrorism in the USA at the turn of the millennium. Sent to twenty-thousand police chiefs. Inconceivable, but true.'

Polly picked the papers up and studied the first page as Alex got out a second file.

'Second phase. The government issues Executive Order 10990 allowing them to take over all modes of transportation and control of highways and seaports. Executive Order 10995: they seize and control the communication media. Executive Order 10998: they take over all food supplies and resources, public and private, *including* farms and equipment. Look, Uncle Jas.'

He pushed the top document across the table.

'It's all here. In black and white. Executive Order 11000 allows the government to mobilize American civilians into work brigades under government supervision; even allows the government to split up families if they believe it necessary.'

Alex rifled through the papers.

'Order 11001: the government takes over all health, education and welfare functions. Order 11002: a national registration of all persons. Order 11003: the government takes over all airports and aircraft.'

Jason turned to Adrian.

'Look, in the USA, the executive orders exist,' Adrian said, matter of factly. 'They have their equivalents in Europe and the UK. Think about the strategy. The international banking cartel achieves its objectives: eliminate all opposition: reduce,

310

then chip the population; unimpeded survelliance and control; further centralization of their financial pyramid scheme of money as debt. A complete destruction of the US constitution.'

Alex looked triumphantly at Adrian.

'That's *exactly* right, Mr President.'

Adrian looked at Alex, gently.

'This stuff's been doing the circuit for decades, Alex,' he said in a fatherly tone. 'It's disinformation, son. You and a million others sucked in to a deliberate accumulation of disinformation. Security agencies have investigated all of these issues since the 1950s. Majestic Twelve. James Forrestal's supposed suicide. JKF conspiracy theories. Underground bases. Roswell. Area 51. 9/11 conspiracy theories. HAARP. Chemtrails. Black helicopters . . . Martial law. It's all blatant disinformation, Alex. The fodder of Hollywood screenwriters and B-grade graphic novels. I'm sorry, pal. Really. Take it from one who's in the know. There's patently *nothing* there.'

A deep red flush spread from Alex's face down his neck.

'The executive orders?' he muttered.

'They're there as a last resort. A protection for the American people. The same in Europe. They'll never be used, Alex. There will be no martial law. Trust me.'

Shame-faced, Alex closed his laptop.

'He's going to be a great journalist, Jas.' Adrian winked at Alex. 'I'd snap him up and start him in the Vox newsroom if I were you.'

'But you *have* heard of the Mark of the Beast, Mr President,' Polly said, softly.

Adrian looked at her strangely.

'*And he causeth all, both small and great, rich and poor, free and bond, to receive a mark in their right hand, or in their foreheads: and that no man might buy or sell, save he*

311

that had the mark, or the name of the beast, or the number of his name,' she quoted, her voice very soft but like steel.

Jason, Alex, and Lily all gazed in amazement at the normally softly spoken Polly.

'Here is wisdom. Let him that hath understanding count the number of the beast: for it is the number of a man; and his number is six hundred threescore and six.'

'Polly!' Alex frowned at her.

'The Book of Revelation, chapter 13,' Polly said, an icy note in her voice that Jason had never heard before. Adrian loosened his collar.

'And in the latter time of this kingdom,' Polly continued, *'a king shall arise, having fierce features, who understands sinister schemes. He shall even rise against the Prince of princes.'*

Six Secret Service men moved out from the shadows of the garden room and surrounded Adrian.

'Your car is here, Mr President, sir.'

Adrian stood up, strangely pale.

Polly continued, her ethereal features set.

'He will be broken, though not by any human power.'

'You okay, pal?' Jason frowned. Adrian stood ashen, still staring down at Polly.

'Now, Lily,' he said, turned to Lily and kissed her perfunctorily on both cheeks. 'Visit me. You promised.' Lily nodded.

Adrian looked at Polly, who was looking back at him unsmiling. 'And bring Polly,' he added, softly.

Jason's mobile rang. He picked it up, saw Julia's number, then put it back down. Then with a sigh, he picked it up again.

'Yes, this is Jason. Hang on, Julia. Adrian's just leaving.'

He handed the phone to Lily.

'Find out what your mother wants,' he growled.

Jason clasped Adrian's hand.

'See you back in New York, pal.'

'Yes, Mom,' Lily answered. 'Alex'll drop us at New Chelsea before going back to Nick's. Okay. He won't like it. But I'll tell him.'

Lily held out the phone to Jason as Adrian and his entourage walked towards the door.

'She says it's urgent. She won't speak to anyone but you.'

'Oh, so she gave me the silent treatment for two years during the divorce proceedings, but *now* she'll speak to me?'

Jason took the phone back from Lily.

'Yes. It's me, Julia,' he snapped. 'What is it?'

'Impossible! Run that by me again.'

'From France?' He frowned. 'He sent you something from France? You're sure you've got your facts straight?'

Adrian turned at the glass and gold doors and waved. Then disappeared into the Lanesborough.

'Not tonight.' Jason looked at his watch. 'I've got to be somewhere in half an hour. Can't you drop it off at the house?'

Lily glared at him. Jason sighed.

'Yes. Yes, *all right*. I know it's late. Look, I'm going to the country estate – to pay my respects to Father tomorrow morning before I fly. Pick me up at 9 a.m. At Mother's. Belgrave Square. I've got to fly out before noon so *don't* be late.'

He flipped the phone shut and stared silently up at the roof, then looked at Lily strangely.

'It seems there was a note,' he said. 'With information for me.'

He stood up as the waiter put his coat over his shoulders.

'From Nick.'

Adrian walked out of the glass and gold doors of the Lanesborough and towards the Mercedes.

'She wears the Seal,' he said. Perspiration flowed from his forehead. He wiped his brow with a handkerchief, as the constriction across his throat eased.

'It is strong on her. The power of the Nazarene.' He slowly rebuttoned his collar.

'Get me a strategic assessment from Guber. Internment camps. Termination gas chambers in the UK. FEMA in the US. As soon as martial law is declared the first lists will be activated.'

'And the girl?'

'Red or Blue?'

Adrian smiled slowly.

'Black. The Black List.'

CHAPTER TWENTY-SEVEN

Cryptic

Jason sat at the scratched melamine table, two coffee cups already stacked in front of him. He remembered Dylan Weaver from the summers at Cape Cod. Pragmatic. Hard-nosed. A geek. Dylan Weaver had been insistent they meet. But why?

He looked at his watch, then peered out of the window through the drizzle to the wall across the street plastered with seedy posters.

'I hate this weather.'

A young pert Cockney waitress, her red leather miniskirt hiding little, stood over him with a notepad, chewing gum.

'So, mister?'

'I'm waiting for someone.'

She laughed and winked knowingly.

'Sure you are, mister. You're *all* waiting for someone.'

Jason looked at his watch again, then glared up at her.

'Get me another coffee.'

'Not very friendly, are you?'

She looked down at him for a moment.

'You on TV? You remind me of someone.' Jason shook

his head and watched her walk away without taking the dirty cups. He coughed. She turned.

He pointed to the cups. She chewed her gum loudly and leaned over him.

'You ask for a lot mister, don't you? Bleedin' Americans.'

The dilapidated door creaked open and Dylan Weaver, dishevelled and unshaved, walked in, drenched. He had changed out of his black suit, but kept the ill-fitting yellow anorak which scarely covered his hung belly.

'De Vere?'

Jason nodded. Weaver sat down heavily on the frail wooden chair and leaned over the table, his pasty features uncomfortably close to Jason's, breathing heavily.

Jason held out his hand. Weaver ignored it. He looked Jason up and down impassively.

'I thought brothers were supposed to look out for each other.' Weaver took out a well-used laptop from under the yellow anorak, pried open the lid with plump grimy fingers and booted it up.

He looked furtively around.

'They're after me. I can't stay long.'

'Who? *Who* is after you?' Jason asked.

Weaver hesitated. 'I don't know. I'm being followed.'

'What did Nick tell you?'

'That's the point. He didn't tell me anything.'

'Look, pal,' Jason said, 'If you're here to waste my time.'

Weaver stared at Jason grimly.

'De Vere, if it was up to me, I'd never see you again. This is the thing. Nick emailed me the night he died. He was trying to send me something – a *file*. Something he'd filmed. Lily told me he'd left you a message on your answering machine. The same night he died. I need to know – did he say anything about what he filmed?'

Jason sighed.

'Look, Weaver, my brother's dead. No, he didn't tell me anything – just some drug-induced ramble about the Ark of the Covenant, but he was scared. Really scared. It sounded like one of his trips.'

Weaver fished a hard drive out of his rucksack and placed it on the table.

'Well, then I can't help you.'

Jason frowned. 'But the file he sent you?'

'It's blank. I've applied the public key. I know Nick's private key – it should be a cinch, but it's not reading. I've gone through ten million combinations. It's an encryption I've never seen before. A deadlock.'

'You're *sure*?'

'It's my work, De Vere. Clients pay me lots of money to be sure.'

'There has to be something on there. He obviously figured you'd break the code.'

'Look,' Weaver said, packing up, 'whatever Nick filmed – it's gone. There's nothing. There's some high-powered intelligence encryption involved: some agency has tracked his email to my address, used a covert action program, an encryption application with trapdoors, and encrypted Nick's email. This is high-flyer intelligence stuff, De Vere. These hackers kill people.'

He stood up and walked towards the door.

'And they're tracking me. I just needed to know what you knew. Which is nothing.'

'Weaver, you can't just leave it there.'

Dylan Weaver talked quietly without turning.

'There're some high-flying hackers on our payroll in China. Should have been put away years ago but they feed us the information we need. I'll see what they have to say.'

'We're not finished,' Jason said, getting up.

'Time's up, De Vere. I'll be in touch.' Dylan disappeared into the rain onto Shaftesbury Avenue. The door slammed hard behind him.

Alex parked Polly's vintage Mini Cooper in the underground parking space. He eased his lanky frame out of the car and looked over to the reserved sign that read 'NDV'. He sighed, then grabbed his satchel, slammed the car door and walked towards the express lift.

A black Range Rover accelerated out of nowhere and shot straight past him.

'Watch where you're going!' Alex shouted after the fast-disappearing vehicle. He dusted himself off. 'Idiot,' he muttered, walking towards the lift.

A minute later he stepped out into the sky lobby of the London apartment block.

'Hey, Harry,' he greeted the balding, middle-aged concierge.

'You just missed them, mate.' Harry gestured to the lift.

Alex frowned.

'Missed who?'

'Your college mates. Hadn't seen you for months. They passed on their condolences for Nick.'

'You let them in?'

'Nah. Didn't need to. They had their own key, mate. They stayed about half an hour then got tired of waiting.' He looked down at his watch. 'They left five minutes ago.'

'No message?'

Harry shook his head. Alex stared at the concierge, perplexed. He got in the penthouse elevator. A minute later he exited into the lobby of the huge hedonistic bubble that was Nick's London penthouse. The lights switched on automatically. As did the music. He walked straight out from the elevator onto the wrap-around terrace, glancing out at the London Eye and Canary Wharf glistening through the

318

glass walls and continued around past the hot tub into Nick's bedroom.

He stopped in mid-stride. The sleek black drawers of Nick's dressing room had been ripped from the wall, his vast collection of Levi's and shirts strewn across the room. Alex walked out into the open-plan living area, his heart beating violently in his chest.

He stared at the image in the enormous mirror that covered the entire living room wall.

The Chinese lacquered bar had been overturned and the padded, cobalt leather wall of the dining room had been slashed to ribbons. Every drawer had been ripped open.

The penthouse looked like a tornado had been through it.

Alex looked over to the digitally secured safe, normally concealed under Nick's numbered print of Edvard Munch's *Vampire*. The canvas had been torn from the wall and the steel door of the safe was still swinging open.

The safe was empty.

Alex reached for the phone.

'Damn!' Jason muttered, looking down at his watch for the third time in five minutes. He should have got a cab. His schedule was tight and Julia was late. His jaw tightened. 'As usual.'

A loud, incessant hooting broke the silence of the tranquil Knightsbridge neighbourhood. Jason looked out of the drawing room's huge Georgian window.

It was Julia all right. She was sitting smugly in the driving seat of the pert Jaguar, parked on the kerb, wearing a scarf and dark glasses. Jason walked out through the hallway, slammed the oak doors and walked past the gate over to where Julia was parked. He leant over the passenger door and glared at her.

'It's Belgrave Square, not New Chelsea,' he hissed. 'You don't have to wake the whole neighbourhood.' His eyes narrowed at Julia's gloved hand tapping impatiently on the hooter. He glared again and with bad grace opened the low door and jammed his six-foot frame with difficulty in the passenger seat.

'Couldn't you have found something more functional?' he said. 'And you're *late*.'

Julia's mouth tightened in a thin line. She moved the dark glasses onto the bridge of her nose with a sharp movement.

'If you don't like it, get a taxi.'

She snapped her glasses back. Jason scowled, fumbling clumsily with the safety belt. Julia turned the key in the ignition and roared away from the kerb, Jason still stuck with the seatbelt behind his ears as the white Jaguar car sped through the centre of London and then out towards the suburbs.

Jason clutched his bare head, the winter winds freezing with the crosswind. Julia, plus scarf, was windproof.

'It's late December, for god's sake! Why have you got the roof down?'

Julia turned sharp left off the main highway onto a country lane, swerving neatly around a slow-moving lorry.

'Who chooses your barber nowadays?' she said. 'Aunt Rosemary?'

Jason's face was like thunder.

'I *presume* I was the ruthless media tycoon riding rough-shod over all that is pure and righteous in your last book?' he said. Julia's chin set. Irritated. They narrowly missed an oncoming car in the narrow country road.

'God, Julia!' he spluttered. 'What are you trying to do – kill me?'

Julia screeched around the bend, with Jason clinging to

320

the dashboard as they flew past rambling-rose-covered thatched houses.

'If you'd read the book, you would have known I'd already killed you off – violently: a car bomb. It was very therapeutic – saved me a fortune on psychiatrist's fees.'

She turned another sharp left and screeched to a halt outside a small English country church surrounded by fields of grazing sheep.

Julia undid her scarf. Her gleaming blonde hair fell to her shoulders. She turned to Jason.

'I spent the night in a South Bank police station with Alex, if you must know. I'm exhausted. Nick's penthouse was ransacked.'

Ransacked?' Jason looked at her sceptically. 'Was that Alex's definition, or the police's?' he said, sarcastically.

'Both, actually,' she said, frostily.

'How do *you* know Nick's apartment was ransacked?'

She opened the car door, climbed out gracefully and glared at Jason from over the white Chanel sunglasses that matched her white jeans and leather jacket.

'Because I was there with the police and Alex at one in the morning. That's how, Jason.'

She slammed the car door.

'Probably some of his low-life friends,' Jason mumbled, 'looking for cocaine.'

His mouth tightened. He seemed to be having as much trouble getting the seatbelt off as he'd had getting it on.

'You never gave Nicky *any* credit, did you Jason? Nothing at all. You let him go to his grave without talking to him. How *could* you?'

Julia leant over and picked up a bunch of pale pink tulips out of the boot.

'*Now* I get it,' Jason scowled. 'You've brought me all the

way out to my father's grave for a lecture on what a cold heartless swine I am for not forgiving Nick.'

The seatbelt jammed in the door.

Julia started to walk up the winding churchyard path.

'You cut him off, Jason,' she declared. 'You didn't talk to him from that day to this.'

Jason finally managed to get out and strode after her, brushing his hair back in a vain attempt at style.

'He was a brilliant archaeologist,' he shouted after her. 'He threw his whole career away on heroin . . . cocaine . . . whatever it was . . . *and* disgraced the family name. Father *never* got over it.'

A very English vicar appeared from behind a gravestone. He regarded the shouting Jason with obvious disapproval.

'Good morning,' he said.

Jason nodded sheepishly and continued striding after Julia.

Panting, he caught up with her in a secluded corner of the churchyard where she stood at a large, beautifully kept mausoleum. The vicar watched them suspiciously from the path.

Julia knelt and placed the tulips on the grave. 'What do you think?' she hissed. 'Do you actually think I would *choose* to be on my own with you?'

Jason glared at her. 'Living on your own is making you *paranoid*.' He grasped her arm. 'And take those damn glasses off.'

'I am *not* living on my own,' Julia seethed. 'And *don't* you call me paranoid. You always were a pompous ass. Look what you did to Nick.'

Jason rolled his eyes and pointed to James's grave.

'Ssssh – *not* at my father's grave . . . and you leave my brother out of this.'

Julia drew herself up to her full five feet four. Seething,

322

she took off her glasses to reveal tear-stained, red eyes smudged with mascara from crying.

'Your brother – *your* brother. And how much time did you spend with him in the past seven years, Jason De Vere? In between your mergers, your digital platforms, and launching your damn satellites?'

The vicar looked at them disapprovingly again.

'Nick was trying to *tell* you something. Don't ask me why he chose you. But he did. He thought your dad was killed. It sounded like he was in some kind of trouble.'

Jason lowered his voice ominously.

'This isn't one of your books, dammit, Julia. People don't just *kill* people.'

'Lily said he left a cryptic message on your answering machine.'

'He called me, that's all. Typical Nick subterfuge. Sounded like he was on a trip. Now please give me my note and some privacy.'

Julia glared at him, then unclasped her white leather handbag.

'It was mailed from France the night he died.'

She held out the distinctive brown linen envelope.

'And actually the note is addressed to *me*,' she said.

Jason frowned. He took the envelope out of her hands and stared at the Mont St Michel coat of arms, perplexed. Slowly he turned it over.

'It's from Mont St Michel.'

'Of course it's from Mont St Michel,' Julia snapped. 'He spent the day with Adrian.'

'No, he didn't!' Jason declared. Furious.

'What do you mean, he didn't? He phoned me when he was just 40 miles away from the Abbey. The morning he died.'

'What time did Nick phone you, Julia?' Jason asked coldly.

323

'Around 10, 10.30, my time. That made it, say, 11.30 his time.'

'You're mistaken.' Jason turned the envelope over once more.

'*Really?*' Julia put one hand on her hip, her blood boiling. 'Well, as it so happens, I'm *not* mistaken, Jason De Vere.' She groped in her bag for her phone, flipped it open and scrolled down. Seething, she passed her phone to Jason.

'Right there. On the EU GPS satellite reading. Call received from 40 miles from Mont St Michel – 10.37 exactly. Caller ID – Nicholas De Vere.'

'Well he must have changed his mind.' Jason conceded grudgingly. 'Adrian said he phoned but he'd been held up. He never arrived at Mont St Michel.'

'Oh, come on, Jason. He was only 40 miles away when he phoned me. He was headed straight there.'

'*You* know Nick,' Jason shrugged.

'Yes, I *do* know Nick,' she snapped. 'He was headed straight there. If he wasn't there, how did he get the envelope?'

Jason looked down at the Mont St Michel crest.

'I suppose he carried them around in his satchel?' she said sarcastically.

'What else did he say?'

Julia raised her hands.

'He was a bit . . .' She frowned. 'I don't know. Serious. Very serious. He was asking for information. Uncle Lawrence's birth certificate. The names of who's on your Vox board.'

'The Vox *board*?' Jason stared at her, incredulous. 'Oh god, Julia. Nick never looked at a financial in his life. And he wanted a list of my *board*? He had to be on one of his trips.'

'Fine.' Julia raised her hands. 'Have it your way. There's his note. Read it for yourself. And I want it back.'

Jason turned his back on Julia, took the note from the envelope and scanned it for a few minutes.

'He says they gave him Aids,' he muttered. 'He said the same thing on my answering machine.' His voice softened. 'Look, Julia, I know how close you were,' he said, clumsily, passing her back the note.

He took out the photograph.

Julia pointed at Julius De Vere. 'I don't recognize anyone except your grandad and Uncle Xavier.'

Jason's earpiece lit up. 'Yes, Purvis,' he said.

He turned. A chauffeur walked up the path towards him, carrying a white wreath. Jason took the wreath and placed it on James's grave.

'Okay, I'm on my way. Tell Mac to fire it up.'

He looked at his watch and began walking back through the gravestones.

'Tell Levine to make sure he has my briefcase. And two reservations for the Rose Bar. Make sure you get the reservations. It'll be after 9 p.m.'

He clicked off his phone and walked to the Bentley that was parked directly in front of Julia's Jaguar. The chauffeur opened the back door for him.

Jason hesitated. He turned, and waved the envelope at the slight figure in white who was gazing after him. He gave an awkward smile.

'Thanks.'

CHAPTER TWENTY-EIGHT

The Godfather

29 December 2021

Jason stood under the custom-made Venetian glass chandelier in the lobby of the luxury New York hotel. The emotional exhaustion of the past week combined with his current jet lag was beginning to take its toll. He ran his fingers through his hair and looked around at the enormous hand-carved Italian fireplace and roaring fire. The plush red velvet curtains. The epic canvases. The matador's jacket.

Old World grandeur merged with what Nick would no doubt have described as modern aesthetic.

One of the hotel's three penthouses had been Nick's home from home whenever he was in New York. He had called it 'High Bohemia', and loved it.

Jason stood, frozen. Everything, literally everything, suddenly reminded him of Nick.

He checked his watch: 9.30 p.m. precisely. Xavier Chessler would be waiting for him in the Rose Bar. He was a meticulous time keeper and ran his personal life as rigorously as he ran his banks.

Jason stepped into the elevator, then out into the soaring space.

There, seated against the green velvet walls, directly under a Warhol canvas, was Xavier Chessler. Jason sank into a plush velvet antique chair directly opposite him.

He studied his godfather.

Age had treated Xavier Chessler kindly. His mane of thick straight silver hair framed his distinguished features. Xavier Chessler had just turned eighty-four and looked twenty years younger – although Jason did harbour a secret suspicion that thanks to the urging of his ex-fashionista and flamboyant wife, Marina, Botox may have had something to do with the youthful-looking semi-retired investment banker.

Xavier sipped delicately at a cocktail.

Odd. Jason raised his eyebrows deliberately at the elegant old man. His godfather was fastidious about his nutritional habits and rarely touched alcohol.

Chessler looked up at Jason roguishly from under his eyebrows.

'Merely pineapple spiked with ginger and shaken with mint, lemon and a dash of angostura bitters.' Chessler shook his head at Jason. 'Most refreshing, in fact. Though I suppose you'll be wanting the Lagavulin.'

'Unusual for New York.'

'This is quite the place, young Jason.'

He motioned to the chic young crowd that was gathered around the bar. Celebrities. Young investment bankers. The well heeled.

'Nick always felt at home here.'

Chessler motioned to the nearest waitress.

'The Lagavulin.' He pointed at the menu. 'And the same as before.' The waitress left. 'Nick and I celebrated Marina's last birthday here,' Chessler said. 'You were in Beijing. Adrian and your mother paid for him to summer here.'

327

'I didn't know he was here in July.' Jason hesitated. 'I should have taken his calls, Xavier.'

'No time for recriminations, my boy. Life's far too short for regret. Especially when you reach my age.'

The waitress returned with the whisky and a second cocktail.

'You said Nick sent you a note.'

Jason stared into the glass.

'Not really a note. Well, put it this way: he sent Julia the note; he sent me a photograph.'

Jason took the Mont St Michel envelope from his jacket pocket and passed it over the table to Xavier.

'You're in it.'

Chessler removed a pair of silver-rimmed glasses from his spectacle case, placed them over his nose, and studied the photograph.

He looked up at Jason.

'Well . . .' He frowned. 'Of course, I recognize your grandfather. And Piers Aspinall. Ex-Director of MI6. He died last year. Poor fellow had Parkinson's, if I recall.'

He studied the photograph more intently.

'It's old. Very old. Both your father and I must have been in our early forties,' he sighed. 'Ah, the ravages of time, Jason.'

'You've no idea who the other men are?' Jason asked.

Chessler shook his head.

'Look, dear boy, your father and I were on so many boards together. Charitable. Non-charitable. I'm a non-executive director on twenty-six as we speak. I'm sorry, Jason, but I really can't place these men.'

'There's a name,' Jason gestured to the photograph, 'in Dad's handwriting. On the back.'

Chessler turned the photograph over.

'Aveline,' he murmured. 'Yes, that's your father's writing

328

all right. I'd recognize it anywhere. I'll tell you what, Jason. Seeing as it's important to you, and apparently was to your father, if you don't mind my keeping this, I'll do a little investigation of my own.'

'Of course,' said Jason. 'I'd really appreciate it.'

'You said there was a note?'

'To Julia. It was cryptic. Rambling. Typical Nick. I only took the photograph. I'll tell you what *is* strange though.'

Jason pointed to the envelope.

'Mont St Michel's crest. But Adrian said Nick wasn't at Mont St Michel the day he died.' He shrugged.

'These things seem confusing, dear boy.' Chessler removed his glasses, folded them, and placed them back in the spectacle case.

'We've all been shaken by Nick's death.' He tucked the case back in his jacket pocket. 'But I'm sure there's a quite straightforward explanation.'

Jason shrugged. 'I guess we'll never know.'

He raised his glass and looked again around the eclectic candlelit space.

'A toast to Nick.'

Xavier Chessler raised his cocktail glass.

'To Nick. Brilliant archaeologist. Loyal son.'

'And brother.' Jason finished his whisky. He frowned.

'Xavier, listen. I've got a 7 a.m. meeting tomorrow. One of Vox's hedge funds. Can we catch up over lunch? Say Sunday?'

Chessler clasped Jason's shoulder.

'Of course, dear boy. Marina and I are weekending at the Hamptons. Spend the weekend. You know Marina's dying to catch up on all the New York media intrigue. Retirement's driving her crazy. Your presence will be a godsend.'

Jason stood up.

329

'I'll fly down late Friday.'

'You're my only godson, Jason. Three daughters. No sons. You've always been like my own.' He looked Jason in the eye. 'You know there is nothing, I mean *nothing*, that I wouldn't do for you.'

'I know that, Uncle Xavier.' Jason leant down and embraced the old man.

Xavier Chessler watched as Jason walked through the bar.

Jason turned at the door and waved.

Xavier smiled in affection. He placed the photograph carefully in his inner jacket pocket, then clasped his left wrist in agony. He undid his cufflink and stared down in horror at the 'Warlock's Mark'. It was literally smouldering on his skin.

Julius De Vere was torturing him from the grave. From hell itself. He was sure.

He reached for his phone, scrolled down. And dialled.

'I think we may have a problem.' He smiled at the waitress. 'Just the check, please.'

He lowered his voice. 'No, nothing I can't control. I just wanted you to be aware. Yes. It seems Nicholas sent a note. Before he died. Addressed on a Mont St Michel envelope. Yes. I have it.

'Of *course* I'll dispose of the evidence. He's coming to the Hamptons for the weekend. I'll find out what he knows. Keep an eye on him. Inform me via our London connection the minute that meddlesome IT vermin, Weaver, is taken care of.'

He clicked off the phone and stared grimly ahead.

His godson would be a formidable adversary if his suspicions were finally aroused. But, properly handled, that shouldn't be for some time.

Jason De Vere's extermination after the opening of the

Seventh Seal would be imperative. Until then, he would serve the Brotherhood's purpose.

I t was bucketing.

Dylan Weaver stood out of sight from the road, in the doorway of Iceland. He glanced down at his watch, uneasy, then back through the glass doors of the frozen food supermarket chain before venturing out into the almost deserted High Street.

A hundred yards up the road, he could still make out the two black Range Rovers that had been parked outside his second-floor flat since eleven this morning.

He pulled the yellow anorak over his head and emptied the contents of a half-finished packet of crisps into his mouth.

With one last furtive look towards his flat in the converted piano factory, he walked swiftly in the direction of Kentish Town Tube station. He would catch the Northern Line to King's Cross, and the Circle Line to Paddington just in time to catch the last Express to Heathrow.

He grasped the dog-eared aeroplane ticket for what must have been the fifth time in the last hour with sweaty fingers. The high-flying intelligence hackers in Hangzhou had received the hard drive over an hour ago.

He would catch the Virgin Atlantic airbus to Shanghai from Terminal 3 at lunchtime tomorrow. He would be safely in Pudong airport by nightfall.

CHAPTER TWENTY-NINE

Apocalypse

M ichael stood outside Gabriel's chamber watching Gabriel from the doorway.

'Your soul is prepared?' he asked.

'The dreamings.' Gabriel looked up at Michael, worn, his features etched with grief. 'Kingdoms rising ... falling ... the race of men ... Judgement ... the Revelation of the Apocalypse of Saint John. I see the things that are about to be visited upon the world of the race of men first-hand ... As Revelator.' Gabriel trembled. 'As seer.'

Michael looked at Gabriel, without speaking.

'There before me was a Pale Horse.' Gabriel shuddered. 'Its rider was named Death.' He walked over to the terrace and gazed out at the Rubied Door. 'Sword ... famine ... pestilence,' he whispered. 'Hail and fire mingled with blood.' He bowed his head. 'Would that it had never come to this.'

'He has given them opportunity after opportunity to repent.' Michael's voice shook with emotion. 'They choose to follow Lucifer. They reject Christos. They reject the great sacrifice. He has waited *aeons*, Gabriel, restraining the Judgements.'

Michael walked over to Gabriel.

'Yet still he loves them,' Gabriel said, softly.

'His Judgements can be held back no more.' Michael placed his hand on his sword. 'The scales of iniquity in the world of the race of men are full. Our brother Lucifer has ravaged their souls. Judgement has to take its course.'

'Yet still he *loves* them, Michael.' Gabriel swung round to face Michael, his features ravaged with grief. 'Not as we, the angelic. He was born one of them. Walked as one of them.' Gabriel's voice rose in intensity. '*Lived* as one of them.'

'Died as one of them.' A voice came from behind them.

The brothers turned to find Jether outside the chamber.

'He is touched with the feeling of their infirmities, with their weaknesses.' Jether smiled gently. 'He understands all the besetting things that ravage their souls.'

Gabriel stared at Jether. Ashen. 'I have seen things too terrible to utter, Jether. The Seven Seals will be opened. The riders . . .'

'Beloved Revelator.' Jether closed his eyes. 'You speak truly. You have journeyed many nights as a seer. The Four Horsemen of the Apocalypse will soon ride the West Winds of the race of men to unleash their furies.'

'The race of men, their world crumbles.' Gabriel bowed his head.

Jether walked over to him.

'It is a strange thing, Gabriel.' Jether laid his hand on Gabriel's arm. 'I have lived among them as one of the angelic unawares for more than four decades. I have seen evil and wickedness among the race of men that is unimaginable.' Jether closed his eyes. 'And untenable,' he said softly. 'Rapes. Abortion. Cold-blooded murders. The most iniquitous of deeds.'

He opened his eyes.

'And yet . . .' A look of wonder crossed Jether's wizened features. 'And yet, I have seen a love in the world of the race of men that defies even our angelic comprehension.' Jether paused, deeply moved.

'I have seen a mother sacrifice her life to save her child. I have seen grown men in war lay down their lives for their brothers. I have seen first-hand the most base and selfish of the ways of the race of men. And yet' – Jether raised his tear-stained face to Michael in wonder – 'I have seen . . . I have seen their *glory*. I have seen his image, his imprint in them. Oh, what is man that he is mindful of them?' Jether whispered.

'There is worse.' Gabriel spoke with his back to Jether and Michael. 'I see Yehovah weeping.'

Michael drew in his breath. Appalled.

'Yehovah weeps for what is to come.' Jether nodded. 'The Great Tribulation upon the world of the race of men.'

Michael bowed his head.

'In precisely nine moons, Yehovah will hand over the execution of the Seven Seals to Christos. They are his subjects. He is their king.'

Jether gazed out beyond the twelve pale blue moons of the First Heaven, beyond the shooting stars and lightning arcing over the Rubied Door, then raised his palm until the outline of the planet Earth became faintly visible through the shifting lilacs of the horizon.

'At the end of human history,' Jether said, softly, 'Yehovah turns at last from grace to judgement. He has compassionately, so tenderly, invited the race of men, each and every one of them, decade after decade, aeon after aeon, to companionship with him. The End of all Ages is now upon us. He has been their lover . . .'

Jether raised his gaze to the two brothers, his eyes burning, fierce with intensity.

'Now he will become their Judge.'

CHAPTER THIRTY

Bolt from the Blue

Seven Days Later
5 January, 2022

Jason's chauffeur closed the limousine door, as Jason hurried out of the lashing rain, ducking under the white and gold canopy of the Fifth Avenue entrance of his newly acquired Central Park penthouse. The other Manhattan penthouse, which he and Julia had shared for seventeen years during their marriage, had finally been sold. Much to Julia's delight and ensuring her lifetime financial liquidity, no doubt. He scowled.

And Jason, to the shock of his family and associates, had unpredictably splashed out seventy million dollars of his personal trust fund on prime real estate. Now his primary New York residence. Deeded in the name of Lily De Vere.

He strode into the lobby, nodded to the concierge in greeting, and walked straight into the elevator. A pulse-quickening forty seconds and forty-two floors later, its gilded doors opened onto the private elevator landing of the triplex penthouse that spanned the top three floors of the palatial chateau in the sky. Lulu, his Ridgeback, bounded towards him at full speed, her tail wagging. He bent down and rubbed her head affectionately, then headed straight for the bar in the 2,500-square-foot grand salon. Jason smiled.

'To die for,' as Lilian would say. Decades ago it had once been the entertainment hub of the elite of East and West Coast society. The Roosevelts, Kennedys, Reagans, Frank Sinatra and Ava Gardner, Marilyn Monroe, even Laurence Olivier and Vivien Leigh had whiled away days and nights under what was now Jason's roof.

For the last forty years it had belonged to an inordinately wealthy Wall Street tycoon who was a complete social recluse. Jason flung his jacket over a sofa and poured himself a whisky. Smug.

The cycle would continue. Here it would entertain only himself, Lily during her vacations, and Lulu, surely the most pampered dog in Manhattan.

He yawned. He desperately needed some shut-eye.

He walked over to the soaring twenty-foot French doors and went out onto the terrace. The moon was out. He stared out at the panoramic view of Central Park, the skating rink and the glistening city lights. New York at night. Unbeatable.

He sighed. *Tomorrow would be relentless.*

Six a.m. flight to Babylon. Prepping for the early morning summit on the seventh. Lunch with the Iraqi Prime Minister and late-night drinks with Adrian before the big day. Six a.m. – breakfast with the Minister of Telecommunications. Eight a.m. – the Ratification of the Concordat of King Solomon, then 5 p.m., Babylon time – the final signing of the Ishtar Accord.

The biggest media scoop in the world. And thanks to his little brother, Vox had the exclusive. Jason finished his whisky, then retraced his steps back inside and walked over to a marbled desk under the huge Palladian windows.

He rifled idly through the mail laid out by his housekeeper.

337

The usual. Junk mail. Bills. No personal mail. He hesitated, then picked up a cheap blue hand-addressed envelope at the very bottom of the pile. He studied the postmark. *Curious.*

It was mailed from Hangzhou, China.

Slitting it open with a paperknife, he turned it upside down. A tiny disk no larger than his thumbnail fell out, followed by a grubby piece of paper.

Jason unfolded it. The handwriting was a scrawl, but a legible scrawl.

One to follow. Weaver.

Jason crumpled the paper in his hand, picked up the disk and walked the heated marble floors towards his new mahogany library. He switched on his laptop and inserted the disk, sinking down into his leather chair in front of the fireplace, whisky in hand. He studied the screen.

The first document was a letter with his father's signature at the bottom – James De Vere. He'd recognize that forceful italicized scrawl anywhere.

He sighed. He missed his dad. He'd hardly seen him the year before he died.

There was a second document signed in green ink.

Scrolling back, he read James De Vere's letter to Lawrence St Cartier, then leant back in his chair, staring blankly towards the fireplace for several minutes.

He brought up the second document and scanned it.

Requisition for a live biological agent from Fort Detrich. A note of monies paid to low-level thugs in Amsterdam. His gaze dropped to a third file.

Live Aids virus delivered 4 April, 2017. Injected 12.07 a.m. Signed warrant for Nicholas De Vere's execution.

Jason stared at the screen, stunned.

What was it Nick had written in his last note to Julia? *'They gave me Aids.'*

Jason ran his fingers through his hair, perplexed, then drank down the rest of his whisky and flipped open his phone. He scrolled down until he reached Xavier Chessler's name. He paused, then continued scrolling past Smythe, Stephens, and St Clair. He stopped on St Cartier.

Jason had always been fond of the old man. His mother trusted him implicitly. It seemed as though his father had, too.

He studied the three phone numbers for St Cartier.

London. Cairo. Alexandria.

He hesitated. Lilian had said the old man was wintering at his apartment in Cairo. He'd get hold of him there.

CHAPTER THIRTY-ONE

The First Seal

Slowly, the colossal Rubied Doors of Yehovah's throne room swung shut.

Out of the rising mists, the twenty-four ancient kings of Heaven became visible. They were twenty-four High Stewards of Heaven – twenty-four of the wisest and most powerful of the angelic host of the First Heaven – who because of their faithfulness had been endowed with the Seven Seals of the Wisdom of Yehovah. Twenty-four angelic elders of greatest humility who, having proven faithful through a million aeons, had been set in governance of the present end-time age of the race of men.

They walked majestically up the nave of the throne room attired in brilliant white raiments, signifying their refusal to join the rebellion of Lucifer, and wearing crowns of gold that signified their victory in battle with the Fallen. The jewels on each elder's crown represented love, joy, benevolence, serenity, fortitude, humility, forbearance, fidelity, chivalry, and temperance.

Leading them was Jether the Just, the most powerful ancient angelic king of the First Heaven.

'Jether the Just!' an angelic herald proclaimed. 'Steward of Yehovah's ancient mysteries.'

They stopped before the twenty-four golden thrones that stretched in a semicircle on either side of the gleaming sardius altar.

Jether held his gold sceptre high before the angelic host and they bowed in accord as one.

Jether took his throne, followed by Xacheriel who had taken Charsoc's throne at Jether's right hand, aeons before, then the twenty-two remaining elders followed.

'Gabriel the Revelator, Chief Justice. Prince of Archangels,' a second angelic herald proclaimed. 'Long may you reign with wisdom and justice.'

Gabriel gravely followed the ancient kings through the Gates and into the throne room, Michael at his side.

'Michael the Valiant, Commander of the armies of the First Heaven,' the angelic herald proclaimed. 'Long may you reign with justice and valour.'

Michael walked beside Gabriel carrying the Sword of State. Together they walked up the nave of the throne room towards the Seat of Kings. Their knights-in-arms fell into step behind them, solemnly bearing the banners of the Royal House of Yehovah.

As one, the brothers knelt in the burning crimson mists that rose from the sardius altar.

A huge shuddering and roar broke forth as flashes of lightning, rumblings, and peals of thunder emanated from the throne room walls, shaking the entire chamber. The throne room became bathed in the most brilliant and luminous of colours. The walls emanated a deep glimmering sardius, then almost at once transformed into the soft dappled azure of a million burning sapphires. Brilliant amethysts radiated from the immense, circular descending rainbow as still Yehovah's throne descended.

Michael lay prostrate, his face pushed against the crystal floor, trembling.

341

Jether, too, fell prostrate, his mouth moving in supplication and adoration as still Yehovah descended through the open dome. The angelic host fell prostrate as the great and terrible roaring of the Ancient of Days filled the chamber.

Thousands of suns and myriad moons from millions upon millions of galaxies were woven as a living, pulsating tapestry of the cosmos that cloaked Yehovah's being. And still Yehovah descended. From each moon and planet, and from the millions of stars that radiated from the translucent cloak of his radiance, light waves resounded, oscillating throughout universe after universe – an inexorable tsunami of sound.

And still the Ancient of Days descended.

The luminous white light of the chamber transformed into a dazzling amethyst brilliance, which turned to a glimmering emerald, and then a robust sapphire – the spectra of light reflected in Yehovah's mantle. And as Yehovah descended, the rainbow descended also. It seemed to stretch throughout the universe.

Before Yehovah's throne seven blazing torches burned a hundred feet high, as seven columns of the intense white fires of holiness, and in the midst of each torch were the flaming coals of the Spirit of Yehovah – his eyes.

And still the throne of his glory descended with him. As it lowered, the floor of the throne room became as mercury, then transformed from the fluid metal into a sea that was as living, breathing sapphire. It was transparent, and there was no flaw within it. Ear-splitting peals of thunder shook the chambers and it was as though the very atoms of the walls pulsated.

And as the thundering subsided, blue lightning bolts, shot through with white fire, coursed through the Ancient of Days' cloak, lighting up the universe in their wake.

Yehovah's countenance was hidden from view, veiled in burning clouds, but above his robes, in the place where his face should be, a light shone like the orbs of a thousand brilliant suns.

Yehovah – the One before whom all heavens and galaxies fled in the very majesty and awe of him. The One whose hair and head were white like snow from the very radiance of his glory, whose eyes flashed like flames of living fire with the brilliance of his multitude of discernments and great and infinitely tender compassions.

For his beauty was indescribable. His tender mercies and compassions were unfathomable.

And so, as One, he dwelt in the throne room. And as Three.

For they were indivisible. And they were indissoluble.

And when the throne and the One who sat on it had descended, Yehovah's hands became visible through the thick luminous hanging mists of glory.

In his right hand he held an enormous scroll of linen parchment that emitted a burning white light.

Gabriel stared in wonder at the scroll.

'It is the scroll from the Ark of the Race of Men,' he whispered, gazing at the living, glowing golden handwriting covering both the front and back of the scroll.

The ancient angelic lettering emitted shafts of light, pulsing from Hebrew to Greek, to Arabic, then to ten thousand languages, both of the ancient angelic and of the race of men. The scroll was secured at the front by seven vast golden Seals, crafted of fine gold, each with one enormous uncut diamond in its centre.

Except for the First Seal. The First Seal had no diamond. But in its place was a stone of sardius.

Michael raised himself up from the crystal floor, trembling. He looked over to Gabriel.

'It is the title deeds to the Earth.'

Gabriel nodded. 'And the chronicles of the entire universe.

Yehovah holds in his hand the only record of the chronicles of the race of men. Past. Present. And all that is to come. The consummation of all history. The title deeds have resided in the Ark. The Seven-Sealed Scroll has rested hidden below the twelve great codices of the Ark in the lower Western Labyrinths of the Seven Spires for over two thousand years.'

He raised his eyes in adoration to the throne.

'Since the Great Sacrifice of the Lamb,' Michael uttered.

Gabriel nodded. 'Waiting for the very End of Days when it is to be opened. If none from the race of men is eligible to claim the title deeds, the claim will be lost, and Lucifer's reign will never come to an end.'

Michael stepped forward. His emerald-green eyes blazed with righteousness. He raised the Sword of State high.

'Who is worthy in the race of men to open the book, and to loose the Seals thereof?' he cried.

'Who is worthy?' the angelic heralds cried.

Jether and the elders fell prostrate. 'We are not born of the race of men. We are not worthy!' they cried.

'Who is worthy to open the scroll?' the angelic heralds cried a second time, this time to the ten times ten thousand of the angelic host.

'We are not born of the race of men. We are not worthy,' the roar of the angelic host resounded through the throne room.

'Who is worthy in the race of men to open the scroll?' the angelic heralds cried a third time, this time to the millions of the race of men gathered in the throne room, both of the righteous dead and those who had accepted the terrible sacrifice on Golgotha in aeons past.

Jether raised his head. He surveyed Adam, then John the Baptist, then Moses, and Elijah.

Finally John the Baptist stood, his eyes blazing. He fell prostrate.

'I am one born of the race of men. I am not worthy,' he uttered, tears streaming down his face.

Adam fell prostrate behind him. 'I am one born of the race of men. I am not worthy.'

Hundreds, then millions of the righteous dead fell prostrate across the throne room, each crying, 'I am not worthy . . . I am not worthy.'

Jether watched as King Aretas of Petra and his daughter, Princess Jotapa, fell prostrate, tears streaming down their cheeks.

'I am not worthy,' the noble king uttered.

'I am not worthy,' Jotapa sobbed.

'Jether the Just,' Gabriel said, 'read the consequences, according to Eternal Law, if the Seal remains unopened.'

Jether stood.

'If the Seal is not opened, Lucifer's kingdom stands forever sealed on earth. His kingdom comes. Forever and ever, without end. The Fall. The Curse. The utter misery he has wrought in the world of the race of men – his mark of pain and suffering on every living thing – will remain on Earth eternally. There will be no redemption from his kingdom. He will reign eternally as sovereign of the race of men if the Seal is not broken.'

He paused.

'If one of the race of men is found who is worthy, the Earth will finally be reclaimed from Lucifer, the Fallen, and men who have usurped God's ownership.'

Michael walked forward and raised his arms toward the thone and his face to the dome.

'Who is so exalted in rank and might to be authorized, to be worthy to open the Scroll and break the Seals thereof? Who of the race of men is sanctioned to wrest the planet Earth back from the usurper – Lucifer?'

Michael stared around, his eyes blazing.

345

'Who is counted worthy to overthrow the intruder? To rid for all time Lucifer and his legions of the Fallen? Who has the sanction to open the Seven-Sealed Scroll?'

'Only one,' a voice whispered.

And Heaven almost stilled.

John, the Revelator, stood, tears streaming down his cheeks. He raised his arms towards the throne.

'There is only one,' he whispered, in between his wracking sobs.

Staring. Gazing in complete adoration toward the throne at the right hand of Yehovah. He fell on his face like one dead.

Gabriel stared, transfixed.

'He was there,' he murmured. 'The Apostle John that Christos deeply loved.'

Jether walked over to the altar.

'Weep not.' He laid his hands on John's head, then raised his hands to the throne, his eyes closed in ecstasy.

'Weep not,' he cried. 'For behold, the Lion of the tribe of Judah, the Root of David, hath prevailed to open the book, and to break the Seven Seals thereof.'

And suddenly, behind the hundred-foot blazing white columns of fire, in the midst of the throne and of the four mighty cherubim of Yehovah, and in the midst of the elders, stood a Lamb, as though it had been slain. It had seven horns and seven eyes.

Gabriel fell to his knees, his limbs trembling.

'Thou art worthy to take the book, and to open the Seals thereof,' he cried.

Gabriel stared entranced at the image of a Lamb standing, as though it had been slain, having seven horns, and seven eyes, which were the seven Spirits of God, sent forth into all the Earth.

'The Lion that is of the tribe of Judah, the Root of David,

hath overcome to open the book and the Seven Seals thereof,' he said, echoing Jether's words.

And the Lamb metamorphosized into Christos. Gabriel stared entranced at the eyes that flashed like flames of fire. At the strong, imperial face of the slain Lamb – Jesus Christ.

Christos walked, tears streaming down his face, and took the scroll out of the right hand of Yehovah.

The four cherubim or living creatures before the throne and the twenty-four ancient angelic elders fell down before Christos. Tears streamed down Jether's leathered cheeks.

'Worthy art thou to take the book, and to open the Seals thereof,' the twenty-four elders cried in unison.

Gabriel watched Xacheriel. Xacheriel's gaze was riveted on Christos, his eyes ablaze with adoration, his voice resounding with his twenty-three compatriots across the throne room.

'For thou wast slain, and didst purchase unto God with thy blood men of every tribe, and tongue, and people, and nation, and madest them to be unto our God a kingdom and priests; and they reign upon the Earth.'

A thunderous stentorian roar erupted from ten thousand times ten thousand of the angelic host.

'Worthy is the Lamb that was slain to receive power, and riches, and wisdom, and strength, and honour, and glory, and blessing.'

And the sound of many voices resounded from the world of the race of men. Christos removed the keys of hell and death – or keys to the title deeds of the race of men.

Gabriel watched him trembling.

Jether waited.

The twenty-four elders waited.

Ten thousand times ten thousand of the angelic host waited.

Yehovah waited.

Christos looked straight into Yehovah's face. Imperial, his eyes blazing.

And the King of Kings of the Universe and Race of Men broke the First Seal.

Lucifer stood at the edge of the sheer cliff face of Mont St Michel, his hands raised to the darkening Normandy skies, his six seraph wings outstretched.

'I watched as the Lamb opened the first of the Seven Seals,' he whispered, his raven hair lashing his scarred features. 'And I heard one of the four living creatures saying as with a voice of thunder, "Come."'

Lucifer stared at the image of the White Rider, now plainly visible above the Abbey of Mont St Michel. Lucifer stayed still for a moment, his face raised in ecstasy to the fierce Atlantic gales.

'I looked,' Lucifer's voice rose in strength, 'and there before me was a white horse! Its rider held a bow and he was given a crown, and he rode out as a conqueror bent on conquest.'

He turned. Adrian knelt before him, the moon glimmering down on his face, illuminating the beauty of his already striking features.

'The First Seal is opened,' Adrian whispered. 'My reign as the Son of Perdition begins.'

Lucifer laid both hands on Adrian's head.

'Seven years till our victory at Armageddon. Seven years and this planet shall be mine for eternity!'

A thick, dark, tar-like elixir flowed from Lucifer's hands onto Adrian's temple.

'For I so loved the world.' Lucifer cried, an insane fire in his eyes, '. . . that I sent my only begotten son. That whosoever takes the Mark and follows him shall perish and forfeit eternal life.'

348

He turned to the raging seas.

'For mine is the Kingdom!' he cried. 'The Power and the Glory . . .'

He looked straight up at the statue of the Archangel Michael on the church spire towering 560 feet above him. And smiled an iniquitous, triumphant smile.

'Forever and ever . . . Amen.'

The First Seal had been broken.

The White Rider was released.

The rise of Lucifer's son was assured in the world of the race of men.

But my elder brother had once again been short-sighted.

For the breaking of the First Seal of the Apocalypse of St John was to herald in a kingdom that would shake the kingdoms of the damned.

A kingdom that was to herald the end of Lucifer's iniquitous reign on the Earth.

The world of the race of men that we, the angelic, had wept over as it became Paradise Lost, was to become once again Paradise Regained.

But not without the greatest battle that the heavens and the world of the race of men had ever seen.

A battle that would rage for seven years.

A battle that would culminate on the plains of the Valley of Jezreel.

The Battle that would be called in the race of men . . .

The Battle of Armageddon.

THREE AND A HALF
YEARS LATER

June 2025

CHAPTER THIRTY-TWO

The Riders of the Apocalypse

European Superstate Headquarters
Babylon, Iraq

The motorcade of thirteen black Mercedes limousines sped across the sprawling network of Babylon's gleaming new highways.

Adrian sank back into the plush leather seat of the Mercedes. He gazed out through the darkened windows at the masses screaming in adulation, waiting for a glimpse of the motorcade carrying the supreme architect of the new Iraqi State, the rising economic genius of the European Superstate, Adrian De Vere.

Adrian glanced down at his watch. It was a Friday. A far cry from the Friday of nearly 42 months earlier: 7 January 2022.

The day he had dreamed of, since winning his first electoral seat for Oxford in England nearly two decades ago.

The day when, right here in Babylon, the Concordat of King Solomon had been ratified, and the first constituent of the forty-year Ishtar Accord between Israel, the Pan-Arab Union, Russia, the EU, and the United Nations had been signed. A seven-year guarantee by the EU and the United Nations to defend Israel, as a protectorate, bound by international law. According to the Ishtar Accord, Israel, in exchange for its immediate denuclearization, would be protected both diplomatically and militarily by the European Union Superstate and the United Nations against Russia, the surrounding Arab States, and any enemy third parties. Israel would, however, retain its sovereignty and remain a state under international law.

Things had progressed more smoothly than Adrian could ever have hoped for.

Israel had been at peace with every Arab nation on its borders since the Accord and was already forty-one months into the implementation of its seven-year denuclearization strategy.

A UN peacekeeping force now occupied the Temple Mount and monitored Israel's boundaries, which had reverted to the borders of 1967.

Jerusalem was undivided and Muslims, Christians, and Jews now had 'free right of passage to the holy places in Jerusalem regardless of religion, gender or race'.

And the brand new Solomon's Temple – Jerusalem's third Temple – being erected in the Northern Quadrant, was only days away from completion.

Adrian would give Israel a few more months of basking in the statutes of its status as a protectorate . . . before he contravened the Accord.

By that time the denuclearization programme would be irreversible. Israel would be demilitarized for the first time since 1948. Defenceless. Adrian smiled.

He looked up at the vast steel-and-glass horizon that rose a quarter of a mile high and fifty miles wide, courtesy of the two-trillion-dollar investment from the European Superstate and the World Bank.

The first three Riders of the Apocalypse had been released, plunging the entire globe into mass social and economic upheaval. And today ten of the world's most powerful kings and presidents were gathering at the newly erected European Union Superstate Headquarters in Babylon for a world summit on the global famine and economic crisis.

Adrian De Vere had been unanimously elected to serve as Chair.

The motorcade turned a sharp right down Black Gold Boulevard.

Adrian studied the skyscrapers: Saudi Aramco, BP, Royal Dutch Shell, Gazprom, Exxon Mobil, and the newest addition, PetroChina.

A far cry from 2001 when over 90 per cent of Iraq remained geologically unexplored due to years of wars and sanctions. A conservative estimate of Iraq's present oil reserves stood at over four hundred billion barrels.

All under the jurisdiction of the European Union Superstate . . . and Adrian.

Running parallel to the flourishing oil industry was the new media hub of the world. Television networks from every civilized nation on earth now broadcast their signals from the Babylon Plains. He smiled in satisfaction.

Babylon and Europe were flourishing while the entire Western and Eastern world crumbled.

The Riders of the Apocalypse were venting their fury. The first Judgements were raining down.

Eighteen months ago, on what was now known internationally as the World's Black Friday, economic collapse and world famine had struck at the aorta of Western and Eastern society.

Bank balances had been wiped out overnight. A thousand top-ranking banks from London to Tokyo to New York had been in liquidation by morning. Millionaires had become paupers in a day. From Tokyo to Detroit, Los Angeles to Shanghai, entire cities had been looted and burned.

Bread lines had stretched across the streets and sidewalks of every American state. From California to Washington State. And across each British county, from Cornwall to Caithness, statutory instruments had been issued in the UK. Martial law had been implemented across the world.

Executive Orders had been issued by the President of the United States in short succession. The US Government had taken control of all modes of transportation, including highways, seaports, all airports, and aircraft. It had seized the communication media and now controlled all electrical power, gas, petroleum, fuels and minerals, and had direct control over all food supplies and resources, both public and private. And it now operated a national registration of all persons.

By early 2024, Congress had repealed the United States Firearm Owners' Protection Act of 1986. Guns in the United States had been confiscated under threat of death. And then had come the Avian flu pandemic.

Unlike the rest of the world, Adrian had been prepared.

He declared a state of emergency which automatically conferred extraordinary powers to him as President of the European Union Superstate. Martial law and famine emergency law were implemented immediately.

Adrian, with the full backing of the rich and poor throughout Europe, introduced the establishment of a class-less, stateless society based on common ownership.

He abolished the euro and then, in the face of millions' mass panic, introduced the European form of trade for the future – a European-wide trial where an EU social security number was embedded in a chip on the right wrist.

With it the wearer had access to food stamps, to the contents of thousands of Europe's vast grain stores and underground seedbanks that were guarded by battalions of NATO's troops. And to the European Superstate's vast stockpile of pandemic vaccinations.

Without the chip, life ceased to exist.

The Brotherhood immediately released twenty trillion dollars of gold from the International Security Fund's vaults in Switzerland into the European Union's Solidarity Fund; a fund formed to respond instantaneously and to come to the aid of any member state in the event of a major disaster.

Adrian smiled. Funds flowed in short order from the EU's Solidarity Fund to every member state of the European Union, stabilizing their economies. Alleviating famine. Rebuilding health and welfare functions. Julius De Vere's brainchild was achieving its objective. Adrian was fast being hailed as the new Alexander.

The initial stage of his seven-year plan was working precisely according to the Brotherhood's timetable. The world's attention was fixed onto the European Union Superstate . . . and on Adrian De Vere.

The UK, economically bankrupt and brought to her knees by the Avian flu pandemic and famine, had finally come into the fold.

The ratification of the Lisbon Treaty in 2009, during Gordon Brown's term of office, had done only half the job, and while Adrian was in Downing Street, he and his legal teams had drawn up the London Pact.

The 700-page document outlined the inclusion of England, Scotland, and Wales into the European Superstate. It ensured the UK's permanent loss of its UN seat. The European Superstate's total control over British foreign policy. And the UK's complete loss of control over its borders.

Six months earlier, during the Avian flu pandemic, the British Prime Minister, having implemented martial law in England, Scotland, and Wales, and facing full-blooded insurrection from the British public, reluctantly signed the London Treaty behind closed doors at Mont St Michel in Normandy.

Adrian had been well prepared. Britain's reward was four trillion dollars in gold and silver from the EU's Swiss vaults and ten trillion from the International Security Fund, released immediately into the British economy.

In a period of a year, Britain stabilized. Adrian with unmitigated resolve, had single-handedly saved the nation from the brink of disaster.

And today he would unveil his plan to bail out the ten newly appointed world superblocs whose infrastructures had been grieviously shattered by the 'Riders' – a bail-out plan to the tune of fifty trillion dollars, plus loans from the International Security Fund. The opening of the Seven Seals of Revelation was currently moving directly in his favour.

He sighed in satisfaction as the motorcade rode through the Ishtar Gate, newly returned by Berlin in recognition of his service to Europe; the entrance to his new European headquarters.

His plan for a one-world superstate – a New World Order – was well on its way. His next step would be the introduction of the one-world currency.

The trial with the RFID chip for the new credit system had surpassed his wildest dreams, but it was just a minor practice run . . . while Guber and his intelligentsia perfected the ID tag.

Adrian's real coup was a special ink deposited in a unique barcode pattern for each individual, which would be injected under the surface of the skin. Just like a fingerprint.

The prototype was called 'the Mark'.

Guber's face appeared on the limousine's videoscreen.

'Update from the Vatican's scientists on the polar shift, Mr President, sir.'

Adrian nodded.

Feeling the vibration from his mobile, he glanced down. It was Jason.

'Have it waiting for me on my desk,' he said, then flicked his phone on.

Jason's face came into view on the screen. He looked haggard.

'Hi, Jas . . . on my way to the summit. Can't talk.'

'It's Mother, Adrian. She's had a heart attack. Get here as soon as you can.'

'I'll fly in straight after the summit,' he said, softly.

Jason's face vanished. Adrian turned to Chastenay.

'Have Khalid prepare the Boeing. We'll leave for London after the last session.' He looked straight ahead. 'I need to tie up some loose ends.'

CHAPTER THIRTY-THREE

An Uninvited Visitor

Cairo

Lawrence St Cartier sat outside the dirty cramped coffee shop known locally as an *ahwa*. He was huddled over a battered tin table, immersed in a dog-eared, nine-day-old edition of the *Islington Gazette*. A poor substitute for the *Telegraph*, he considered, but given the current socio-economic cataclysm shaking Egypt, he was grateful for small mercies. In the international section of the local newsstand this morning, it had been a choice of the *Gazette*, the *Kashmir Observer*, and the *Socialist Worker*.

'Lawence, Lawence!' Lawrence looked up in the direction of the drinks counter and frowned. Waseem was gesticulating wildly in his direction, pointing at a glass of Turkish coffee, then at a glass of tea with mint.

Lawrence pointed to the coffee and nodded emphatically.

Waseem beamed, negotiating a path through the animated crowd watching TV, past braziers of hot coals and shisha pipes, until he reached Lawrence's table on the pavement. It was two in the morning and despite the bread lines and social turmoil, Cairo was in full swing. No martial law here . . . yet.

Waseem set down the Turkish coffee in front of Lawrence.

'Yemeni beans?' Lawrence raised his eyebrows. Waseem nodded vigorously. Lawrence smiled. Amid all the devastation, finding Yemeni beans now in Cairo was like finding black gold. He sipped delicately at the glass of the steaming Turkish coffee.

'Ah.' He closed his eyes, drinking in the intense cultural experience.

'Aromas of the Ottoman Empire.' Waseem watched him in fascination.

A loud outburst of jubilant shrieking erupted from the table behind Lawrence.

Lawrence opened his eyes. Turning to the table, he gave a thumbs-up to the excited winner behind him. They erupted in shrieks all over again. Lawrence beamed.

'Backgammon,' he declared. Waseem nimbly laid out a backgammon board in front of Lawrence, then shook out pegs and dice from a small cotton bag. Lawrence took a large slurp of his coffee, then nodded to Waseem who rolled the dice.

Lawrence did the same, then stopped. Frozen. Slowly he rose from the table and stared out past the few crazed drivers who were operating solely on black-market fuel. He raised his gaze to the forest of satellite dishes, in the direction of his rooftop apartment in the faded splendour of downtown.

Rolling up his paper, he walked straight through the crowds, wending his way through haphazardly parked cars, motorcycles and horse-drawn carts. Waseem ran after him.

'Malik Lawence . . . Malik!' Waseem panted.

Lawrence turned sharp right at a sign that read 'Obey the road rules', then dodged his way nimbly through four lanes of chaotic traffic, narrowly missing a donkey-drawn cart. He hovered, trapped between the unmarked lanes, shaking his head at the crazed and honking drivers, then hurried across the road, disappearing into the crowd.

Lilian had tubes attached to her nose, mouth, and forearm. She was sleeping. An intensive-care nurse checked her readings then disappeared. A second nurse entered.

Jason stared down at Lilian, then gently released her thin hand from his grasp. He looked over towards Rosemary who sat reading in the far corner of the room. She looked up.

'You got here fast.'

'Summering in Rome. The States are out of hand. Can't walk through Manhattan without being accosted by the military on every corner. FEMA's gone mad. Give me the detail, Rosemary.'

Rosemary frowned.

'She collapsed on the pavement outside a house in Wimpole Street at around ten this morning. She had had an appointment of some kind. That's all I know. The ambulance came immediately and brought her here. She was in a coma, then woke up hallucinating. Then she asked for you. Fell asleep when she was sure you were on your way.'

The second nurse rechecked Lilian's readings and her tubes, then exited.

Jason looked at his watch.

'Adrian should be here before ten. Try to catch some sleep.'

Rosemary smiled.

'I'll snatch an hour when Adrian gets here. He said he'll hold the fort till I'm rested.'

Lilian's eyes fluttered open.

Jason took her hand. 'It's me, Mother. Jason,' he said, softly. 'I'm here.'

Lilian tried to draw herself up into a sitting position. Both Jason and Rosemary stared at her in alarm.

'They took my baby.' She stared right through Jason, her eyes wide with trepidation.

Jason and Rosemary exchanged a glance.

'Mother, you're hallucinating,' Jason said, softly.

Lilian pressed Jason's hand.

'Jason – you're my son?' He nodded.

'Of course I'm your son.'

Rosemary shook her head. 'It's the drugs.'

'Jason.' The heart monitor fluctuated noticeably. He looked over to Rosemary in alarm.

'The doctor says you're not to strain yourself. Mother, the medication is making you confused. Don't try to talk. I'm right here.'

'Rosemary, get the staff nurse,' he ordered.

Lilian shook her head, her eyes full of fear.

'Just rest, Mother,' he murmured.

'Jason, there are things . . . things that your father and I never told you. You have to know. You have to protect yourselves from them.'

'Mother, please – you're confused.'

Lilian mustered all her strength and clasped Jason's hand so tightly he winced.

'They murdered Nicholas, Jason. They'll come for me. Then they will get to you.'

She struggled to raise herself.

'You *must* protect yourself. In my safe . . .' Lilian struggled for breath.

'Your father – a set of papers arrived from his lawyers yesterday.'

Jason frowned. He looked at her, completely baffled.

'Mother, Dad's been dead for four years.'

She grabbed Jason's hand.

'A black file – with his gold crest. Get it to Lawrence, Jason: Lawrence St Cartier. Promise me. You can trust Lawrence . . .'

The staff nurse entered followed by Rosemary and a specialist.

'Mr De Vere . . .' The doctor looked at Jason, sternly. 'Your mother is not to be excited under *any* circumstances. She has had a major coronary.'

They pulled the curtains around the bed. The nurse prepped Lilian's arm and deftly inserted a needle into her arm. The doctor stood in front of Jason. 'If you'll please excuse us.'

'Jason,' Lilian cried in agitation. '*Promise.*'

Jason struggled for control of his emotions.

'I promise, Mother. The black file to Lawrence St Cartier.'

Lilian's panic started to diminish as the sedative began to take effect.

Her eyes closed.

'I love you, Jason,' she whispered.

Then she fell into the blissful succour of oblivion.

Lawrence stood outside the imposing turn-of-the-century apartment block from old downtown Cairo's *belle époque*, staring up towards his apartment on the tenth floor.

Waseem ran up to him, out of breath. Lawrence placed his finger on the boy's mouth.

'It would seem, Waseem, that we have an uninvited guest.'

Lawrence shook his head and pointed upwards. Waseem frowned darkly.

They walked past the decorative iron railings and stone cornices into the hallway and opened the iron lift doors. Lawrence pressed a button and the lift moved upwards at a snail's pace.

The lift stopped with a thump on the tenth floor.

Lawrence got out, followed by Waseem, into the long hallway.

He hesitated outside a beautifully crafted doorway.

'A most *unwelcome* guest.'

Lawrence raised his hand slightly. The door opened slowly.

Standing on the balcony, his hand raised in greeting, stood Charsoc.

Lawrence walked inside and closed the door sharply.

'I should have let you know I was coming, Jether,' Charsoc said, languidly. 'You could have prepared me some tea.'

Lawrence looked Charsoc up and down. He was still in human form. Six foot three. Hooked nose. Cropped iron-grey hair.

'Kester von Slagel, emissary to Lorcan De Molay, I presume.'

'Pleased to make your acquaintance.' Charsoc bowed. 'Professor Lawrence St Cartier, antiquities expert.' He smiled thinly and removed his gloves. He watched as Lawrence metamorphosized into his angelic form as Jether.

'Forgive me if I don't follow suit,' Charsoc said. 'Yehovah's addendum to Eternal Law as regarding my entry through the Portal of Shinar put rather – let me just say – a damp-ener on things.'

Jether nodded to Waseem, who transformed into the youngling, Obadiah.

Charsoc raised his eyebrows.

'I see we have a youngling too. My, my, Jether! How circumspect of you. Hired help.'

'Obadiah.' Obadiah nodded and disappeared out of the door. Jether looked down at Charsoc's dog collar and frowned.

'Flattering, don't you think?' Charsoc smiled. 'Robes. Crucifixes. Continual black attire. Somewhat macabre. But the rings are magnificent. *Luridly* ornate. Quite to my taste.'

He looked fondly down at the huge uncut stone on his signet ring.

'Bloodstone – a variety of chalcedony. Legend has it that the bloodstone was formed from the blood of Christ dripping on the green earth and solidifying.'

His eyes narrowed.

'I'm being groomed ... coached ... *primed*, Jether. As Grand Inquisitor of the Ruling Body of the Global Congress of Churches.'

'The False Prophet of Revelation. Why am I not surprised?' Jether said, drily.

'A new order.' Charsoc raised his arms to Cairo's skies. 'The Inquisition reborn.'

Jether walked out onto the balcony.

'You outstay your welcome.'

'I took a minibus,' Charsoc said, ignoring Jether's comment. He dusted off his robes gingerly. 'Crowded. Bald tyres, ripped seats. Fifteen piestres.' He shook his head distastefully. 'You could have least have taken up residence somewhere more civilized.'

He hesitated, looking out at the view of Old Cairo at night.

'London ... Milan ... Or are you here because of sentiment perhaps?' he hissed. 'Egypt protected the Nazarene, and so fulfilled what the Lord had said through the prophet: "Out of Egypt I called my Son."'

'What do you want, Charsoc?' Jether said, his voice like ice.

'Tetchy. Tetchy, Jether. Have it your way. I am here to deliver a message.'

'Of *course* you are.' Jether looked at him with disdain. 'From second-in-command of the high ancient kings of Heaven to Lucifer's errand boy. A message from your master.' Charsoc glared at Jether with undisguised loathing.

'A message from my Master concerning the forthcoming evacuation of the Nazarene's subjects,' he said. 'They are more than an irritant, Jether. They greatly obstruct our progress in the realm of men.'

Charsoc removed a parchment missive from his carpetbag.

'You know I have always been a stickler for legal protocol. I hold Yehovah's guarantee – the Rubied Seal.' Charsoc held out a parchment missive with a glimmering Rubied Seal to Jether. 'My Master demands its immediate implementation.'

Jether slowly took the missive from Charsoc's outstretched hand.

'The Rapture,' Charsoc hissed, 'as it is called in the world of the race of men.'

'It is imminent,' Jether said, his voice very soft.

'Imminent is not soon enough. They plague us with their confounded supplications. The incursions of the angelic hosts through the Portals to assist them must stop.'

Charsoc swung around.

'The Nazarene,' he spat. 'Visitations to this wretched planet. Nightly.'

'They are his subjects. He is their king. He comes in answer to their supplications.'

'Precisely. *Their* removal ensures *his* removal. And it ensures our victory. From the hour the Ishtar Accord was signed we had seven years until the Final Battle. Forty-two months are all but gone. We are running late.'

'But *we* are right on time, Charsoc.' Jether's voice was very soft. He looked down at the missive in his palm.

'We *demand* their removal,' Charsoc snarled. 'According to the precepts of Eternal Law.'

'You can make no demands. You abide by Yehovah's jurisdictions only.'

'Then you leave me no alternative.'

Charsoc carefully removed a pair of vermilion slippers

from the bottom of his carpetbag, then a turquoise eye mask and nasal spray. Jether watched as he removed a bottle of blood pressure pills.

'Matter!' he muttered. 'Inferior. This infernal body constantly needs retuning. I have become finicky over the past four decades.'

Jether rolled his eyes. 'You were *always* finicky, Charsoc.' He stared down at the Rubied Seal on the missive. '*You* leave *me* no alternative. The prospect of your company is more than I can stand.'

A strange smiled flickered on Charsoc's lips.

'I see we understand each other.'

'Let us dispense with superficialities,' Jether said, frostily. 'At the passing of the Pale Rider through the Kármán line – the boundary between the Earth's atmosphere and outer space sixty-two miles above us – his subjects shall be removed.'

'The Pale Rider.' Charsoc smiled in satisfaction. 'Ah . . . the Fourth Seal: Nisroc's gruesome precursor to the Sixth Seal.'

He replaced his slippers and the eye mask in his carpetbag.

'*And I beheld when he had opened the Sixth Seal, and, lo, there was a great earthquake; and the sun became black as sackcloth of hair, and the moon became as blood.*'

Charsoc unscrewed the cap of his blood-pressure pills and slung two in the back of his mouth. He swallowed, then grimaced.

'*And the stars of heaven fell unto the earth . . . And the heavens departed as a scroll when it is rolled together; and every mountain and island were moved out of their places.*'

'Breathtaking. Seeing I am trapped in this infernal human form, I shall invest in a small cabin in the highest mountains of this planet immediately on my return to Normandy as a safeguard to ensure my survival.'

And snatching the missive with the Rubied Seal out of Jether's palm, he walked through the chamber out into the lobby, past the trembling Obadiah, and into the open elevator.

Jether stood in the doorway watching him in silence.

Charsoc looked back at Jether, then studied his rings and yawned deliberately.

'Of course, no one will ever realize that the Rapture even occurred,' he said, nonchalantly.

The iron gates of the elevator began to close.

'The disappearance of the "Christians" will be passed off as a complete non-event. Overlooked in a natural disaster and its resulting pandemic that caused the death of untold millions.'

He pulled down the brim of his fedora hat.

'As they say in some sectors of this planet,' he said crisply, 'have a nice day.'

Jether watched as the elevator disappeared from view.

He hesitated as though hearing something, then turned to the youngling. 'Obadiah, hold the fort until my return.' He made the sign of the cross. 'I have urgent business to attend.'

CHAPTER THIRTY-FOUR

Dossiers Secrets du Professeur

Jason got out of the army van and thanked the lieutenant out loud, and Adrian silently, for arranging him a special pass. Although the London Pact had been signed six months ago, the UK curfews implemented in 2023 were still in place. It was five minutes past nine and the Belgravia streets were deserted. He walked towards the front door. Maxim waited for him on the brightly lit porch.

'Master Jason,' Maxim said, wringing his hands in distress. 'How is Madam Lilian?'

'She's stable,' Jason said, softly, walking into the hall. 'In intensive care, but stable.'

He removed his jacket and handed it to Maxim. 'It's a waiting game.'

He loosened his collar and rolled up his shirtsleeves.

'Master Adrian called from Babylon at lunch,' Maxim said.

'I talked to him from the hospital,' Jason replied. He looked at his watch. 'He should be landing any minute. Mother's tough, Maxim. The doctors say she'll pull through.'

'Tough as an old boot,' Maxim said, taking a handerchief

from his top pocket. He dabbed his eyes, then blew his nose in loud decibels.

Jason opened the drawing room doors.

'Mother's not herself, Maxim,' he said, softly. 'She's hallucinating. Kept saying they took her baby.'

Jason looked up at Maxim, pale and drawn. 'Maxim . . .' He hesitated.

'After Nick's death, Weaver, Nick's old school friend, sent me a disk with information Nick had emailed him before he died. It was a copy of a letter from my father. And some other documents. I sent them to St Cartier for safekeeping.'

He studied Maxim closely.

'You knew my father. Knew him well. I was too young to notice anything . . . or care. Was there ever any evidence that Dad was involved with anything *clandestine*?'

Maxim looked into Jason's eyes for a long time, then finally spoke.

'It came to my knowledge that Master James was a long-term member of a secret society of the elite, Master Jason. I once was a reluctant witness to a fight between Master James and Madam Lilian. Unfortunately I heard more than was necessary for me to be privy to.'

'And?'

'It was about your grandfather, Julius De Vere.'

'Julius? He kept to himself.'

'The father was different from the son,' Maxim said, quietly. 'There were things Master James would have to do that he felt violated his moral code. He despised himself for being a part of it. He did it to ensure that you boys would remain unharmed. And free from their clutches. That is all I know.'

'Thank you, Maxim.' Jason stood in the hall deep in thought. It was not the answer he wanted to hear.

'Maxim, what was the appointment Mother had in Wimpole Street?'

'She was on a call to Wimpole Street two days ago, Master Jason. I assumed it was the doctor's.'

Jason frowned.

'That would explain it.'

'All I know is she took a taxi yesterday morning. Refused the chauffeur. Said it was private. I should have told you.'

'You did fine. Now get some rest. I'll stay up in case the hospital calls.'

Maxim bowed.

'Your whisky is on the cabinet. Poured.'

'Maxim, one last thing. Mother was very confused. She mentioned a document that had arrived.' He paused. 'A document from my father.'

'From Master James?' Maxim frowned. 'But Master James is deceased.'

Jason nodded.

'Yes, Maxim, we know that,' he said patiently.

Maxim wrinkled his brow.

'A Fedex package *did* arrive on Tuesday addressed to Madam. She signed for it. She refused supper that night.'

'Thank you, Maxim.'

With a bow, Maxim closed the heavy mahogany drawing room doors.

Jason walked over and switched on a small sidelamp on the liquor cabinet, then picked up the whisky Maxim had poured. He gazed silently ahead out of the large arched drawing room window into the night sky, then reached over and switched on the television remote.

He switched from Sky to CNN, then to Vox USA. The usual images of looting and soldiers patrolling the curfewed streets of New York filled the screens. He watched the bread lines in Los Angeles and sighed. America had collapsed into anarchy. The United States was unrecognizable. Indeed, it

372

was being divided into thirty-three regions that very month. Each region's government would be autonomous.

Thank god he'd moved Vox headquarters to Babylon when he did – thanks to Adrian.

The grandfather clock struck 2 a.m. He switched on to BBC News 24 and sat down on the sofa. He watched in the dim half-light as Adrian's face came onscreen.

'*Adrian De Vere, President of the European Superstate, ended the World Summit today with the unveiling of a bailout plan to the tune of fifty trillion dollars . . .*' Jason flicked the remote off and pressed the video player remote. Pictures of Adrian, Nick, and Jason when they were young flickered onscreen. He sighed and leaned back into the sofa, his feet up on the coffee table, to watch a young Lilian holding Nick on her lap as he blew out three candles on a huge birthday cake. Jason and Adrian stood behind dressed in bow ties.

Jason recalled his seventeenth birthday party. It was at the De Vere mansion in Narragansett. Nick had run around with a camera snapping Jason, Adrian, and anything that moved.

Nick. Jason sighed. It had been over three years since his brother's death and he still wished with every passing day that he could have had just one chance to put things right. He looked down at his phone. A new text from Aunt Rosemary. Adrian had just arrived at the hospital. Lilian was sleeping. Stable. *Mother.*

He turned to look at the original painting by Annigoni hanging over Lilian's writing desk, then rose, walked across the room, and carefully removed the painting from the wall.

Facing him was a small iron safe. He stared down at a black-and-white photo of his father, then punched in a combination.

The safe door sprang open. Jason reached inside and

brought out a wad of aged and bulging files. Carefully, he sifted through them.

James and Lilian's marriage certificate. James's death certificate. Nick's death certificate. He paused. Copies of Julia and Jason's marriage certificate and Lily's birth certificate.

Why on earth did she keep this stuff? He shrugged.

There, right at the bottom, exactly where Lilian had said it would be, lay the thin black file with James's private De Vere insignia embossed on the front.

Jason took it out and placed it on Lilian's writing desk, then replaced the files in the safe, and relocked the combination.

He poured himself a second whisky, sat back on the sofa, and opened the file, sifting through the top papers.

Three records of money deposits ... bank account numbers ... no names. Nothing else except an innocuous-looking bulky blue linen envelope. He looked at the postmark and frowned. The Isle of Arran, *Scotland*?

He opened it. Inside was a wad of cheap lined paper of the sort available at any corner shop in England.

He studied the ten stapled pages of shaky black handwriting, then flipped through to the end. He stared at the signature.

'Hamish MacKenzie. The Gables Retirement Home'.

He started to read.

CHAPTER THIRTY-FIVE

Aveline

2017
Gables Retirement Home
Isle of Arran, Scotland

Professor Hamish MacKenzie – now nearly ninety-seven, sat at a writing desk in his bathchair. He gazed out through the window at the vast Scottish loch that glimmered in the early morning mist at the edge of the manicured lawns of the Gables.

He picked up his pen with trembling fingers.

30 December 2017

To James De Vere

Please do not dismiss what I am about to disclose to you as the senile ramblings of a very old man. As I write this I am ninety-seven, and my time on this earth is complete. They cannot harm me now.

I am not a religious man. My god was the God of Science.

But before I meet my maker, I feel it essential that I divest myself of the great burden of conscience that I have carried for over three decades.

Proof of these incidents have been lodged with my lawyers for decades, but my lawyers were paid huge sums of money to mislay them. What you have in your hand is the only actual proof that any of the events I am about to disclose to you ever happened.

Jason picked up the top document and then laid it down. He turned the page.

When I was younger I was like many genetic scientists of my era – driven and ambitious to find the elusive at any cost. I placed science and the pursuit of know-ledge above moral ethical considerations . . . I was the epitome of this to my shame.

MacKenzie dipped his nib in the violet ink and continued his meticulous scratching on the page.

In 1962, I concluded the successful nuclear transfer from a diploid cell of a frog to an unfertilized egg cell from which the maternal nucleus had been removed.

From there my work came to the attention of global intelligence agencies. And to the attention of the Directorate of Operations, the branch of the CIA that ran covert operations: UFO design and testing, HAARP technology, anti-gravitational propulsion research, and a host of macabre black-ops programmes, including a highly advanced covert eugenics and biogenetic engi-neering programme.

For over two decades I conducted thousands of macabre experiments in the military's deep underground bases – the core of the Directorate's operations and the Military Industrial complex. I journeyed between Groom Lake, Dreamland, Area 51, Los Alamos, Dulce – to name just a few.

We performed gruesome experimentation on thousands of supposedly abducted and missing children. We used young women as incubators for our grisly hybrid experiments. We conducted alien–human genetic research in our covert laboratories far below the surface of the Earth. I will spare you the lurid details, only to say it is a part of my life I deeply regret. By 1976, I was regarded as the top genetic scientist in the world.

Unbeknown to the general public, in 1974 we already had successfully cloned five equivalents of 'Dolly the sheep', and were just weeks away from the first human cloning.

Hamish MacKenzie put down his pen and looked out at a gardener trimming the edges of the manicured lawns.

In February 1981, my black-ops handlers were approached by their extremely powerful masters. A covert organization – a shadow government, if you will. Controlled by a mysterious Jesuit priest.

I was personally offered multiple millions for my research to insert a genome provided by them into an unfertilized egg whose genes were to be removed. There were mutterings about the Immaculate Conception.

I was not a religious man. I asked no questions. Obeyed my masters. Did as I was instructed. To the letter.

In December of 1981, I had one ambition – to leave the world of depraved covert biogenetics behind.

With the money I earned from this project, I planned

to create my own foundation – The Aveline Foundation for Genetic Research – and return home to my native Scotland.

2025
The De Vere Mansion
Belgrave Square, London

'Aveline.' Jason scrabbled in Lilian's desk drawer for a pack of cigarettes.

She didn't smoke, but he knew she still kept a pack of James's favourite brand even years after his death. They were there, just as he'd thought.

'Aveline.' The name rang a bell. He shook a cigarette out of the packet. Julia had always disapproved of his smoking. *C'est la vie.*

He took out James's lighter and lit the cigarette.

'Of course! Aveline was the name on the back of the photograph his father had sent Nick.'

Jason looked at his watch, then picked up his phone and dialled.

2025
St Bernadette's Hospital
Hyde Park Corner

Adrian stood over Lilian. Her face was covered by an oxygen mask. His mobile phone rang.

'Yes, Jas,' he said, smiling down at Lilian. 'Relax. Mother's fine. She's stable. I've sent Rosemary off to get some shut-eye. Yes, of course I'll stay with her until she wakes. I'll let you know as soon as there's any change. Bye.'

The De Vere Mansion
Belgrave Square, London

Jason clicked off his phone, then continued reading.

2017

Gables Retirement Home
Isle of Arran, Scotland

I had never seen genetic material like that before. Not even in my experiments with alien DNA. The genome was unequivocally not of human matter. Its genetic make-up was like nothing I had ever encountered.

Hamish MacKenzie gazed out at the still grey surface of the loch.

I well remember that day. The day when he came to the safe house in Marazion. He was dressed in the black robes of a Jesuit priest.

I never knew his name.
But I will never forget his face.

CHAPTER THIRTY-SIX

Nightmare Hall

1981
Northern Gate, The Asylum
Marazion, Cornwall, England

The driving rain lashed down onto the sleek black antique Rolls Royce Phantom Two as it purred past the towering, centuries-old iron gates of the Asylum. It turned down into a narrow cobblestoned lane, its blinding headlights illuminating the stark forbidding walls of the Gothic Revival mansion that was positioned against a vast disused copper mine.

A blinding flash of lightning crashed through the heavens as the Rolls drew to a halt under the austere gaze of the monstrous stone griffins perched on the turrets either side of the northern entrance.

Two clean-shaven bodyguards exited in full military uniform. The first opened the passenger door of the Rolls. The second stood quietly at attention.

Two feet in a pair of black Tanino Crisci limited edition patent shoes set down on the gravel, followed by a silver cane in a gloved hand. Standing up, the tall robed figure walked up the short pathway to the entrance, his features hidden by the circular brim of his *cappello romano* hat.

He paused to look out past the griffins into the black Cornish skies that loomed above him as a myriad of strange spherical objects flashed in the sky overhead at lightning speed – then disappeared.

Lorcan De Molay smiled slowly in approval. He smoothed the black robes of the Jesuit order and adjusted the large crucifix that hung from a cord around his neck.

This was the abode of his Dark Slaves of the race of men, who ran more than a thousand of the sprawling underground cities of the Brotherhood, and the abode of the Fallen. He nodded to his bodyguard, who knocked loudly on the monstrous wooden door.

Slowly the wooden facade slid open, revealing a one-foot-thick steel door. The door slid open and De Molay walked past Hamid into the yawning vestibule, where ten soldiers in full battledress stood at attention.

De Molay nodded to the Serbian officer.

'Colonel Vaclav.' Vaclav saluted, trembling visibly.

De Molay removed his hat. He nodded to a tall, flat-faced Russian.

'General Vlad.'

An ear-splitting siren sounded. Vlad saluted nervously as two thick steel doors slid open on the far side of the vestibule. De Molay removed his black kid-leather gloves, as Moloch and seven more of the Fallen lumbered towards him.

Moloch towered over the terrified Vlad, leering, his long, black, stringy hair masking his contorted craggy features, then grasped Vlad's throat with one monstrous hand and held him two feet off the ground. De Molay raised his hand. Moloch scowled, instantly dropping the suffocating Russian to the floor.

'You spoil my sport, Master,' Moloch growled, his voice a mixture of dark discords.

'You will have your sport later. Where is the Halfling?' De Molay demanded.

'The Halfling awaits you, My Lord,' Moloch growled.

A hefty, thick-featured, Germanic woman, dressed in a black siren suit, appeared behind him.

'Your communication implied that the nuclear transfer has been successful, Fraulein Meeling?' De Molay asked tersely.

Frau Meeling saluted, staring up at him in terror.

'Jawohl, Your Reverence. Professor MacKenzie has been successful.'

De Molay nodded and Meeling led the way down the huge corridor, then turned a sharp right where a posse of black-suited soldiers wearing the sand-coloured berets and the cap badge of the SAS stood guarding an enormous cavern – the entrance to a sprawling underground complex.

They saluted as one at De Molay as he rounded the corner. The party boarded a large silver railcar and strapped themselves in. The railcar erupted at Mach 2, passing the split-second light of hundreds of other railcars as it sped through the subterranean tunnel seven miles beneath the surface of the dramatic wild countryside of Cornwall and under the Atlantic – its final destination Reykjavik, Iceland.

Ninety minutes later, the railcar stopped outside a steel gate which opened into a sprawling underground city.

Meeling led the way past the NATO military guards into a steel lift. As the operator powered up, hundreds of crystals emitted a purple-bluish light and the lift car plunged downwards at high speed past levels two and three, still downwards past levels four and five. It stopped abruptly at level six.

Lorcan De Molay and Frau Meeling exited from the lift and walked through a second energy field. Armed Nephilim, genetic hybrids – part human, part angelic – covered their faces from him as he walked. He stopped before a huge pulsing screen that read *Level Six: Genetic Halls – Human, Not Human* in English, Icelandic; and in a language of fallen angelic symbols.

De Molay walked through the *Not Human* entrance, through a second steel gate and into the lobby of Level Six.

A thousand bloodcurdling screams of insanity echoed through the maze of winding Gothic corridors.

'Nightmare Hall,' De Molay murmured. 'The Twins have excelled themselves, don't you think, Frau Meeling?'

The corridors of Nightmare Hall were punctuated by hundreds of cells with small iron barred windows. The inmates shrieked in terror as De Molay strode past multi-limbed humans and vats of seven-feet-tall, bat-like humanoid creatures. They passed a large cell, the inmates of which were dwarves and children with severed limbs and strange staring pale blue eyes.

'We finish the work begun by our medical hero, Josef Mengele, the Angel of Death, Your Reverence,' Meeling whispered, in awe.

She inserted a pass key in the scanner, then waited while the doors clicked open. She pushed through them, then headed straight for a second set of large institutional-looking doors at the far end of the research laboratory marked *Psychosurgery – Restricted Entry Only*, guarded by nine-foot Nephilim.

A second set of steel doors opened to reveal a small laboratory. On the glass panels was written *Genetics Department* in large black letters.

Frau Meeling bowed and turned on her heels, leaving De Molay alone with the elderly man who was huddled intently over state-of-the-art cloning equipment.

De Molay smiled thinly.

'Our "special undertaking" has been successful'?

Professor Hamish MacKenzie turned to face De Molay, who surveyed him with mild distaste. MacKenzie's baggy old cardigan was wrongly buttoned and his worn trousers were sagging at the knees. There were day-old egg stains on his shirt. He ran his veined fingers through his sparse white hair; a strange exhilaration lit his watery blue eyes.

'Successful beyond all imagining, Your Reverence,' he murmured.

MacKenzie continued, euphoric, unaware of De Molay's disapproval.

'Precisely one hundred and twenty days ago, I inserted the genome of alien matter into an unfertilized egg whose genes I had removed.'

De Molay's gaze moved from the unkempt MacKenzie to the state-of-the-art laboratory filled with centrifuges, thermocyclers, molecular phosphorimagers, cloning cylinders, hybridization chambers, and plating devices.

MacKenzie walked to a second unmarked door, his eyeline in direct parallel to a small steel machine that instantly emitted a purple laser directly into his iris. The steel doors opened.

De Molay followed MacKenzie through a smaller, pristine laboratory that opened into a glass-domed chamber some twenty feet high.

As De Molay entered, the laboratory plunged into darkness. The only light emanated from the solitary glass incubating chamber, covered by a muslin cloth.

MacKenzie removed the cover from the artificial prototype womb.

The four-month-old foetus was suspended in a translucent fluid-filled sac, its heart visibly pumping, sleeping as soundly as if in its mother's womb.

'The fertilized egg is now growing and developing,' MacKenzie said. His eyes gleamed in exhilaration.

'With only the donor's nuclear genetic code. Of alien matter and yet . . .'

'And yet, it develops as a human,' De Molay murmured. He took a step nearer, as though magnetized, to the incubator. The foetus's heart began to beat more rapidly.

MacKenzie stared at the foetus, confused. The monitor's readings were escalating out of control. Trembling, he checked the readings. The foetus's heart was now pounding at 300 beats per minute.

De Molay placed his hand on the glass dome. MacKenzie watched in horror as the heartbeat escalated to 340 . . . 360 . . . 400. A bright purple light pulsed from the foetus's chest cavity. MacKenzie was flung to the floor, temporarily blinded, his hands over his ears, screaming from the excruciating pain that coursed through every cell of his body.

De Molay caressed the glass dome and the foetus's eyes opened. De Molay stared, mesmerized into the foetus's glowing violet gaze.

MacKenzie looked up just as its eyes emitted a savage electrical current that struck through the incubator's glass dome, striking the dome of the laboratory.

'My only begotten son . . .' De Molay murmured. Then abruptly removed his hand.

2017
Gables Retirement Home
Isle of Arran, Scotland

MacKenzie stopped writing. He shuddered, then leant back in his bathchair, fighting nausea. He took a deep breath and picked up his pen.

1981
The Laboratory
Reykjavik, Iceland

Instantly the lights and electrical apparatus switched back on. The foetus's heartbeat slowed to 80 beats per minute.

MacKenzie, paralyzed with terror, looked up from the ground, staring up at the Jesuit priest.

'As per our agreement, you will receive fifteen million dollars,' De Molay said softly. 'One third transferred to your account on the clone's birth, the next instalment when he turns eighteen. In the event of your death by natural or any other causes, on his fortieth birthday, the final instalment will be transferred to your scientific foundation, the Aveline Institute.'

2025
The De Vere Mansion
Belgrave Square, London

There was that name again. 'Aveline'.

Jason took a sip of whisky and turned the page.

1981
The Laboratory
Reykjavik, Iceland

MacKenzie rose to his feet, trembling visibly.

He looked at De Molay, who was still staring mesmerized at the clone.

'Forty million dollars,' MacKenzie said. His voice was very soft.

'I have deposited copies of every piece of correspondence,' he continued. 'Our agreements, my procedures with lawyers in London.'

He glanced at the foetus, then back to De Molay.

'Every conversation anyone in your organization has conducted with me months before my furlough here began, I recorded. Every cloning blueprint has been scanned and already transferred to my outside sources.'

He stood staring at De Molay. 'I remain convinced that you and your elite minions will go to extreme lengths to ensure the secrecy of this project.' He hesitated.

'Your organization's name is mentioned, as is the head of MI6 – Piers Aspinall – along with seven others. I think the few remaining nobler elements of the British and US governments will find the incriminating evidence precisely what they've been hoping for, and will connect it with Los Alamos.'

The professor smiled slightly. 'Maybe even Dulce . . .'

'You see, Your Reverence, I am many things . . .' He hesitated. 'A coward, perhaps . . .' He looked into De Molay's watery pale gaze. 'But a fool – no. The microdot is a copy. In the event of my untimely death or disappearance, the contents will be communicated to every opponent of your Shadow Government in the Western and Eastern hemispheres. Your operation will be permanently jeopardized.'

'You have no idea who you are dealing with,' De Molay said, evenly.

MacKenzie reached into his pocket and brought out a large handkerchief and wiped his brow.

'I have no next of kin to blackmail me into submission. My life is dedicated only to science.'

De Molay studied MacKenzie intently.

Finally he spoke. 'Forty million.' He paused. 'You are no fool, Professor.'

'And you' – MacKenzie stared straight into De Molay's eyes – 'are no priest.'

MacKenzie turned back to the foetus. When he looked up a moment later, De Molay had vanished.

2025
The De Vere Mansion
Belgrave Square, London

J ason slowly stubbed his half-smoked cigarette out in an ashtray. He turned the page.

I am ashamed now, so many years later, of my greed. But I was a most ambitious man. And the money set my foundation up for my lifetime. And the next.

Thirty seconds after I successfully delivered the clone I was escorted by security agents to Stansted Airport in London. I was flown back by an unmarked jet to Area 51.

The next day, a mysterious fire broke out in the safe house in Reykjavik. The laboratory in Iceland and years of research documents were destroyed. All my research staff suffocated in the fire.

Five days later, the first ten million was transferred to my account.

J ason reached for the papers with the bank account numbers. There it was in black and white. A transfer of ten million dollars on 26 December 1981. He shrugged. He still didn't get it. What did this have to do with anything? Especially with his father?

. . . and, unknown to the whole world, at 2 p.m. on 21 December, 1981, the world's first nuclear genetic clone was succesfully delivered.

I retired from my intelligence work two months later and relocated to Scotland where I set up my research quarters in Edinburgh.

CHAPTER THIRTY-SEVEN

A Death in the Family

2025
St Bernadette's Hospital
Hyde Park Corner

Adrian looked down at his phone. It was Jason. Adrian turned to the nurse.

'Private call.' He gestured to his phone. 'Give me two minutes. No disturbances.' The nurse nodded.

'Yes, of course, Mr President, sir.'

'Jason, Mother's heavily sedated,' he said, 'but she's stabilized. Fast asleep. Don't bother to come over. You get some sleep. I'll stay with her till Rosemary returns. Great. I'll phone you if anything changes.'

Adrian clicked off his phone. Lilian's eyes flickered open.

'The Vanderbylt connection has been most advantageous, Mother,' Adrian smiled down at Lilian. 'Especially with the Israelis. But when all's said and done, the Accord has been signed and sealed for three years.'

He paced the hospital room.

'James? He knew too much. He was about to talk. I had

no option, Lilian – I had to kill him. As for Melissa,' Adrian said, matter of factly, 'she and her father were becoming a liability. And Nick?' He shrugged. 'I liked Nick.'

Lilian struggled to reach her mask.

'He was innocuous enough. That wasn't in the plan.'

She tore the mask off with all her remaining strength.

'You . . .' Ashen, she stared at Adrian. Her hands trembled violently. 'They got to you. They promised to leave you alone.'

'Mother,' Adrian smiled, 'I *am* "they" . . .'

Lilian stared up at Adrian, her eyes wide with horror and rage.

He walked round to the oxygen flow meter. 'But you see, Lilian . . .' His fingers moved casually over the tubes to Lilian's breathing cannula. 'You've been getting too clever. And you *are* in the plan. You see, Lilian, you signed your own death warrant. The information you so cleverly tracked down at the Medical Library in Wimpole Street is just *far* too incriminating to let you stay alive.'

Lilian tried desperately to lift herself up.

'Jason.' She looked beseechingly at Adrian.

'Oh, Jason's your first-born all right. A real chip off the old block, as they say. Your second son was strangled at birth – the babies exchanged – by order of the Grande Druid Council. The execution papers were signed by Julius De Vere. And now, Mother, your meddling has sealed Jason's fate.'

Lilian closed her eyes. A single tear fell down her cheek.

Adrian smiled. 'You want to plead for your eldest son's life?'

A male nurse entered quietly and Lilian reached out her hand towards him.

'Help me, please,' she sobbed.

The male nurse nodded to Adrian, and Lilian watched in

horror as the nurse metamorphosized into a Warlock right before her eyes.

As she reached for her rosary, her voice was shaking, barely audible.

'Michael, the Archangel, defend us in the hour of battle,' she whispered. 'Be our safeguard against the wickedness and snares of the devil.'

Lilian stared up at Adrian, afraid but resolute.

'May God rebuke him we humbly pray, and do thou, O Prince of the heavenly host' – Lilian clasped the rosary tightly to her breast – 'by the power of God, thrust down to hell Satan' – she struggled to breathe – 'and all the evil spirits who wander through this world . . . seeking the ruin of souls.'

Adrian looked down at her, watching her face turn blue.

'They won't hear the alarm, Mother,' he murmured, 'I had it disconnected ten minutes ago.' He stroked her hair. 'It was good while it lasted.'

'Lawrence,' Lilian murmured. Adrian's eyes narrowed. He sensed it.

The Presence. He followed her gaze towards the door but there was no one there.

'I knew you'd come, Lawrence,' Lilian whispered in elation.

The Warlock retched violently. Adrian snatched the rosary from Lilian's fingers and nodded to the Warlock, his eyes black with malice.

The Warlock swabbed Lilian's skin, then held up a hypodermic syringe.

'The fact that you were Jewish was unavoidable,' Adrian murmured as the Warlock slowly injected Lilian with one ampoule of concentrated potassium chloride.

'But this will make up for it.'

Precisely ninety seconds later, Lilian De Vere was dead.

Jason walked through to the kitchen, letter in hand. He put the letter down on the kitchen table, grabbed a cafetière from above the Aga cooker, then a package of Lilian's favourite Columbian coffee and switched on the electric kettle. He idly studied the branding on the package of coffee – mass market from her local grocery store. He shook his head.

He'd never understood it. No matter where she travelled, Lilian swore that nothing matched up to the coffee he now held in his hand.

He measured out two scoops into the cafetière, unaware that at the precise moment, Lilian was being murdered by his younger brother.

He flicked the kettle off, poured the water into the cafetière and pressed the plunger down.

'She is far beyond your reach now,' Jether said.

Adrian leaned against the wall of the toilet in Lilian's hospital room, sweat pouring from his brow, avoiding Jether's gaze. He slid to his knees, retching violently.

'The Nazarene,' he uttered. 'You have been with him.'

Adrian gazed up at Jether with loathing. His eyes glowed strangely, like intensely burning coals.

'His presence torments you,' Jether said. He bowed his head.

'You were too late,' Adrian rasped, 'to save her.'

'No,' Jether said, softly. 'It was her time.'

Adrian's breathing became easier.

'Do not think your secluded Portal in Alexandria will

remain intact without a fight, Jether the Just,' he spat. 'The Monastery of Archangels is a military target. High on the list of the Fallen.'

He raised himself unsteadily to his feet. Recovering rapidly.

'I will win.'

Lilian's rosary, still in Adrian's left hand, began to smoulder. Opening his hand, he stared down in horror as the sign of the cross branded itself into his left palm.

'The Nazarene,' Jether said, softly. 'He will defeat you on the Plains of Megiddo.'

And he vanished before Adrian's eyes.

2025
The De Vere Mansion
Belgrave Square, London

Jason poured the coffee, then pulled out a kitchen chair and sat. He took a sip of the coffee, then picked up the coffee carton.

'Not bad, Mother,' he muttered. Then he picked up Hamish MacKenzie's letter and continued reading.

1998
The Aveline Foundation
Edinburgh, Scotland

MacKenzie was sitting at his desk when an orderly entered clutching a postal sack. He emptied it out onto the table and MacKenzie watched as the envelopes and papers fell out onto his desk.

'Alien watchers, cult watchers, threats, Doc – they're calling you a satanist this time.' MacKenzie shook his head and scanned some of the papers.

The orderly leaned over.

'The old man is here again,' he said. 'He's causing a ruckus, Hamish. It's bad for the Institute.'

MacKenzie took off his glasses and sighed. He rubbed his eyes wearily.

'All right, I'll see him. Rescue me after two minutes.'

'He's at the door.'

The orderly opened the door and ushered a grubby old man inside. The old man stood nervously in front of MacKenzie, clutching his plastic bags.

MacKenzie gestured to the chair in front of him. 'Please sit.'

The old man shook his head. He stared around the room, obviously petrified.

'I can't be long. Have to stay on the move. They're everywhere.'

MacKenzie frowned, confused at the man's eloquent enunciation. The man pushed a paper over the desk to MacKenzie.

'My credentials.'

'Fellow of the Royal College of Obstetrics,' MacKenzie read aloud. 'Member of British Foetal Medicine, Perinatal Medicine.' MacKenzie looked up at the old man in faint recognition. 'Why, you're Rupert Percival.' He stared in shock at the filthy homeless man before him. 'You were the obstetrician in the St Gabriel's case?'

The old man nodded, a bit calmer now. 'I received my medical degree at Trinity College, Dublin, and did my obstetric internship at Guy's. I was highly respected in my field. Look, my time is short. They'll get to me. They get to everyone eventually.' He darted a glance out of the window, then back at the door.

'There was an incident. I was highly sought after. My practice was in Harley Street. I selected my patients from the elite. The prenatal genetic diagnosis for one of the mothers I looked after was oligohydramnios.'

'Too little amniotic fluid?'

Percival nodded.

'There was no doubt of the poor foetal growth. A lagging fundal measurement of over 3 centimetres. Because of the status and wealth of this particular family – he had a top White House job, very wealthy, banking, oil; they were in London for the summer – no measure was spared. DNA samples, weekly ultrasounds and measurements of the baby's head, thigh bone, abdominal circumferences. In the last two-thirds of pregnancy the amniotic fluid comes from foetal urine, and since lung formation is dependent on breathing in amniotic fluid, the lungs of these babies with very severe dysplasia are very underdeveloped.

'I set the Caesarean date for 20 December 1981.

'Certain powers that be did everything they could to take me off her case and replace me with a fellow of the Monash Institute, but the mother would have none of it. She insisted that I, and only I, treat her.

'I delivered the baby on the set date at St Gabriel's Nursing Home in Knightsbridge. As expected, the baby had very severe dysplasia and no kidney function at all and as a result was placed immediately in intensive care.

'I didn't expect it to be able to survive more than a few hours after birth because of the poor lung function. Well, the following morning I came in at dawn for my routine visit. The baby's functions were perfect. It was a *completely different baby.*'

'You're sure you couldn't have been mistaken?' MacKenzie asked him.

'I am a specialist, MacKenzie. There was no mistake. I sounded the alarm. But all details in the file had been changed to coincide with the replacement. The nursing staff I'd worked with on the previous shifts were all mysteriously unobtainable and the mother – of course never having seen the baby – insisted it was a miracle.

'The powers that orchestrated this were very wealthy and very, very powerful. Within twenty-four hours, I was made out to be a madman.

'On reaching my surgery in Harley Street, I found my office ransacked, all files confiscated – by M16, I was informed.

'I was immediately suspended and my name was dragged through the mud by the British press.'

'Gross misconduct,' MacKenzie whispered, remembering. 'They said you had been drunk while operating, that you had a long-standing alcohol problem.'

'A dry sherry at Christmas, that was the extent of my drinking. They shut me out and shut me up, MacKenzie. Took my credibility. I lost my family, my career, my *life*. They turned me into this.'

Percival scrabbled in one of his shopping bags.

'Unbeknown to them, I had executed two sets of tests, one immediately after the birth, a separate one the following dawn. I had filed those papers immediately with the Redgrave Medical Library in Wimpole Street, under a fictitious case name. They have lain there undisclosed for over seventeen years. They will be your proof.'

2025
The De Vere Mansion
Belgrave Square, London

Jason put MacKenzie's letter down and riffled through the file. Scrawled on the back of the last page was 'The Redgrave Medical Library, 64 Wimpole Street'.

'Wimpole Street,' Jason said to himself. 'So that's what Mother was looking for.'

1998
The Aveline Foundation
Edinburgh, Scotland

'I had taken a sample of the newborn's DNA early that morning when I came in. I still had a sample of the foetus's original DNA.'

Percival took a small steel tin from his plastic bag.

'I'm dying, MacKenzie. I have six weeks left, maximum. They can't get to me any more. I needed an expert in the field. Someone I could entrust this to.'

Opening the steel tin, he placed two laboratory slides on the table before MacKenzie.

'It's the DNA of the surrogate. I had never seen genetic make-up like that in my life before.'

Percival looked up at MacKenzie. His lip trembled.

'It was non-human.'

MacKenzie walked over to a large microscope in the anteroom leading from his office. Percival's hands trembled as he passed the first slide over.

'The DNA belonging to the original baby.'

He passed the second slide. 'The surrogate's DNA.'

MacKenzie stared out towards the loch, his eyes distant. 'That was the first time I ever knew . . .'

2025
The De Vere Mansion
Belgrave Square, London

Jason continued reading . . .

The genetic make-up of Percival's 'surrogate infant' was the exact replica of the nuclear genetic clone that I had produced years before in my laboratory. There could be no mistake.

I knew the clone's genetic markers in my sleep.

It was the DNA belonging to the clone.

Born twelve hours after the Caesarean birth of Percival's infant.

'They' had calculatedly removed the original infant and switched it for their own genetic clone, unknown to the parents, for some veiled malevolent scheme.

Percival's body was discovered a week later with a gunshot through the chest. In a rubbish dump.

Gables Retirement Home
Isle of Arran, Scotland

A ruddy-faced old lady, her hair covered by a purple scarf, pushed a tea trolley into the room and smiled kindly at MacKenzie.

'The usual, Professor?' she asked.

MacKenzie nodded. 'Thank you, Bridget.'

As she poured him a steaming cup of tea, MacKenzie folded up the letter and pushed it into a pale blue envelope. He licked and sealed it and with shaking hand wrote on the envelope:

James De Vere – Personal
c/o Thomas Nunn
Adler, Nunn, and Greenstreet Solicitors
Vestry Hall, Chancery Street
London WC2A.

Bridget placed the tea down next to him on the desk.

'Three sugars, Professor?' MacKenzie nodded.

'Bridget.' He took her leathered hand in his and placed the blue envelope carefully in it. 'Get this in the last post.'

Reaching in his bathrobe, he brought out a battered old wallet and carefully counted out three pound coins and a couple of twenty pence.

'Register it, Bridget, and bring me the receipt.'

'Of course, Professor.' She gave him a cheery smile. 'I'll see you later.'

The door closed and MacKenzie picked up his tea, relief written all over his face. He closed his eyes.

CHAPTER THIRTY-EIGHT

Skeletons in the Closet

2025
The De Vere Mansion
Belgrave Square, London

Jason looked up, ashen. Maxim stood in the kitchen doorway, his dressing gown awry.

'I . . . I'm afraid I have terrible news, Master Jason, sir. From the hospital.'

Jason stood up and felt in his pocket for his phone.

'Damn.' He'd left it in the drawing room all this time.

'It's Madam Lilian, sir.'

Jason steeled himself.

'She passed away ten minutes ago.'

Jason sat heavily in the kitchen chair. He stared up at Maxim, speechless.

Maxim walked over to the pantry, then reappeared a minute later holding a whisky bottle in his right hand. He laid the bottle and one glass down in front of Jason.

'You don't approve of my drinking, Maxim,' Jason said, frowning.

'Madam Lilian's last instructions before she died, Master Jason, sir.' Maxim's voice shook with emotion.

Jason held up the bottle and looked at it.

'It's over seventy years old,' he whispered, reading the label. 'Macallan Fine and Rare Collection. These bottles are out of circulation.'

'Seventy-two years old to be precise, Master Jason, sir. Madam Lilian acquired it for thirty-eight thousand pounds in 2008.'

Jason shook his head in disbelief. He looked at the blue ribbon tied around the neck of the bottle, then opened the card. It was Lilian's handwriting, dated the day before she had collapsed on Wimpole Street.

To my beloved eldest son.

I have kept this for you as a token for over fifteen years.

Yes, you well know I don't approve of your drinking. I never have.

But if ever there was a moment for a toast, surely it is now.

I have lost your father. I lost Nick.

And I now know that Adrian was never mine to lose.

You, my beloved son, are all I have left.

Look after Lily for me. And Julia. She loves you, Jason.

Be strong, my son. Be courageous.

And fight for the truth, no matter where it may lead you.

Do not fret for me, for I am in a much better place.

I wish you love. I wish you peace.

But most of all – I wish you faith, Jason.

I will love you always,

Mother.

Jason looked up at Maxim. He wiped the tears from his cheek.

'She knew . . .' His voice broke. 'She knew she would die.'

Maxim nodded, unable to speak. He poured the whisky into Jason's glass then raised his own glass of elderflower cordial.

The phone rang in the hallway. Maxim went to answer it.

Jason picked up the card and reread it.

Maxim walked back into the kitchen.

'Master Adrian has just left the hospital. He's coming straight over.'

Jason sat at the kitchen table, the half-finished glass of single malt in front of him. He turned to the last page of MacKenzie's letter.

I have followed the genetic clone's rise intently since that day in 1998.

In December of that year, he graduated with five A levels from Gordonstoun.

In 2002 he received his BA (Hons) in politics, philosophy, and economics from Oxford.

In 2005, after two years at Princeton, he spent a year specializing in Arab studies in Georgetown.

From 2006 to 2010, he served as a director in the family business. Asset management.

He became Chancellor of the Exchequer in 2010.

In 2012 he became British Prime Minister.

This is the secret I have held for over three decades.

His father was James. His mother, Lilian.

Jason stared at the last sentence in disbelief.

The clone incubated in the Jesuit laboratory all those decades ago is none other than the present Prime Minister of the United Kingdom – your son – Adrian De Vere.

The whisky glass slid out of Jason's fingers and smashed to the floor.

He sat staring at the shattered pieces of glass for a full minute. Slowly he got up, then walked over to the kitchen door and unlocked it, the blue envelope still clutched in his hand. He paced restlessly around the rose beds, threw down his fourth cigarette of the evening and stubbed it out with his heel, then took out the packet and immediately lit another one, his fingers trembling.

He inhaled deeply, then turned, hearing a sound directly behind him.

The cigarette slipped out of his hand onto the gravel.

He looked up into the intense grey gaze of his younger brother.

Nick.

The story continues in A Pale Horse,
now also available where good books are sold.

CHRONICLES OF BROTHERS
– BOOK TWO –
A PALE HORSE

Gabriel

G abriel lowered his pen.

'The Fourth Horseman is released.' He gazed out of the cloister window to the rows of cypress trees in the outer courtyard of the Monastery of Archangels. Jether stood at the chamber door.

'The Three Riders of the Apocalypse traversed the West Winds, venting their fury. Now Niscroc, Prince of Death and Hell, rides the Pale Horse, wielding his scythe.' Jether inhaled sharply.

'The plagues will be fearsome.'

Gabriel pushed his platinum locks away from his forehead. He raised his face to Jether.

'It is as I saw in my dreaming,' he whispered. 'A fourth of the race of men slain by sword, famine, pestilence.'

'We must steel ourselves.' Jether's expression was grim. 'For there is far worse to come. The Fifth and Sixth Seals will be broken swiftly after the Fourth. The First Six Seals are the Wrath of Man. At the breaking of the Seventh Seal . . .'

'Everything will change,' Gabriel said, finishing Jether's sentence for him.

'The Pale Rider enters the Kármán line, sixty-two miles above the Earth's surface, even as we speak,' Jether said, staring out of the cloister window at a grey-hooded horseman astride a horse, its colour a sickly ashen. It was drawing rapidly nearer. The horseman brandished a scythe in his left hand.

Gabriel looked up at Jether.

'Then it is the appointed time.'

'Forty-two months have passed. Nisroc rides,' Jether murmured. 'The Rapture is imminent.'

Gabriel rose and walked over to join Jether at the window.

'We enter the End of all Ages.' His hand rested on the Sword of Justice.

Jether returned Gabriel's steady gaze, then bowed his head.

'The Great Tribulation has begun.'

The Characters

EARTH: 2021
The De Vere Dynasty

Jason De Vere – Eldest brother, De Vere dynasty. US media tycoon. Chairman, owner, and CEO of multi-billion-dollar media corporation Vox Entertainment. Married to Julia St Cartier for twenty years; now divorced. One daughter, Lily De Vere.

Adrian De Vere – Middle brother, De Vere dynasty. Ex-Prime Minister of the United Kingdom newly appointed President of the European Union. Nobel Peace Prize nominee. Currently negotiating the 'Ishtar Accord'; the Third World War peace treaty. Widowed. No surviving children.

Nick De Vere – Youngest brother, De Vere dynasty. Archaeologist. Celebrity playboy. Dying of Aids. Currently in relationship with Jotapa, Princess of the Royal House of Jordan.

James De Vere – Father of Jason, Adrian, and Nick De Vere. Deceased.

Lilian De Vere – Chairwoman of the De Vere Foundation. Mother of Jason, Adrian, and Nick De Vere.

Julius De Vere – Grand Master of the Brotherhood. Warlock. Chairman of De Vere Continuation Holdings AG (1954–2014). Father of James De Vere. Grandfather to Jason, Adrian, and Nick De Vere. Deceased.

Julia St Cartier – Former editor of *Cosmopolitan*. Present: Founder/CEO of Lola PR. Married to Jason De Vere for twenty years, now divorced. Mother to Lily De Vere.

Lily De Vere – Julia and Jason De Vere's daughter. Confined to a wheelchair following a car accident.

Melissa Vane Templar De Vere – Adrian's wife. Died in childbirth.

Rosemary De Vere – James De Vere's half-sister, Lilian's companion.

Maxim – James and Lilian De Vere's butler.

Pierre and Beatrice Didier – James and Lilian De Vere's chauffeur and housekeeper. Currently working for Adrian De Vere at Mont St Michel, Normandy.

The De Vere Dynasty, Extended Circle Friends/Associates

Lawrence St Cartier – Jesuit priest; retired CIA; antiquities dealer. Julia St Cartier's uncle.

Alex Lane-Fox – Investigative journalist in training. Close family friend of Julia, Jason, and Lily De Vere.

Rachel Lane-Fox – supermodel. Julia's best friend. Killed in an aircraft on 9/11.

Rebekah and David Weiss – Rachel Lane-Fox's parents.

Polly Mitchell – Lily De Vere's best friend. Alex Lane-Fox's girlfriend.

Klaus von Hausen – Youngest Senior Curator of Department of the Middle East, British Museum. Ex-lover of Nick De Vere.

Charles 'Xavier' Chessler – Warlock. Previously Chairman of Chase Manhattan Bank. President of World Bank. Retired. Jason De Vere's godfather.

Callum Vickers – (early 30s), top London neurosurgeon. Seeing Julia De Vere.

Dylan Weaver – IT specialist holding high-level freelance positions with global banks, institutions, and various software companies. Nick De Vere's old schoolfriend.

Jontil Purvis – Executive assistant to Jason De Vere for nineteen years.

Levine and Mitchell – Jason De Vere's aides.

Kurt Guber – Adrian's head of security at Downing Street, now Director of EU Special Services Security Operations. Also, an exotic weapon specialist.

Neil Travis – Former SAS head of security for Adrian De Vere.

Anton – Adrian De Vere's butler.

Father Alessandro – Vatican Priest and scientist from the Vatican.

Waseem – Lawrence St Cartier's assistant.

Frau Vghtred Meeling – Austrian employee of De Vere's household: Nanny to Jason, Adrian, and Nick. Also, Abbess Helewis Vghtred.

Brother Francis – Monk, Alexandria , Egypt.

The Brotherhood
(Illuminati)

His **Excellency Lorcan De Molay** – Ex-Superior General of the Jesuit Order. Supreme High Priest of the Brotherhood, Jesuit Priest. Birthplace: indeterminate. Current age: indeterminate.

Kester von Slagel (Baron) – Lorcan De Molay's emissary.

Piers Aspinall – Head of MI6/British intelligence.

Charles Xavier Chessler – Previously Chairman of Chase Manhattan Bank. President of World Bank. Retired.

Ethan St Clair – Grand Master of the Scottish Brothers.

Dieter von Hallstein – Ex-German Chancellor.

Naotake Yoshido – Chairman of Japan's Yoshido banking dynasty.

Raffaello Lombardi – Patriarch of the black nobility family of Venice. Director of Vatican Bank.

Julius De Vere – Grand Master of the Brotherhood. Warlock. Chairman of De Vere Continuation Holdings AG. Father of James De Vere. Grandfather to Jason, Adrian and Nick De Vere. Deceased.

Jaylin Alexander – former Executive Director of the Central Intelligence Agency.

Commander General Omar B. Maddox – Commander of NORAD (North American Aerospace Defence Committee).

Gonzalez – US Secret Service Presidential Protective Detail.

Lewis – Deputy Secretary of Defence.

Drew Janowski – Special Assistant to the President for Defence Policy and Strategy.

Werner Drechsler – President of the World Banks.

Vincent Carnegie

The Royal House of Jordan

King of Jordan – Jotapa, Faisal, and Jibril's father. Deceased.

Jotapa – Princess of Jordan. In relationship with Nick De Vere. Namesake of ancient Princess Jotapa who lived over 2,000 years ago.

Jibril – Jordanian King's youngest son. Appointed Crown Prince.

Faisal – Jordanian King's oldest son.

Safwat – Head of Security and Jotapa's personal bodyguard.
Crown Prince Mansoor of Arabia.

Other Characters

Professor Hamish MacKenzie – Genetics scientist and world expert on animal and hybrid cloning.
Jul Mansoor – grandson of Abdul-Qawi, Bedouin archaeologist.
Waseem – Laurence St Cartier's assistant.
Abdul-Qawi Aka Jedd – Bedouin archaeologist.
Matt Barto – Vox's Tehran Bureau Chief.
Jordan Maxwell III – Investment Banker, Neal Black Securities.
Powell – Neal Black's Vice-President of IT.
Von Duysen – Colleague of Jordan Maxwell.
Laurent Chasteney – Assistant to Adrian.

First Heaven

Jesus – Christos; the Nazarene.
Michael – Chief Prince of the Royal Household of Yehovah, Commander-in-Chief, First Heaven's Armies. President of the Warring Councils.
Gabriel – Chief Prince of the Royal House of Yehovah; Lord Chief Justice of Angelic Revelators.
Jether – Imperial warrior and Ruler of the twenty-four ancient monarchs of the First Heaven and High Council. Chief Steward of Yehovah's sacred mysteries.
Xacheriel – Ancient of Days Curator of the sciences and universes, one of the twenty-four kings under Jether's governance.

Lamaliel – member of the Ruling Council of Angelic Elders.

Issachar – member of the Ruling Council of Angelic Elders.

Methuselah – member of the Ruling Council of Angelic Elders.

Maheel – Members of the Ruling Council of Angelic Elders.

Joktan – Ruler of Gabriel's Revelator Eagles.

Obadiah, Dimnah – Younglings, an ancient Angelic race with characteristics of eternal youth.

Sandaldor, Zadkiel – Gabriel's generals.

Zalialiel – Guard of the Portal of Shinar.

The Fallen

Lucifer – *Satan*, King of Perdition. Tempter; Adversary; Soverign Ruler of the race of men, Earth, and the nether regions.

Charsoc – Dark Apostle; Chief High Priest of the Fallen. Governor of the Grand Wizards of the Black Court and the Warlock Kings of the West.

Marduk – Head of the Darkened Councils and Lucifer's Chief of Staff.

The Twin Wizards of Malfecium – Grand Wizard of Phaegos and the Grand Wizard of Maelageor. The super-scientists.

Mulabalah – Ruler of the Black Murmurers.

Astaroth – Commander-in-chief of the Black Horde. Michael's ex-general.

Moloch – Satanic prince. 'Butcher' of Perdition.

Sargon the Terrible of Babylonia – Champion of Gehenna. Great Prince of Babylonia.

Balberith – Lucifer's chief attendant.

Nisroc the Necromancer – Keeper of Death and the Grave.

The Dark Cabal Grand Wizards – 666 Black Murmurers.

Dracul – Ruler of the Warlocks of the West and Ancient Leader of the Time Lords.

Nephilim – A hybrid between the angelic and the race of men.